THE CASSANDRA PALMER COLLECTION

KAREN CHANCE

THE CASSANDRA PALMER COLLECTION

Author's Note

Over the years, I have written a number of short stories and novellas to accompany the Cassandra Palmer novels. These were gifted to my readers on my web page, where they remain. But some people wanted them revised and gathered together into a single anthology, which is how this collection came about.

I should note here that do not include the Lia de Croissets shorts, which were written for anthologies and over which I do not have the rights to self-publish. I have, however, included the Pritkin POV scene from *Tempt the Stars,* which is also on my web page, as it was as much a short story as a missing scene. I hope you will enjoy.

TABLE OF CONTENTS

The Gauntlet 3

The Queen's Witch 71

The House at Cobb End 127

Shitty Beer 161

A Family Affair 176

Shadowland 277

Pritkin POV from *Tempt the Stars* 380

The Day of the Dead 394

Black Friday.. 444

Set in the England of Elizabeth I, "The Gauntlet" features Kit Marlowe as a newly created vampire and Gillian Urswick as a witch with a penchant for highway robbery. That hobby had landed her in trouble with the Silver Circle, the self-appointed guardians of the magical community, who didn't like thieves, particularly not when they were also members of the Druid covens that had been nothing but thorns in the Circle's side. Gillian had a date with a noose as a result, and only Marlowe had a chance to break her out of the Circle's prison in time.

The Gauntlet

Chapter One

The sound of a key turning in the rusty old lock had everyone scurrying forward with hands outstretched, begging for food, for water, for life. Gillian didn't go with them. Trussed up as she was, she could barely move. And there was no life that way.

The burly jailer came in carrying a lantern, with two dark shapes behind him. To her surprise, he didn't immediately kick the women aside with brutal indifference as usual. Instead he let them crowd around, even the ones who had been there a while, and whose skeletal hands silently begged with the others.

"This is the lot, my lord," he said. "And a sorry one it is, too."

"Why are some of them gagged?" The low, pleasant tenor came from one of the shapes she had assumed to be a guard. The speaker came forward, but she couldn't see much of him. The hood on his cape was pulled forward and a gloved hand covered his face, probably in an attempt to block the stench.

She smiled grimly and let her head fall back into her arms. It wouldn't work. Even after two days, she hadn't become inured to it: the thick, sickly-sweet odor of flesh, unwashed and unhealed.

"Some are strong enough to curse a man to hell otherwise," the jailer informed him, spitting on the ground.

"Show me the strongest," the stranger said, and Gillian's head jerked back up.

The jailor grumbled, but he ordered his men to drag the bound bodies that had been shoved to the back of the room to the forefront. The stranger bent over each one, pushing matted, filthy hair out of their eyes, as if looking for someone. Gillian didn't watch. She concentrated everything she had on biting through the remaining mass of cloth in her mouth, her eyes on the open door behind the men.

The guards came only once a day, doling out water and a thin gruel, and she didn't know what kind of shape she would be in by tomorrow. Even worse, she didn't know how Elinor would be. She glanced over at the child's huddled form, but she hadn't moved. Not for hours now, a fact that had Gillian's heart clenching, part in fear, part in black rage.

If those whoresons let her daughter die in here, she'd rip this place apart stone by stone. Her arms jerked convulsively against the shackles, but they were iron, not rope. If she couldn't speak, she had no chance of breaking them.

It didn't help that she hadn't had water in more than a day. The guard assigned to that detail last night had been one of those she'd attacked on arrival, in an aborted escape attempt. He'd kicked her in the ribs as he passed, and waved the ladle under her nose, but not allowed her so much as a drop. If he'd followed orders, he might have noticed what she was doing, might have replaced the worn woolen gag with something sturdier.

But he hadn't.

"That one's dead," the jailor said, kicking a limp body aside. He quickly checked the others, pulling out one more before lining up the remaining women at the stranger's feet. Most were silent, watching with hollow, desperate eyes above their gags. A few struggled weakly, either smart enough to realize that this might be a way out, or too far gone to understand what was happening.

"What about this one?" A hand with a square cut ruby ring caught Gillian's chin, turning her face up to the light.

"You don't want her!" the jailer said, aiming another kick at her abused ribs.

"The agreement was, in good condition," the stranger said, blocking the booted foot with his own.

Gillian barely noticed. Up close, it was obvious that she was in even more trouble than she'd thought. The fact that the stranger was dead wasn't a good sign. That he was still walking around was worse.

Vampire.

They stared at each other, and he smiled slightly at her start of recognition. He had a nice face—young, as if that meant anything—with clear, unmarked skin, a head of dark brown curls and a small goatee. The last would have been amusing under other circumstances, as if he was trying to make his pleasant face appear more sinister.

She wondered why he didn't just bare his fangs.

"I don't see as it makes a difference, if you're aiming to feed off her," the guard said, angry, but smart enough not to show it.

Those liquid dark eyes swept over her. "What I do with the woman is my affair."

"Ahh. Some sport beforehand, then. I'd not risk it, meself. One of my men tried the night she was brought in, and the bitch cursed him. He's in a bad way, still."

"How tragic," the vampire sounded amused.

The guard must have thought so, too, because his already florid features flushed even darker. "See if you're laughing with a pillicock the size of a pin!" he spat.

The vampire ignored him and put a hand beneath Gillian's arm, helping her to stand. "I'd let you out of those, but I'm afraid you'd hex me," he said cheerfully, nodding at her cuffs. "And I like my privities the way they are." He glanced at the guard. "Tell me about her."

"One of them that's been operating out of the thicket," the man said resentfully, referring to Maidenhead thicket on the road between London and Bristol, where Gillian's group had had some success relieving travellers of their excess wealth.

"Ah, yes. I met a robber there myself, not long ago." The vampire smiled at her. "He was delicious."

Gillian just stared. Did he always talk to his food this much before eating it?

"But I must say," he commented, his eyes on her worn gown, greasy red hair and dirty face. "For a member of one of the most notorious gangs of thieves in England, you do not look very prosperous."

Maybe I would, she thought furiously, *if I didn't have to spend most of my time avoiding people like you.*

Once, she'd had protection from his kind. She'd been a member of one of the Druid covens that had ruled the supernatural part of the British Isles for time out of mind. But that had been before the arrival of the so-called "Silver Circle," an ancient society of light magic users who had brought nothing but darkness to England.

They had arrived in force ten years ago, as refugees of a vicious war on the continent. The religious tensions that had culminated with Spain launching the Armada had offered an opportunity to one of the Circle's oldest enemies. A group of dark mages known as the Black Circle had joined forces with the Inquisition under the pretense of helping to stamp out heresy. And by all accounts, they had been brutally efficient at hunting down their light counterparts.

But their suffering hadn't made the Silver Circle noticeably gentler on anyone else. They had but one goal in mind—to rebuild their forces and retake control of magical Europe. And they intended to start with England.

Gillian's coven was one of those who had refused their kind offers of "protection," and preferred to continue determining their own destiny.

In return, they had been subjected to a witch hunt mightier and more successful than anything the Inquisition had ever managed. By the time they realized just how far their fellow mages would go to support the idea of a unified magical community, the covens had been decimated through deceit, betrayal and murder.

But they haven't killed all of us, Gillian thought viciously. Not yet. It was a fact that would someday cost them dear.

The vampire had been watching her with interest. She didn't know how he could tell anything past the folds of the gag, but apparently, he saw something that pleased him. His smile became almost genuine.

"See my man about payment," he told the guard, his eyes never leaving her face. "I'll take this one with me."

"Take her?" The guard's scowl became more pronounced. "Take her where?"

"That is my affair," the vampire repeated.

"Not if ye're planning to make off wi' her, it damn well isn't! No one will much care if she doesn't last long enough for the rope, but it's as much as my life is worth to let her go beyond these walls. She's dangerous!"

"I do truly hope so," the vampire said oddly.

A beefy hand fell on his shoulder. "If ye want to make a meal off her, that's one thing. But all the gold in yer purse won't save me once they discover—"

In an eye blink, the guard was slammed against the wall, held several feet off the floor by the slim hand around his throat. "Perhaps you should be more concerned about your immediate future," the vampire said softly.

Gillian didn't wait to see who would win the argument over which one would be allowed to kill her. The soggy threads finally came apart in her mouth and she spat them out. But with no saliva left, and a throat still throbbing from the elbow blow it had taken days ago, she couldn't speak. She swallowed convulsively and concentrated everything on making some kind of sound—anything.

An incantation rolled off her tongue. It was a dry whisper, but it was enough. With a rusty creak, the shackles parted around her wrists and ankles, and she was free.

Her limbs were stiff and uncoordinated, and her head was spinning from the power loss. But then she caught sight of Elinor and nothing else mattered. She lurched forward in a scrambling crawl, making it a few yards before rough hosed legs blocked the way.

"Where d'ye think you're going?" the other guard demanded, grabbing her by the back of the collar. She slung a spell at him, but the angle was off and it missed, exploding against the low ceiling of the room.

Had the roof been in proper shape, the spell would have either dissipated or ricocheted back, depending on how much power she had been able to muster. But whoever had owned this heap of stones before the Circle had skimped on repairs, and the once stout wood had seen one too many winters. What felt like half the roof suddenly rained down on their heads, sending her stumbling back and burying the guard under a pile of weathered beams.

Gillian clutched the wall, blinking in the wash of brilliant sunlight that streamed through the ruined roof. It was blinding after two days of almost complete darkness, and the struggle with the guard had disoriented her. She was no longer sure where Elinor was, and when she tried to move forward, she was battered by screaming, panicked women.

"Elinor!" she yelled as loudly as her parched throat would allow, but there was no answer.

Her eyes finally adjusted and she caught a glimpse of her daughter's slight form huddled against one wall. She was rocking slightly, staring at nothing, her hands bound to an iron ring. Gillian crawled over and started to work the leather bindings on her wrists off. They were so tight that the circulation to her hands had been partially cut off and her small fingers were swollen like sausages.

Elinor didn't fight her, although she couldn't have seen much through the glare or heard her mother's whispered assurances over the din. She was trembling from a combination of exhaustion, shock and fear. Dark blue rings stained her eyes and her beautiful blond hair hung limp and lifeless, like her expression.

The last stubborn strap came loose and Gillian pulled her daughter into her arms. She started to rise when one of the bound figures on the floor rolled into her, struggling in vain to throw off her bonds. The old woman was in irons and gagged, as Gillian had been, with no chance to escape if she couldn't speak.

Gillian pulled a disgusting scrap of cloth out of her mouth, to give her a fighting chance, while scanning the room for any way out besides the door. "Release me," the woman gasped, on a rattling breath.

"Release yourself, old mother," Gillian told her distractedly. "I need what strength I have left."

She could already hear soldiers on the run, thudding their way up the tower's wooden steps. There was only one way down—and it was the same path the guards were taking up. She might make it alone; she had that much pent up rage. But not with Elinor.

"Mind your manners, girl!" she was told, right before wrinkled, age-spotted fingers reached out and gave her a pinch. Gillian grasped the woman's hand, intending to pry it off her flesh. But then she looked down-- and stopped cold.

Crisscrossed by delicate veins and almost buried under a layer of grime were faint blue lines, etched onto the woman's inner wrist. Gillian stared at the curling, elegant pattern, one older than the walls that imprisoned them, older than almost anything else in these isles, and felt her skin go cold. The three-pointed triskelion was worn only by the leaders of the great covens.

A cannonball had landed a dozen yards from her once, and it had felt like this, like being knocked flat even though she hadn't moved. She had never really believed that it might work, this plan of extermination. The covens could be hurt, but they would come back, as they'd always come back, through every war, invasion, and black time that littered their past. But if the Circle could reach even to the heart of them, could reduce one of the Great Mothers to this...

They could destroy us, she thought blankly. *They could destroy all of us.*

Chapter Two

Another pinch interrupted Gillian's thoughts, this time feeling like it took a hunk of her arm along with it. "Stop daydreaming," she was told tetchily. "And do as you're told!"

It wasn't a request, and obedience to the elders was ingrained from birth. The requisite spell all but leaped to her lips. But the iron was corroded, or perhaps her power was fading, because it took a second application before the old hinges finally gave way. And by then, reinforcements had arrived.

Gillian could hear them in the corridor, being hit with spells from the few witches still capable of throwing any. Someone screamed and a body crashed into the heavy wooden door, slamming it shut and momentarily interrupting the attack. But it would be a moment's reprieve at best. And when the guards broke through, she didn't think recapture would be their main concern.

The Great Mother latched onto her arm with a strength she hadn't thought the woman had. "There." She pointed to a corner of the room that had emptied of prisoners. A splash of sunshine, mid-afternoon and richly golden, highlighted a patch of bare worn boards. They were old and slimy, scattered with rat bones and smeared with human waste. But unlike the roof, they were solid.

"I can't," Gillian confessed. She knew without trying that she didn't have the strength to destroy the floorboards. They were good English oak, as hard as the stones that made up the tower's walls, and just as immovable. "We have to find another—"

"Stop arguing," the eldest snapped, cutting her off. "And take me."

Gillian took her. She didn't know what else to do. They were trapped.

Even worse, the vampire was standing off to the side, casually observing the chaos. She scowled; she should have known that sunlight wouldn't kill him. If he was that weak, he'd have come at night. He'd retreated further into the hood of his cape, leaving him a long column of black wool, but otherwise appeared unconcerned.

He didn't move, but Gillian carefully kept the sunlight between them nonetheless. She pulled Elinor and the eldest along the wall, hoping that the glistening beams would provide some kind of protection. His head turned, keeping them in view, but he said nothing.

"In the middle. There!" the Great Mother gasped, and again Gillian followed orders, only to have her arm gripped in a steel-like vise. Cloudy blue eyes met hers, almost sightless, but somehow penetrating all the same. "In times like these, we do what is needful—what we must to survive, for us and our folk. Do you understand, girl?"

No, Gillian thought frantically. What she understood was that the door was about to open and they were all going to die. That was pretty damn clear. "I do not think they mean for any of us to survive," she said, her throat raw.

The Great Mother's grip became positively painful, arthritic fingers digging into the flesh of Gillian's arm. "It matters not what they mean! Will you *fight*, girl, for what is yours?"

"Yes," she said, confused. What did she think? That Gillian planned to simply lic down and die? "But it is not likely to be a long one. I have little power left, and the Circle--"

"You will find that you have all the power you need."

Gillian didn't understand what she meant, and there was no time to ask. The door burst open, but she barely noticed, because the frail body on the dirty boards had begun to glow. Power radiated outward, shimmering beneath translucent skin like sunlight through moth wings. It flooded the ugly room, gilding the old bricks and causing even the guards to shield their eyes.

Elinor made a soft sound and hid her face, but Gillian couldn't seem to look away. For one brief moment, the Old Mother looked like an exquisitely delicate statue, a fire-lit radiance flowing under the pale crepe of her skin. And then Gillian's own skin began to heat, the flesh of her arm reddening and then burning where the thin fingers gripped her.

She cried out and tried to jerk away, but the Old Mother stubbornly held on. Her skin was shining through Gillian's hand now, so bright that the edges of her flesh were limned with it. But she couldn't feel her anymore. She couldn't feel anything but the great and terrible power gathering in the air, power that whispered to her, wordless and uncontrollable.

It exploded the next moment in flash of brilliant fire. Gillian threw her body over Elinor's, trying to shield her from the searing heat and deadly flames she expected. But they didn't come. And when she dared to look again, the old woman's body was gone—and so was half the floor.

The thick oak boards had dissolved, crumbling into nothingness like charred firewood, leaving a burnt, smoking hole looking down into the room below. Gillian crouched beside it for a moment, her heart pounding, knife-edged colors tearing at her vision. Until a glance showed that the guards had fled in fear of magic they didn't understand.

She didn't, either, but she recognized an opportunity when she saw one.

Elinor was clinging to her neck, hard enough to strangle. It was far from comfortable, but at least it meant she didn't have to try to hold her as she lowered them onto one of the remaining rafters of the room below. It was the gatehouse, where a contingent of mages usually stayed to watch the front of the castle and to guard any prisoners in the room above. No one was there now, everyone having run up the stairs to secure the door or having scattered after the escapees.

For a brief moment, they were alone.

Gillian's arm throbbed under the burnt edges of her sleeve, but she ignored it and started making her way along the beam to clear the pile of smoking shards below. Yellow sunlight struggled through the haze, enough to let her see stone walls spotted in a few places by narrow, arrow slit windows, a few stools and a flat-topped storage trunk that was being used as a table. The remains of someone's lunch was still spread out over the top of it.

There were no obvious ways out. The only door let out onto the ramparts, which were heavily guarded. And even if they had been able to fit through the tiny windows, the main gate was protected by two towers filled with archers. Anyone trying to leave that way would have to traverse a quarter mile of open fields, the local forest having been cut back to give the archers a clear shot.

Gillian thought that she could just about manage a weak shield, but not to cover two, and not to last the whole way. And Elinor couldn't help or even protect herself; she was barely seven and her magic had yet to manifest. The eldest should have saved her sacrifice, she thought grimly. They weren't going to get out of this.

"Could I be of assistance, at all?"

Her head whipped up to see the vampire's curly mop poking through the charred edges of the hole. She threw up a shield, silently cursing him for forcing her to use the power, and jumped to the floor. Shards of wood and a few old iron nails dug into her bare feet, but the pain was almost welcome. It helped to push away the gut-wrenching panic and let her think.

A guard was sprawled on the floor nearby, half hidden by the fall of wood and debris. He wasn't moving, and one hand was a bloody mess—he must have used it to try to protect himself. The other gripped a long piece of wood that was partially concealed by his body. She crouched beside him and started tugging on it, while keeping a wary eye on the creature above.

"My earlier jest may have been . . . ill-timed," the vampire offered. "I do not, in fact, intend to dine upon you. Or your lovely . . . daughter, is it?"

Gillian's head jerked up. "Touch her and they will never find all the pieces," she snarled, pulling Elinor behind her.

But the creature made no move toward them, other than to spread his hands, showing that he held no weapons. As if he needed any. "I assure you, I pose no threat."

"A harmless vampire." She didn't bother to keep the mockery out of her voice.

"To you." A smile came easily to that handsome face. "In fact, I work with a party in government charged with maintaining the security of these lands."

"You lie. Vampires work for their makers."

"Yes, but in this case, my mistresses' interests align."

"And what would those interests be?" Gillian asked, not because she cared, but to buy herself time to find out if the item in the guard's hand was what she thought it was.

"The queen's enemies are not composed of humans alone," he told her, as easily as if he carried on conversations upside down every day. Which maybe he did, she thought darkly, images of bats and other unsavory creatures coming to mind. "Ever since England became a refuge for the Silver Circle, she has been a target for the dark. And the assassination attempts grow with each passing day."

"And why should a vampire care about such things?"

"We must live in this world, too, Mistress—"

"Urswick," she panted. Curse it—the guard weighed a ton!

"I am pleased to make your acquaintance, Mistress Urswick," he said wryly. "I am Christopher Marlowe, although my friends call me Kit."

"You have friends?"

"Strangely enough, yes. I would like to number you among them, if I could."

Gillian was sure he would. But while she might be a penniless thief, her coven ruined, her friends scattered or dead, neither she nor her daughter would be feeding him this day. "Don't count on it," she snapped, and jerked the slender column of wood free.

It was a staff as she'd hoped, but not of the Circle's make. The surface was satiny to the touch, worn smooth as stone from centuries of handling. The oil from all those hands had cured it to a dark mahogany, blending the black glyphs carved along its length into the surface. She traced one of the ridges with a fingertip and didn't believe it, even when a frisson of power passed through her shields to jump along her nerves.

Her fingers began to prickle, black fury rising in front of her eyes, as she stood there with a Druid staff in her hands. It wasn't enough that they were persecuted, imprisoned, and murdered. The Circle had to steal what little of their heritage they had been able to preserve, as well.

"At the risk of sounding discourteous, may I point out that you are in no position to be choosy?" the vampire said, right before the door to the room slammed open and half a dozen guards rushed in. And then blew back out as the staff turned the door and half the wall into rubble.

"Perhaps I spoke too soon," he murmured, as she pulled a white-faced Elinor through the red bite of heat and the smell of smoke to the now missing door.

Outside, the castle's walls hemmed them in on all sides, gray stone against a pewter sky. A battle was going on to the left, with the prisoners trying to get down the stairs. They looked to be holding their own, with one witch's spell sending a guard flying off the battlements into the open courtyard. But that was about to change.

Reinforcements were already running toward the battle from either side. And they were the Circle's elite corps—war mages, they called them—instead of the talentless scum employed as jailers. The witches from most of the covens were well trained in self-defense, but their weapons had been confiscated when they were taken. Without them, they wouldn't last long.

She'd barely had the thought when a group of the Circle's dark robed mages broke off from the main group and started her way. In front of them was a lethal cloud of weapons, iron dark against the pale sky. Gillian didn't try to run; there was no time and nowhere to go. Against the Circle's harsh alchemy of steel and iron, she called Wind, and it answered far more quickly than usual. She was only dimly aware of a blizzard of debris behind her back and the mages' squawks of alarm as their weapons went tumbling back at them.

For a moment, the roar of her element filled her senses in a heady rush, billowing out her tattered gown, matting her hair and blowing into her eyes. She didn't bother to brush it away. It felt good. It felt like power.

But it didn't last. Within seconds, the wind was already dying. The staff was magnifying her strength, but she had so little left. And when it gave out—

"My offer of assistance remains open," the vampire said casually. He'd jumped down from the second floor and was leaning against the shattered wall, watching the chaos with the mildly interested glance of someone at a bear baiting with no money on the outcome.

"It's well known that your kind helps no one but themselves!"

"Which is better than attacking and imprisoning our own, would you not say?" She didn't see him move, but he was suddenly beside her, the wind whipping his curls wildly around his face.

"Why should you want to help me?" she demanded harshly.

"Because I need yours in return."

Despite everything, Gillian almost laughed. He stood there in his fine clothes, smelling of spices and sporting a jewel worth the price of a house. And she was supposed to believe that he needed anything from the likes of her?

"'Pon my honor," he said, seeing her expression.

"You may as well swear on your life! Everyone knows that vampires are selfish, base, cruel creatures who only want one thing!"

"And everyone knows that coven witches are weak, treacherous and easily corrupted," he shot back. "Everyone is often wrong."

Gillian started to answer, but a harsh clanging echoed across the keep, cutting her off. A small group of witches had cleared the stairs and were making a break for the gates. But the heavy iron portcullis guarding the entrance had slammed down before they could reach it, trapping them in the middle of a sea of enemies. Gillian's hands clenched at their desperate cries for help, but there was nothing she could do but die with them.

And she had Elinor to think about.

She spun on her heel, brushing past the vampire and racing back inside the small gatehouse. The trunk was still there, with its bit of stale loaf. She brushed it aside and threw up the heavy lid, hoping for weapons—charms, potions, protection wards—anything designed to hold a reservoir of magic for use in times like these. But there was nothing, aside from a few scattered rat droppings.

She slammed the trunk shut in frustration, wishing she had the strength to throw it at the wall. The guard must have taken the staff as a trophy. Because wherever the Circle was storing their weapons, it wasn't here.

"The other gate is still open," the vampire said, from the doorway. "And I am skilled at glamourie. Let me inside your shields and I can hide you and the girl. We can walk out of here while the fight distracts the guards."

"Why should I trust you?" she demanded, desperate for a reason, any reason.

"What choice have you?"

Gillian didn't see that they had much either way. Getting outside the walls would do them little good if it left her drained and defenseless, and at the mercy of a creature whose kind were well known to have none. But with no weapons and her magic all but exhausted, staying here would mean certain death at the hands of the Circle.

The vampire's head suddenly came up, reacting to something beyond the reach of her senses. "Help me and I'll help you," he said urgently, holding out his hand.

Gillian hugged Elinor against her, every instinct she had screaming that she was mad to put their lives in the hands of a creature who saw them merely as prey. But if her only choice was between dying now and dying later, she would take later. "If you betray me, I will use my last breath to curse you!" she promised.

"I would expect nothing less."

Gillian licked dry lips. She didn't believe him, didn't think for a moment that he really wanted to help. But the wind had died and booted feet were pounding up the stairs, and she was out of options. She readied a curse, hoping it wouldn't be her last. And dropped the tattered remnants of her shield.

Chapter Three

*T*his *was typical*, Kit thought, slamming them back against the wall as a mob of mages rushed in. Find the perfect candidate and, naturally, everything went to hell before he could get away with her. Unfortunately, his lady was not one to understand unforeseen difficulties. He really did not want to think of the reception he was likely to get if he returned empty-handed.

Of course, at the moment, he would rather settle for returning at all.

"Search every inch," the dark-haired leader snapped, and Kit silently cursed.

He'd been hoping for a group of slow-witted guards who might have assumed that the witch had somehow slipped past them in the confusion. But judging from their windblown hair and murderous expressions, these were the men she'd attacked outside. And he couldn't take a half dozen war mages on his own.

At least, he didn't think he could, having never before tried. And he discovered that he wasn't all that keen on finding out. He decided some subtlety was in order and started shuffling his little party toward the ruined door.

He thought their chances of making it out undetected were reasonably good. He'd used one of the talents he'd manifested since becoming a master and gone dim as soon as he heard the men approaching. Dim wasn't invisible—he could still be seen if someone was looking right at him. But even then he'd be only a faint, indistinct outline, like a haze of black smoke. And with all the real smoke choking the air, who was going to notice?

A war mage, apparently. He'd almost reached the door, where only a single mage stood guard, when one of the nearby searchers suddenly changed direction and grabbed a fold of his cloak. "Sir! They're—"

So much for subtlety. Kit seized the man's arm and slung him into the mage guarding the door, hard enough to send them both staggering backwards off the ramparts. Then he snatched the child into his arms, grabbed the witch by the waist and bolted.

It wasn't the most elegant escape he'd ever made, but a lifetime of close scrapes had taught him not to be picky. He dodged a spell that came blistering through the air after him, sidestepped a small battle, and headed for the stairs. And then pulled up abruptly and spun them back against the wall.

"What is it?" the witch demanded. "Why are we—" She stopped, catching sight of the same thing that he had.

The stairs were choked with guards and the courtyard of the castle had turned into a particularly colorful hell. The flimsy wooden shacks that housed the kitchen, stables and blacksmith had caught alight and were burning merrily, with spell-fire tinting the billowing smoke in glowing colors. Horses were neighing, people were screaming, and spells were exploding on all sides.

In other words, it was the usual battlefield chaos, which was what gave him pause. On any given battlefield on any given day, there were about a hundred ways to die—and that multiplied tenfold if it was a magical battle. He going to have to—

A spell he hadn't seen coming hit them broadside before he could finish the thought, sizzling against the shield the witch had managed to raise before flaming out in a burst of acid green sparks. And while no one might have been able to see them, that spectacle had been all too visible. Even worse, the effects didn't dissipate; instead, a glowing nimbus pulsed in the air around them, like the corona of the sun on a foggy day.

"Marker spell," the witch gasped, before he could ask. "They used them to hunt us in the forests, to make it impossible for us to hide. You can't conceal us now and I cannot protect all three of us!"

She started struggling, probably deciding to use her remaining strength to save herself and the girl. But it wouldn't be enough and Kit knew it. They had to stay together, and they had to get out that gate, but the stairs were impossible. He could probably survive the assault of the guards; but not the witches.

That left only one option.

"Hold on," he said grimly, renewing his grip on them.

The witch was quick; he'd give her that. "Are you mad?" she stared from him to the chaos below and back again. "We can't go down there!"

"And we cannot stay here! We're sitting ducks. The smoke should hide us."

"Hide our bodies, mayhap," she snarled, struggling to get away.

Kit held on and dragged her to the edge of the rampart, trying to spot the least lethal landing place. But mages were converging on them from all sides, and there was no more time. He jumped, right before a bolt of pure power tore through the air he'd just vacated.

It hit the side of the stairs behind them, blowing a hole in the stone and sending shards raining down onto the crowd below. The screaming and cursing and spell throwing from the witches increased four-fold, but Kit barely noticed because something hit him full in the face.

It wasn't a spell, unless the mages had invented one that smelled like burnt feathers and tried to peck your eyes out. He cursed, but couldn't do much more with his arms full of witches. But whatever-it-was went into a frenzy anyway, squawking and flapping its wings wildly, as if he was attempting to murder it.

And then the ground tilted under his feet and he landed on his arse.

It took him a few seconds to realize that he hadn't hit the ground at all, but the edge of a cart full of woven cages of chickens. Half of them had broken open in the battle and the contents were floundering around in the mud or getting roasted mid-flight by the spells crisscrossing the air. Except for the one which had somehow gotten its claws trapped in the wool of his doublet.

The witch had righted herself and her daughter and was hunkered down beside the cart, watching in disbelief as he did battle with the guards' dinner. Kit had the distinct impression that his credibility might have just taken a hit, especially since he seemed to be losing. And then wounded dignity was the least of his problems when a dark-haired mage jumped off the stairs and landed on the cart's other end.

Kit went flying into him, bird and all, and the three of them tumbled off the back of the cart. The mage was cursing and trying to raise a shield, while Kit attempted to drain him before he could manage it. They were both half successful. The mage snapped his shields shut, but they didn't completely stop the flow of blood that Kit was leeching out of him through the air.

In a panic, the man sent out a cluster of levitating magical weapons. Half of them collided with crazed birds while the rest attempted to bury themselves into Kit's flesh. He swatted at them, but like a storm of angry bees, they kept buzzing around, rushing in to stab at him whenever they got the chance.

"You're losing as much blood as you steal, vampire!" the mage crowed, attempting to gut him with a sword.

"But I can replace mine," Kit said sweetly, sending the sword spinning across the fight with a well-aimed kick. "How about you?"

"Well said," the man replied, and kicked him in the square in the groin.

Kit stumbled back, fervently wishing that padded cod pieces hadn't gone out of style, and landed in the cages of squawking fowl. His impact burst most of the ones left intact and sent up a whirlwind of flapping wings and clawing feet. He fought his way free, finally tearing his own damned passenger loose and tossing it aside. But by the time he got back to his feet, the mage was gone.

And so was the witch.

"God's Bones!" he hissed, staring around wildly. But she and the girl were nowhere in sight. That could mean that a mage had her, but he doubted it. The spells the Circle's men had been casting weren't the kind they used when they wanted to take prisoners, and he didn't see her body.

No, it was a safe bet that she'd run off somewhere while he was distracted. The question was, where?

He glanced at the secondary gate, or what he could see of it through drifting clouds of smoke. It was temptingly close, and the mages hadn't yet managed to lower the portcullis. It looked like they'd tried, but the witches had hit it with something that caused the metal to run like honey. And enough had dripped into the crevices of the track to cause the gate to stick partway down.

There was room to squeeze out underneath, but that required getting to it first. And that didn't look likely. The Circle had placed a double line of guards across the opening to act as a human buffer, leaving their own men free to slowly decimate the witches who were gathering in force nearby. In between the two groups was a hell pit of smoke, spells and running, screaming people.

If she'd headed that way, she wouldn't last long.

It had seemed such an easy task, Kit thought grimly, as he ducked and dodged his way through the melee. Interrogate Lady Isabel Tapley, a coven witch lately apprehended by the mages who was suspected of being in league with the Black Circle. There were rumors that another plot was brewing against the queen, whom the dark blamed for sheltering their enemies, and Kit had been sent to find out if there was any truth to them.

But nothing had gone right from the beginning. Lady Isabel had poisoned herself before he arrived, leaving him to question a corpse, and not the animated kind. The fact that she'd resorted to such extreme measures made him that much more convinced that the plot was genuine, but she'd left no papers behind and her servants knew frustratingly little about their mistress' plans. The only thing he had been able to glean was that she had a meeting in three days' time with several men newly arrived from Spain.

And that one of them shared the name of a noted Black Circle member.

Kit needed to be at that meeting. And for that, he needed a credible Lady Isabel. But young, red-headed, coven witches were a little thin on the ground these days, thanks to the Circle. And his request to be allowed to borrow one had been flatly refused. He had therefore gone to the source and bribed the guards, only to land in this mess.

The more sensible side of his brain offered the observation that, really, there had to be other witches who fit Lady Isabel's description. And some of them might be found in somewhat less trying circumstances. The other part of his brain, however, the one that was always getting him in trouble, was dead set on this woman. He'd bled for her; he would have her. And the Circle would not.

Assuming he could find her before they did.

Chapter Four

So much for my knight errant, Gillian thought, watching her rescuer getting beaten up by a half-roasted bird. She was about to go rescue the creature when one of the war mages dove off the side of the ramparts, flinging a curse in front of him. She acted on instinct, dropping her all-but-useless shields and throwing up a *declive* instead. It took most of her remaining strength, but it worked; the protection spell acted like a mirror, reflecting the caster's magic right back at him.

It caught him in the middle of his leap, popped his shields and sent him crashing headfirst into the cart. The vampire had landed on the other end, and the two-hundred-pound mage smashing down at the edge of the cart caused him to go flying, chicken and all. And then she didn't see any more, because strong arms clapped around both of hers from behind, lifting her completely off the ground.

She tried to mutter a curse, but found she couldn't draw a breath. The guard—and it had to be a guard, because she was still alive—was doing his best to squeeze her in two. She couldn't aim the staff with him behind her, so she brought it down on his foot instead, as hard as she could. The man bellowed and dropped her, and Gillian scrambled away, only to be dragged back by the ankle.

She rolled over to try to free herself, and then had to roll again as a knife flashed down, ripping through her gown and missing her by inches. As he wrenched it out of the ground, she caught a glimpse of Elinor behind him, her face pale and her eyes huge. And then the guard dropped his knife and started screaming.

Gillian scrambled to her feet, ready to grab her daughter and bolt, assuming he'd been hit by a stray spell. And then she realized—it was a spell, but it hadn't gone astray. A coiling ribbon of reddish gold flame had snaked out of a burning hut and hit the man square in the back.

At first she thought Elinor must have done it, despite the fact that it was years too early for that. But a searing pain in her arm caused her to look down, and she saw the fire glyph on the staff glowing bright red. She stared at it in disbelief, because she couldn't call Fire.

All coven witches had to specialize in one of the three great elements—Wind, Fire or Earth—when they came of age, and hers was Wind. She'd never been able to summon more than one; no one could except the coven Mothers, who could harness the collective power of all the witches under their control. But she could feel the drain as her magic pulled the element through the air, as she called it to her.

She just didn't know how she was doing it.

And she didn't have time to figure it out. The guard had made the same assumption she had and spun, snarling, on Elinor. Gillian had a second to see him start for her daughter, to see his fist lash out—

And then she was looking at the hilt of a knife protruding from the burnt material of his shirt.

The smell of the charnel houses curled out into the air, mixing with the tang of gunpowder and the raw-lightning scent of spent magic. The guard fell to his knees, the blood gushing hot and sticky from a wound in his side, wetting her hand on the hilt of his blade. She let go and he collapsed, a surprised look on his face and blood on his lips. And then Elinor was tugging her away, shock and pride warring on her small face.

Gillian didn't feel pride; she felt sick. She wiped her sticky hand on her skirts, feeling it tremble, like her the breath in her lungs, like her roiling gut. But the guard's death wasn't the cause. She pulled her daughter into her arms and hugged the precious body against her, her heart beating frantically in her chest. She'd almost lost her; she'd almost lost Elinor.

She crouched down beside a nearby well, the only cover she could find that wasn't burning, and stared around desperately for some opening in the crowd. Panic was making it hard to think, but she shoved it away angrily. She couldn't afford weakness now. Weakness would get them killed.

A group of nearby witches was attacking the stables, but Gillian couldn't see the point. The horses' faster pace might get them beyond range of the archers before their shields gave out, but that was assuming they made it out at all. And while the portcullis wasn't completely down, a mob of guards and who-knew-how-many protection spells stood in their way.

No. No one was getting through that.

But they might cause a great deal of commotion trying.

She blinked, her heart drumming with sudden hope. She stared from the battlefield to the high, gray walls surrounding it. And then she scooped up Elinor and took off, weaving through the remaining sheds and outbuildings that hugged the castle walls.

She stopped when they reached the far side of the structure, squatting beside a wagon piled high with empty barrels, breathing hard. She didn't think they'd been seen, but she couldn't be sure. There were guards here, too, although not as many. Most had joined the fight and the rest were staring at it, as if watching her people be slaughtered was great entertainment.

She probably had a few minutes, at least.

She tugged Elinor behind the wagon and started working on the ropes holding the barrels, tearing her nails on the tight knots. "What are you doing?" Elinor was looking at her strangely.

"Getting us out of this place!"

"There's no door here," Elinor said, staring past her at the carnage.

"Don't look at it," Gillian told her harshly. "And no door doesn't mean no exit."

But not getting one of the barrels loose might. The knots must have been tied before the previous night's rain and they'd shrunk. Try as she might, she couldn't get them loose, and while it would be easy with magic, she didn't have it to spare. She was ready to scream from frustration when she spied a little barrel on one edge of the cart that no one had bothered to strap down.

She rolled it onto the ground and stood it on its end, glancing about. She didn't know if she could do this once, but she certainly couldn't manage it twice. The moment had to be perfect.

It came an instant later, when the guards on the ramparts above them reached the farthest end of their patrol. It left a brief window with no one on the walls directly overhead. Gillian stepped back, pointed the staff at the barrel and cast the strongest levitation spell she could manage.

For a long moment, nothing happened, the small container merely sat there like a stone. But then, as she watched with her heart in her throat, it quivered, wobbled slightly, and sluggishly lifted off the ground. She breathed a sigh of relief and jerked the staff towards her. The barrel followed the movement, but slowly, as though it weighed much more than empty wood should. But she didn't start to worry until it began to shake as if caught in a high gale.

And then started cursing.

A stumpy little leg poked out the bottom, with a big toe sticking out of a pair of dirty, torn hose. Then a plump arm pushed through the side and a head topped by wild red curls appeared where, a moment before, the round wooden lid had been. The head was turned the other way, but the barrel was slowly rotating, so it wasn't but a second before a small, furious face came into view.

It had so many freckles that it was almost impossible to see skin, but the militant glint in the hard, green eyes was clear enough. "Goddess' teeth! I'll curse you into oblivion, I'll gouge out yer eyes, I'll cut off that bald-headed hermit twixt yer laigs and feed him to—" She paused, finally getting a good look at the woman standing in front of her. "Gillian?" The tiny woman's gaze narrowed and her head tilted. "Wot's this, then?"

"Winnie," Gillian said hoarsely, her brief moment of hope collapsing as the barrel resolved itself into a stout, four-foot-tall woman in a green Irish kirtle. "I didn't recognize—"

"I should demmed well hope not," Winnie said, flexing her small limbs. She gently floated to the ground while rooting around in her voluminous skirts. "'Ere. You sound like you need this mor'n I do."

Gillian took the small bottle her friend proffered and downed a sizeable swallow before realizing it wasn't water. Now she couldn't talk *and* she couldn't breathe. "What?" she gasped.

"Me special brew."

"Didn't they take it from you, when you came in?" Elinor asked suddenly. Seeing a familiar face seemed to have done her good, and she had always liked Winnie.

"Naw. Made it look like a growth on my thigh, I did. Hairy." She nodded archly. "Lots o' moles. The guards din' want ter get too close."

Elinor looked suitably impressed.

Gillian gave Winnie back the "brew"—her wits were addled enough as it was—and the small woman tucked the possibly lethal concoction away. "Right, then. Wot's the plan?"

"The plan was to levitate one of these barrels and ride it out of here!" Gillian croaked. "There's about to be an assault on the front gate. If it draws enough attention, we might be able to slip away while the guards are—"

"Don't matter," Winnie broke in, shaking her head. "The Circle's got charms on the walls, don't they? Try ter go over and poof," she gestured expressively. "The spell breaks and ye fall to yer death. Saw a witch try it a minute ago."

So much for that idea, Gillian thought, swallowing. But Winnie's wouldn't work, either. "They'll check for those in hiding," she said, trying to keep the panic out of her voice. "As soon as they've rounded up those who chose to fight!"

"Aye," Winnie said, imperturbably. "And mebbe they'll find me and mebbe they won't. But fightin' war mages is nothin' but a quick death—if yer lucky."

"If we had our weapons, they wouldn't kill us so easily!" Gillian said passionately.

"But we don't. They're up there," Winnie pointed at a nearby tower. "And ain't no reaching 'em."

"What?" It took a moment for her friend's words to sink in. And then Gillian turned her face upwards, staring at the massive cylinder of stone that loomed above them, blocking the sun. "They're right there?"

"Don't go getting any ideas," Winnie told her, watching her face. "I know how ye are about a challenge, but this one's a beggar's chance. There's a mass o' guards on the door and probably more inside. I heard a couple talkin' about bein' kept on duty to help secure the place."

"That's never stopped us before," Gillian murmured, feeling a little dizzy at the sudden return of hope.

"This ain't a job, Gil," Winnie said, starting to look nervous.

Gillian rounded on her, eyes flashing and color high. "No, it's not *a* job, Winnie. It's *the* job. Our last, if we don't do this!"

"But we can't—"

"It's just another robbery! Only we need this one more than any gold we ever took."

Winnie put a small hand on her arm. "Gil, stop for a minute. Stop. Yer're not gettin' through that door."

"Oh, don't worry," Gillian told her, staring upwards. "I'm not planning on it."

Chapter Five

Kit reached the hell pit only to have to jump aside to avoid a group of stampeding horses, which some enterprising witches were using to try to storm the gate. And then a rogue spell blistered past, caught the edge of his wool cape and set it on fire. He flung off the now deadly garment and started to stamp out the flames, when he caught sight of a nearby guard.

The man had taken a break from combat in order to besport himself with a pretty blond. He had the struggling girl on her back, her dress over her head and his knee between her thighs—until Kit tossed the length of burning wool over his head. It was rather more pleasurable, he decided, stamping out the flames this way, although the guard didn't seem to agree.

The girl did, though. She scrambled to her feet and kicked the man viciously before sprinting off. But after only a few yards, she turned around, came back and kicked him again. Then she looked at Kit, dropped a small curtsy and fled.

He stared after her, shaking his head. Witches. He was starting to think they were all a bit addled.

And then he was sure of it, as he caught sight of his own particular lunatic attempting to ride a levitating barrel over the walls.

For a moment, he just stared, sure his eyes were playing tricks on him. Until he spied no fewer than five mages heading for the cask and its glowing cargo. Devil take the woman! He sprinted across the battle, cursing, as his witch floated gently to the top of the East Tower.

About halfway across the courtyard, he realized what she was doing. That tower was used as the armory, and it was a safe bet she was trying for the weapons. But he didn't give much for her chances. The Circle surely had a ward on them, if not on the—

It was on the window. He watched her reach the only one on this side, an elongated type barely wider than the average arrow slit, and cry out. Then a burst of power flared and the barrel shot away from the tower like a ball out of a cannon.

It went sailing off through the air with the witch's slumped form miraculously still attached. Not that that was in any way positive. She'd have been better served had she fallen off; she might have only broken bone or two that way. As it was, she was headed straight for the heart of the battle.

Kit's eyes flicked around, even as his brain told him that it was over, that there was nothing to be done, that this was *not going to happen*—

Then he was running and leaping and grabbing for her as she shot past. Because he'd obviously gone mad at some point and hadn't noticed. But at least it couldn't get any worse, he thought, as he hit the side of the cask and held on for dear life.

Until it rolled over and he ended up dangling upside down.

The only reason they weren't spotted immediately was the thick smoke cover, but there were alarming gaps in it and a hovering cask with two glowing riders was a bit hard to miss. But, on the positive side, his impact had caused their mad conveyance to change course slightly, allowing them to miss the thick of the fight. On the negative, they were now careening for the west wall of the castle at an alarming rate.

He tried to grab the witch and jump off, but she wouldn't budge. It took him a vital few seconds to realize that she'd lashed herself in place with rope, and by then, it was too late. A huge gray expanse filled his vision and, even with vampire reflexes, they were out of time. He threw his body to the side, causing the barrel to spin—right into the wall.

The impact didn't break the wood, because it never hit the cold, unforgiving stone. Kit did, at a rate of speed not recommended for vampire-kind. For a moment, it felt like his body had actually merged with the rock, and he wasn't sure that it hadn't. Because when the barrel suddenly jerked and pulled away from the wall, it felt like some of his hide stayed behind.

There was no time to check, however, because they weren't slowing down. The impact should have absorbed most of the forward momentum, but they hadn't simply wobbled off a few yards and stopped. Instead, the barrel seemed to have a mind of its own, and it was quite obviously demented.

Kit held on, fingers clenched white against the wood, as they swooped around the edge of the ramparts, causing several of the guards who had remained at their posts to have to hit the ground face-first. But others retained their dignity—and their ability to fire. The barrel rolled and plunged, weaving in and out of the cover of smoke, as a rain of arrows shot by. One of them grazed Kit's arm, leaving a stinging track across his skin, while another buried itself in the wood between his spread legs.

He stared at it wildly—there were certain things he was not willing to sacrifice for queen and country—only to have the witch start kicking at him. It looked like she wasn't dead, after all, he thought, as a dirty heel smashed into his nose. He grabbed it, trying to see past the blood flying in his face, and caught sight of wild red hair and glaring gray eyes.

"Let go!"

"Do you promise not to kick me again?" he demanded thickly.

"Yes!"

He released her and she jerked her foot back, only to bury it in his throat a moment later. Kit would have cursed, but he thought there was an outside chance he might never talk again. And then a mage jumped him.

Their demented ride immediately took them into the open air once more, the mage holding onto one of Kit's boots as the vampire tried to kick him off. He finally succeeded, losing a fine piece of footwear in the process, only to have another mage jump at them from the ramparts. Kit tensed, ready for a fight, but the barrel suddenly stopped dead and the man sailed on by, more than four feet off course.

Kit turned his head to grin at the mage and received another kick upside the jaw.

"I'm trying to help you!" he told the witch indistinctly.

"It's a weak charm! You're going to wear it out!"

Kit personally thought that would be a vast improvement, particularly when the crazed cask suddenly went into convulsions. He held on, feeling rather like he was trying to break a particularly cantankerous horse, as it bucked and shuddered and shook. And then it suddenly flipped and dove straight for the ground—with him underneath.

He cursed as he was dragged across the battle, through the sides of burning sheds and over piles of debris. The fire worried him most—he'd lost his cloak and his doublet was quickly being shredded, leaving little barrier between the deadly embers and his skin. Thankfully, the barrel didn't seem to be the patient sort, and a moment later they were back in the air.

Kit decided that enough was enough and snapped the rope holding the witch, preparing to leap off with her, only to be smashed in the face by something huge and heavy. It took him a moment to realize that it was the side of the tower. They had circled back to where this whole crazy ride had started.

And then the equally crazy witch lunged for the spelled window ledge again. "Are you mad?" he asked, grabbing her.

"Let me go!" Her elbow caught him in the stomach, but he grimly held on.

"You'll get yourself killed! The ward—"

"Is down," she gasped, struggling. "It expended its energy last time—I can get through now!"

"You can get trapped now," he shot back. He didn't understand enough about magic to fully follow what was going on, but the guards running for the base of the tower were all too familiar. As was the spell that hit him in the back a moment later.

For an instant, he thought the witch had thrown it, but she wasn't even facing his way. As soon as the stun loosened his hold, she grabbed the window ledge and, with a wriggle and a twist, squeezed through. Kit slumped over the barrel, staring blearily down at a red-headed dwarf at the bottom of the tower, who was pointing the witch's staff and glaring menacingly up at him.

There was little he could do if she chose to hit him again, but instead she glanced behind her at the approaching guards, grabbed the little girl's hand and towed her away. Kit concentrated on not falling off the barrel, which he might survive, into the forest of guards, which he probably wouldn't. His head was numb and his fingers clumsy, but he managed to grab the window ledge on the third try and somehow slithered through the opening.

"You complete *ass!*" The woman looked at him as he collapsed to the floor. "Did you push it away?"

"Push what away?" he asked thickly, trying to figure out which way was up. The stunner had been a strong one, and while he could throw it off, it would be a few minutes. And he wasn't sure they had that long.

"The barrel!"

She leaned dangerously far out the window, and cursed. A moment later, he managed to sit up, only to have the blunt end of a pike hit him upside the temple. It was a glancing blow, but it slammed his head back into the wall. He sat there, watching the room spin, as several witches fished around outside the window with the sharp end of the pike.

They resolved themselves into one madwoman a moment later, about the time he heard the approach of far too many mages on the stairs. Of course, in his condition, one might be enough to finish him off. Kit staggered to his feet and started toward the door, only to have the witch flap a hand at him. "I warded the room!"

"It won't hold them for long."

"It won't have to." She'd hooked the barrel—Kit could see it bobbing outside the window—and was in the process of loading it with the contents of a large trunk. "Well, don't just stand there!" she said frantically. "Help me!"

"Help you do what?"

For an answer she shoved a double handful of wands, charms and bottles of odd, sludgy substances into his hands. He didn't know what half the things were, but although some of them buzzed, chimed and rang like a struck tuning fork against his skin, nothing appeared to be attacking him. For a change.

"Put them in," she said impatiently.

"Put them in the barrel?" he asked slowly, wondering if he was following this at all.

"Yes! By the Goddess, are you always this slow?"

Kit thought that was a trifle unfair, all things considered. But then the door shuddered and he decided to worry about it later. He threw the weapons into the cask, turned and almost bumped into the witch, who was right behind him with another load.

He sidestepped and dragged the heavy trunk over to the window, earning him a brief glance of approval. "I don't see what good this is going to do," he pointed out, as they finished cramming the barrel full of the trunk's contents. "The fight is halfway across the courtyard—"

"As this is about to be." The witch started to climb out the window, onto the overstuffed cask, when a spell came sizzling through the air. Kit jerked her back and it exploded against the stone, leaving a blackened scar on the tower's side.

"God's Bones, woman!" he cursed, fighting an urge to shake her.

"It wasn't meant to happen this way," she said, staring blankly at the window. "I planned to have the weapons out before anyone noticed."

"They appear to have noticed," Kit said grimly, looking for other options. Unfortunately, there didn't seem to be any. The room was small and wedge-shaped, with but one door and window, both of which the Circle was now guarding.

She rounded on him. "You should have stayed out of it! If you hadn't jumped on board, they might not have spotted me!"

"If I had stayed out of it, madam, you would be dead," he snapped. "And I was not the one sending us careening about like a drunken hummingbird."

"Neither was I!" Gray eyes flashed like lightning. "Winnie thought you were attacking me. She was trying to shake you off."

"Winnie would be the demented dwarf?"

"She isn't either," the witch said heatedly. "And say that sometime in her hearing!"

"I will, should I live so long," he replied, as the door shuddered again.

The witch stared at it, and then back at the barrel. And then she snatched a wand from the chest and aimed it at the fully-loaded cask.

"What are you doing?" he demanded, grabbing for her arm. But the stun had made him clumsy and before he could knock it aside, their only way out of this death trap went flying off like a bullet.

"Giving us a fighting chance."

"That was our chance!"

The witch shook her head violently. "None of us have a prayer if they don't get that gate open!"

"And now what?"

"Now this." She rotated her wrist and the barrel followed the motion, spewing its contents across the smoke-blackened scene.

"That wasn't what I meant!" Kit said, giving into temptation and shaking her. "How do you plan to get out of here?"

She licked her lips. "We fight."

"With what? You've just sent our only weapons to the other side of the castle!"

"Not all of them," she protested, glancing at the pieces that lay scattered across a nearby table. "As long as it's only guards, we should be—"

The sound of a heavy fist, pounding on the door, cut her off. "Open in the name of the queen!"

"She isn't my queen!" the witch yelled.

There was a pause, and then another voice spoke. "Then open in the name of the Circle."

Chapter Six

Gillian stared at the vampire, who looked blankly back. She didn't have to ask if he had any ideas. His face was as pale and tight as hers felt.

Outside, someone's spell smashed the barrel into a thousand pieces, but too late. There was a huge shout from the crowd as the witches realized what had just rained down on them like manna from heaven. And then the fighting resumed, far more viciously than before.

It was what she'd wanted, what she'd worked for. There was no way of getting Elinor out of here if the gate stayed closed, and no chance to break through without weapons. But the plan had been to ride the barrel back down before sending it off into the fray. Not to get trapped five stories off the ground with the Circle on either exit.

"Master Marlowe," the mage's voice came again. "We know you are in there with the witch. Send her out and you may leave peacefully."

"Peacefully?" The vampire snorted. "Your men attacked me!"

"Because you were protecting the woman. Cease to do so and we will have no quarrel with you. We promised your lady safe passage and we will honor that agreement."

Gillian braced herself, sure he would take them up on the offer. She had friends who would have abandoned her in such a situation, and she wouldn't have blamed them. And this man owed her nothing.

But he surprised her. "I have need of the witch," he said, gripping her arm possessively.

"Then you can petition the council."

"Would that be the same council that sentenced her to death?" he asked cynically.

"Send her out, or we shall come in and take her."

The menace in the man's voice made Gillian shiver, but the vampire just looked puzzled. "Why?" he demanded. "Why risk anything for a common cutpurse? She is of no value to you, while my lady would reward you handsomely—"

The mage laughed. "I am sure she would! Do not think to deceive us. A common cutpurse she may have been, but the guards saw what the old woman did. We know what she is!"

The vampire looked at her, a frown creasing his forehead. "What are you?" he asked softly.

Gillian shook her head, equally bewildered. "Nobody. I . . . nobody."

"They appear to feel otherwise," he said dryly. Sharp dark eyes moved to the table. "I don't suppose any of those weapons—"

"Magical weapons are like any other kind," Gillian told him, swallowing. "Someone has to use them."

"And I'm not a mage."

"It wouldn't matter. Two of us against how many of them? No weapon would be enough to even the odds, much less—"

A heavy fist hit the door. Gillian jumped and the vampire's hand tightened reflexively on her arm. It shouldn't have been painful, but his fingers closed right over the burn the eldest had given her. She cried out and he abruptly let go, as the mage spoke once more.

"Master Marlowe! I will not ask again!"

"Promises, promises," the vampire muttered.

Gillian didn't say anything. She'd pushed up her sleeve to get the fabric off the burn, but no raw, red flesh met her gaze. Instead, she found herself staring in confusion at an ancient, graceful design etched onto her inner wrist.

Her fingers traced the pattern slowly, reverently. It wasn't finished, with only two of the three spirals showing dark blue against her skin. But there was no doubt what it was. "The triskelion," she whispered.

"The what?" the vampire asked.

She looked down, in the direction of his voice, and found him sprawled on the floor for some reason. Her head was spinning too much to even wonder why. "It's the sigil used by the leaders of our covens."

His eyes narrowed. "A moment ago, you claimed to be of no importance, and now you tell me you're a coven leader?"

"But that's just it, I'm not! At least . . ." Gillian had a sudden flash of memory, of the Great Mother's hand gripping her arm, of how she had refused to let go even in death—and of the ease with which the elements had come to her aid thereafter. She had put it down to the staff magnifying her magic. But no amount of power should have allowed her to call an element that was not hers.

"At least what?" he asked, getting up with a frustrated look on his face.

"I think there's a chance that the Great Mother . . . that she may have—" she stopped, because it sounded absurd to say it out loud—to even think it. But what other explanation was there? "I think she may have passed her position to me."

She expected shock, awe, disbelief, all the things she was feeling. But the vampire's expression didn't change, except to look slightly confused. And then his head tilted at the sound of some muttering outside. It was too low for her ears to make out, but he didn't appear to have that problem.

"They've sent for a wardsmith," he said grimly. "Before he arrives and they rush the room and kill us both, would you kindly explain what that means?"

"They offered you safe passage," Gillian reminded him.

"And I know exactly how much faith to put in that," he said mockingly, hopping up onto the table. "Now *tell me*."

She took a deep breath. "Every coven has a leader, called the Great Mother or the Eldest. In time of peace, she judges disputes, allocates resources and participates in the assembly of elders at yearly meetings. In time of war, she leads the coven in battle."

He'd been trying to press an ear against the ceiling, but at that he looked down. "And you agreed?" he asked incredulously.

"She asked if I was willing to fight for my own," Gillian said defensively. "I thought she meant Elinor, to get her out of this . . ."

"So, of course, you said yes!"

"I didn't know she was putting me in charge!"

"That is why the mages marked us," he said, as if something had finally made sense. "I wondered why they were focused on you when there were dozens of prisoners closer to the gates."

Gillian shook her head. "They don't want me, they want this." She held out the arm with the ward.

"For what purpose?"

"The triskelion gives the Great Mother the ability, in times of danger, to . . . to borrow . . . part of the magic of everyone under her control," she said, struggling for words he would understand. "It's meant to unite the coven in a time of crisis, allowing its leader to wield an awesome amount of power, all directed toward a single purpose. It's why the Circle fears them so much, why they've hunted them so—"

She broke off as her voice suddenly gave out. The vampire frowned and pulled a flask from under his doublet, bending down to hand it to her. She eyed it warily, thinking of Winnie and her brew, but it turned out to be ale. It was body-warm and completely flat, and easily the best thing she'd ever tasted.

He balanced on the edge of the table in a perilous-looking crouch, regarding her narrowly. "If the ward is that powerful, why did the jailers not take it off the witch once they had her in their grasp?"

"They didn't know who she was," Gillian gasped, forcing herself to slow down before she spilled any of the precious liquid. "I didn't even know. She was dressed in rags, her hair was dirty, her face was haggard— she must have been in disguise and was picked up in a raid."

"But do not magical objects give off a residue your people can feel?"

"Yes, but the ward isn't like a charm—it holds no magic itself when not active. And non-magical items can occasionally be missed in searches."

"But if it's so powerful, why didn't the witch use it herself?"

"She was gagged," Gillian said, thinking of the disgusting scrap of cloth she'd pulled from the eldest's mouth. "And by the time I freed her, she was too weak to fight. Goddess knows how long she was in there."

"So in return for your help, she saddles you with the very thing most likely to get you killed," he said in disgust.

"She wanted to save her people, and she needed someone strong enough to use the ward!"

"Then I suggest you do so. There are four guards in the chamber below and at least five in the corridor outside—and that is assuming no one is hiding under a silence shield. Above us is the roof of the keep, guarded by four more men who can be called down if needed. And then there's the two below the window, who are doubtless hoping we'll poke our heads out again and get them blown off!"

"*Fifteen men?*" Gillian repeated, appalled. That was three times as many as she'd expected, especially with an escape in progress. What were they all doing here?

"Fifteen war mages." He smiled grimly. "There is a price to be paid for breaking into the most secure part of the prison."

"But . . . how do we to get past so many?"

"We don't. I can take three, possibly four with your help. No more. We need a diversion to draw the rest away to have any chance at all."

Gillian licked her lips, staring at the blank space on her arm where the third spiral of the triskelion should have been. The ward looked oddly lopsided without it, the pattern disjointed and incomplete. Like the connection it was meant to make.

"I . . . don't think I can," she confessed.

"I beg your pardon?" the vampire asked politely.

"This isn't a complete ward," she explained. "The triskelion should have three arms, one for each of the three great elements. And this has but two. The other hasn't manifested, and until it does, the ward won't function."

The vampire jumped off the table and grabbed her arm. "You're sure it had three, when you saw it on the old woman's wrist?"

"Her title was Eldest and yes! They all do."

"Then where is the other one?" he demanded suspiciously.

"Well, I don't have it hidden in my shift!" she said, snatching her arm back. It throbbed with every beat of her heart, a pounding, staccato rhythm that was getting faster by the minute. But she couldn't afford to panic. Not here, not now. She had to figure this out, and there was an answer—she knew it. Magic had rules and it followed them strictly. She just had to find the ones that applied here.

The vampire must have thought the same, because he straightened his shoulders and took a breath. "How is the sigil usually passed from person to person?"

"There's a ritual," she said, trying to concentrate. "The last time it happened in my coven, I was a child. My mother wouldn't allow me to attend—she thought it too gruesome—"

"Gruesome?"

Gillian hugged her arms around herself. "The new Mother has to run a gauntlet, to prove her fitness to lead. She must summon each of the three elements to her aid, and each time she calls one successfully, that element becomes active on the sigil."

"What is shocking about that?"

"If she fails, she dies," Gillian said simply, her chin lifting. Her tone challenged him to denigrate the covens' traditions as the Circle constantly did. Barbaric, they called them, and backward and crude. But it was for instances like this one that the ritual had been instituted. Only someone with a firm belief in her abilities and an utter devotion to her coven could pass the gauntlet, because only someone with that level of commitment could lead in times like these.

That was the kind of woman the eldest had been, capable and strong, in spirit if no longer in body. But Gillian wasn't that person. She wasn't anything anymore.

"And then what?" the vampire demanded.

"Nothing, I . . . that's all I can remember. Call the elements and the sigil activates."

"Well, you must have called two already," he said, pointing to the two arms of the triskelion. "Which ones?"

"I remember calling Fire," Gillian told him. "It was in battle. I looked down because my arm hurt and saw the glyph glowing on the staff. I wondered why I was able to summon it when I never could before."

"And the other?"

"That has to be Wind—my own element. It didn't hurt, so I can't be sure, but I think it came in when the Circle's men attacked us the first time."

"When you blew their weapons back at them."

"Yes."

"Then which one is missing?"

"Earth," she whispered, her eyes going to the window as the full implication hit.

His eyes narrowed at her tone. "Why is that a problem?"

"Because Wind comes from air and I was standing right by a burning hut when I called Fire!"

"And?"

"And I need to be near an element to summon it."

His own eyes widened as comprehension dawned. "And we're five stories up."

Chapter Seven

Gillian didn't have a reply, but she couldn't have made one anyway. Because the next moment, the assault on the door resumed. Only this time, it sounded like a battering ram had been brought up. The door shuddered under massive blows, the ward around it sparking and spitting.

The vampire swore. "I didn't think they would find a wardsmith so quickly."

"They didn't, or they wouldn't be trying to batter their way in! They were probably lying before, hoping you'd hear."

"Then we're safe for the moment?"

"No," she admitted. "Wards like this are tied to the integrity of an item. Just as a shattered charm loses its magic, the ward will fail as soon as the door suffers enough damage."

"And when will that be?"

She stared at the tiny fractures already visible in the wood and swallowed. "Not long."

"It doesn't make sense," he said angrily. "If you were going to use the sigil, you would have done so before now. They must know that you can't. Yet half the war mages in the prison are here, instead of at the gates!"

Gillian shook her head. She'd had the same question, and he was right, it didn't make sense. She couldn't direct the fight from here, not that anyone was likely to listen to her anyway. The witches had fled before the eldest died; they hadn't seen what had happened.

She was, she realized with sudden clarity, about to die for a position nobody even knew she had.

"You've already sent most of the weapons that were here to the battle and the Circle has men watching the window in any case," the vampire fretted. "They can't be concerned about you sending more. Why waste this many men on a single woman who isn't even a threat?"

Gillian started to shake her head again, but then she stopped, staring down at her wrist. And just like that, she understood. "They're not," she said blankly.

"They're not what?"

Her hand closed over the ward, but she could still feel it, carved into her flesh like a brand. "They're not aiming for one witch," she said, looking up at him as it all came together in a rush, like a riddle that had needed but one final clue. "This is about destroying all of us!"

"I don't understand."

"There is no such thing as a one-way street in magic. Anything that can give power can also be used to take it!"

"You're talking about the triskelion."

She nodded frantically. "It links all the witches under the eldest's control. If the Circle gets their hands on it, they can use it to bleed each and every one of them dry! It doesn't matter if they run, if they hide—" she broke off abruptly, thinking of Winnie. Gillian had given her the staff, hoping its power would allow her to hide herself and Elinor. But if the Circle obtained the ward, it wouldn't matter how well they were hidden.

They could be killed just the same.

Gillian felt her blood run cold.

"But the ward isn't complete," the vampire protested. "If you cannot use it, how can they?"

"By putting me under a compulsion, by forcing me to call the last element—and then using me to drain every last person here!"

"But surely, not everyone here was a member of the same coven."

"It doesn't matter! Magical objects follow simpler rules than humans do. And a coven, in the loosest sense, is a group of magic workers under the leadership of an elder. And she was the most senior witch here."

"You're saying that the ward thinks the whole prison was her coven?" he asked doubtfully.

"Which she passed on to me," Gillian said numbly, staring at the window. The setting sun was shining through drifting clouds of smoke, casting a reddish light into the room. She couldn't see the battlefield from where she stood, but it didn't matter. The real battle wasn't going to be fought down there.

It seemed hopeless. The Circle held all the cards; they had from the start. There were too many of them and too few coven witches, and unlike the Great Mothers, they had no sense of community, no reverence for the ancient ways, no respect for a magic so different from their own. They had never meant to work with anyone. From the beginning, their strategy had been subjugation or destruction.

It was their game, and they had already won.

But they wouldn't win completely.

"Kill me," Gillian said harshly, as the pounding on the door took on a strange kind of rhythm, like the furious drumming in her chest.

"What?" The vampire had been staring at the window, too, as if in thought. But at that, his eyes swiveled back to her.

"I won't let them do it," she told him flatly. "I won't let them use me to destroy everyone else. I can't save myself, but I'll die on my own terms, as the old Mother did. A free coven witch and damn them all!"

"And yet you'll still be dead," he said sharply.

"Nothing can stop that now."

"Perhaps, perhaps not. If you will give me but a moment to think—
"

"We don't have a moment," she said, grabbing his arms. "Do as I ask or it will be too late!"

"You don't understand," he told her, and for the first time since they'd met, he looked unsure of himself. "The thought occurred to me, as well, but it isn't that simple."

"Your kind does it all the time!"

"We do no such thing!" His dark eyes flashed. "Those who join us are chosen very carefully. Not everyone is fit for this life, and it does little good to go to the trouble of Changing someone merely to have them—"

"Changing?" It took her a moment to realize what he meant, and then her fingers dug into his arms. "You're saying that—you mean can—" she broke off, the implications staggering her.

He was talking about making her into one of them, about turning her into a monster. She shuddered in instinctive revulsion, her skin going clammy at the very thought. Walking undead, drinkers of blood, merciless killers—every horror story about the breed she'd ever heard rang in her mind like the clanging of a bell. She *couldn't*—

But it would work. Coven magic was living magic, based on the deep old secrets of the earth. And its creations were living things, tied to the life of the one who bore them. If she died, the ward died with her. It was why they had to be passed from elder to elder before death, or new ones had to be created.

And it didn't get much deader than a vampire.

It was the only way to survive this. The only way to see Elinor again, to be there as she grew up, to protect her. It wouldn't be anything like the life she'd hoped to have, the one she'd dreamed of for them. But it would be *something*.

And that was more than her own kind were willing to offer.

"Do it," she told him. "Make me one of you."

The vampire scowled. "As I informed you, it is not that easy. And there is a chance that it could make things even worse."

Gillian severely doubted that. "The Circle promised you safe passage if you ceased to protect me," she reminded him. "If they find me dead, there's a good chance they'll leave you alone rather than risk making an enemy of your mistress. They have enough of those as it is!"

"That isn't the point—"

"Then what is?" she demanded desperately. The wood of the door was starting to splinter. They had minutes, maybe less, and she wasn't sure how long the process took.

"The point is that I am not sure how," he admitted, with faint spots of color blooming high on his cheeks.

"But . . . but you're a master," she said, bewildered. "You have to be! You've been running about in broad daylight for the last hour!"

"Yes, but . . ." he sighed and ran a hand through his curls. "It is too complex to explain fully, but essentially . . . my Lady Pushed me."

"Pushed? What—"

"It is done when a master wishes to elevate a servant's rank quickly. A great deal of power is . . . is shoved through a subject all at once," he told her, swallowing. "It is rarely done, because many times, the subject involved does not survive. But the threats against her Majesty were grave enough to make my Lady decide that she needed someone on the inside, and no one in her stable was qualified. But a newly-made vampire has many weaknesses that—"

"Newly-made?" Gillian grasped onto the one thing in all that which made sense. "How new?"

He licked his lips. "A few years."

"A few *years*?"

"If you round up."

Gillian felt her stomach plummeting. "You're telling me you've never Changed anyone before?"

"I never had cause," he said, looking defensive.

"Didn't they train you?" she demanded, suddenly furious. She had found a way out of this, against all the odds, she had found a way. And he *didn't know how*?

"It is rather like sex," he snapped. "The theory and the practice being somewhat different!"

"You have to try!"

"You don't understand. It is a little-known fact that newly-minted masters, even those who took centuries to reach that mark, often have . . . mishaps . . . before they succeed in making their first Child. If I do this incorrectly—"

"Then I'll be dead," she said harshly. "Which is what I will be when the Circle finishes with me in any case." She took off her kerchief, baring her neck before she could talk herself out of this. "Do it."

For a moment, she was certain he would refuse. And why shouldn't he, she thought bitterly. It sounded like masters changed only those who could be helpful to them in some way, and she'd been little enough use to anyone alive. Why should dead be any different?

But then he swallowed and stepped closer, his hands coming up to rest on her shoulders. There was fear in his eyes, and it looked odd on that previously self-assured face. Like the bruises purpling along his jaw and cheek, wounds his kind weren't supposed to get. Her hand instinctively lifted to touch them, and found his skin smooth and blood warm, nothing like the stories said.

She stared at him, wondering if his kind felt pain, if they felt love, if they *felt*. She didn't know. She didn't know anything about them but rumors and stories, most of which, she was beginning to realize, had likely been fabricated by people who knew even less than she.

"Try to relax," he murmured, and she wasn't sure whether he was talking to her or himself. But then his eyes lightened to a rich, honey-gold, as if a candle had been lit behind them. The pounding on the door receded, fading into nothingness, and the cool breeze flowing through the window turned warm. Incredibly, she felt some of the stiffness leave her shoulders.

For a moment—until his lips found her neck and she faltered in cold panic, the soft touch causing her heart to kick violently against her ribs. Her hands tightened on his sleeves, instinct warring with instinct—to push him away, to pull him closer, the will to live fighting with the need to die.

"I'm not doing this correctly," he said, feeling her tremble. "You should not feel fear."

"Everyone fears death, unless they have nothing to live for."

"And you have much."

She nodded, mutely. She hadn't realized until that moment how focused she'd been on all that she'd lost, instead of on what remained. She didn't want to die. She wasn't *supposed* to die, not here, not now. She knew it with a certainty at war with all reason.

"I cannot do this if you fight me," he told her simply. "Humans tell stories of us forcibly Changing them against their will, but that rarely happens. It is difficult enough when the subjects are willing, when they want what we have to offer."

"And what is that?" she asked, trying for calm despite the panic ringing in her bones.

"For most? Power, or the possibility of it. Wealth—few masters are poor, and their servants want for nothing. And, of course, the chance to cheat death. Quite a few transition in middle age, when their bodies begin to show wear, when they realize how short a mortal life really is."

Gillian shook her head in amazement, that anyone would throw away something so precious for such scant reward. "But few become masters, isn't that right?" He nodded. "So the power is in another's hands, as is the wealth, to give or withhold as he chooses. And as for death—" This didn't feel like a cheat to her. It felt like giving up. It felt like the end.

The vampire smiled, softly, sadly. "You are a poor subject, Mistress Urswick. You are not grasping enough. What you want, you already have; you merely wish to keep it."

"But I'm not going to keep it, am I?" The terror faded as that certainty settled into her bones. She had one chance, here and now, and it would never come again. She could let fear rob her of it and die, or she could master herself and live. A strange life, to be sure, but life, nonetheless.

"Do you wish to proceed?" he asked her, watching her face.

Gillian took a deep breath, and then she nodded.

Chapter Eight

He didn't tell her again that this might not work. He didn't tell her anything at all. But golden threads of a magic she didn't know suddenly curled around her hands where they rested on his arms. She had always thought vampires were creatures of the dark, but the same bright magic shone around him as his hands came up to bracket her face.

"I don't know your first name," he whispered, against her lips.

"Gillian," she told him, hearing her voice tremble.

"Gillian," he repeated, and her name in his voice was full of so much longing that it coiled in her belly, dark and liquid, like her own emotion. And perhaps it was. Because when he suddenly bit down on her lower lip, the sensation left her trembling, but not with fear.

He made a low noise in his throat and pulled her close. The same strange magic that twisted around them sparked off his fingers wherever they touched her, like rubbed wool in winter. The tiny flashes of sensation had her arching helplessly against him, one hand clenched on his shoulder, the other buried in the silk of his hair.

She could taste her own blood, hot and coppery, on his tongue as he drove the kiss deep, and it drew a sound from her, something animal and desperate. She gulped for air when he pulled back, almost a sob. She wanted—she wanted more than this; his hands on her body, his skin against hers, his tongue tracing the tiny wound he'd made—

But when he returned, it wasn't to her lips.

A brilliant flash of pain went through her, like a shock of cold water, as his fangs slid into the flesh of her neck. She drew in a stuttering breath, but before she could cry out, a rush of rich, strong magic flooded her senses, spreading heat through every fiber of her body. She'd always thought of vampires as taking, but this was giving, too, an impossibly intimate sharing that she'd never even dreamed was—

He didn't move, but it suddenly felt like he was inside her, thrusting all that power into her very core. She shuddered and opened to him, helpless to resist, the vampire shining on her and in her, elemental and blazing and gone past human. The pain was gone, the magic driving that and everything else away, crashing over her like ocean waves, an unrelenting and unending tide. She screamed beneath it, because it couldn't be borne and it had to be; because there was no bracing to meet it and no escape; and because it would end, and that would be even harder to bear.

"Gillian." It took her a moment to realize he had drawn back, with the tide of magic still surging through her veins. It felt like the sea, ebbing and flowing in pounding waves that shook the very foundations of—

She blinked, and realized that it wasn't just the vampire's magic making the room shake. It wasn't even the pounding on the door, which seemed to have stopped in any case. She frowned and watched as the few remaining charms jittered and danced off the table, all on their own.

"What is it?" she asked, bemused. The vampire pulled her to the window, and leaned out, dangerously far. "What are you doing?" she tried to pull him back. "They'll kill you!"

"I don't think so," he said, his voice sounding as stunned as she felt. "Why not?"

"Because I believe you may have completed that ward, after all."

He backed away from the window and she moved forward, in time to see what looked like a black wave crash into the side of the tower, shaking it to its very foundation. She blinked, dizzy from blood loss and still burning with that strange energy. And then another wave started for them, rising out of the earth of the courtyard, and she understood.

"In defense of your life," the vampire said, with quiet irony.

Gillian looked down to see the third spiral of the triskelion, glowing bright against her wrist. She traced it with a finger and power shivered in the air for a moment, before melting back into her skin, joining the tide swelling within her.

"I think it might be best if it didn't hit," he said, glancing from the approaching wave to the cracks spidering up the old walls. "Can you stop it?"

"I don't want to stop it," she told him, flexing her fingers and feeling the warmth of deep rich soil beneath her hands, the whisper of the age-old magic of the earth in her ears. But there was something else there, too, alien and strange, but powerful, all the same. It wasn't the vampire's rich, golden energy, but colder, more metallic, more—

She laughed, suddenly understanding what the Old Mother had meant. "You'll have all the power you need," she repeated.

"What?"

"The Mother didn't just link the witches into her coven," she told him delightedly. "She linked the mages, too!"

He stared at her, and then back at the awesome power of the land rising to meet them. "That's . . . very interesting, but I think we had better jump before the next wave hits."

"Let the Circle jump!" she said, and pushed *out*.

The magic flowing along her limbs followed the motion—and so did the earthen tide. It paused almost at the tower base, trembling on the edge of breaking like a wave about to crest. And then it surged back in the other direction.

Masses of black soil rippled out in concentric circles from the base of the tower, flowing like water toward the old fortress walls. They hit like the surf on the beach, crashing into stone and old mortar already riddled with tiny fissures from years of neglect. The fissures became cracks, the cracks became gaps, and still the waves came. Until the earth shifted beneath the foundations and the stones slipped loose from each other and the walls crumbled away.

There were shouts and curses from the guards who fell with the walls, and from the bewildered mages who suddenly found themselves at the center of a pile of spread-out rubble. But the witches were eerily silent, turning as one to look up at the tower for a long, drawn out moment. And then they gave an ancient battle cry that raised the hair on Gillian's arms.

And charged as one.

* * *

"Nope, nothing." The distant, muffled voice came from somewhere above him, right before something was slammed down through what appeared to be acres of dirt, barely missing his head.

Kit swiveled his eyes to the side to stare at it. It was wood, as thick around as his wrist and pointed slightly at one end. A fine specimen of a stake, he thought, with blank terror.

"Are you sure you saw him over here?"

That was the witch. Gillian. He tensed at her voice, trying to force something, anything past his lips. He wasn't sure if he succeeded, but the stake was removed.

"Aye, although I don't know why ye care," the other voice said. "He's a vampire. He'll just feed off ye again."

"He didn't feed off me the first time," the witch said. "I told you, he was helping me."

"Strange kind 'o help that leaves ye pale and sweating," the other voice grumbled, right before the stake was slammed down again—between his legs.

His alarmed grunt must have been audible that time, because the witch's voice came again, closer this time. "Don't move, Winnie."

Kit lay there, his heart hammering in his chest in rapid beats that his kind weren't supposed to have. But then, they weren't supposed to panic, either. And that was clearly a bunch of—

"Found him!" The witch's excited voice came from just above him, and there was a sudden lessening of the weight of the earth pressing down on his limp body.

It took ten minutes for them to haul him out, either because the witches had expended their magic destroying the jailers, or because no one cared to use any on a vampire. Certainly the sour-faced dwarf who finally uncovered his head looked like she'd much rather just heap the dirt back where they'd found it, possibly after using her massive stake one more time. But the witch got hands under his arms and pulled him out of the hole in a series of sharp tugs.

She laid him on the ground and bent over him, her unbound hair falling onto his filthy face. "Are you all right?" she asked distinctly.

Kit tried to answer, but only succeeded in causing his tongue to loll out of his mouth. He tasted dirt. She pushed it back in, looking worried.

"What's wrong with him?" she asked the dwarf, who was suddenly looking more cheerful.

"One too many stun spells, looks like to me," she said cheerfully. "And he didn't get out 'o the way fast enough when the tower came down." She poked at him with her toe. "Be out of it for a while, he will."

She moved away, probably off to terrorize someone else, and the witch knelt by his side. "We can't stay," she told him, trying to brush a little of the caked dirt off him. "The Circle probably knows about this already, or if they don't, they soon will. We have to go while we still have a head start."

Kit coughed up a clod of dirt from lungs that felt bone dry. He strongly suspected that he'd swallowed a good deal of it, too, but mercifully, the witch had found his flask and filled it with water. He gulped it gratefully, despite the unpleasant sensation of mud churning in his stomach.

It managed to rinse enough soil loose from his vocal cords for a dry whisper. "You . . . came back," he croaked.

She brushed dirty hair out of his eyes, causing a little cascade down the back of his ruined shirt. "Of course. What did you expect?"

"I . . . wasn't sure." He licked his lips and drank a little more with her help. "We . . . had a deal, but . . . many people . . ."

She frowned slightly. "What deal?"

"I help you . . . you . . . help me."

"I did help you," she said, the frown growing. "Winnie wasn't the only one who wanted to stake you."

He shook his head, sending a cloud of dust into the air. "No. You promised . . ."

"I'm not going with you," she told him flatly. "I have a child to think about. I have to get her out of England."

"You . . . you're Great Mother now," he protested. "You can't leave."

"Watch me," she said viciously. She gestured around at the tumbled rubble. "This is what the Circle brings. Nothing but ruins and destruction, everywhere they go. I'm not raising a child in constant peril!"

If he'd had any saliva, Kit would have pointed out that the Circle hadn't turned a perfectly good, if slightly dilapidated castle into a pile of rocks. But he didn't, and she didn't give him the chance in any case.

"And as for the other, you cannot have a coven of one. And I'm shortly going to be the only one left. Everyone else is going back to their own people, to regroup, to plan, to hide . . ." she shrugged. "It's a new world, now that the covens are gone. And we each have to find our own role in it."

He lay there, watching the last rays of the setting sun blaze through her glorious hair. And wished his damn throat would unfreeze. He had a thousand things to say and no time to say them. "If you're not . . . going to stay. Why look for me?" he finally managed.

She bent down, her face softening, sweet lips just grazing his. "To say thank you," she whispered. "Winnie will never understand but . . . I was there. I know. You could have finished what you started."

"Not . . . unwilling."

She smiled, a little tearfully. "And if ever anyone was to convince me . . ."

He caught her hand as she started to rise. "Stay," he said urgently. "You don't . . . I can show you things . . . wonders—"

"You already have."

She kissed him, with feeling this time, until his head was spinning from more than just the spells. She didn't say anything when she drew back, but she pushed his hanging mouth closed with a little pop. Then she jumped to her feet and ran for the distant tree line.

But after only a few yards, she stopped, paused for a moment, and then ran back. And relieved him of his ring. "Traveling money," she said, with a faintly apologetic look. And then she took off again.

Kit stared after her until the gathering shadows swallowed her up. Witches. He'd been right all along. They were completely mad.

He smiled slightly, his lips still tingling from her final touch. But what glorious madness.

Author's Note: "The Queen's Witch" is the companion novella to "The Gauntlet" and continues the story of Kit Marlowe and Gillian Urswick.

THE QUEEN'S WITCH

Chapter One

Light from inside the weather-beaten structure leaked out through the shutters, striping the plank of driftwood over the door in flickering bands of gold. There was no name on the sign, but most of the tavern's clientele couldn't read anyway. And the image it bore was really quite good enough.

The corpse-green paint was starting to peel, adding to the gruesomeness of what appeared to be a rotting body surrounded by waving tentacles. In fact, the *Dead Spaniard* was named after an unfortunate sailor who washed ashore while it was being built, wrapped in seaweed like a shroud. I'd always thought the name appropriate, considering the tavern's reputation as the best place to get a knife in the back in London.

Not that anyone was likely to bother stabbing me. Two days in a stinking jail and another three on the run had left me looking like a beggar, with the filthy gown, dirty face and bug eyes of a madwoman. Anywhere else, I'd have worried about my reception; here, I fit right in. I skirted a

THE CASSANDRA PALMER COLLECTION

puddle of sick, ducked under the low hanging sign and pushed open the door.

Ahead was a small hallway that let out into a big main room dimly lit by fire and rush light. It was more crowded than usual, because a new rogue was being admitted into the company of thieves who used the tavern as their base. A young man with a thin face and bleary eyes stood on a chair, grinning gamely as his brothers in crime dumped a massive flagon over his head.

At least it might kill a few lice, I thought, and started forward— only to have a staff catch me in the belly.

"Wot's the word?" the old man holding it demanded, while his pet monkey watched me with round, black eyes from a perch on his shoulder.

"I was in jail last week; I don't know the word," I said, trying to push past.

The staff was removed from my flesh only to be slammed into the wall in front of me, hard enough to drive another dent into the pockmarked wood. "Then ye don't get in."

"You know me!" I said impatiently, but I didn't attempt to remove the barrier.

Solomon le Bone didn't look like much. His hair was a wispy yellowish gray—what little he had left of it—his hands were twisted and gnarled from age, and one of his eyes was milky white and unseeing. But his magic was as strong as ever, whereas mine was all but depleted.

"Don't matter. Ye need the word." He squinted at me suspiciously through his good eye. "Could be one of the demmed Circle, under a glamourie."

He was referring to the ancient group of light magic users which had recently established themselves as the guardians of the supernatural community—whether it liked it or not. "They're the ones who threw me in prison!" I said heatedly, pushing limp red hair out of my eyes.

"Aye. And when they take somebody, they don't come back. Yet here ye are." Sol said it with the air of a senior barrister making a brilliant closing argument.

Fulke, the old man's son, shot me a sympathetic glance from behind the counter, but made no move to intervene. Clearly, I was on my own. I stood there trying not to sway on my feet, because showing weakness here was a good way to get a knife through the ribs.

Or to lose one's purse.

I felt my belt suddenly get lighter, but before I could react, the damned monkey was back on his master's shoulder, chattering at me in what sounded suspiciously like laughter. I made a grab for him, but missed when he performed an impossible acrobatic maneuver and ended up hanging by his tail from a rafter. He managed to twist his neck so that his head was upright, allowing him to watch me smugly while dangling my purse just out of reach.

"Give that back!" I ordered. His only response was to show me a withered arse before beginning to paw through his prize.

I glared at him, wishing I had enough strength left for one good *immolate*. He'd always been a flea-ridden, smelly, evil creature with a habit of throwing feces at anyone who displeased him. Everyone had breathed a sigh of relief when he finally died three years ago. The relief hadn't lasted long. Old Solomon had just enough necromancy to bring the little horror back, but not enough to make him look like anything more than what he was—an animated sack of fur and bones with, if possible, even more of a bad temper than before.

That was demonstrated when he managed to get the purse strings untied. He stared at the pebbles in his paw for a moment, before chucking them contemptuously at my head. I lifted my staff—I might not be able to throw a spell, but I could at least club him with it—but he flipped back onto the beam, skittered along its length and leapt onto a table, upsetting a patron's trencher as he made his escape.

The man mostly looked relieved, as anyone who had ever tasted the tavern's fish stew could understand, and the miscreant vanished into the shadows at the back of the pub. "Useless thing," Sol said, frowning. "I've trained him better than that."

"I should damned well hope so," I said, surprised to get even that much of an apology out of the old man.

"He ought to know the difference by now between a purse o' coin and a bag of rocks," he finished tetchily. "Where do y'keep the real one?"

"I don't. Thanks to the Circle, I don't have a penny for a pint right now!"

"Another reason not t'let ye in," he said complacently, tipping his stool back against the wall.

I fished a ring out of my real purse, a pocket sewed inside my kirtle. It was set with a large square cut ruby of a deep blood red hue, a good stone. It should be enough for what I wanted.

"Not a penny," Sol mocked, as I handed it over.

"Not in coin, no. I took that off a vampire."

"Best be careful, girl," he told me, fishing a jeweler's loupe off a string around his neck. "Stealing from their kind is a dicey business."

"That's the only good thing about being locked up," I said bitterly. "There's not much more can be done to you."

Sol cackled delightedly. "Ye stole it off him *while in jail*?"

"I needed traveling money."

"And what was a vampire doin' in a mage's prison? I thought they policed their own."

"He wasn't a prisoner," I said shortly, wanting to hurry this up. I could almost feel the Circle's noose closing in. And considering how many people they'd lost in the escape, a noose is exactly what it would be as soon as they caught me.

But Sol didn't appear to feel the same. Usually terse to the point of rudeness, he must have had a pint or three before I arrived, because tonight he was almost chatty. "Then what was he doin' there?" he asked again, taking his time examining the jewel.

"I don't know. Some damn fool story about working for the queen and wanting my help."

"Wanting ter help himself to dinner, more like."

I didn't reply. I also didn't touch the spot on my throat, under my shift, where he'd bitten me. The interlude had been a strange one, and I wasn't sure what I felt about it. Not that it mattered; I'd never see him again.

If I was lucky, I'd never see anyone in England again.

The thought sent an unexpected pang through me, but I shoved it away. "You've seen it," I said impatiently. "What'll you give?"

KAREN CHANCE

But Sol's beady eye was no longer fixed on the ring. The legs on his stool hit the floor with a thump and he wheezed out a breath through his missing front teeth. "Where did ye get *that*?"

He was staring in disbelief at the staff in my hand. The long piece of wood was ebony dark, cured by centuries of careful handling. It felt satiny smooth under my touch, with a faint tingle where my fingers rested. I couldn't blame him for his surprise; it wasn't every day that an ancient Druid weapon was spotted in the hand of a dirty thief.

Of course, until a few days ago, it had been in worse ones. One of the mages serving as jailers had taken it from its rightful owner, a leader of one of the great covens. He had died soon thereafter, in the fighting that had led to my escape, and I'd somehow ended up with it. I was a thief, but this I would have returned, had there been anyone left with a right to it. But the Old Mother had died in jail, and the covens were scattered and broken, their leaders dead or in hiding.

Like the staff, coven witches were becoming a rarity in England.

"The Circle confiscated it from one of their prisoners," I said tersely. "I confiscated it from them."

As usual, Sol didn't ask for specifics. "What're ye wanting for it?"

"I'm here to trade for the ring."

"I c'n buy rings anywhere. I want the staff."

"You'll take the ring or nothing."

"Nothing then." He carelessly tossed the ring back at me.

"I'll go elsewhere," I warned. "It's a good quality stone, no visible flaws. Plenty of people—"

"Will turn ye into the Circle and collect the reward, which is more than the ring is worth," he finished for me. "Ye're a wanted woman, Gillian. Not one ter be making threats."

And they called me the thief.

The staff was a treasure of my people; it deserved a better fate than this. But I didn't have a people anymore, nor a family, save one. And her safety was worth any price.

"What'll you give?" I asked harshly.

"What'll ye take?"

I'd have preferred to discuss that somewhere other than the doorway, but the ribald party going on inside made that impossible. I waited while a couple of men came in. One was promptly allowed inside; the other, a curly-haired sailor type, paused just beyond the thresh hold, cursing and wiping the remains of someone's dinner off his boot.

"A license to travel, for me and Elinor," I said quickly, referring to my daughter. "Money—enough to make a decent start elsewhere. And safe passage to the continent."

The wily old man contemplated this for a minute, while I watched the patterns the firelight painted on the floor and tried not to look as desperate as I felt. Despite what he seemed to think, this wasn't the only place in town to make a sale. But I didn't know how many of those establishments the Circle's men might be watching.

"The money's no problem; safe passage neither," he mused, lighting up a long pipe. "But the license, that's another thing. We don't need 'em."

"But humans do. And that is what I must appear to be. I was almost recaptured twice on the way here."

I glanced over my shoulder, but all I saw was the sailor who'd stepped in the puddle of sick. It had somehow smeared onto his hose, too, which he'd stripped off a hairy leg. Now he was balancing precariously on one foot, hose in one hand and boot in the other, looking bemused. It looked like he'd started the night's revelry a little early.

"Aye. 'Tis the way of the world, lass," Sol said, with the air of someone imparting great wisdom. "Power shifts and we have to shift with it, if we want to keep our heads."

"Thank you for that," I said, through gritted teeth. "Now can you get me a license or not?"

"I can. But I'm thinking ye'll not be needing it where ye're going."

It took my tired brain a vital few seconds to catch up. Then I glanced at the counter, where Fulke should have been, and found it empty. *Goddess teeth!*

I sprang for the door, cursing Solomon's filthy hide, only to have it slam open and a group of mages rush in. Fulke's traitorous hulk was visible just behind them and there was no question where he'd been—or why.

~ 63 ~

The Circle's men would have had me before I could turn around, but the sailor took that moment to pass out on the lintel, causing the mage in front to trip. And the others ran into him in their eagerness to get at me.

The accident bought me a precious moment and I turned toward the main room, intending to run out the back. I might have made it, if Solomon hadn't kicked my legs out from under me. I rolled and brought the staff up, only to have Fulke leap from the doorway and make a grab for it.

"No!" Sol screeched. "Don't touch it, ye idle-headed lout!"

Fulke was not the swiftest thinker, but he'd spent years suffering under his father's lash for the smallest infraction. He jerked his hand back as if burned and I whirled on Sol, who dove for the door in a move that belied his age. He scuttled behind one of the mages, a young sandy-haired blond, who surged back to his feet and grabbed the staff.

I hadn't uttered a spell, hadn't even formed one in my mind, yet power pulsed under my fingertips before spilling down the wood like liquid. The mage froze as it flowed onto his hand, spread up his arm and covered his body. And then he started screaming.

I jerked back, but he didn't let go. Instead, his hand came away with the staff, in a stringy, gooey mess that in no way resembled flesh any longer. The small, pale finger bones melted through the slimy mess and rattled against the floor. I stared in horror from the shining arm bone hanging out the end of his flapping sleeve to his face, where round eyeballs lolled in fleshless sockets as the skin dripped down his bones.

He stopped screaming about the time he collapsed into a heap of clothes and spreading ooze. But I could still hear it in my head, a high-pitched, half-hysterical sound that I vaguely realized was in my own voice, and then someone grabbed me. I looked up to see the vomit-smeared sailor, who had apparently sobered up quickly.

"Run!"

Sage advice, had there been anywhere to go. But the appalled silence of a moment before had disintegrated into utter chaos, as the drunken patrons of the bar met the small contingent of mages in a tangle of thrashing limbs, shrieks and curses. One of the latter shot by my face, close enough to singe my hair, and caused the sailor to jerk back with an oath.

Having been in more tavern brawls than I cared to recall, I hit the ground and started crawling. The *Spaniard* was built on a slant to match the bank of the Thames, with an extra story on the river side. The lower level was used for storing whatever illicit merchandise Sol was dealing in this month, and had a convenient ramp leading down to the water. If I could get to the staircase, there was a chance I could get out before the Circle noticed I was—

A curse sizzled over my head before exploding against the wall in a shower of sparks. It looked like they'd noticed. I picked up the pace, only to catch sight of Fulke waving his arms and looking panicked.

"No! No fire spells. *No fire spells!*" he bellowed, loudly enough to be heard over the din. No one else paid him any attention, but then, they didn't know what Sol had downstairs. I didn't, either, but when Fulke picked up the monkey and ran for the entrance, leaving the till behind, I decided I didn't want to find out.

I reversed course, hoping to slip out the front door in the chaos. But my hair had come loose from its fastenings and someone stepped on it, slamming my head down onto the roughhewn boards and making my ears ring. And then someone else's boot made contact with my ribs, hard enough to knock the wind out of me. Worse, it jolted the staff out of my fingers. I scrambled after it, through a forest of legs and spilled ale, and managed to get my hand on it—

And looked up to see a mage leveling a flintlock at my head.

I stared at it stupidly, still stunned and breathless. I had the staff, but didn't have the energy left to use it. And this man was either better versed in Druid magic than the other, or he'd seen what had happened to him. Because he carefully kept out of reach as he prepared to blow my head off.

But then his face paled and the weapon dropped from his fingers, his eyes going dead before he hit the floor. I stared past him at the sailor, whose hand was outstretched but didn't hold a weapon. And then he grabbed me around the waist and hurled us at one of the windows.

"No," I gasped, "there's no—"

I cut off as we crashed through the old wooden shutters and out into thin air. A few dizzying seconds later, we landed hard on the ramp Sol used to roll barrels up from the water. Only we rolled down it, straight into the slimy waves lapping at the bottom.

That turned out to be fortunate. The side of the tavern blew out a moment later, in a rush of heat and noise that sent blazing boards scattering far into the night. The sailor cursed and ducked under water, although most of the pieces went flying over our heads to flame out against the Thames.

"—land down there," I finished. I gazed numbly at the merrily burning building—for a brief moment, until a heavy hand grabbed the back of my neck and I was jerked to within an inch of the sailor's face.

But it wasn't his any longer. It suddenly smeared, like someone had taken a cloth to a dirty window. Parts of it became streaked and blurry, while others went missing entirely. In their place were bits and pieces of another picture: the jaw line became stronger, the cheekbones became more pronounced, and the unkempt beard was replaced by a neatly trimmed goatee. But the cap of dark curls and the outraged expression remained the same.

"You," the vampire told me viciously. "Had best be worth this kind of trouble."

Chapter Two

An hour later, I was in hot water again, but this time, I was enjoying it. The vampire had a small ship, the *Bonny Lass*, which had been anchored not far from the tavern. We'd swum out to it in order to avoid any of the Circle's men who had survived the explosion, and were now in the process of washing off the river stench.

At least, I was. I doubted that even someone as wealthy as the vampire appeared to be had another luxury like this aboard. I leaned over to refill my wine glass, then settled back against the soft sheets cushioning the side of a large, wooden tub. And sighed.

The sigh soon turned into a yawn, the hot water lulling me into sleep I couldn't afford. I had somehow kept hold of the staff in the confusion, but I'd lost the ring. I needed to find some other source of funds and do it quickly. Elinor was safe with friends, but she wouldn't stay that way for long. Neither of us would, as long as we remained within the Circle's reach.

The question was: where to go?

Being a witch in her majesty's most Protestant England had once been considerably easier than life on the Continent, where the Inquisition had been joined in its efforts to wipe out magic users by a group of dark mages known as the Black Circle. Having been excluded from the magical community for years, they lusted after its demise and their own subsequent rise to power. And their magic combined with the Inquisition's numbers had insured that the number of real witches meeting a fiery end had recently shown a dramatic increase.

As a result, a flood of magical refugees had started arriving in England, determined to rebuild their power and retake the continent. Anyone who resisted the new order imposed by this "Silver Circle" was suspect. But members of the once powerful, independent covens or—worse—outlaws who refused to abide by anyone's rules but their own, were anathema.

I was the Circle's worst nightmare, for I was both.

No, neither the continent nor England was safe for a coven witch these days. I'd heard the Circle had few allies to the East, where the Asian covens paid them little respect and no heed. Of course, they might have no more for a couple of penniless refugees, but I could try.

It was a sound plan, I decided, even as the thought of leaving for good caused another pang. It wasn't sadness, wasn't even anger, although both of those were present. It was more of a soul deep feeling of *wrongness*. England was home; England was *ours*.

I pushed the thought angrily away. I couldn't fight these kinds of odds; no one could. But I could live. I could see to it that my daughter lived. Against the Circle, that was the only kind of victory anyone could expect.

"You're supposed to be relaxing, yet you look as though you're planning another battle."

My eyes flew open to see the vampire standing beside the tub, watching me with faint amusement. He caught the hand I raised to slap him, which I belatedly noticed was holding my wine glass. He refilled it as I stared at it, wondering how it had ended up empty again.

No wonder I was tired.

"A gentleman would have announced himself!" I told him, pressing against the side of the tub.

"And a scoundrel would have joined you."

I started to make the kind of reply that deserved when I caught sight of his right hand. The ruby gleamed black in the low light, but with glints of red fire. It seemed I wasn't the only one who had rescued something from the evening.

"Then what does that make you?" I asked instead, moderating my tone.

"As with most of us, it depends on the circumstance."

I stood up, running a soapy hand up his chest as I did so. There was muscle, firm and warm, under the loose shirt. "And which way are you leaning?"

I didn't get an answer that time, at least not in words.

He had amazing hands, I discovered, slightly coarse in texture, but warm and skilled. Later, I'd be able to remember each movement, each individual touch, but at the moment it all washed over me in a jolt of sensation. Warm: hand at the nape of my neck, chest hard against my own, palm smoothing down my back; hot: mouth against mine, tongue stroking in; sharp: teeth nipping at my lower lip. Rough here, smooth there, hard and solid everywhere.

It had been seven years since my husband died; almost two since I'd lost my last lover in a robbery gone wrong. And there had been no one since, the never-ending struggle to survive precluding everything else. I'd forgotten how good it felt, another's hands on my body, another's breath in my mouth—

He suddenly pulled me hard against him, and that answered one question about vampires, at least. He was still in his disguise as a sailor, wearing the usual loose-fitting breeches. It was easy to slip a hand below the slack waste band, to smooth down over soft skin and hard muscle, to find the source of his desire.

I wrapped my free hand around him and heard him draw in his breath sharply. His own hand moved abruptly lower, clenching well below my waist, causing me to moan softly. For a moment, I almost forgot what I had been doing.

Hot, moist breath stirred my hair. "Mistress Urswick—"

"Gillian." Formality seemed somewhat superfluous now.

"Gillian, then," he said, sounding a bit strained. "I believe I need to make something clear."

"And what is that?"

He caught my other hand and brought it up to his lips, before forcing the palm open. "I am not a fool," he said, and retrieved his ring for the second time.

Devil take him!

I broke away and he let me go, casually stripping off his soaked shirt and going to a chest to fetch a dry one. I glared at the long line of his back for a moment, then climbed out of the tub and wrapped myself in one of the spare sheets. I turned, a suitable comment on my lips—and stopped dead.

He hadn't been going to fetch a shirt, after all, and the view was undeniably attractive. But that wasn't what had my breath catching in my throat. That was reserved for the small chest in his hands.

"If you are so fond of jewelry," he said wryly, "perhaps you can tell me what you think of these."

I tucked in the top of the sheet and quickly took him up on his offer. He sat the little chest down on the table with the wine and I started pawing through it. There was gold in abundance—chains, rings, bracelets and trinkets. But the majority of the chest held more precious contents still: jewels in every color and cut gleamed, sparkled and glimmered in the lantern's soft glow.

And there were no commoners here, no jaspers or moss agate, no chalcedony or onyx. No, spread out before me was the royal court of jewels, diamond and ruby, emerald and sapphire. And pearls, ropes and ropes of precious, precious pearls. I picked up a strand of black ones, my breath catching in awe. They were the size of large grapes and almost the same color, a dark, rich plum that shone with an iridescent luster.

The most sought after of gems, pearls were prized by every lady from the queen to the fishmonger's wife, to the point that laws had had to be passed limiting their wearing to the upper classes lest the supply run out. One rope of these would solve my need for coin for many a year to come. Two might well do so permanently.

I looked up, smiling brilliantly, and he laughed. "I am glad to see that something I have pleases you."

I blinked in surprise. I had actually been thinking that this might be one of the more pleasant challenges I'd had in a while. But before I could frame a response, he stepped out of the wet breeches and into the bath, giving me a brief view of the lamplight playing over smooth skin and hard male strength. And the words dried up in my throat.

"This lot was confiscated from a house in Portsmouth a fortnight ago," he told me, soaping up. "Three men and a woman are suspected of plotting against the queen. Two of the men were killed in the raid, and the Circle picked up the woman, Lady Isabel Tapley, yesterday. I was at the jail to question her."

"And did you?" I asked, a little hoarsely.

"It is difficult to question a corpse, which is what she was after ingesting some kind of poison," he said dryly. "And we have yet to locate the third man, leaving us with little to go on, other than what they left behind."

I glanced from him to the jewels, torn between two very attractive options. Greed won. "I take it she was fond of jewelry," I said, idly picking up a ring set with a large rectangular emerald.

His lips twisted. "I know the contents of that chest by rote. If anything goes missing, I will have to search you for it."

"I'll try to put it somewhere interesting," I murmured, examining the stone. It was cut in the new hog back manner, with a flat top and beveled sides. I'd only seen a few done in that fashion, which increased the jewel's natural fire. But in this case, it wasn't the cut that interested me.

"The coffer didn't belong to the witch," he said, scrubbing his hair. "We found it in the house owned by the two men. As neither was wealthy, nor part of the local guild, it made us think that the jewels might be important."

"Who is 'we,' Master—" I stopped, realizing that I'd forgotten his name. "You said you work for the queen," I finished awkwardly.

"I said that I work on her behalf," he corrected, before ducking under the water. He came back up, dark hair curling around his face and water dripping off his lashes, and grinned at me through the wet strands. "I am Kit Marlowe, by the way, in case you've forgotten."

"I hadn't," I lied. The name didn't suit him, but then again, I wasn't sure what would. Most men I could size up in a matter of moments, but this one was an odd combination of wit and deadly danger, and it was throwing me. The monsters weren't supposed to have a sense of humor.

They weren't supposed to kiss that well, either, but I pushed that thought away.

"You never explained why a vampire should care who is queen in England, Master Marlowe."

He settled comfortably back against the tub, arms spread along either side, wine glass dangling from one pale hand. "We have a government as well; it is called the Senate."

"I know that."

"Then perhaps you also know that their only real rivals for power are the mages. As long as the magical community remains as it is, divided and quarrelling among itself, they are no real threat. Allowing any one group to gain supremacy, on the other hand—"

"Might lead to more competition," I finished for him.

"Yes. At the moment, the haven provided in this country for the Silver Circle has allowed it to rebuild its strength. Should that haven be removed, it might well be overcome and the mages united under the Black. The Senate has every reason to wish the queen well."

"Unlike the covens," I said bitterly. "She has been a party to everything that was done to us. She let this happen—to her own people!"

"It is difficult these days to know who one's enemies are," he shrugged. "She was informed that many of the covens on the continent had joined the Black Circle, and some of their leaders work closely with the Spanish—"

"They aren't dark," I said tightly. "They're trying to survive! After the Circles began their war, the covens on the continent were told the same thing we were—give up your traditions, your leaders, your power to protect your people, and bow to our rule. Or we'll destroy you before you can ally with our enemies!"

"I heard that the covens didn't make things any easier on themselves," he said, sipping his wine. "That they refused any compromise."

"Why should we compromise?" I demanded. "We are English, and have been these many centuries! They are nothing more than foreign refugees. They need to bow to our leaders' authority, not the other way around!"

"It seems a middle ground must be found, if both are to survive."

"We haven't survived!" I hissed. "Or did your eyes fail you at the prison?"

"Yes, I saw." For the first time, he looked serious. "And that is precisely why you must help me. If we can find out what this group is planning, if we can stop it, it may prove to the queen that—"

"She isn't *my* queen," I said, low and even.

"Very well. Help me for your own sake, then. I overheard what you said to that old villain at the tavern. I can get you the passage abroad you desire, as well as money, papers, whatever else you need. Assist me in this and I will see you and your daughter safely away from these shores."

I crossed my arms, struggling to get my temper back under control, to remember the main concern here. "What do you want?"

"To start with, I was hoping you could tell me something about this lot," he gestured at the jewels. "The Circle's agents at court could only say that neither the coffer nor its contents were cursed."

"And what makes you think I can do better?"

"As you demonstrated at the prison, the coven's magic differs from the Circle's."

"Ours is based on that of the fey," I said, going back to examining the jewel. "Or it once was. It's a bit of an amalgamation of human and fey these days, which is one reason the Circle doesn't trust it."

"And I thought that was due to the fact that the covens are run exclusively by women."

"They're not," I said, frowning at the ring. Its setting was loose, having been damaged on one side, and I didn't like what it showed me. "That's another of the Circle's lies."

"And yet I've never heard of one lead by a man."

"It's rare," I admitted. "Our particular brand of magic is often stronger in women. But it does happen."

"Do you sense anything amiss with that, then?"

"No." I tossed the ring back on the pile with a grimace. "It's harmless enough. They all are, for that matter."

He picked it up, looking frustrated. Apparently, that hadn't been the answer he'd wanted. "You're sure?"

"If they were cursed, I'd have felt it before I ever touched them."

He scowled and twisted the emerald around so that it caught the light. "My lady's favorite," he said sourly. "I suppose I could make her a gift."

"Your lady?"

"She who made me vampire. She came from the desert, and says the color reminds her of growing things."

"Well, I wouldn't give her that one," I said wryly. "Unless she's fond of fakes."

He looked up. "I beg your pardon?"

"It's counterfeit. A good one, I grant you, but—"

"How do you know?"

I raised an eyebrow. "Do you have a knife?"

"There's one in my boot."

I leaned back in the chair, giving in to temptation. "Can you get it for me?"

He looked surprised for a moment, and then his lips twitched. He slowly stood up, the lantern light shining on wet curls and water slick skin. He didn't bother to dry off before climbing out of the bath and walking to the door, giving me a view of the flex and roll of sleek muscle. He bent over and retrieved the knife from his boot, then returned, standing in front of me with a dark smile.

"You enjoy living dangerously."

I licked my lips. "Is there any other way, these days?"

The stone was already loose, and came out easily. I handed it to him and he leaned over to hold it closer to the lantern. "It looks genuine."

"It is. But submerge it in your wine glass for an hour. You'll find you don't have one stone but two. They glued a thin upper layer of poor-quality emerald to a lower one of dark green glass. The glass makes the emerald look darker, and therefore more expensive, as well as making it appear to be a larger stone."

"How can you tell?"

"Out of the setting, you can see the difference in color along the side," I said, pointing out the thin line with a fingernail. "Where the layers come together."

He picked up a beautiful carconet of sapphires and moved behind me, pushing my wet hair aside in order to drape them around my neck. "And this?"

"The stones are genuine," I said, leaning back into the feel of those strong hands. "But of low quality. They've been backed by colored foil to make them appear to be more expensive, brilliant blue ones."

"How did you know?" he asked, his hands smoothing over my bare shoulders.

"I've learned to check for such things. You'd be surprised how many times we relieved a fine lady or gentleman of their jewels only to discover when we went to sell them that they were paste. Or to have a buyer tell us they were paste, when they were the real thing."

"No honor among thieves?"

"Not the thieves I know," I said, thinking of Sol. "After a few such times, I found someone to teach me the difference."

"Then these are all cheap imitations?" he asked, as those hands moved lower.

"Not cheap," I corrected, my eyes sliding closed as the sheet slipped to my waist. "The cheap ones are quartz or rock crystal dipped in liquid glass, or glued to colored paste. And their settings are nothing more than tin covered with a thin layer of gold. These are real jewels, as are the settings."

"But sapphires—even poor-quality ones—and gold are expensive. Why pay good coin for fakes?"

"Pride," I said, my breath hitching as calloused thumbs began stroking back and forth over sensitive skin. "A lady might order copies of her jewels should the real ones have to be sold to pay debts. If the fakes are good enough, no one need ever know."

"Except her heirs," he said sardonically. "Who can't then sell them themselves."

"Or because the cost of the latest fashion is too high. To be in style at court these days, a lady must wear ropes of pearls as well as sprinkling them about her clothes. But there are few who can afford so many of the real thing. Many embroider fakes onto their doublets or gowns, in case they lose them, and keep the real ones safely locked in settings about their necks."

"Making imitation stones is not illegal," he said thoughtfully. "Yet these men were skulking about as if they had a cellar full of priests."

I swallowed, caught between the warmth of his hands and the cool, cool feel of the jewels. "It isn't illegal unless you pass off the fakes as real."

"I am not interested in counterfeiters," he told me, resting a chin on my shoulder. "Even good ones. I need to know if these pose a threat to her majesty."

"Only to her purse, if she bought them."

He sighed, his breath hot against my throat. "The meetings may have meant nothing; merely rogues running with rogues. But I must be sure. We're going to have to do this the hard way."

I blinked and twisted my neck around to look at him. "The hard way? And that would be?"

He smiled slowly. "The reason I need you."

Chapter Three

Ten minutes later, I was face down on the vampire's bed, wondering how I managed to get talked into these things. "I'm beginning to think this is a bad idea," I panted.

"It isn't my fault," he complained, with a move that had my breath catching. "It simply won't fit."

"You're not really trying."

"I assure you, I am."

"Are you certain you've done this sort of thing before?"

"I do seem to recall," he grunted, "a few occasions."

"Well, were you paying attention?"

He did something that felt like it permanently rearranged my insides. "Was that better?" he asked sweetly.

"You're learning," I gasped, rolling over and snatching the dress off the end of the bed. "Now, let's see if this miserable thing fits."

Kit let go of my stays and stepped back. "I don't know why noble women's clothes are so demmed complicated," he complained. "With peasant girls, it's a shift and a kirtle and done."

"And your experience with peasant girls is extensive, is it?"

He crossed his arms. "There's no reason to be short with me, simply because the woman was a few inches—"

"She was not thinner than me," I said, gritting my teeth as I adjusted the tight bodice enough that I could breathe. "You didn't lace me correctly the first time."

"My apologies. I thought this would go more smoothly if you did not pass out on the lintel."

I glared at him, temper high, until I found myself stuck in the folds of the cursed woman's farthingale. "She must have been built like a boy," I complained, and he sighed and came over to rescue me.

"I admit to not paying close attention at the time. I was more concerned with not allowing her to murder me."

He was talking about the witch who had been working with the counterfeiters. She'd been from one of the English covens which had apparently decided that, if their own country didn't want them, perhaps they would throw in their lot with its enemies. Almost the only thing he'd discovered from questioning her servants was that she was supposed to meet with a member of the Black Circle tonight.

The idea, of course, was for me to replace her.

Kit stepped back, eyeing me up and down, while I tried not to fidget. The low-cut French gown of deep red velvet was fit for a queen—a very small one. I was glad I'd put her stockings on before we started, because bending over was no longer an option. But the size wasn't the main reason the get up was making me uncomfortable.

"I make a credible lady's maid," he said, breaking into a smile.

I didn't smile back. "I'm not a lady."

"You speak as one."

"My mother was one of our healers; she saw to it that I received an education," I said, sitting at the small table where I'd spread out the woman's toiletries. "But my skills are not those needed to impersonate someone used to fine company."

"What type of education?" Kit settled himself beside the table, chin in hand.

"I was a wardsmith," I told him, sorting through the little pots. I couldn't remember the last time I'd worn paint, but the dress looked strange without it. I pushed the one containing ceruse away; one of the advantages of being a redhead was that my skin was pale enough.

"And yet you turned to thievery?"

I looked up, bristling. "After the Circle convinced the queen to give them monopolies over our traditional livelihoods, yes! I can't create wards or even sell the charms I've already constructed without paying them for the privilege. And I would rather starve!"

"I meant no offense," he said, passing me a pot of something. "I find your solution . . . enterprising."

My eyes narrowed, but he looked sincere. And he didn't strike me as someone who worried overmuch about the law, if it inconvenienced him. He had helped me escape from prison, after all.

I opened the pot and took a sniff, before recoiling at the stench of sulfur. Vermilion. "Returning to the point," I said. "Lady Isabel was of noble birth. How do you know I won't give myself away in the first five minutes?"

"Because I will be standing at your side, playing the part of your nefarious vampire lover."

I looked him over. He had donned a black leather jerkin over a doublet of blood red samite and black slops. He looked sleek, dark and dangerous—until he smiled as if this were all a huge joke, and ruined the effect.

"You could at least look a little nervous!" I said, setting aside the stinking rouge. "If we're found out—"

"If I looked uneasy, it would only help to ensure that," he said mildly. "Take it from an old hand—a little bravado goes a long way. Act as if you belong and no one will question it."

"They will if they've heard of the witch's capture," I pointed out. The closer it came to time to leave, the more I was regretting agreeing to this. Having the wherewithal to get Elinor away would do me little good if I didn't live long enough to use it.

"The Circle kept that very quiet, at our request," he assured me. "But if challenged point blank, you can always say you escaped." His lips twisted. "It will even be true."

"And if this man has met her?" I demanded, trying to darken my lashes with the woman's expensive imported kohl. It was worse than the vermilion, I thought darkly, as it smeared everywhere.

He laughed and wiped a thumb across my cheek. "You look like a painted Indian."

"I cannot believe women wear this every day," I said, scowling. "It's vile!"

"T'is the fashion. They all wish to look like the queen—pale skin, red hair, black teeth—"

I put the pot down. "She does not."

"Oh, I assure you, she does. It's become quite the thing, to blacken one's smile before going to court. In sympathy, as it were."

"I'm not doing that."

"And plucking one's hairline back several inches," he teased, as I reached for the brush. "To get a proper high forehead—"

"I'm not doing that, either!"

"Clear skin, natural blush, and white teeth—I shall be ashamed to be seen with you."

"Just answer the question!"

He grinned at me, unrepentant. "He hasn't met her. Angus Trevelyan is Cornish, but he hasn't set foot on English soil since the late queen was on the throne. He was banished by the covens for dealing in banned substances in Queen Mary's reign."

"What kind of banned substances?" I asked warily.

He shrugged. "Poisons, mostly. He fled to the continent, and the Black Circle soon enough found a use for his talents. The rumor is that he's risen quite far in their ranks."

"We're visiting a notorious poisoner?" I asked, putting the brush down abruptly.

"The best, from what I hear."

"I trust he isn't serving dinner!"

"Oh, I shouldn't worry about that. His weren't the kind you ingested. He typically fused them with an object, something worn against the skin. T'was said some of the more virulent needed only a touch to have a man screaming in—"

He cut off when I suddenly bolted for the door. "He'll have no reason to poison an ally," he told me, suddenly appearing between me and the only way out.

"I'm not an ally," I said heatedly.

"He won't know that—"

"He doesn't have to! You want me to play the part of a coven witch—when he hates the covens!"

"That was a long time ago," Kit said soothingly.

"What if he has a long memory?"

"Gillian." Kit let his forehead fall against mine. It shouldn't have been comforting, but for some reason, it was. "What more could he do to the covens?" he asked simply.

I swallowed. There was that. Whatever revenge this Trevelyan might have wanted, the Circle had already done for him. I didn't agree with what Lady Isabel had been doing, but I understood it, understood the impotent rage behind it. The urge to strike out, to do *something*—

"He was banished before she was even born," Kit said softly. "And her family played no part in it. He has no cause to wish her ill."

"I know nothing about why they're meeting," I pointed out. "If they ask me any questions—"

"I'll handle them."

I stared at him, wanting to believe him—needing to. But I didn't trust people easily, and that went double for strange vampires. "You'd better!"

"I shall," he said easily, leading me back to the table. "Your role is merely to get me in. As soon as we find out what they're after, my people will do the rest."

"I don't know why your people can't do all of it," I said, snatching up the hood that matched the gown.

"We tried that in Portsmouth. It netted us a cask of fake jewels and two dead bodies, nothing more. I won't risk that again."

"Let us hope there are not two more dead bodies tonight," I said darkly, settling the awkward thing in place.

"You look lovely," he assured me. "They won't suspect a thing." I shot him a look he didn't see because he'd gone to rummage through the witch's trunk.

"At least everything fits now," I said, twisting about. The dress was stiff with embroidery and heavy from more yards of fabric than were in my whole wardrobe. But the ramrod stiff posture required by the bodice and the glittering, elegant folds of the skirt combined to lend me an odd sort of grace. I looked in the mirror and, for a moment, I didn't recognize myself.

"So it does," he said, rejoining me with a suspiciously innocent look. I belatedly noticed that he was holding something wrapped in linen.

"What is that?" I asked warily.

"Her shoes."

I said something extremely unladylike, and he laughed.

* * *

Getting in didn't prove to be the problem. A portly butler with a comically self-important expression took one look at the staff and became positively obsequious. He stepped back to let us through the door of a fine, half-timbered house along the Thames, not far from the ruined hulk of the *Spaniard*.

It looked like the Black Circle paid well, I thought, gazing about at gleaming plate, fine Turkey carpets and vast, echoing rooms. But they were all dark, lit only by the circle of light thrown off by the gleaming silver candelabra in the butler's hand, and the place was as silent as a tomb. The analogy did not improve my mood, and neither did the fact that we did not stop at a receiving room, as I'd expected. Instead, we were led straight to the master's chambers.

As with most of the upper classes, Trevelyan used his bedroom as a place for intimate gatherings of friends. And with only four people, we certainly qualified. So much for losing myself in the crowd, I thought grimly.

But as it turned out, it didn't matter. The faint iridescence of a ward shimmered in the air above a table draped by a fine cloth, its contents throwing off a thousand prisms of light as it slowly revolved. And no one had eyes for anything else.

"Lovely, isn't it?" Trevelyan asked, leaning over my shoulder, close enough that I could smell the brandy on his breath. He looked more like a tradesman—beefy arms, too-pronounced jowl and scattering of gray stubble—than the fearsome dark mage I'd been expecting. But there was an oily, slick feel about him that made my skin crawl.

But I couldn't argue with the sentiment. "It's magnificent," I said fervently.

Suspended in the air behind the almost invisible ward was the most spectacular jewel I had ever seen. At the center was a gold mounted, square cut table diamond, easily half the size of my closed fist. Sparkling like fire in the candlelight above it was another the size of a quail's egg. But neither held my eyes, because neither was the real showpiece.

Of all the jewels, pearls brought the greatest price because they were the rarest. And of all the pearls, the one most prized by ladies of the court was the large, single teardrop that occurs so rarely in nature, but hangs so beautifully from a pendant. Hanging below the center stone of this necklace was the single largest pearl I had ever seen, easily the size of my thumb, pure as new fallen snow and perfectly pear-shaped.

I'd never seen anything remotely like it.

Kit squeezed my thigh under the table, I don't know why. Perhaps I was drooling. But Trevelyan seemed pleased.

"It quite took me that way, as well, when first I saw it," he said. "Still does in truth. But then, they only managed to pry it out of the king's hands a fortnight ago. Blasted man owns half the world, but do ye think he'd turn loose of the one thing likely to give him the rest of it?"

"He was wise to be cautious," the handsome Spaniard to his left said. He'd been introduced simply as 'Señor Garza.' Judging by the size of his ruff and the small fortune in jewels he wore, that was almost certainly false. But then, no one had questioned my introduction of Kit as George Dunn, so I couldn't really complain.

"His father wouldn'a been so timid."

"His father lost the Armada," Garza said sharply. "His son would prefer not to lose anything else in these isles. And *La joyel de los Austrias* is a great prize."

"It's nothing next to the prize to be won!"

"Which is why you now have it."

Trevelyan shook his head. "T'wasn't so easy," he told me. "We had t'show him those demmed Venetian doodads that your lot intended t'use before he'd see reason."

For a minute, I had no idea what he meant. And then a vague memory stirred. "Murano," I said, glancing at Kit. The island off the coast of Venice was famous for the quality of its fake pearls. They were so good that the penalty for selling them as real was the loss of a hand and a ten year exile. But Trevelyan didn't seem to agree.

"Glass pearls," he snorted. "No disrespect meant to yer ladyship, but those scoundrels sold you a bill 'o goods. You would need a glass eye not to know they was fake."

"I thought they were credible," I said, remembering the ropes of black beauties in Kit's little chest.

"To the layman, perhaps," the Spaniard said condescendingly. "But not, I think, to the queen."

"Aye. If there's one thing that old harridan knows, it's pearls," Trevelyan said, getting up to refill my glass himself, as the servants appeared to have been banished for the night. "Particularly those. She paid three thousand pound for 'em, back when the Queen o' Scots needed some quick coin."

"I'm surprised she'd part with so much," Kit commented mildly.

Trevelyn shook his head. "Bargain 'o the century it was; not even half their value."

"Nonetheless, when you consider how tight she is—"

"But they're unique," Trevelyn interrupted eagerly. "Something that no one else has. That's what hooked her before, and it's what'll do her again!"

"But we cannot risk a substitution," Garzas said, looking from me to Kit and back again. "After so long, I am willing to wager that she could tell in the dark whether they were hers or no."

"Aye," Trevelyn said amiably. "T'is better this way."

"And what way would that be?" Kit asked casually.

"The *joyel de los Austrias* contains two named stones, *La Estanque* and *La Peregrina*," Garzas said, gesturing at the gleaming jewel behind the ward. "The first is the large center diamond and the second is the pearl— believed to be the largest in the world. His Majesty's father gave it to the late queen when he came to England to marry her, and she wore it almost constantly thereafter. Naturally, the present queen assumed it would be hers upon her sister's death, only to find that it had been quite properly returned to the prince in Queen Mary's will."

"Rumor was, she was furious," Trevelyan added, grinning. "But she was also new ter the throne and couldn't risk makin' an enemy over something as trivial as a jewel. But she'll not let it slip away a second time."

"I am not sure I'm following you," I said, actually afraid that I was.

"*La joyel de los Austrias* will be presented to the queen in open court, as a peace offering from his Majesty," Garzas said, with a twist to his lips. "And if her people manage to so much as see it before she snatches it out of the ambassador's hand, I will be shocked."

Kit's hand clenched on my leg, hard enough to make me wince. I didn't need the hint; it was clear enough what they planned. People had been trying to assassinate the queen since before she even took office. There had been numerous plots to shoot her, stab her, or foment rebellion against her; it wasn't a great leap to imagine one to poison her.

"You seem to have it all arranged," I said, sinking my own nails into Kit's silk-covered thigh.

"Aye," Trevelyan said, shrewd brown eyes narrowing. "But the question is, will the covens rise, once the deed is done?"

"I . . . will need to discuss that with the elders," I temporized, only to have him scowl.

"None of that, now. You wanted proof that we can do as we say, well here it is. The ambassador will be here in an hour to pick it up, and tomorrow he'll present it. A day after that, the country'll spiral into chaos

while the privy council scrambles to find an heir. She's never named one—
"

"It is assumed by most at court that the king of the Scots will succeed," Kit broke in.

"But he's in Edinburgh, in't he?" Trevelyan shot back. "An' like as not, he won't risk starting for London only to have someone else named while he's still on the road. He'll wait to be invited, and while the court squabbles an' he paces in his castle, we'll have our chance!"

"And once England has been added to the empire, I assure you, the covens will find themselves in a much more advantageous position," Garzas informed me, leaning over the table. "We have seen how you are treated here, your skills devalued, your ancient knowledge wasted. But we will restore you to your past greatness. We will give you back that which is lost."

They were both staring at me, obviously expecting a decision. "I believe I've seen enough," I said, my head reeling. "If the curse works as you say, my coven will be ready."

"And the others?" Trevelyn said sharply. "Ye promised at least three."

I hadn't thought there were three intact covens in England, other than those which had buckled under the Circle's demands. Or had seemed to do so.

"Yes, well, where ours leads, the others will follow."

"You must be sure," Garzas told me. "We cannot do this by magic alone. We need men, if we are to hold this land. But most of those loyal to our cause are in the north and will need time to shift their armies here. Just as we need it to transport ours across the channel. You must buy us that!"

"You'll have our aid," I said evenly. "As soon as you keep your side of the bargain."

"Then we will have it tomorrow," the Spaniard told me. "And tomorrow, we will have England."

Chapter Four

I t took another ten minutes of drinking and well-wishing before we could finally make our escape. The river's stench had never smelt so good, I thought fervently, leaning against the side of a building down the street, heedless of the fine fabric of the witch's cloak. My insides felt like someone had stirred them with a stick, but it was over. It was over and we'd done it.

I didn't quite believe it.

"You were right," I told Kit, feeling a little giddy. "That wasn't so bad. There were a few rough moments, I grant you, but all in all—"

"Return to the ship and give this to my man," he said, cutting me off and pressing something into my hand. "Tell him what passed this night, and the danger in which the queen lies. He will see to it that you receive what I promised you."

He strode off back the way we'd come as I stared in confusion at my palm, where his signet ring gleamed softly in the dim light. And then I picked up my skirts and chased after him. "What are you talking about?" I asked, catching him up. "Where are you going?"

"I'm going back."

"Back?" I stared at him, wishing I could see his expression. But the only light came from a few weak moonbeams that had managed to fight their way through the clouds, and the pinprick of a lantern in the Spaniard's blackened guts, doubtless from some scavenger. Still, the features I could make out looked serious. "Back where?" I asked, hoping I had misunderstood his meaning.

"You heard the mage. The ambassador will be here in half an hour. I must get the jewel before then."

He started off again, but I grabbed his arm. "Why?" I asked incredulously. "Simply tell the queen to refuse the gift. Now that you know the plan—"

"It is not so simple."

"And why not?" I demanded.

"Because they chose the bait too well," he said, sounding aggrieved. "If the queen has a weakness, it is for pearls. She wears seven strands of them on a daily basis, and more on state occasions. They are the symbol of virginity, and she is the virgin queen. She identifies with them closely."

"Why does that matter?" I asked heatedly. My initial elation had evaporated, leaving me angry and confused. We were out; we were *free*. We needed to get as far away from this place as possible, not talk of going back!

"It matters because she has what may be the finest collection in Europe. She has given explicit instructions to her sea captains to seize pearls for her whenever they have cause to raid another ship. Drake once told me he thought they would win a man a knighthood faster than any amount of gold."

"Then surely she has enough!"

"There is no such thing," he said dryly. "She once forced one of her ladies-in-waiting to present her a magnificent black velvet, pearl-embroidered gown as a gift—and the woman was wearing it at the time! White and black are the queen's favorite colors, and pearls her favorite adornment, and no one is allowed to outshine her in her own court. Or anywhere else."

"You cannot believe she'd risk her life for a single jewel!"

"Not just any jewel, no. But for *La Peregrina*—"

"But it's *cursed.*"

"Yes, but it will not appear to be so," he said impatiently. "Trevelyan was a coven mage before he was banished. If he's cursed the stone using earth magic, the Circle won't detect it. Their advisors at court will tell her that there's nothing wrong with it."

"But you can tell her differently. You can—"

"I do not have direct access to her Majesty," he said, starting back for the house and forcing me to jog alongside. "My lord Walsingham did, but since his death it has been far more difficult to gain her ear."

"You must have some way—"

"Yes, but the queen may well choose to believe those who tell her what she wishes to hear, or pick up the king's gift before anyone can tell her anything at all!"

Suddenly, I could see it—the jewel in a beautiful presentation box, the ambassador opening it before the throne, the queen's astonishment. My own fingers had itched to touch it, to feel the pearl's glossy perfection and prove to myself that it was real. Anyone's first impulse would be to pick it up.

And even if her mages stopped her, if they made her wait while they inspected it, they would find nothing wrong. Only a coven witch might detect whatever malediction Trevelyan had used. And the Circle had ensured that there were none of those at court.

We reached the mage's house and I dug in my heels. "You can't go in there!"

Kit shot me an exasperated look. "I have explained why I must."

"But you'll die!"

His lips quirked. "In case you failed to notice—"

"Make a joke now," I told him seriously, "and by the Goddess—"

I cut off as someone threw open a window above us. Kit snatched me back into the shadow of the house as a single candle was thrust out into the night, shining bright as a beacon in the darkness. It highlighted Trevelyn's stubble as he peered up and down the street.

I held my breath, pressed hard against Kit's chest, as the candlelight struck glints off the gold in the witch's gown and a few drops of hot wax splattered the street in front of her dainty shoes. But the mage never looked down. I finally realized that he hadn't heard us; he was looking for his guest, who was due any minute now. After a long moment, he closed the shutters once more and I let out a shaky breath.

"You must go," Kit whispered.

"And you must *listen*," I said, in a furious undertone. "That isn't an ordinary ward in there—it's a *mortuus* field. Any living flesh that passes through it dies."

"Which should prove no hindrance for me."

I rounded on him. "You may not be alive in the human sense, but your body is animated by living energy—energy that the field will suck right out of you. It might not kill you, but it will drain you dry, thus leaving you at Trevelyan's mercy—or lack of it!"

That wiped the perpetual smirk off his face, at least. "How can you be certain?"

"Because I was a wardsmith. And that's a Druid ward."

He was silent for a moment. "Then I'll hook it with something and pull the jewel out."

I shook my head. "Nothing but flesh can pass through the field, but only the caster's is immune. He can reach safely through; you can't."

Kit's eyes narrowed as he stared up at the window. "Does he have to be alive at the time?"

I glared at him. "You do not want to take on a dark mage on his own territory!"

"I will do what I must," he told me, with a stubborn glint in his eye.

"Listen to me," I said, resisting a strong urge to shake him. "Trevelyn is a Black Circle mage with the added benefit of earth magic. He's also an expert poisoner, who has littered Goddess only knows how many traps around the place. I'm telling you plainly: go in there and you will not come out."

"And yet I must have it, Gillian." And I finally found out what he looked like when he wasn't joking. I decided I preferred the jovial mask to this glitter-eyed stranger.

I stared at him, angry and confused. "If this is about your lady, surely she will—"

"This is about my queen," he said furiously. "She may not be yours, but she is mine. And I will not fail her in this!"

He started to climb up, but I held on. "But . . . but you mocked her," I said, in disbelief. "She's old, her teeth are bad, she's cheap—"

"She is all of those things, as well as stubborn and vain and childish and mercurial and a thousand others. She is *England*," he hissed, gesturing sharply. "With all its faults and frailties, its pettiness and posturing, and its stubborn will to survive. She should have been dead a thousand times by now, we all should—when Rome invited most of Europe to invade, when the Queen of Scots fomented rebellion within her very borders, when the Armada came. And yet she lives, and so do we, Protestant and free in spite of it all, because of that willful, stubborn, impossible, indomitable woman!"

I blinked, finally catching up. "You're not doing this because you were ordered to at all, are you?"

He drew himself up. "My lady instructed me—"

I crossed my arms and just looked at him.

He scowled. "Go and do as I asked. Tell my man what you heard and then depart this country as quickly as you can. If this fails, you need to be far away from here before Trevelyn and his ilk come to power."

He grasped hold of the lower story, preparing to lever himself up. Preparing to die, if necessary, for the country he loved and the woman who embodied it—for all of us. He was completely mad, but I was no better. England was mine. It might have forsaken me, but nothing changed that. And I couldn't watch its ruin any more than he could.

Goddess' teeth.

I pulled him back down. "I'll help you," I said sourly.

"But you said—"

"I know what I said! But despite everything, I do not believe we would be better off under foreign rule." I crossed my arms. "There's a damn sight too many foreigners here already, if you ask me."

"Help me how?" he demanded. "You said the ward is impenetrable."

"It is." I stared past him into the dark, where the lantern was still bobbing here and there amid the wreckage of the Spaniard. We were closer now, allowing me to pick out Fulke's hulking shape in the shadows. And something more besides. "But I think I might have an idea."

* * *

Twenty minutes later, my idea was sitting on Trevelyn's table, scratching its arse.

"What is it doing?" Kit asked, hanging off the roof to peer into the window.

"What does it look like?" I asked crossly, trying to keep a tenuous grip on the mage's wet shingles. On top of everything, it had started to rain, and the gown was taking on water at an alarming rate. Any minute it was going to drag me off the roof to my doom.

"Why?" he asked incredulously. "It cannot possibly have fleas. What would they live on?"

"Vitriol," I said sourly, glaring at the disgusting lump.

Sol's moth-eaten pet had been clinging like a limpet to Fulke's sweaty neck as he sifted through the burnt-out hulk of the tavern, looking for the till he'd left behind. In return for not beating him into a pulp, he had loaned the thing to us. Not that it had done a damn bit of good, so far.

"Are you certain he can penetrate the field?" Kit demanded.

"Yes! At least . . . fairly certain."

"Fairly certain?"

I transferred my glare to him. "I haven't had cause to try this before! But it should work. Zombies are controlled by magic, not living energy. As flesh, he should be able to pass through the field; but with no life to drain, the ward can't hurt him."

"More's the pity," Kit muttered, as I glanced nervously behind me.

The main entrance to the house was around the corner, but the light spilling from the open front door was casting wavering shadows into the road. There were three of them, the two mages and—I assumed—the butler who had greeted us. But they wouldn't be there for long. I'd cast a spell imitating the sound of horses' hooves to get them out of the room, but when they didn't find their illustrious guest waiting on the doorstep, they'd be back.

And our one chance would be lost.

I looked back to find that the monkey had transferred his attentions to his armpit. He was less than four feet from the slowly revolving necklace, but was paying it no attention whatsoever. Perverse damn thing. Any other time, he would have been all about a bit of shine, but because for once I wanted him to steal something, he wasn't interested.

"The wretched thing hasn't been the same since his death," I said, wishing he was still alive so I could choke the life out of him.

"It does take it out of one," Kit agreed, letting himself down through the open window.

"What are you doing?" I whispered. "Get out of there!"

"Nothing bothered him," he pointed out, disappearing inside.

"He's already dead!"

A curly head poked back out briefly. "As am I, and we're out of time. Stay here."

I cursed, thinking of the few hundred snares Trevelyn could have placed around the room. And then I wriggled my fifty pounds of waterlogged velvet through the window after him. I lost one of the witch's shoes, but I made it in—just in time to see the monkey take a swipe at Kit's head.

"You're lucky," I panted, as the creature scampered up the bed curtains. "At least he doesn't throw excrement anymore."

"Only because he doesn't make any," Kit said, shooting me a glance. "And I thought I told you to stay put."

"And I thought I told you not to come in here!"

"We don't have time for—" his head jerked up at the sound of horses' hooves on the street—real ones this time. "—anything," he finished, jumping up and grabbing for the monkey.

He moved almost too fast to see, just a blur against the pale walls, but the monkey moved faster. It had the liquid speed of the undead, too, and the added advantage of a compact little body. With a derisive clucking of his tongue, he ducked under Kit's hands and jumped to the rafters, skittering along a beam with his shadow rippling grotesquely along the wall.

I turned to the window in time to see no fewer than five cloaked figures clatter past on horses. I didn't get a power reading off the one in front—the ambassador, I assumed. But the other four were practically glowing against the night. I didn't know what the Black Circle's equivalent of war mages were, but I had a feeling we were about to meet them. Briefly.

"We have to go," I told Kit, spinning around. "Now!"

"Thank you for that," he said, from atop the large, center beam bisecting the room. He made another grab for the monkey, just as the thing jumped for a different rafter. The creature somehow reversed course mid-air, ending up back where he'd started, but Kit didn't. He did manage to land on his feet—mostly--and glared up at the thing. "Get down here!"

I rolled my eyes. "Yes. That'll work."

"Do you have a better idea?"

I stared up at the little horror, which was currently showing us his withered bits. He wasn't my zombie; I couldn't control him. And Sol was who knew where right now, not that the bastard was likely to have helped in any case. And his creature was no better, as conniving, contrary and obstinate as his owner, always doing exactly the opposite of what was—

I blinked, and then quickly decided that it couldn't hurt. I limped over to the table and placed my nose close enough to the ward to feel the slippery static of its surface. "What a beauty," I cooed.

"He can't understand you," Kit said, looking at me strangely.

"He understands the general idea," I said, as the monkey turned his tiny face toward me. I ignored him, concentrating on the ward. "Such a pretty, pretty thing," I breathed. "Must be worth a fortune. I'm glad it's so well protected."

"Unlike us," Kit said grimly, staring at the door.

"What is it?"

"They're coming up the stairs."

I stared in desperation at the necklace, so temptingly close, so impossibly far away. My fingernails made a whispering across the outer membrane of the ward as I curled my hands into fists. I could practically feel it, the smooth contours of the golden rose that formed the setting, the cool, slippery gleam of the jewels. But it might as well be on the moon.

And then I blinked and it was gone—and so was the monkey.

"Grab him!" Kit said, jumping for the window.

I turned in time to see a furry blur making a break for freedom, and then the door slammed opened and things became a little confused. Someone shouted and someone else leaped for us, a curse flying out in front of him. I spun, acting before I thought, and lashed out with a declive that flung the mage's spell right back at him. Whatever he'd cast must have been pretty brutal, because it caught him in the middle of his leap and sent him crashing back into his party.

"Caught him!" Kit crowed, from somewhere behind me and I didn't hesitate.

"Then catch this!" I told him, throwing a leg over the staff. He grabbed me around the waist and swung on behind me as I flung us into space, using the staff as a platform for a levitation spell in lieu of a broom.

It worked—a little too well.

I'd forgotten that the staff multiplied my power considerably. Instead of merely flying out the window as I'd planned, we burst through in an explosion of wooden slats, taking one of the shutters along with us. To make matters worse, the voluminous skirts flew up in my face, ensuring that I couldn't see anything as we hurtled through the air.

For a very long moment, there was nothing but the monkey's angry chatter and Kit's curses as I fought with seemingly unending yards of fabric. And then the velvet cloud parted and I stared around, to find us pelting through the air above London at an unbelievable speed. I stared around in awe. I'd never been so high before.

Then I remembered that we weren't the only ones who could fly. I glanced behind us, half expecting to see the Black Circle's mages gaining fast. But there was nothing besides dark blue clouds stacked high above skirts of rain, with lightning flashing bright in their bellies.

"What are you doing?" Kit shouted in my ear.

"Getting us out of trouble!" I said, my face cracking into a grin.

"And into worse one?" Judging by his expression, I'd finally found something that he didn't find amusing. "Get us down from here!"

I laughed, exhilaration rushing through my veins. "As you like!"

I pointed the staff's nose downward and we plunged back toward the ground, Kit's arm tight around my waist, his scream ringing in my ears.

We skimmed along above the Thames close enough to smell it, until the ship rose up ahead, like a leviathan out of the mist. The moon hung behind the sail, illuminating it so that the seams stood out like the intricate veins of a leaf. Beautiful.

Several sailors were on deck, having a late-night drink, until they saw us and dropped the bottle, their mouths hanging open in shock. We landed nearby, as unsteady on our legs as two drunks, with me laughing like a child. Kit thrust the smelly monkey at one of them, pushed me into the side of the cabin and kissed me, heedless of the staring men.

"Witches!" he gasped, when we finally broke for air. "You're all completely mad!"

"It does help," I murmured, collapsing against him in a fit of helpless giggles. "And at least they didn't follow us."

"Follow us? I doubt they so much as saw us!"

I grinned. I doubted they had, either.

"It isn't funny!"

I grinned wider and tried to rearrange his wayward curls. They were everywhere. "Yes, it is."

"Sir?" One of the sailors approached tentatively.

"What is it, man?" Kit demanded, his eyes never leaving mine.

"Beggin' yer pardon, sir," the sailor held up the monkey. "But what were ye wantin' me ter do with this?"

"Take it below. And don't touch the necklace."

"Yes, sir. As you say, sir." But the man just stood there.

Kit was looking at me with a strange expression on his face. "What is it?" I asked.

"I am trying to decide whether to kiss you again, or to throw you over my knee!"

"Let me know when you make up your mind," I told him. I thought both had possibilities.

Kit glanced at the sailor, who was still just standing there. "Well, what are you waiting for? You have your orders."

"Yes, sir." The sailor shifted from foot to foot, but didn't go anywhere. "There's just one thing, sir."

"God's bones, man! Spit it out."

The man held up the monkey, whose little hands, I finally noticed, were empty. "What necklace?"

Conclusion

The next morning, I was in the witch's gown again. An hour of hard work had made it presentable, if not precisely wrinkle-free. That was fortunate, because there was nothing else in my possession fit for an audience at court.

Not that I'd had one, so far. Nor was I so eager, I thought, as a vase came flying out of the door beside me like a cylindrical bird. It crashed against the far wall, scattering shards everywhere and making several passing courtiers jump.

Kit followed quickly on the heels of the vase, hugging the wall beside me. "There are days I truly miss Lord Walsingham," he told me fervently.

"I told you not to mention the necklace."

"I didn't have a choice! If we'd lost it near Trevelyn's house, and he'd been able to trace it—"

"How do you know he didn't?"

"The several thousand dead fish that washed ashore this morning would suggest otherwise," he told me dryly.

"The vindictive little bastard," I said, in disbelief. "He dropped it in the river rather than let us have it."

"So it would appear."

"Are they going to try to recover it?"

Kit suddenly grinned. "Do you know, that was Her Majesty's question."

I looked at him warily. "Why is that amusing?"

"Because a number of the lofty leaders of the Circle are down at the riverbank right now, knee deep in slime and rotting fish, attempting to do just that. And that was after having to admit that they were not entirely certain that they could detect a coven ward."

My lips twitched for a moment, until I made the obvious connection. "You never promised that I would do it!" I said, panicking. "The curse will have worn off by now, even assuming I could—"

"It's worn off?" Kit's grin widened. "That's even better."

I grabbed his shoulders. "Did you tell her?"

He laughed and settled his hands on my waist. "No. But I did point out that this incident has demonstrated that there is more to magic than the Circle knows."

"Meaning?" I asked warily.

"That they might overlook threats that come from magic unlike their own."

"But the Circle has a coven wizard at court," I protested.

John Dee had long been their link to the queen, the filthy bastard. He was English, although you would never know it considering how he had immediately chosen the Circle over the covens. Perhaps because his magic was second rate, ensuring he'd had little power within the old hierarchy. But the Circle valued him for his connection to the queen, and with their backing, he'd gone far.

"Yes, but he doesn't appear to be able to help in this instance," Kit said, innocently. "I pointed out to Her Majesty that coven magic usually flows easier through the veins of women, much to Master Dee's annoyance."

I stared at him a moment, and then felt a grin split my face. Now that was funny.

"It was therefore decided," he continued, "that while the queen may have a wizard, she needs also a witch."

It took me a moment to understand what he was saying, as I was still enjoying the mental image of Dee humiliated before the court. And then my eyes widened and I tried to jerk away. "No. I'm leaving England, that was our agreement!"

Kit's hands tightened, refusing to let me flee. "And it stands," he told me quickly. "I will provide what I promised, if that is what you wish. But I thought there was a chance you might prefer to stay and fight."

"No one can fight the Circle," I said, before I even thought. And then was appalled to realize how quickly that sentiment had sprung to my lips, how thoroughly I had come to believe it.

"Not outright, perhaps," he agreed. "But there are other ways to obtain your desires. The Circle did not rise to ascendancy in England by combat, but by influence. There is a chance, should you prove of service to Her Majesty, that the same could prove true for the covens."

I stared at him, my immediate response anger at the thought that we should have to compete for what was rightfully ours. But I never uttered the words. That was the sort of attitude that had come close to destroying us.

"It isn't fair," Kit said, reading my face. "But we live in this world as it is, not as we would necessarily like it to be. Isn't that how you've survived, Gillian? Making the best of a bad set of circumstances? Now you have the chance to do the same for your people."

"And what does the Circle think about this?" I asked, stalling for time.

His eyebrow went up. "As they do not yet know about it? Nothing."

"And when they do?"

"The Circle does not control the queen," Kit said flatly. "It is by her sufferance that they are allowed to remain. Should they challenge her, their counterparts abroad would be only too pleased to help her rid herself of them. They may have the magic, but she holds the power in this land. And rarely are they allowed to forget it!"

I stared over his shoulder for a moment, out one of the long set of windows running down the hall. The rain of the previous evening had vanished, leaving behind a perfectly clear, pale blue sky. It contrasted nicely with the red stone of the palace, the green of the fields spreading out in every direction and the distant ribbon of river snaking its way through a land my people had protected from time out of mind.

The thought of leaving it forever had felt like it ripped a hole in my very soul. The thought of staying . . . Not that Kit's plan was a certainty, but in life, what was certain? It was a chance, which was more than I had ever thought we would have.

He must have read my face again, because his hands tightened on my waist. I looked at him, and felt my face break into another smile. "Master Marlowe, I do believe the queen just bought herself a witch."

Author's Note: This was written in answer to a question that came in for a Facebook Q&A asking: *"How old is Pritkin's house in Stratford? In the book he stated that he had owned it for over 100 years, but I wondered when the house was actually built and if someone had owned it before him."* I started to answer it in the Q&A, but thought it deserved better. So here it is.

THE HOUSE AT COBB END

Chapter One

John had started out impressed. Not at the gilt edging on the book's antique vellum pages or the hand carving on the heavy wooden cover. But at the fact that, even though this was merely an estate agent's manual, someone had lavished care into a spell that changed the usual listings into perfect three-dimensional representations of the properties on offer. Every time he turned a page, a new vista spiraled up into the dim office light, in a sparkle of distant sunshine and a cascade of carefully tended cobblestones.

Or, in this case, a spread of rolling hillside.

He sat up a bit straighter.

He'd been at this for over two hours, only to find his initial amusement fading as he discovered that all of the best places were already taken. And the remaining ones . . . Well, it might be charming to see bluebirds nesting in the thatch of a miniature roof, or to peer into a tiny cracked window and have one green eye and a strand of blond hair be reflected back at him. But it also meant that the houses in question would require extensive renovation, and he simply didn't have the time.

It was also a factor that most of the available homes were in town, hidden from the usual occupants of Stratford-upon-Avon by clever spells and throngs of tourists. John didn't like towns. John liked . . . well, he liked this.

Instead of covering only one page, as was the norm, this particular magical diorama had elbowed its way onto two. And thereby squeezed the small garret flat that had been occupying the other page into a third of its original space, leaving it sadly crumpled and annoyed looking. John didn't care.

John cared about the rolling green grasses spilling across a partly wooded hillside. He cared about the ribbon of river, surging like a liquid bookmark down the center of the page. He cared about the house sitting in late medieval splendor on the crest of a hill, surrounded by trees and vines and acre upon acre of fine British farmland, without a single neighbor in sight.

It looked a little overgrown, but he could put up with that. For blessed country solitude, he could put up with a great deal. He looked at the clerk. "What about this one?"

A long beak of a nose peered around a tottering pile. "I thought you said that you preferred a free-standing property."

It took John a moment to notice that the tiny eyes above the beak were, incredibly, focused on the scrunched-up flat in the corner, rather than on the gleaming vista doing the scrunching. "Not the garret," he said impatiently. "The other one. The farmhouse."

The small eyes widened. "The farm—oh no. No, that is not available."

"Then why is the border green?" John indicated the discreet outline, which in this case was less of a rectangle and more of a rugged coastline, hedging the scene. "I thought that indicated—"

"I didn't say it was let. I said it was unavailable."

"Then why is it in the book?"

"Because it refuses to leave!" The clerk glared at the offending, cheerful scene. "We've tried excise spells, erasure spells, and half a dozen others to at least get it back into its proper place, but without effect. It's one of the oldest properties listed, you see, owned by one of our first adjutants. And it would appear that the book equates age with importance."

John wasn't interested in the clerk's struggles with his magical library. He was interested in the house. "I would like to tour this one."

"It is not available."

"Yes, so you said. My question was why?"

The sunlight leaking through the room's old, leaded windows turned the clerk's skin a sickly yellow. Or maybe it was always that way. John had never seen anyone who looked more like he'd spent the morning sucking on a lemon. "There have been . . . issues . . . in the past."

"What kind of issues?"

"The kind of issues that make it off limits, Mr. Pritkin." The voice was as emphatic as the book snapping shut in his face.

John had a vision of the clerk's wispy gray mane bursting into flame like the wick of a particularly sallow candle. But he reigned in the impulse, and also swallowed the sharp comment that sprang to his lips. He was a desperate man and he was running out of time.

"I'm to be married in less than a month," he said, trying to appeal to the blasted man's sympathy, since camaraderie was getting him sod all.

"My felicitations."

"And my fiancé is not a war mage, nor a civilian aide, and will therefore not be permitted in barracks."

"I should hope not!" The clerk looked appalled at the very thought. That was absurd, as there were a growing number of female members of the War Mage Corps, the body charged with protecting the magical community. However, that was over the protests of some of their male counterparts, less because of misogyny than the prevailing assumption that powerful female magic workers must be coven-trained. And the covens, especially those in Britain, had a long and bloody history with the Circle.

Of course, the fighting was long since over, but tensions remained, causing the female recruits no end of problems. John could sympathize. There were those who hadn't wanted him in the barracks, either.

After all, at least the women were human.

"Then, as you can see, I need a house," he soldiered on. "Within a month. Less, really, as there will doubtless be repairs to be made, and I will need to buy—"

"What you need is to look elsewhere." The clerk shoved the massive book into the warded cabinet behind his desk. "Or wait for Jenkins to vacate his cottage, as I said. The other property is not available, and therefore its state of repair is irrelevant."

"But Jenkins isn't moving until after—"

"Thank you, Mr. Pritkin."

"Yes, but why is it un—"

"Thank you and good day."

The last two words must have triggered some kind of spell he hadn't detected. Because the next thing John knew, he was sitting in the cramped, wood-paneled hall outside the clerk's office, being trampled by several more bright-eyed hopefuls on their way in. Good luck, he thought viciously, and swept off down the hall, wondering for the thousandth time what he was doing working with the damned Corps in the first place.

And then he remembered, when he almost ran the reason down. Not that the man noticed. The slightly pudgy fellow coming out of the loo had hair the color and shape of a dandelion pouf, and blue eyes that couldn't see his hand in front of his pleasant round face. At least not without his spectacles, which he appeared to have misplaced judging by the way he was assaulting some poor recruit.

"Benedict?" Jonas Marsden squinted at the young man. "Is that you?"

"Uh, yes sir." The recruit looked a little startled that a brigadier general would even know who he was, much less bother to address him. Or maybe it had something to do with the fact that his superior was all of an inch from his nose.

"What are you doing with that?" Jonas demanded.

"With what, sir?"

"With that!" Jonas gestured at the straw boater the man had yet to remove.

"You . . . you mean my hat, sir?"

"No, I mean *my* hat. What are doing with my hat?"

The young man looked around for help, but everyone else had scattered to the four winds. Except for John, and it only seemed to make the man more nervous when he recognized him. Now he had the second-in-command of the Corps and its infamous half-demon adjutant both staring at him. "Er, well, actually, sir, it's . . . well, in fact, you see, it's *my* hat."

The man sounded almost apologetic at having to point this out.

But Jonas wasn't having it. "Then where is mine?" he demanded.

"I . . . I'm afraid I don't really—"

"On the peg board behind you," Pritkin said, less to be helpful than to hurry this along.

Not that it did, of course.

"Nonsense." Jonas drew himself up. "I think I know where I left my own hat!" And onto the dandelion it went.

"On someone else's head?" John asked, plucking a black bowler off a peg and tossing it to the young man. Who caught it and then just stood there, looking at it. John sighed.

Jonas turned that sharp blue squint on him. "John?"

"Yes, and I have a bone to pick with you."

Jonas muttered something that sounded like 'what a surprise,' but John decided to let it go since he needed the man's help. "I want you to talk to Edwards for me."

"Edwards?"

"In allocation. He's being a stubborn git—"

"Job requirement."

"Well it's damned irritating! I was told—by you, I might add—that I was to be allowed Circle housing—"

"Well, of course. Working for us, even unofficially, tends to make a person enemies. Particularly with that nasty group of Velos demons you've been helping to round up—"

"Which is my point! But I've been here all morning and Edwards has been no bloody help at all. He found me three options, none of which are remotely suitable—"

"None?"

"The first was a dump, the second far too small, and the third still has a tenant—who intends to retain possession until at least the New Year."

"Yes, well, that's when assignments get changed around, you see," Jonas said, eyes crossing as he squinted upwards.

"But that's five months away and I need something today. And Edwards won't even show me the only property I really liked—nor so much as tell me why. Do you understand the problem now?"

"Yes," Jonas said, taking the boater off his head and looking at it strangely. "This isn't my hat."

"Damn it, Jonas—"

"It's him!" Jonas pointed at the confused young man, who had simply been standing there, cradling his superior's lost bowler carefully in his hands. "He's at it again!"

"But, sir," Benedict said, looking alarmed. "I didn't . . ."

"Oh, for the love of—" John snatched the boater, stuck it on the recruit's head, took the bowler from the idiot's hands and stuck it on Jonas's. "Now, will you please go talk to Edwards?"

"Of course, dear boy." Jonas pushed flyaway golden hair under the old black brim, watching the recruit narrowly all the while. "No need to fret. This is a simple matter. Won't take a moment."

Chapter Two

"Than Edwards is a git," Jonas puffed, slashing at the overgrown grasses with a cane.

"And you're his superior," John pointed out. "You could have simply ordered him to—"

Jonas made an irritated sound in his throat.

"You're intimidated," John accused.

"I am no such thing," Jonas slashed a bit harder. He seemed to have some sort of vendetta against the grass. "But the man controls my housing, too, you know. And I very much like where I am at the moment."

"As opposed to an attic garret?"

"Precisely."

They topped the hill, which was steeper than it had looked in the housing office, Jonas puffing a little harder now. He saw John noticing and scowled. "It's what happens when you get promoted. Too much demmed paperwork, not enough time in the field."

"Well, you're in a field now."

"Yes, but is it the right field?" Jonas asked, looking about. He'd dressed for the occasion, all country squire tweed except for the long silk aviator's scarf blowing dramatically in the wind. Fair enough—he'd flown them around all morning looking for the right set of topographical features. But the aviator goggles and scarf, along with the fluffy dandelion on his head, did make him look slightly mad.

"I think so," John said. "I didn't get more than a glimpse in the office, but the river's in the right place. And it was called Cobb End, and this is Cobb Hill . . ."

"Doesn't necessarily follow, old boy."

"I know that," John said irritably. "But without an address, it's the best I could do. And the damned man wouldn't give me one!"

"Of course not," Jonas said, like someone who already had a perfectly comfortable flat waiting for him. "It's not only war mages who use protective housing, you know. What if one of our adjutants went rogue and told someone the location? Can't be too careful where families are concerned."

Which was the point, Pritkin thought. He'd assumed that his on-again, off-again relationship with the Circle was in jeopardy when he'd decided to marry. He wouldn't risk his fiancé's life for a job, even if the Circle did know far too little about some of the things they hunted. They were just going to have to fend for self, however unfortunately that might play out—unless he found this house, of course.

Which, ironically, they were making as difficult as possible.

"We could get back in the air," Jonas said, "take another look 'round." He sounded oddly hopeful. And adenoidal.

John slanted him a look. "You have hay fever?"

"No," Jonas said stoutly.

"Your eyes are red and you're breathing like a freight train."

"My eyes are the same color they always are, and I'm breathing this way because you dragged me up this blasted hill! Now, is it here or not?"

"It's here," John said. He was sure of it. But the area was larger than he'd recalled, nothing but flowing green grasses and nodding wildflower heads, picture-postcard pretty under a gentle afternoon sun.

And no damned help at all.

Not that he'd expected it to be easy. A portal system linked approved residential areas directly to HQ, as well as to popular areas around Britain, allowing people to enter and leave their homes without ever being seen in the vicinity. And the environs around them were heavily warded to prevent stray tourists from accidentally stumbling across them.

Of course, if one was outside the portal system, it worked rather well on mages, too, John thought, as a smug butterfly flitted past his nose.

And then he heard it.

"I don't know why you can't live in town with everyone else," Jonas was grumbling, poking at the air with his walking stick. "Nature!" It was disparaging.

"I like nature," John murmured, tilting his head and trying to recapture that elusive sound, just a note on the wind.

"Yes, but does it like you?"

"Normally," John said, wishing his friend would be quiet and let him concentrate. Instead, the impatient war mage released a torrent of cacophonous magic that assaulted John's ears like nails down a blackboard, and sent the poor butterfly wheeling into the air. Damn it!

"You see?" Jonas gestured, as his reveal spell revealed exactly squat. "Nothing."

"Perhaps we should split up," John said tightly. "We'll cover more ground that way."

"And where would you suggest I go?"

"Back down," he waved a hand. "Toward the river."

"But you said it was at the top of the hill!"

"I may have been mistaken."

"Do you mean to tell me I trudged all the way up here for—"

"You trudged up here because you wouldn't order a certain officious clerk to do his job," John reminded him, which won him a squinty-eyed glare. But it also resulted in his companion stomping back down the hill, in a manner that made it clear that he was unlikely to stomp back up again.

That was all right. If John was correct, this wasn't a problem Jonas could solve.

He didn't bother going any further, since it wouldn't help. Instead he sat down, the rough bark of a tree at his back, and closed his eyes. And listened.

He always found it odd when people talked about the quiet of nature; to him, it was louder than any town, with thousands of creatures chirping and buzzing and hissing and slithering and eating and mating on the hillside that was their world. To one with ears to hear, it was deafening. It was also irrelevant, at least to his current search, and after a few minutes John managed to filter it out.

There were human noises, too, the harsh shrill of a train's horn, the distant metallic snick-snick of some kind of farm equipment, and the sound of inventive cursing from Jonas. Who had reached the river again judging by the frenzied splashing. John smiled. And then he filtered that out, too.

For a while there was nothing else, just the wind in his ears and the smell of grass and good English earth in his nose. He extended his senses, not straining because this was not something force would help, but just mentally touring the area. Unlike Jonas's attempt to bludgeon his way through the hillside's defenses, John melted into them. This time, there was no painful flash to sear his mind, just the soft shushing of grass as his sense form waded through it, feeling it brush against him now, thigh high, a warm, dragging caress.

Before long, he was smelling honey. And then more than smelling; it was a taste, a burst of sunshine on his tongue. He licked his lips, enjoying the delicate flavor, smelling the clover that had fed the bees, feeling the warmth of the sun on their hive through long summer days. He chewed the comb until his jaw was stiff with it, until the wax softened in the heat of his mouth, until it released the last of its sweetness.

Until it came again, that single note on the breeze.

It was as delicate and fleeting as a whisper, blown along like a leaf and as ephemeral as the air that carried it. But John had heard such songs before, and he knew the way of them. He waited until it was closer, a sweet chime, like the taste of honey distilled, but with a faint plaintive appeal underneath. And then he sang a single note back, not a word, not even a thought, more of a question mark in musical form—

And it had barely left his lips when a song, full-blown and loud, exploded around him in a cacophony of excitement. Little trills ran up and down his spine, into his ears, and across his tongue like small bursts of happiness. It warbled at him, so fast and so excited that he couldn't keep up, much less find a break in which to—

He stumbled. Which was fairly surprising as he hadn't realized that his body had been following the lead of his senses. Not until his shin barked up against something solid and unyielding, blocking his path.

It was a fence, old and weathered and draped in swathes of honeysuckle. Golden coin sunshine flickered down through the branches of several old apple trees, dappling the boards and the verge of a path leading up to them. It took him a disorientated moment to realize that he'd skirted half the hillside, ending up almost completely opposite from where he'd begun, where the grasses and genteel decay had hidden the little tableau.

Not that anyone would have expected to find a fence there, as it was busily guarding . . . absolutely nothing. At least, nothing that John could see, besides a tangled bit of undergrowth and a few more scraggly apple trees. But there was something there, nonetheless. Something glowering at him from the space between the trees. Something strong with resentment.

Power. Anger. Challenge.

And underneath that, a great and powerful sadness, hopeless and dark, that hung in the air like a dirge.

"Any luck, then?"

John jumped slightly at the sound of Jonas's voice carrying up the hill. It sounded like the braying of a donkey for a moment, as harsh and discordant as the magic the man had used a few moments ago. Until John's ears adjusted back to human levels, and he swallowed and answered.

"Not yet. And you?"

"Nothing. John, are you sure—"

"No. Now that I think of it, I may have misremembered the area."

"You misremembered?" John looked over the side of the hill, to see an outraged little war mage with wet trouser cuffs waving a grass-tipped cane. And spouting something John didn't bother to listen to because he was busy listening to the fence, which was still burbling happily. It would be the easy part—or at least, it would be, if Jonas would ever shut up.

"Yes, I know. My apologies," he yelled down, with no sincerity at all. "Do have a nice flight back."

Jonas cut off mid-sentence to glare at him. "A nice flight."

"Good day for it," John grunted, tugging at a heavy stone that had been pushed up by one of the apple tree's roots, shoving the fence slats out of place.

"You aren't coming?"

"No. I thought I'd stay for a bit, go over it again. Best to be sure, you know."

"You could make sure by coming back to the office and checking the book again," Jonas said suspiciously.

Bollocks. "Yes, but that would require dealing with that benighted fool Edwards, and I find I'm no longer in the mood."

That, at least, was true.

"No longer—" Jonas broke off with an oath. "And I wasn't in the mood to go trudging 'round the wilderness, either, before you dragged me out of my office!"

"We're fifteen minutes from Stratford, not the middle of the Sahara. And it was the loo. You need to get a sight spell, Jonas."

"What I need is to get my head examined. Every time I listen to you—"

"Yes, thank you for the help," John said brightly.

Jonas didn't bother to reply to that. John waited another moment, but he didn't hear any more cursing. And when he crept quietly to the side of the hill again, his annoyed sometimes employer was nowhere in sight. John heaved a sigh of thanks, stripped off his coat and squatted down beside the fence. And got to work.

Chapter Three

The problem wasn't the fence itself, but the spell woven into it. It was a cloak designed to shield the property from intruders' eyes and to raise an alarm at the presence of unwanted guests. It was fairly standard—at least for the fey, which was who had set it up long ago.

John hadn't been sure of that on hearing that first, elusive note. He'd known it was elemental magic—there was no misjudging that—but it could have been Druid. Should have been, really, because true fey magic was rare on Earth these days. But then, Druid wasn't all that common anymore, either, at least not in the Circle's backyard.

But no, it was fey, chiming away like strings of tiny bells all along the length of the fence. But also jangling, discordant, and off tune in a dozen places, and here and there making some truly frightening sounds.

But not half so much as what was coming from the other side.

John blocked that out for the moment, and just listened to the fence for a while.

Unlike human magic, which decayed quickly after the death or departure of the spell caster, the fey variety lived on. Literally, in this case, as it had bound itself to the flowers, the trees, the earth, drawing the strength to continue from their living energy. But without anyone to direct it, it gone a bit . . . off. Grown wild and cheeky over the centuries, but lonely, too, which was why it was so pathetically glad to have someone to talk to.

For his part, John was rather grateful it was here, since he was out of practice and the problem further in was intimidating the hell out of him. But this was a happy, silly little thing, and bound to wood, thankfully, which was always easy. Anything that had once been alive and growing was, the cells fusing with the magic like notes from an instrument accompanied by a human voice.

He cleared his throat, feeling a little strange. How long had it been since he sang a song for something important, for something other than calling the woolen fibers in his socks to knit back together? He couldn't remember. Of course, he'd sung spells frequently as a boy, taught by the fey who'd come to look him over because any fey blood gives a claim. One negated, in his part, by the demon blood that no fey line would have.

But they had been beautiful, those laughing faces, so unlike any he'd expected. Stories were told of them, dread stories of deceit and treachery and murder. And some of those stories were true. But they left out the dancing and the laughter and the generosity of the creatures who had spent a summer with him, singing to him, teaching him, even though one look had told them that they wouldn't be taking him home.

They'd been regretful, because he picked up the old ways so easily, astounding the Druids he met thereafter, whose magic had once derived from the same source. He'd been good at theirs, as well, since it was merely a mixture of two he already knew, two different strands of his heritage. But it had surprised them, since almost all of their adepts were women.

John had often wondered about that. It wasn't that men couldn't do the spells—the difference between humans was, after all, fairly small, and in any case, it had never prevented male fey from mastering their magic. It had never prevented him, and his fey blood was miniscule. But most men could not. The Corps could not, leading to their contempt and fear of a magic they didn't understand, a magic that whispered instead of roared.

John eyed the fence.

And then he sang to it, in the old language, because he'd never spell-sung in any other. Sang the songs the golden ones had taught him, some of the words of which he didn't even understand. But he knew most of them, and he felt the rest in his bones. And it seemed that he hadn't lost the knack, after all, because all the broken pieces of the fence happily listened when he sang about getting in line, coming back to true, behaving themselves. And soon it was all nice and solid again, with a tinkling melody twining merrily about the posts.

John patted it absently. So much for the easy part.

A gate in the fence opened effortlessly under his hand, but he didn't walk through, unsure if he wanted to open this particular can of worms. If the situation was what he thought it was, it could be dangerous—would be, really—and he didn't owe the house, or its owner, anything. This wasn't his business, he told himself; wasn't his problem.

Just like a wild, half-demon child hadn't been the fey's.

Yet they had stayed, and helped him, and taught him the magic that had saved his neck more than once. And whatever fey blood was coursing through his veins wouldn't let him leave with that debt unpaid. At least, he assumed that was why his feet were carrying him up a winding garden path that materialized like mist as he trod on it. He certainly hadn't told them to do it, he thought testily, and then he saw the house.

And suffice it to say, the estate agent's book had been somewhat . . . out of date.

What emerged from the mist was a queer, lopsided thing, late medieval by the look of it. Two story, with wattle and daub walls and heavy shutters closed against the sun. And it was completely overrun with plant life.

Grass had turned the sloping roof into a recreation of Jonas' hairstyle, only in green. Heavy vines had eaten into the walls, to the point that it looked like the house had veins coursing under its skin. And, most disturbingly, a forest of half-dead apple trees had crowded next to the foundation, so numerous that their almost bare branches still managed to block most of the sun. Yet they were strangely orderly, like parishioners in a church.

Or mourners at a funeral, John thought grimly.

He moved cautiously forward.

The place was utterly, deathly quiet. No birds called, no small animals scurried for cover; even the burbling fence was no longer audible. It was like stepping into an alien world, and not one happy to see him. John had the distinct impression that the door would have been locked against him, if an apple tree's roots hadn't propped it into a perpetually open position. He edged around the frame, careful not to touch it, careful not to touch anything.

It was dark inside, to the point that he could make out little past the swirling motes of dust disturbed by his careful entry. He started to call light to him, but some instinct told him that it would be a very bad idea. There was magic here already, magic in droves, tingling through the soles of his feet, crawling over his skin, boiling in the very air before his face, like an unseen, potent liquor that he drew into his lungs with every breath. He almost immediately felt giddy with it, reckless.

And that, he thought vaguely, would be an even worse idea.

He forced himself to get a grip and to look around. And after a moment, that became easier as his vision adjusted. There was light, and not only from the door. A few stray rays had somehow made it through the undergrowth and shutters both, spearing the darkness here and there in crisscrossing beams. It was enough.

It was more than enough, he thought in wonder, staring at huge old vines, some bigger around than his leg, that tangled on the walls and drooped down from the ceiling, and at the forest of roots sprouting up from between the floorboards, threatening to trip him with every step. Together, they'd pulled the room, which had once been a kitchen judging from the fireplace and shattered pots, so out of whack that it looked almost round. That was odd, but not particularly disturbing.

No, the disturbing part was welded to the middle of the kitchen floor.

John approached cautiously, awe and fear and shock running in equal parts through his veins, despite the fact that he'd known what he would find. Known what had to be here to explain the surfeit of magic that had no place to go, and no way to die. He knelt on what remained of the floorboards, which had once been oak but which were now . . . something Other.

He didn't touch it. The very idea made his skin crawl, although he'd technically seen worse. At least, he'd seen things that were supposed to be worse, although at this very moment and at this very time, he couldn't actually think of any. Because blood and gore and even death were natural, and there was nothing natural about this.

What lay in the darkness under its shroud of leaves was in the shape of a man. It wasn't one—it never had been—although at one time it had been flesh and bone instead of wood, and muscle and sinew instead of ropy vines, although a casual onlooker might be forgiven for not noticing the change. The oak had pushed up from the floor in an exact replica of once noble features; the tiny vines spreading around it perfectly mimicked flowing hair. Even the pattern—ironically leaves and vines—on a long-dissolved coat had been scrupulously reproduced, as if carved by a loving hand out of wood.

But no sculptor had done this. There were no chisel marks on this masterpiece, and even the greatest of sculptors can't make the rings and swirls in wood conform to their vision. A living being had lain here once, who knew how many centuries ago, in exactly this manner.

And unless John was very much mistaken, he lay here still.

Chapter Four

"**W**hat the hell is that?"

John jumped and spun, his heart in his throat and a gun in his hand. Which he lowered when he recognized the distinctive silhouette in the doorway. "Damn it, Jonas!" he holstered his weapon. "I thought you'd gone."

"Obviously." The word was dry. "And you did not answer my question."

"It's not easy to answer."

"Try." And the voice was no longer that of his slightly eccentric friend, but of a senior war mage with the authority to make John's life a living hell if he didn't like the answer. And he wasn't going to. Hell, John didn't like it himself.

"It's a fey," he admitted.

"That is a fey?"

"Well, it was. Or, rather, it is."

Jonas just looked at him.

"It's not dead . . . exactly," John explained. Badly. But he was still fairly shaken, and this wasn't the sort of thing that English was equipped to handle. Or any other spoken language, for that matter. It wasn't even something the fey discussed; it was simple felt.

But he didn't think that telling Jonas to get in touch with his feelings was a great idea.

"And how does one not die exactly?" his superior asked, predictably.

"One is fey."

Jonas scowled. "That's less than helpful, John!"

And yes, it was. But the magic in the air was swirling about, making it hard to think, even about much less difficult subjects. Probably in response to the emotions emanating from one very unhappy war mage.

"You mustn't use magic in here," John cautioned. "It . . . wouldn't be the best idea."

"And why not?" Jonas demanded, but he reigned in the anger radiating off him, and the power using it as a conduit. And as soon as he did, the room quieted. Slightly. John had the feeling it was never truly still. But then, how could it be?

He licked his lips and tried again. "The fey don't live as we do, therefore it should come as no surprise that they don't die as we do, either."

"Following you so far," Jonas said, his eyes moving from the not-corpse on the floor to the walls and vine-draped ceiling and back again.

"They don't have a spirit as we understand it. Or rather, they do, but it is fused with their bodies, indistinguishable from them in life, and accompanying them in death."

"I thought you said they don't die," Jonas said, edging a little closer, even while his eyes continued to flick around nervously.

John really couldn't blame them.

"They don't die as we do. It is more of a . . . a merging with their world. Their bodies are reabsorbed, and so is their spirit. The prevailing belief is that, just as the bodies rejoin the soil whence they sprang, to be reformed into something new—to be reborn, as it were—the soul does as well."

"Because it does not leave the body."

"Yes."

"And this . . ." Jonas paused, searching for the right word. He didn't find it. "This is what results?"

"Not in Faerie, no. But this fey died on Earth. But for some reason, no one returned to look for him."

"And that is unusual?"

"Very. The fey always retrieve their dead. Even in time of war, they make provision for it. Particularly when that fey is outside of their world."

"And if they do not?" Jonas asked, kneeling on the other side of the creature, fascination and repulsion warring on his face.

"This," John said simply. "Or so it would seem." He felt like pointing out that he was hardly an expert on the subject, but it didn't seem like a good time.

"And what precisely is this?"

"I can only guess, based on what you see. He should have been returned to Faerie, where his spirit and body would have been reabsorbed by the world that gave him life, to someday live again. But that didn't happen. And when it did not . . ."

"He tried to merge with our world," Jonas said, catching up. Sometimes John forgot how very quick the man could be.

"Yes."

Jonas surveyed the scene in front of him. "I take it that was not a great success."

"I don't understand it," John said, frowning. "The fey have a great deal of facility with nature, more in their own world, of course, but it should have been possible—"

He cut off at a warbling cry, which he belatedly recognized as from the fence outside. It cut through the deadly quiet like the alarm it was, but before he or Jonas could react, there were new silhouettes in the doorway. Familiar ones.

"Bollocks!" John threw himself at his superior, tackling him and rolling both of them through a connecting door—right before a wave of venom slashed through the space where they'd been standing.

"What are you doing?" Jonas spluttered. "We have to fight, man!"

"Those are Velos!"

"I know what they are!"

"Then stay the hell down," John hissed, pushing the man behind the flood of roots gushing down some stairs. "And don't raise a shield," he added, as he felt Jonas' power gather in the air once more.

"What the—have you gone mad?"

"Velos' venom eats through shields," John explained curtly, as all hell broke loose next door. "And anything else it comes in contact with. Shields won't help you."

"Then what do you suggest we do?" Jonas demanded, getting back to his feet and trying to peer over John's shoulder.

"Nothing."

"Nothing? And how is—" Jonas cut off, having finally managed to maneuver into a view of the vine-draped door. And of the kitchen beyond, where half a dozen Velos were making the acquaintance of an ancient, infuriated fey.

"Well," Jonas said, watching as the room came alive, and the Velos came apart. Vines surged down from the ceiling like boa constrictors, grabbing two of the more or less man-shaped Velos and squeezing for all they were worth. Another surged out from a wall and grabbed a third demon's legs, and then went wild, thrashing him back and forth across the room, slamming him between the rock-covered face of the fireplace and the old, hard wood of the opposite wall, over and over and over again.

The other three had already realized that their would-be ambush of the mages had gone somehow, hideously wrong, and were trying to get back out the door. Only to be met with a positive hail of apples from the trees outside, causing them to slip and slide and duck and fall, straight into the embrace of the roots reaching out from the floor. Roots that wrapped them up like mummies, or more correctly, like victims in a spider's web.

And then pulled their thrashing prey down, down, down, churning up the broken boards and the underlying soil until not even the creatures' grasping hands were visible any longer.

And suddenly, all was still again.

John had been watching the show that the roots had put on, and so hadn't seen the fate of the other three demons. But they weren't there when he glanced around the room. Only a single shoe was left, sitting atop a gnarled old root like a trophy.

He swallowed.

"Yes. Yes indeed," Jonas said, apropos of nothing. But then, John didn't have anything more eloquent to offer himself. He sat down on a step, pulled a flask out of his coat and belted back a long one. Then he handed it to Jonas.

"Always carry my own, old boy," Jonas said, pulling a bottle out of his sock.

For a while, they just sat, letting the alcohol sooth jangled nerves and blur memories that were too new and too stark to process. But before long, Jonas got around to the point. "We can't simply leave it," he pointed out. "It's an ambush waiting to happen for anyone who wanders in here. And sooner or later, someone will."

"I've no intention of leaving it," John said, draining his flask. Because he needed it. And because this might be one of those things that was easier when drunk off his ass.

He made his way into the next room.

The fey was still there, of course. And still as intimidating as hell. But for some reason, despite the scene that he'd just witnessed, John didn't find it as terrible as before. Maybe it was the alcohol, or maybe just the time he'd had to adjust, but all he could see now was a being stranded far from hearth and home, with no hope of getting back.

Forgotten, by friends and foes alike. Left to molder here, on distant shores. Left to rot.

He didn't blame it for being angry, this solitary trapped soul. Didn't blame it for anything. He just wanted to help.

"To get you home," he murmured, and something in the air shifted. John sat down, and then glanced up at Jonas. "You should go. In case this goes wrong."

Jonas regarded him for a moment, and then perched his plump bottom on a conveniently bench-shaped root. He didn't say anything, and John gave up. It wasn't like the cat wasn't already very much out of the bag.

He turned his attention back to the fey.

Like the fence, its magic carried a song, one that John had been determinedly blocking out. He let it flow over him now, and for one, brief moment, he panicked. It was so dense and layered, with notes piling on top of notes and chords resonating off every surface. And the rich, varied and impossibly complex melody was made infinitely more so by all the other songs running through it: the sweet trills of air, the surging lilt of river, the chorus of plants, the deep boom of earth.

John had no idea how to start singing with it at all.

So he just sat there for a while, feeling overwhelmed and dizzy and quite, quite useless. As it must have sat, possibly for centuries. Alone and running wild, like an untended vine—

He stopped in sudden comprehension. It was like a vine. It was exactly like one, in fact, or like the fence outside, which had twined around any and every source of life that it could find, melding its song with the strange melodies of this new world. But unlike the fence, the fey hadn't fully committed, hadn't fully surrendered. It had taken enough energy to retain consciousness, to retain memory, to remain. But not enough to become one with this strange new world.

Not enough to live again.

But time had done what it wouldn't. As its real body decayed, it had stubbornly built another out of whatever was available, and in doing so, fused with the earth and the wood and the house itself. It was the same way rocks and grass and weeds in a long-overgrown stone wall come together, into one, almost symbiotic whole.

There was no way to separate them. Not after so long. There was no way to send him home.

And what was left of the fey knew that, John realized, as acknowledgment thrummed through the melody, dark and dense and hopeless. It had always known. The reason it hadn't released into the Earth was less about ability than stubbornness, refusing to accept this new world, refusing to let go and discover what it might offer because it was too busy remembering all that it had left behind.

John knew the feeling.

But it was listening now, for whatever reason. Possibly because it was tired of this, too. Or possibly because it had recognized something in this strange visitor that felt eerily familiar.

And so he sang, not with it, because that was far beyond his gifts. But to it. And the subject wasn't the fey and his circumstances, because

John didn't know anything about those. But rather the only thing he did know that might be relevant.

He sang about himself.

He sang about being lost, too, for most of his life: fey but not, human but not, demon but not. He sang about being an odd fusion of all three, and of therefore fitting in nowhere. About being rejected by his birth family, by his fey visitors, by everyone but his demon father, who only accepted him in order to use him.

And the fey was listening. He had been rejected, too. John couldn't understand all of it, or even most of it, but he had been young, hotheaded, reckless, and he had done something . . . the song became so loud, so discordant there, that John was forced to block it out for a time. And when he listened again, it was quieter. Exiled, unwanted, anathema.

John understood this.

And so he sang to it the rest of the story, because his was not yet done. He sang of finding a place in a world, one that wasn't his, no, not entirely. But one he hoped would someday become his. He sang about letting go of old dreams and dead hopes, of disappointments and failures, and of looking to the future with, if not optimism, not yet, then something edging cautiously up to it.

He sang about not going home, but making one.

And then he opened his eyes.

Postscript

John flipped over another page, and was confronted with another derelict cottage, this one wedged between a bakery and a green grocer. It was advertised as "picturesque ambiance," which apparently was estate agent-ese for cracks in the walls and stains on the ceiling. He leaned forward. He was fairly sure he smelled mildew.

Bugger.

And then something obscured the sad little sight, something big and legal-looking that half disappeared into the flat before him. He looked up, confused, only to get a face full of dandelion fluff. "Sorry," Jonas said, shuffling back a step. "Demmed cramped in here."

"The corridor is more spacious," Edwards noted acidly.

"Good point," Jonas said, and pulled John out the door.

The corridor was not, in fact, more spacious, being one of the older parts of the rabbit warren of tiny halls that connected the various areas of HQ. Most were narrow and all were higgledy piggledy, with this particular bit also boasting a sloping ceiling that made it impossible to stand up straight. But right then, John didn't care.

"What is this?" he demanded, thrusting the paper at Jonas.

Jonas rocked back on his heels, looking pleased—until he bumped his head. He glanced up at the ceiling resentfully, and then back at John. "Well, what does it look like?"

"It looks like a deed."

"And so it is." Jonas smiled beneficently.

"To what?" John asked suspiciously.

"Well, what do you think? We can't put just anyone in a haunted house—"

"It isn't haunted. It was never haunted."

"—and in any case, you did clean it up, so to speak. Although I must say, you're still going to have some work ahead of you. The, er, former tenant may be gone, but there's no proper kitchen or bath, and those vines—"

"Jonas—"

"—may be better in the not-attacking-anyone sense of the word, but they're still wafting about in a way that makes a man nervous—"

"Jonas—"

"—and then there's the fact that you were owed a commission for cleaning out the rest of those nasty Velos, and the Corps would vastly prefer to pay in the form of a dilapidated property no one else will touch with a ten-foot pole than to have to actually pony up—"

"Jonas!"

"Hm?" The almost shout seemed to finally get through, and his superior blinked at him myopically. "What's that?"

"Are you trying to tell me that I now own Cobb End?"

"Well, yes, of course. What else have we been talking about?"

"I'm . . . never quite sure," John admitted, feeling stunned and a little giddy.

He'd been avoiding Jonas since that night, when he'd opened his eyes on starlight glimmering through windows that were no longer clogged with vines, but open and clear. Like the walls and ceiling. And the floor, where he had found himself staring at bare boards as whole and smooth as they had been when some hand planed them long ago. There had followed an almost entirely silent flight home, each man lost in his thoughts.

Thoughts which John had assumed must have included some deductive reasoning on Jonas's part about a mage who was part fey, part demon and in possession of magic he should never have had.

He had been braced for an inconvenient revelation, or at least a quick ouster from the service.

He certainly hadn't expected a gift.

He looked up to find his superior watching him, blue eyes keener than he normally allowed. "I thought it was fitting," he said simply. And then he was off, in a bustle of tweed and a waft of fluff, leaving John staring down at his own name in someone's cramped handwriting.

And what do you know, he thought, feeling a grin breaking out across his face.

He had a house.

Author's Note: "Shitty Beer" is a short story/missing scene from the second Cassie Palmer novel, *Claimed by Shadow*, and should be read after that book to avoid spoilers.

SHITTY BEER

"I, for one, like a good cheap beer," Mac said, tilting his chair back against the wall behind his shop, careful not to let his skin touch the burning brick. The sun had been on it for hours, until finally sliding off to torment some cacti around the corner, assuming the cacti minded. John didn't know. He found the flora in Nevada as strange as that in some of the hell regions, which was fair considering the average temperature of the place. He wiped some sweat off his temple, before it could roll down the side of his neck, and took a swig from the bottle Mac had provided.

"Water," he said, because there was no discernible difference.

But Mac didn't seem to take offense. "It's not water, it's beer. It's just shitty beer."

"And you drink this why? Have they suddenly stopped paying your pension?"

"Like I'd notice if they did," Mac said dryly. War mages, especially ex-war mages, were not over paid.

It was probably why his friend had turned a hobby into a second profession. John watched as a painted snake that had been hiding in Mac's long mustache suddenly dropped out of sight, only to reappear on his chest and upset an eagle tat, which pecked at it savagely. The snake slithered off under Mac's stringy bicep, and his friend took another swig, as if he hadn't noticed.

Maybe he hadn't. He only had about a hundred of the things, magical tats of all types and descriptions, covering his body in colorful perfusion to compensate for his inability to shield. He'd once been a war mage, as spit polished and disciplined as any. But ever since a curse stripped away his shields, and thus his career, he'd been looking more and more like a man with no purpose, doing tats for the magical community and waiting . . .

For what John didn't know.

Maybe for better beer.

"There's a liquor store around the corner," he offered idly. "I could make a run—"

"You're not listening," Mac told him, squinting against the sun, which was now behind John's head. "I *like* shitty beer."

"You like shitty beer."

"Yes."

"So, if I were to go get, say, a Newcastle, or a Black Sheep, or that damned chocolate stout you used to favor—"

"Then you could drink it yourself."

"Since when do you champion fizzy, ice cold, tasteless crap?"

"Since I moved to Nevada," Mac said, shooting him an amused look. "Climate changes a man. A good, strong lager and a warm fire pair up nicely when your bollocks are about to freeze off. But here," he waved a hand from the heat shimmering off the nearby road and the dry as dust desert, "not so much. I used to laugh at American beers, too, until I realized why they brew them like they do."

"They brew them?" Pritkin said dourly, and drank his slightly sour soda pop.

"Laugh all you want. But I have learned to appreciate paying a fiver for a six pack, less if I get it on sale. I've learned that, sometimes, I want to sit back with some carbonated barley water and watch the sun set, rather than have my taste buds assaulted by hops, or feel like I'm drinking a bottle of syrup with some of the imperial stouts. I've learned to appreciate grabbing a shitty beer when I'm out at the bars, because it doesn't make me feel like a pretentious SOB, and I'm not paying fifty bucks to get drunk."

"You've thought about this," John said dryly.

"I have." Mac held up his brew, which had started out ice cold, but was now sweating as much as they were. "I salute you, shitty beer! You serve a purpose, and a damn noble one. Give the people something they can enjoy while doing chores or at a barbeque. Give people something they can share with their friends and not worry about the budget. Give people something they can buy at every grocery store, jiffy stop, and gas station to quench their thirst and get a slight buzz. There are better beers, but none dearer to my heart." He drank deeply.

John sighed and did likewise.

It was still shit.

"So, did you just come by to insult my beer, or is there something else?" Mac asked, while fishing them a chaser out of a cooler filled with ice.

He handed a bottle to John, and the nut-brown skin of his hand was hardly discernible against the same-colored dirt. Mac looked like he'd been born here, like he'd risen whole from the baked earth, with cut offs and crow's feet and a long, droopy biker 'stash instead of Adam's fig leaf. It was less like he'd gone native than that he'd absorbed the place into his genes.

John grasped the bottle, expecting to see a serious contrast in their skin tones, since he was less than a year out of the London office and a still pasty transplant. Only to notice that a faint tan had started to cling to him as well. Like the desert hues had bled onto his skin, beginning to claim him for its own.

He stared at his hand, suddenly feeling more than slightly off balance. Like the world had tilted, or like he'd blinked and it had changed. Maybe because it had, shattering in a million pieces just this morning, when his life took less of a turn and more of a jack knife. What it would hold now, how the picture would look when all the scattered shards fell into place, he had no idea.

It was a dizzying prospect for someone who had avoided thinking about the future for as long as he had.

He swallowed and took the beer, and looked up to see Mac eyeing him narrowly.

"Anything you care to share?"

"No," John said hoarsely, and looked around for the opener. Only to realize that Mac had left it inside.

But then, he didn't need it. John watched as his friend held his own brew up to his shoulder, where a painted jaguar sprang at it, grasping it between its paws and gnawing it enthusiastically. Only to spit the sadly mangled bottle cap into the dirt a moment later, a smug look on its tiny face. John eyed the thing warily, then used the underside of a small table to open his own.

And scowled.

"You know," Mac told him. "I could wrestle up a soft drink, if you're really *that*–"

"It's not the beer," John told him, "It's the girl."

Mac blinked. "What girl?"

"The one who may be coming by here later." Or might not, he thought, recalling the sight he'd been left with: a blonde falling out of a too tight, sequined bit of nothing sliding onto the front seat of a luxury sedan. She'd had a hole in her tights, cobwebs in her hair, and blood on her left knee where she must have skinned it during their morning's adventures. Yet there'd been a small smirk on her face, because she thought she'd won.

And she had, at least for the moment. She had driven away, leaving him bleeding in the dust, and fuming, because he couldn't do a damned thing to stop her. Couldn't even argue, for fear that the two incubus-possessed humans with her might recognize him and say something that gave away his heritage.

And wouldn't that just help him make his case?

But he'd wanted to. He'd wanted to rage at her, to say that he wasn't there to hurt her, which should have been obvious since he'd just saved her life! And likely ruined his, because he'd been seen helping a fugitive to escape when he had orders to kill her on sight. As the premier magical authority on earth, the Silver Circle wasn't used to having its rules thwarted by anyone, much less one of its own. He probably had a bounty on his head by now, too, and plenty of people only too happy to collect, many of whom had never thought that a half breed demon spawn belonged as a war mage in the first place.

Well, he likely wasn't one now, he thought grimly.

"John?" Mac was looking at him over the bottle.

"I . . . put my foot in it this morning," he said, wincing at the understatement. "There's a new Pythian candidate—have you heard?" Mac shook his head. "You remember that disgraced heir who ran away a few decades ago?"

"Of course. Elizabeth O'Donnell. Front page news for weeks, only they never found her."

"No. They never did." And if she was anything like her insane progeny, John could understand why. "She's deceased, but it seems she had a daughter, and the Senate found *her*–"

"The vampires?" Mac sat up in his seat, beer forgotten. "You're telling me they have a Pythian acolyte?"

"Not an acolyte; she was never trained. Which is the damned point!" John said, suddenly exploding. He'd been holding his temper all day, never an easy task, and doubly so with that hellion not listening to a damned word he said. And then siccing those three ancient terrors she'd been hanging around with on his friends—his former friends—ah, bollocks!

John drank more shitty beer.

"She's supposed to show up here later," he told Mac, who was looking at him expectantly.

"A Pythian acolyte is coming *here*?" Mac abruptly stood up. His dour, jaded ex-partner suddenly looked as flustered as a boy on his first date. Why John didn't know. The average acolyte—the ones he'd seen, at any rate—were almost silent girls in virginal white who wafted about as if their dainty slippers never touched the polished floors of the Pythian Court. He'd always found them vaguely creepy, and suspected that they practiced their knowing looks in a mirror in order to fluster people.

They'd never flustered him.

If they really had received any visions about his life, they'd have fled screaming when he walked in the door.

"You can relax," he said dryly. "You're not likely to meet her."

"But you said she's coming–"

"I think she told me that to get rid of me. The Circle has a bounty on her head and she doesn't trust me, even though I'm the reason they failed to collect. But I'm going to have to track her down somehow. I need her to help me go after Myra, Lady Phemonoe's heir–"

"What?"

"–who should have been proclaimed Pythia already, but there's reason to believe that she poisoned the Lady–"

"What?"

"–and now she's fled into Faerie and is plotting with our enemies as we speak. Which is why the Circle designated me to go after her—they don't dare to set foot there, but I have some experience with the place. But not enough, not for something like this, which is why I need you. You have tats that work in Faerie, don't you?"

Mac just looked at him for a minute. "I think I need another beer," he finally said, sitting back down.

"You *have* a beer, and I need an answer!"

"In a minute," Mac said. John had never been able to rush him. "Let me get this straight. The heir to the Pythian Throne has gone bad?"

"Yes. And I've been sent to bring her back to justice or kill her, and it was made clear that the Circle would prefer the latter."

"And, at the same time, this other possible heir pops up out of the woodwork as the vampires' protégé–"

"Yes."

"–and now the Circle wants her dead, too?"

John made a disgusted sound. "They think it's better that than she inherit, and we have a vampire-controlled Pythia to deal with."

"Yet you protected her?"

"She's young," John said, shifting uncomfortably. And remembering the first time he'd seen her, a little over a week ago. She'd been in another ridiculous outfit, this time a bright yellow happy face tee, which might not have looked so bizarre if she hadn't been wearing it in the middle of the Vampire Senate!

The ruling body for all North American vampires intimidated even senior mages, and that was when they were playing nice. They hadn't been that day. He'd come in to find her sprawled in the middle of the floor, being menaced by a grim-faced relic out of a Victorian nightmare.

And all alone. Just a tiny figure in that ridiculous T-shirt, with no weapons and no one at her back. Yet she'd been defiant. Obviously terrified, yet unbending, staring the embodiment of death itself in the face.

And not blinking.

He looked up to find Mac's shrewd gaze on him, and a little smile flirting with the corners of his mouth. "She's a pawn," John snapped. "Little better than a child; the vampires are using her. Does she deserve to die for that? And without a trial? The Circle put a bounty on her because of who she is, not what she's done. Is that who we are now? Is that what we do?"

"No," Mac said flatly. "We must protect her."

"*I* must. You must stay out of this. I just need—"

"You can't do this alone, John," Mac said stubbornly. "And we're partners, remember? And war mages—"

"We aren't anything of the kind," John said tersely, because this wasn't the discussion he wanted to have. "They all but ran you out the door, and I'll be lucky to get away with the same. We're not anything anymore—"

"We're *war mages*. You wouldn't have done that this morning if you weren't; I wouldn't be helping you now if I weren't."

"You'll help me?"

"Did you have any doubt?"

John sighed. No, he hadn't. But he also had no intention of dragging Mac into this. This was his fight. Mac had already had his, and barely survived. It was enough.

But his friend didn't seem to think so. "War mages protect the Pythia," he said quietly. "That is who we are. *That* is what we do."

"She isn't Pythia yet."

"And she may never be without our help."

John shook his head. "And if the Circle finds out? You could be charged as an accessory. I'll tell them you didn't know, but—"

"You can tell them any damned thing you want. *I'll* tell them that it isn't about the uniform, or the title. It's about the *job*. I took an oath to stand against the tide trying to swamp us, to take everything the other side can throw and hurl it back in their faces. We are the light in the darkness, the circle that hedges the world of men, the guardians—"

"I know the oath."

"Then I assume this conversation is over."

Not by a long shot, John didn't say, because it wouldn't do any good. Mac was a better man than he was; Mac probably believed the oath and the brain washing that went along with it. The whole velvet robed ceremony, kneeling with swords a-glitter, as if the Circle was some chivalric order out of the Middle Ages instead of a modern military/police force, with all the backstabbing, deal making, and politics of any such group.

Mac had been in it, but never *of* it. He'd been able to see this person or that one as corrupt, but not the Circle itself, not the Corps he loved. But the Circle had changed, and since it commanded its military wing, the Corps had as well. John couldn't trust them anymore, not after they decided to murder an innocent girl. Or even a not-so-innocent one. Even Myra deserved a trial, not that she was likely to get one, and the Palmer girl even less so. And the damned thing about it all, the fact that took it from fuck up to farce, was that he didn't even know that saving her made sense.

If the Circle had gone bad, surely they needed a proper Pythia to help root out the rot? But what did they have instead? A possible murderess on the one hand and a . . . John didn't even know what on the other. He saw the Pythian acolytes again: cool, calm, serene, otherworldly. And then he saw her, blonde hair falling in her face, sweat on her brow despite the casino's overpowered air conditioning, grunting and cursing as she crawled down the middle of a deadly hallway, through the only safe zone in the casino's menacing wards.

Was that a Pythia?

Instead of all knowing, she'd looked as confused as he was. Instead of cool and collected, she'd been complaining half the morning and alternating between whimpering and screaming the rest. Instead of otherworldly, she'd been only too human, all panicked blue eyes and swollen lower lip from biting it too often.

Was that who was supposed to take on the corruption in the Circle, to lead the supernatural community, to fight a *war*?

John didn't think so. But a look at his friend's face told him that Mac didn't share his opinion. For once, it was free of roaming artwork, leaving the thin, un-lined features bare and visible, not that John needed them. The expression blazing in the eyes would have been enough.

For the first time in a while, Mac looked like himself. A war mage and a true believer. John almost envied him.

He wasn't sure what he believed in anymore.

"The power chooses the Pythia," Mac reminded him. "That's its job. Ours is keeping her alive long enough for it to decide."

John nodded tersely. Arguing would be useless, so he wouldn't. He would get what he needed and get out, before Mac got hurt. He would find this girl, use her to find Myra, and get the truth out of the two of them.

And then they would see.

"Come on," he said, putting the bottle down in the dirt. "Let's get to work. I'll fill you in as we go."

* * *

John let the door close behind him on its own.

It was dark inside the little pub, and cramped, with a ceiling that brushed his head until he moved down three steep steps onto age-old boards. The steps were an abrupt drop off from the door, a trap that most new comers didn't see in time, and so ended up sprawled in the floor. It had become almost a rite of passage through the years; John had witnessed dozens of fresh-faced recruits rise stiff and red-faced after a spill, including one youthful Archie McAdam, sans mustache and with a head full of ginger hair.

He paused at the spot Mac had fallen, all those hears ago, and recalled how easily he'd played it off. Jumping back to his feet, asking if he had slid farther than anyone. And when he was told no, that that honor belonged to a long-ago recruit who had slammed head first into the bar and left a still visible mark, he had offered to go back out and try it again.

Mac had immediately fit in around here, at the unofficial war mage pub in Stratford, the home base for the Corps. John never had. And it was particularly foolish for him to be here today, less than twenty-four hours after breaking with the Circle, with a bounty on his head and a whole phalanx of allies-turned-enemies on his trail.

Like the ones who swiveled from the bar, long coats swinging out over enough hardware to tear him apart a hundred times over. There were two of them, plus three more at a cramped table under the eaves. And another just coming in from the washroom in back, drying his hands on a paper towel because there was no room for a trash can in there, before stopping on a dime.

And staring.

John didn't move. He knew them—most of them, anyway—like he knew the bartender. Grizzled Jeroboam, almost two hundred years old and legally blind, who saw through the eyes of the pet hawk on his shoulder. Master and bird were staring at him now, too, like everyone else in the pub, staring but not moving as he stood there for a moment.

And then walked slowly and deliberately across the small space to the back room.

It wasn't any bigger, but it was brighter, although not because of the lighting. Thousands of small, circular pins studded the walls, the ceiling, and the two sturdy columns helping to hold up the roof, reflecting the light like tiny mirrors. Or like someone had decided to wallpaper the place in silver.

It wasn't far from the truth.

John walked along the walls, searching. Some of the pins were polished and bright, looking brand new. Others were older, their color dimmed by tarnish and age. Here and there, one was mangled or burnt almost to a crisp, or speckled with something dark that had never been washed away, because that was tradition, too. Another rite of passage, the last one. Like the pub's name, this was Journey's End for members of the Corps.

The pins were those given to every new mage in the ceremony of joining. They'd been useful once, to close the cloaks earlier war mages had used to conceal their arsenal. Now they were merely ceremonial, and often tucked away, as Mac's had been, amidst his medals and commendations, the little velvet box all but forgotten until John broke into his apartment and retrieved it.

That had been foolhardy, too, but he couldn't trust anyone else to do this. Mac hadn't been active duty when he died, at least not as far as the Corps was concerned. And this wasn't a room for mages who had passed after a long retirement, much less those who had gone rogue and defied the Circle. This was a room for heroes, and they wouldn't have believed Mac qualified.

John knew better.

He finally found a place, a small piece of blank wall at eye level, far in the back. The pin bit into the old waddle and daub easily, sinking into place as if it had always been meant to go there. John stared at it blankly, fingers lingering on the smooth surface.

This was what you did, after a brother died in battle. This was where you brought him, the final act you did for him. John waited, wondering if it was supposed to bring him some measure of peace, some kind of closure.

If so, it wasn't working.

Mac had sacrificed his life to save their new Pythia, and John had thereafter assumed his role as Pythian Protector. He didn't know what he'd been thinking. He wasn't a white knight, wasn't a true believer, wasn't even a Corpsman anymore, and she . . .

God help them all.

But she had Lady Phemonoe's blessing, which was something. And more luck than she deserved. And stubbornness, resiliency, a reckless bravery that reminded him terribly of Mac, and an odd vulnerability that he didn't know what to do with.

John could only hope it would be enough.

He turned around and went back into the bar.

The tableaux hadn't changed, except that there was now a beer at the end of the battered old counter, the kind he usually drank. John looked at it, and then at the other offerings on tap. And made a different selection.

"You're sure?" The venerable barkeep kept staring straight ahead as usual, but his creature levelled a wall eye at John.

"I'm sure."

The pour was made and sat before him, and for the next half hour, he leaned on the bar and drank his shitty beer.

And then left, unmolested.

Author's Note: "A Family Affair" is a novella set between *Curse the Dawn* (Cassie Palmer #4) and *Hunt the Moon* (Cassie Palmer #5). It contains spoilers for Cassie Palmer books 1-4.

A FAMILY AFFAIR

Chapter One

The double doors were painted white with gold trim and had fussy gold door handles. They also had one of the new, high-priced protection wards with none of the traditional potion stench or oily residue. Or any protection worth a damn, John thought darkly.

He was scowling at it when something hard bumped into his back. He flung an arm across the doorway to keep himself from falling into the useless ward. "Wait a minute."

"You wait a minute." The impatient voice came from behind him. "This is heavy!"

"Then put it down."

"I'm going to. Inside."

John forced himself to count to ten. Guarding the Pythia-elect, the woman soon to become the world's chief seer, was no easy task. The fact that the supernatural community was currently in the middle of a war didn't help. But it was her penchant for running headlong into trouble that regularly threatened his nerves—and his sanity.

"The wardsmiths haven't been here yet," he explained. "There's only the standard protection."

"So?"

"So I know of at least a dozen ways around this particular type, and that is assuming the would-be intruder is human. Which considering your talent for making enemies, is by no means—"

"I'm about to rupture something," he was informed, as the big, gaily wrapped box she was carrying smacked into the small of his back again. She had an uncanny ability to hit the same spot every time.

"We'll add additional weight training to your routine," he told her evilly, and threw a shield over one hand. He ran it cautiously over the doorway, checking for traps or the tell-tale holes in the ward's surface that an intruder would likely leave behind.

"Pritkin, it's a hotel room, not a death trap!" A glance over his shoulder showed him impatient blue eyes under a fall of messy blond curls. "Anyway, you're here."

"I can't protect you from everything," he forced himself to say, because it was true. It was also frankly terrifying in a way that his own mortality was not. He'd never had children, but he sometimes wondered if this was how parents felt when catching sight of a fearless toddler confidently heading toward a busy street. Not that his charge was a child, as he was all too uncomfortably aware. But the knowledge of just how many potentially lethal pitfalls lay in her path sometimes caused him that same heart-clenching terror.

And the same overwhelming need to throw her over his lap and spank the living daylights out of her, he thought grimly, when she suddenly popped out of existence. "Cassie!"

His only answer was a loud groan from indoors. He ripped through the ward and bolted inside, gun drawn and heart in his throat. Only to see her staring in annoyance at six huge vampires lounging in the suite's sizeable living room.

Marco, their leader, was a great bear of a creature, a foot and a half taller and at least ten stone heavier than the small woman facing him. But he was the one who looked alarmed. Possibly because she'd just appeared out of thin air barely a foot in front of him.

And she wasn't backing up. "What are you doing here?" she demanded.

"It's not my idea of fun, either, princess," he told her defensively. "Master's orders."

"Oh, for—Casanova was just here!" she said, referring to the hotel's manager. "He checked everything out this morning."

Marco sneered. "Yeah. Like I'm gonna trust that pansy-waist incubus to check anything. Everybody knows what they're good for."

John ignored the unintended jab in favor of grabbing Cassie's arm. "You're not moving until I check it out."

"We're inside a vampire stronghold!" she said, thrusting the package at him.

He thrust it back. "That's what worries me."

She sighed and shoved the box into the nearest vampire's gut instead. "Don't drop it," she warned, before turning her attention on his boss.

"Hey!" Marco protested as she tugged his polo shirt out of his pants and pushed it up, revealing an angry red scar bisecting a thick mat of black hair.

"I knew it!" She looked at him accusingly. "You aren't healed."

"Close enough," he said, trying to pull his shirt back down.

He stopped when Cassie slapped his hands. Then her touch gentled, and she traced the ugly, livid mark with one finger. The simple movement sent an unexpected shiver along John's spine, perhaps because he recalled what those soft little hands had once felt like on his own scars, moving over his skin . . .

He shook himself and shoved the image away.

Marco didn't seem to be having the same reaction, but the obvious concern on her face brought a softer look to his. "I'm okay."

"You almost died, Marco—less than two weeks ago," she told him severely. "You are *not* okay!"

"I'm not planning on running any marathons. But I couldn't stay in that damn hospital bed one more day. Those nurses are complete bastards."

"Just because they wouldn't let you bring in vodka and cigars."

"Or my laptop."

"And why did you need a laptop?"

He looked shifty. "You know, for games. And . . . stuff."

Cassie rolled her eyes. "You needed to rest."

"That is resting!"

She gave up with a little snort and started for the bedroom. John had anticipated that and stepped in front of the door. "Shift inside and I will make your life hell," he said pleasantly.

"You sound like I'm about to run headlong into danger—"

"As you just did? As you always do?"

"—when you know the room has already been checked out. Twice."

He crossed his arms and didn't budge. He'd found out the hard way—give the woman an inch and she'd shift to another continent when he wasn't looking. She was the oddest combination of contradictions he'd ever met: innocence and sensuality, candor and diplomacy, anxiety and utter fearlessness. He hadn't even begun to figure out how her mind worked.

But she was damn well going to live long enough for him to try.

She put her hands on her hips and glared at him. "This is ridiculous! I'm not going to live my life in constant fear, do you understand?"

"Better than not living it at all," he snapped. And for once, he received a semi-sympathetic glance from Marco.

Cassie threw her hands up in a gesture that reminded him vaguely of someone, although he couldn't place it. "Fine," she said, obviously annoyed. She took the heavy package back from the vamp, probably so she would have something to complain about later.

"We already did that," Marco said mildly, as John pushed open the bedroom door with his foot.

"And now I'm doing it again."

Marco bared a lot of gleaming white teeth, several of which were pointier than they should have been. But he didn't argue. They each had abilities the other lacked, and there was a chance a mage might detect something his men had missed. And whatever else John might think about the creature, it was clear that he took his job seriously.

So did John, and he wasn't happy about this latest move. The ongoing repairs from the hotel's most recent disaster had forced Cassie to switch suites, requiring that all protection spells be redone and a new security workup be created. The extra labor was annoying, but the real issue was that it left worrying holes in the security net for however long it took for the wardsmiths to show up.

He went over the bedroom and attached bath twice, just to be sure, switching from Arcane to Druid to Fey magic to detect different types of spells. But it looked like the vampires had done their job. He didn't find so much as a decayed eavesdropping charm.

As soon as he gave the all clear, Cassie pushed past him and staggered inside, carrying her precious burden. She dropped it onto the king-sized bed next to the panoramic view of the Vegas skyline, then collapsed beside it with a theatrical groan. An outside observer might have been forgiven for concluding that she was on her last leg, but John knew better. And sure enough, by the time he returned from checking out the rest of the suite, she was sitting cross-legged on the bed, trying to get the cherry red ribbon off the package.

"What are you doing?" he demanded.

"Opening my gift."

"You don't know what it contains."

"I didn't find it on the doorstep," she said impatiently. "Ming-de sent it to me."

That did not reassure John greatly. Ming-de was a first-level master vampire and empress of the powerful Chinese court. More to the point, she was currently in a cut-throat competition with the Consul, the leader of the North American vampires. And Cassie was viewed by most vamps, however inaccurately, as one of the Consul's chief supporters.

Vampires were a short-sighted breed when it came to getting what they wanted, or in most other ways. And he wouldn't put it past Ming-de to try to weaken the competition by removing one of the Consul's assets. Not to mention that he'd heard rumors of a long-running affair between the empress and Mircea, the vampire Cassie was currently dating.

"I'll open it," he said decisively, holding out a hand.

"Are you sure you don't want to submerge it in the bathtub first?" she asked sarcastically.

"That's not a bad idea." He pulled it out of her hands.

"Stop teasing! It could be something delicate, like porcelain. Or . . . or silk." She reached for it, her eyes hopeful.

"I will be careful," he said patiently. "But I'll open it in the next room."

She looked like she planned to argue, but thought better of it at the last minute and flopped back onto the bed. He decided that he needed to run her around the track a few extra times every day. It cut down on arguments.

He took the package outside. Giving gifts to the Pythia-elect was traditional, but it was yet another headache for her security. That was especially true in this case, when half the senders had been loudly denouncing her for a month, and a good portion of the rest had been trying to have her killed.

Under the circumstances, her guards had no choice but to open each and every package before Cassie saw it, looking for booby traps, poison and malignant spells. And that was after everything had been gone over with a fine-toothed comb by Casanova's people in the lobby. But a brief perusal of this particular gift had his lips twitching.

It seemed that politics wasn't the main thing on Ming-de's mind.

He left most of the box's contents in the front hall, re-entering the bedroom carrying something that resembled a thin soft drink can. He handed it to Cassie, who took it, looking puzzled. "What is this?"

"Bird spit."

She blinked. "I beg your pardon?"

"It's made from the oral secretions of a certain type of bird. They build nests out of it."

Cassie examined the can as if she thought he might be making the whole thing up. "Ming-de sent me bird spit?"

"They sell it in the salon downstairs," Marco chimed in. "I think they harvest it somewhere high in the mountains in China. I hear it's pretty hard to get because the birdies nest so high up."

"Why would anyone bother?" Cassie asked, looking revolted.

"It's good for the skin," John said, waiting for it.

"What?"

"It's supposed to improve the look and texture of the skin."

Cassie's frown took on a new quality as the implication set in. "Ming-de sent me *bird spit* because she thinks I have *bad skin*?"

"I thought women liked cosmetics," he said innocently.

"She sent me a *case*, Pritkin!"

He started to reply, when a presence slammed into him, hard enough to send him staggering. It was the buzz that came from a powerful demon, and there was no question which one. The familiar, hated aura was like a prickle of acid against his skin.

"Pritkin?" Marco's amused dark eyes went suddenly sharp. But this wasn't something any vampire could fix.

"I just recalled . . . an errand," he said, his breath hitching on a snarl. And then he was out the door, before Cassie could figure out that a much bigger threat than a spurned lover had just arrived.

Chapter Two

John scanned the sea of kitsch, looking for the deadly threat that every sense told him was there somewhere. He didn't find it. The flock of tourists, cowboy-goth employees, and dancing neon cactuses conspired to confuse his human vision.

The hotel where Cassie was currently residing was themed after Dante's *Inferno*, with a lobby complete with fake stalactites that shot out geysers of steam on a regular basis. The main drag had tried to combine this with a homage to Nevada's wild west roots, resulting in an explosion of tastelessness that still made him wince, even after a month's exposure. He finally blinked, transitioning to the type of sight he rarely allowed himself, and there it was—an acid green flame shining through the windows of a nearby bar.

John pushed open the swinging doors—authentic right down to the wood grain in the fiberglass—and glanced around. If possible, the bar was even worse than the faux ghost town outside. It featured mementoes of colorful characters from the region's past—colorful in the sense that most of them had ended their lives splattered red from a gunfight gone wrong or black and blue courtesy of a hangman's noose. He finally found the demon he sought sitting under a framed wanted poster for Butch Cassidy, entertaining a small child.

The child was perhaps two, dressed in a yellow romper that left its gender in question and a pair of tennis shoes with bear faces on the tops. It was watching the demon with fascinated brown eyes. Or to be more accurately, it was watching the napkin the creature was holding up.

"You see? Merely a plain piece of paper," the blond devil said solemnly, turning it around so that the tot could see both sides. "But with a little magic . . ." his voice trailed off and the napkin suddenly flew up from his hand in the shape of a hummingbird.

It fluttered around the delighted child's head, prompting squeals loud enough to threaten John's eardrums and to turn the head of a nearby waitress. "Lisa!" The woman, dressed as a saloon girl, had they had favored neon-yellow polyester and black lace, hurried over. "I'm sorry. I told her to wait in back."

"Think nothing of it. I do so enjoy children." The demon caught John's eye. "Most of the time."

"You're a magician," the waitress said, smiling. But unlike her daughter, she wasn't looking at the napkin.

The creature reclined back against the leather booth, all tousled golden hair and lips red from the wine he'd been drinking. "Something like that," he agreed easily.

"I haven't seen you in here before."

"I'm from out of town."

"Way out," John said sourly.

The woman glanced at him, and did a quick double take. She looked between the two of them for a moment, clearly confused. "Are you two related?"

"No." It was emphatic.

"Yes, in fact," the demon said brightly. "He's my son."

"Really?" The waitress took in the creature's unlined face, clear green eyes and youthful body. It was on display in a scoop-neck tank with a silver sheen under a light gray suit. The skin was flawless and sun-bronzed, the nails were buffed to a high shine, and he smelled of some kind of exotic spice.

Then she glanced at John. He didn't need her expression to know that, of the two, he looked older. Crow's feet were beginning to form at the corners of his eyes, his complexion was weathered and his hands had never seen a manicure. He also hadn't had a chance to bathe since chasing a very grumpy young woman around a makeshift gym for two hours, resulting in damp hair and a sweat-stained t-shirt.

He strongly suspected that he stunk.

He also didn't give a damn.

"You don't look old enough to have an adult son," the woman told the demon doubtfully.

"You're too kind, Jessica."

Her nametag said Brittany. She looked down at it, and then back up at him. "I lost my tag a few days ago and had to borrow one. How did you—"

"Magic." He smiled charmingly. "I'm Rosier, by the way."

"That's an unusual name. First or last?"

He took the hand she rested on the table—the one with the wedding ring. "Whichever you prefer."

She leaned closer, wetting her lips. "You know, my shift is over in a few minutes—"

"And you'll need to take your child home at that time," John said, putting a hand on her shoulder. He'd expected to have to disperse the gathering threads of a spell, but there wasn't one. The demon looked at him, amused, and the woman flushed.

"Yes, I . . . yes." She turned and hurried off, without remembering to take his order or to retrieve her child.

"I don't really need the help," the demon told John, pulling out a slim silver case and tapping a cigarette on the table. "Neither would you, if you took some pains. You look like hell."

"You should know."

The creature ignored that. "You can't starve the incubus out, no matter how hard you try. You are what you are. Someday, you're going to have to come to terms with that."

"Wait for it."

"I have been. For entirely too long."

John choked back the reply that sprang to his lips. He was not going to get into a dialogue with the creature. Not over this; not again.

His eyes fell to the little girl, who was still trying to catch the paper bird hovering just out of reach. "I'm not going to kill you in a casino full of people," he told the demon tersely. "You don't need a shield."

"And yet I feel so much better with one. At least until we reach an understanding."

John refrained from commenting on the likelihood of that. "Why are you here?"

"Sit down, Emrys. At least pretend to be civilized."

"That's not my name."

"It's better than what you call yourself these days. A prince of hell named John." He looked pained.

"Why. Are. You. Here?"

The demon held up his hand and a whorl of fire danced over his fingers. He lit the cigarette and sat back, regarding John through a haze of smoke. "To do you a favor."

"I doubt that very much."

"That depends. On whether you're still defending that unbearable harpy."

John felt a quiver of rage rake along his nerves. "I am sure you meant to say Lady Cassandra."

"Yes, do use the title. That makes it so much better."

John's hand clenched at his side, his mind automatically working out the logistics for turning the monster into a puddle of goo while sparing the child. It could be done, he decided. Just.

"Oh, sit down," Rosier snapped. "I'm here to help."

"That would be a first." Of the many assassination attempts that had been made on Cassie's life in recent months, some of the deadliest had been engineered by the creature opposite him. But as her bodyguard, John couldn't afford the luxury of telling the bastard to go to hell. At least not until he learned why he'd left it.

He sat down.

Rosier signaled the waitress. "Another for me and one for my son."

"I don't want a drink," John said flatly.

Rosier let out a breath of smoke that floated lazily upwards. "Don't be so sure. You haven't heard why I've come yet."

The waitress had two glasses on the table in record time. "I believe she's tired," the demon said, passing the sleepy child to her mother after finally allowing her to catch the elusive toy. She looked disappointed to find that, after all, it was merely a piece of paper.

John wondered what kind of deception was about to be dangled in front of him.

* * *

Casanova was warm, and there was the seductive slide of silken flesh against his own. He let his hand slowly fondle the nearest pert backside without bothering to open his eyes. 'Ticia, he identified lazily. Or possibly Berenice. He decided he was hungry and threw a leg over whoever-it-was, pressing the giggling bundle further into the soft folds of the feather bed.

Berenice, he decided. She really did have the most delightful—

The covers were abruptly stripped away, and a puff of air conditioning hit his bare ass. The girls squealed, more out of cold than modesty, he suspected, although there was a strange man in the room. *Very strange*, Casanova thought resentfully, finally opening his eyes and catching sight of a familiar scowl.

"Get up," he was told brusquely.

"The hotel had best be burning down," he said, rolling over and reaching for his robe. 'Ticia grabbed it first and fled, followed by Berenice. The blond took her time, and didn't bother to cover up her best asset as she swayed out of the room. She did, however, throw a coy glance over her shoulder in the direction of the war mage.

No accounting for taste, Casanova thought darkly, as Jason's red head popped up over the far side of the bed. He looked around blearily, wincing at the light. Pritkin hiked a thumb at him. "Out."

"Just because you've chosen the life of a eunuch—" Casanova began hotly, cutting off when his clothes hit him in the solar plexus.

"Get dressed."

"Who the hell do you think you are?"

"It's who *in* hell," Pritkin said, with a strange smile.

It took Casanova a second to get it, because it was the middle of the day—far too early for him to be vertical. And because it was so bizarre. "Since when do you claim your title?"

"Whenever it's useful to me. Now get dressed. Unless you intend to go naked."

"Go? Go where?"

"Ealdris escaped again."

Casanova stared at him, his clothes clutched to his chest. "Ealdris? Ancient demon battle queen with a grudge against the world, that Ealdris?"

"That would be the one."

"But . . . but you just put her back in prison!"

"And now she's out again."

Casanova stared at him, feeling slightly ill. Not that he'd had anything to do with it. When one of the ancient horrors escaped their very just imprisonment, it was a problem for the demon lords, not the minor-level incubus with whom he shared body space. But he was marginally acquainted with the lord who had returned this particular horror to captivity, and beings as old as Ealdris took a wide-ranging view of retribution.

He suddenly wanted Pritkin gone for an entirely new reason.

"What do you expect me to do about it?" he demanded. "I wouldn't last ten seconds against one of those things!" He shivered. "Hateful, filthy beasts. I don't know why the council didn't destroy them all, years ago—"

"Probably because it had enough trouble merely imprisoning them."

"Which is my point! If the council itself couldn't deal with them, what use do you think I'd be?"

"None whatsoever."

"Then why in the name of all that's unholy are you dragging me—"

"I'm not dragging you anywhere. You're going upstairs."

"Up—" Casanova stopped, a horrible idea surfacing. "No. Oh, no. Please tell me that that complete disaster of a—"

"Careful."

"I knew it!" Casanova raged. "It's that awful, awful woman, isn't it? She's somehow involved in this."

"She isn't involved."

"This used to be a nice, quiet operation—"

"Run by a mob boss."

"—and then she showed up and look at it! Someone is always trying to kill her, or kidnap her or do *something* to her and what happens in the process?"

"A good woman is put through hell for no reason?"

Casanova frowned. "No. My hotel is slowly being destroyed! Every other week it's either raided or bombed or taken over by a bunch of deadbeats. And now there's an ancient nightmare coming to finish off what's left!"

"Ealdris has never heard of Miss Palmer."

"How the hell can I be expected to show a profit when—" Casanova stopped, as the mage's words sunk in. "She hasn't?"

"To my knowledge, no."

"Then why are you—"

"Because Rosier has."

Casanova felt his demon curl into a tighter ball somewhere under his sternum. Or maybe that was his stomach. It tended to give him problems whenever the Lord of the Incubi decided to pay a visit. "What does he have to do with this?"

"He's offered me a deal. I recapture Ealdris, and he refrains from further harm to Miss Palmer."

"And you *believe* him?"

"He swore a binding oath. If I succeed, he will have no choice but to honor his commitment or the curse will kill him."

"And this involves me why?" Casanova demanded, dropping the wrinkled mass of clothing and stalking over to the closet for something more suitable.

"Because I don't trust him."

"And you do me? I'm possessed by one of his subjects, remember?"

"Which is why you'll be able to detect a demon presence, should one show up. And I trust your enlightened self-interest. What do you think Mircea would do to you if you let his golden goose get killed on your watch?"

Casanova scowled, and yanked on a pair of boxers. "If you're so concerned, tell Rosier to go hang. Stay and watch the damn girl yourself!"

"I can't afford to do that."

"And why not? We've managed to keep her alive so far without making deals with the devil—any devil."

"We've been lucky so far. But I can't protect her 24/7. Neither can you. Neither can that fool of a vampire, who believes that if he surrounds her with enough of his creatures, no one can touch her."

Casanova shifted slightly, uncomfortable with criticism of his other master. Even if he somewhat agreed with it. "You can't protect her at all if you're dead," he pointed out.

"That is my problem. Yours is making sure that nothing happens while I'm away."

Casanova scowled and pulled on a honey-colored shirt that set off his olive skin. "She's a time traveler, isn't she? Why not have her shift a few weeks into the past until you deal with this, take in a movie?"

"Because that would require telling her why she needs to go. And that would result in her deciding to help me—whether I like it or not!"

"But even Mircea has trouble keeping up with her. How am I supposed—"

"I'm sure you'll think of something."

"I could chase her around the training salle like you do, but I'm not that frustrated," Casanova said caustically. "I prefer a different kind of swordplay with nubile young—"

"Anything that touches her gets hacked off when I return."

"Walking disaster areas are not my type," Casanova sneered. "You can save the threats." Besides, Mircea had already made them all.

"Can you think of no way of amusing a young woman for an afternoon besides sex?"

Casanova blinked. "Why would I want to do that?"

The mage took a deep breath for some reason. "I don't care what excuse you use, merely that you stay with her. Her bodyguards won't notice a demon presence until it's too late, but you will.

"Making me the chief target! Is that supposed to make me feel better? Because—"

He broke off when the mage grabbed him by the shirt and slammed him into the wall. "I don't care how you feel," he hissed, looking a lot like his father suddenly. "I care about what you do. Allow me to spell things out for you. I *will* be back. And if she's dead, so are you."

Casanova watched him leave, feeling his demon curling within him. "Well, shit," they said.

Chapter Three

The street of the soul vendors looked deserted. Dim moonlight filtered down through a heavy lid of clouds highlighting soot-stained brick buildings, most with empty, dark windows reflecting the empty, dark street. Only a single ifrit, glowing coal-red against the darkness, was in sight, and it was in a hurry. Its bouncy, jittering movement left a trail of sparks on the cobblestones as it rushed past.

That wasn't entirely unexpected in an area where the shoppers were often as incorporeal as the items for which they bartered, but the place felt empty, too. The clammy mist of spirits that usually flowed around him, ruffling John's hair and sending chills across his flesh, was simply gone. But at least the small shop he wanted was open, spilling rich golden light into the muddy street.

He crossed the lane and pushed open the door. This place hadn't changed, at least. It still looked like a Victorian-era apothecary, with a scuffed wooden floor, gas lights overhead, and shelves of glass jars lining the walls. The owner was the same, too, hurrying out of the back as soon as the string of bells over the door announced a customer.

And then trying to hurry back inside once he saw who it was.

"Hello, Sid." John reached over the counter and grabbed him by the scruff of the neck, causing the demon to curse and spit. A trail of ooze started sliming down the wall, eating into the plaster and leaving an ugly burnt scar, as John jerked the creature back against him. "That was unwise."

"Instinct," his captive babbled, the ruddy face breaking into a nervous smile. "Just instinct. You startled me."

"Then you must be startled constantly, if this place is as busy as I remember."

"My other customers aren't outlaws!"

"Neither am I." John released him. "The council has given me a weekend pass, so to speak."

"Why?" Sid demanded, turning around.

He looked like a small, bald man with a pleasant, round face and pronounced jowls. It was an illusion, of course, like the rest of the shop, like the street outside, for that matter. What he actually was might have scared off the occasional mage who ventured here for supplies, and Sid wasn't about to lose a sale.

"They hate you," he pointed out.

"Fortunately, they hate Ealdris more."

"Ealdris?" Sid sounded like he'd never heard the name. John shot him the look that deserved. Sid had been a fixture among the incorporeal demon races for longer than anyone could remember, and he paid attention. "Oh, yes," Sid looked diffident. "That Ealdris."

"Rosier has offered me a deal. I recapture her, and he refrains from attempting to murder the new Pythia."

"And you *believe* him?" Sid's bushy eyebrows met his nonexistent hairline.

John sighed. He was already getting tired of that question. "I believe that he doesn't want to go up against her himself. But it's one of his responsibilities as a member of the council."

"He wouldn't be on the council if he wasn't strong enough to handle it," Sid pointed out. "Why does he need you?"

"Because she's hiding here."

That was the part that didn't make sense to John. The Shadowland was a minor demon realm that had risen to prominence as a marketplace, to facilitate trade between the various dominions. But then the leaders of the main factions had started moving in, establishing secondary courts where they could meet without the danger of entering another's power base. Over time, the demon council had begun meeting here as well, making the unprepossessing hunk of rock the *de facto* capitol of hell.

And a damn strange place for a wanted ex-queen to choose for a hide out.

"This isn't a run of the mill demon we're talking about," Sid said, wiping his shiny brow. "The ancient horrors were locked away by the council because even they couldn't control them. What do you think you're going to do if you find her?"

"I dealt with her before."

"She was on Earth for the first time in six thousand years! She was confused and disoriented, and she underestimated you. I wouldn't bet on that happening twice."

"I'll keep it in mind." John leaned on the highly polished counter. "Where is she, Sid?"

"I don't know," the demon's pudgy hands nervously smoothed his pristine white apron. "And I wouldn't tell you if I did. People have been going missing, John—a lot of people—and everyone else is lying low. Which is what you'll do if you have any—" he suddenly cut off, staring at the darkened windows over John's shoulder. He must have sensed something that John couldn't, because his face closed down, becoming business-like.

A second later the bells tinkled again, announcing a new customer. John moved away to peruse the shelves, leaving them to it. If it had been another time, he might have been tempted to do some shopping. The small slotted drawers on the lower half of the antiquated fixtures held the kind of potion supplies almost unobtainable on earth, and when they were the cost was staggering.

He tried to keep his eyes on the drawers, but the shelves up above were impossible to ignore. The glimmering contents of the rows of apothecary jars writhed and twisted in a spectrum of colors—pale amethyst and deep green, brilliant turquoise and ruby red, glittering white and darkest obsidian—with glints like captured fire. But what they contained was far more precious, and far more destructive.

He stepped back, but the shop was small and jars ringed the walls, as well as being stacked high on display tables. His hand brushed against one behind him, and for an instant, he caught a flash of the wonders it promised: *cool green water slipping over his skin, a darting school of tiny fish up ahead, their scales gleaming in the light that dappled the shallows. He surged after them, faster and sleeker, the joy of the hunt thrumming through his veins, scattering them like sliver petals in the wind—*

He snatched his hand away, but they were all around him, whispering, promising, yearning. They sang to him with siren songs and glimpses of wonders, of colors that had never lived in human imagination, of music beyond the range of his senses, of the sounds and scents of worlds long dead. He'd been shielded when he came in, but he'd let them drop to save strength, knowing that Sid's protection was the best available.

He'd forgotten; in this particular shop, the real dangers were already indoors.

"Almost irresistible, isn't it?" a rich voice asked.

John's head jerked up, only to see one of the Irin standing in front of him, its faint glimmer dispelling the shadows for two full yards around him. This one was tall, as they all were, and powerfully built, with skin the color of burnished bronze and ebony hair that spilled onto its spotless wings. It regarded John kindly, out of a face so beautiful, so perfect, it almost made him want to weep.

He squashed that impulse by asking himself what exactly it had done to get barred from the heavens.

"Living another's life," the Irin continued, picking up the jar, "seeing what they saw, experiencing what they felt . . . It's almost like being another person for a time, isn't it?"

"Yes." John shoved his hands deep into the pockets of his coat, and deliberately didn't look at the seductively twisting colors.

"I try to draw out the experience with the more interesting ones," the creature told him. "Allowing me to visit them over and over. I like to think that it permits them to live again, in a way."

"They're dead," John rasped. "They'll never live again."

"No, I suppose not." The Irin tipped its head, looking at him consideringly. "I must confess, I was surprised that a human could interact with them. I had always understood that to be impossible."

"I don't—" John began, only to be cut off as the scene in front of him rippled and changed.

The shop was the same size, but now it had a dirt floor and a thatched roof. Instead of gas lights, there were rough tallow candles, and the windows were merely dark open spaces letting in the sound of crickets and the smell of peat. The same slightly anxious Sid stood behind a rough wooden counter, a homespun apron serving as a handkerchief for his perpetually damp palms. But instead of the Irin, Rosier stood at his side.

In his hands was a clay bowl filled with shades of honey, gold and burnt sienna. They swirled together in glittering bands, bright as jewels in the candlelight, mesmerizing. "Excellent work, Sid," his father said, "I admit, I didn't think you could do it."

"I wasn't sure myself. It took two of my best hunters the better part of a month, but there you are. Nothing good comes easy, I always say."

"And this is very good." Rosier placed the bowl carefully in his son's hands. "I explored one of these as a child; enjoyed myself no end. They're a sort of merpeople, for lack of a better term, in one of the minor water realms."

Emrys took the bowl gingerly, with both hands, and was surprised to find it so light. As if it contained air. As if it contained nothing at all.

"But . . . how can you—"

"A spell," his father said easily. "It captures a being's memories in the moments before death, preserving them for us to study."

"Then I can see through anyone's eyes?" he heard himself ask, amazement in his voice.

"It's better than that," his father said, putting an arm around him. "For a short time after use, you'll retain their abilities. In a real sense of the word, you can be anyone."

Emrys stared at him, speechless, the possibilities spinning around in his mind like the colors in the bowl. His father saw his expression and clapped him on the shoulder, laughing. "What's the matter, boy? Didn't I promise you wonders?"

John shoved the memory away, brutally enough to make the Irin flinch. "My apologies," the creature said. "My people communicate mentally, and sometimes I forget . . ."

John stood there, panting, so angry he could barely see. It hadn't forgotten a damn thing. Like most of the stronger denizens of the vast network of realms that humans dismissed as "Hell," it had simply taken what it wanted.

But it wouldn't take anything else.

John's shields slammed into place, and this time, he didn't ward with his usual water, but with ice. The temperature of the room plummeted dramatically, enough to freeze the mud that had been tracked in the entrance and to send a frozen scale creeping across the boards. Sid gave a bleat of alarm over by the old cash register, and the Irin raised a single elegant brow.

"It appears I have offended. Again, my regrets." The words and tone were contrite, but it flashed him a knowing smile as it turned to leave. "Enjoy your purchase."

John stared after the creature as it swept out, wondering how much more it had seen. Enough to guess that its parting shot would hit home. "Don't pay any attention to him," Sid said, as John rejoined him at the counter. "He's just jealous. The Irin can only take one kind of energy, and your line can absorb almost anything. Well, not legally, but you know what I—"

John had pulled out a map from under his coat as Sid talked. Now he spread it on the counter and grabbed one of the pudgy white hands the shop owner was flailing around. "Just point," he said harshly. He wanted out of there. He wanted out now.

"I don't want to get involved," Sid protested, while he scribbled something on the portion of the map hidden by the cash register's iron bulk. "I'm not a warrior. I can't afford—"

"I understand, although the council may not. You should expect to receive a visit from them shortly."

"They'll have to catch me first." Sid leaned across the counter to flip over the OPEN sign in the nearest window. "That was my last delivery and the rest can go hang. I've decided to take a long overdue vacation. If you're smart, you'll do the same."

John took the hint and the map, pocketing it before turning away from the counter. He stepped out of the smothering warmth and back into the blessed chill of the night. He didn't make a purchase before he left.

Chapter Four

"**B**oiled," Marlowe said, nodding solemnly. "In one of his own pots no less. Henry thought it was fitting."

Cassie looked up from unwrapping another parcel to stare at the curly-haired vampire. "Fitting?"

"Well, the man did try to poison him . . ."

"Henry VIII boiled one of his own cooks?"

"Alive." Marlowe added helpfully.

Her blue eyes narrowed. "You're making that up."

"I heard it from one of the servants who was there. Said the stench lingered for days. Scouts honor."

"You were never a scout."

"True." He grinned. "But then, I never had any honor, either . . ."

She snorted and went back to tackling her gift. "See? I knew you were joking."

Casanova rolled his eyes. It wouldn't surprise him if Marlowe had lit the match.

Almost as if he'd heard him, that sharp brown gaze turned in his direction. Casanova quickly went to fix himself a drink, in order to have some excuse to linger. It was just his luck to have arrived at the girl's suite to find the Consul's chief spy ensconced on the sofa, amusing her with more of his gruesome stories.

He didn't appear to be in a hurry to leave, and he kept glancing at Casanova as if wondering what he was doing there. Casanova was starting to wonder the same thing. Counting him and the spy, there were no fewer than eight master-level vampires prowling around the suite, with two more stationed outside.

Demon or not, no one was getting through all that.

A brief exploration of the bar's fridge turned up three tiny bottles of vodka and he used them all. They were too cold and there was no lime, but today was obviously about hardships. He turned back around to find Marlowe still watching him.

"Can I get you anything?" he asked acerbically.

"I was wondering the same about you," Marlowe said mildly, as Pritkin entered pushing a room service cart loaded with gifts.

Casanova was about to ask him what he was still doing there when he felt it—a familiar power prickling along his skin like a feathering of knives. There was no mistaking what it was—or where it was coming from. He started to shout a warning, but before he could so much as utter a syllable his vocal cords seized up, as if an invisible hand had suddenly clenched around his throat.

"More of them?" Cassie moaned, staring at the cart.

"Don't you like receiving tokens from your admirers?" Marlowe asked.

"They're not my admirers," she said, frowning. "Half these people were calling for my head less than a month ago. They're only sucking up now because it looks like I might live long enough to be Pythia, after all. And the rest are trying to bribe me."

Casanova exerted enough power to punch through a wall, and managed to jerk his glass all of half an inch. A few drops of clear liquid spilled over the side and slid slowly down his hand, cool, cool, against his skin. But he couldn't wipe them away. He couldn't, in fact, seem to move at all.

"So young to be so cynical," Marlowe reproached.

"Oh, really? Look that this," Cassie held up a blue velvet jewel case with a family seal stamped in gold on top. "Some Dutch count wants me to do a reading, but not for him. Oh, no. It seems that his wife has found out about his long-term mistress and is threatening to throw him out, and she's the one with the money. So, he wants me to tell her that she got it all wrong—he's pure as the driven snow."

"I don't blame you for being insulted," Marlowe said, picking up the case and perusing the contents.

Cassie nodded. "I know, right? I've never even met this guy and he expects me to lie for him!"

"For something like that, he could at least have sent diamonds." Marlowe held up a pale blue necklace. "I mean really. Aquamarines!"

Cassie narrowed her eyes at her guest. "I'm serious, Marlowe! There's like a metric ton of this stuff, and virtually all of it comes with some kind of strings."

The chief spy shrugged. "What did you expect? People have been attempting to bribe Pythias since ancient times. It's tradition."

"And what did those other Pythias do?"

Marlowe's cell phone rang. He fished it out of a pocket and glanced at the display. "Took the gifts as their due and told the petitioners whatever they liked."

"That's so wrong!"

Marlowe rose to his feet and took her hand, kissing it with an ironic air that said he knew such things were out of style—and didn't give a damn. "You'll get used to it."

Casanova cursed inwardly, since that was the only way he could do it. The damned creature pretending to be Pritkin was leaning against the wall, arms crossed, with a faint smirk on his face. He was obviously waiting for the chief spy to clear out, which it looked like he was about to do. Casanova didn't know the details of what was scheduled to happen then, but he could make a damn good guess.

He didn't bother trying to appeal to the creature's better nature, because he didn't have one. He focused instead on the tight little ball curled beneath his rib cage. *"Let me go, Rian."*

There was no response.

"Damn it, I know it's you," he thought viciously. *"Demon lord or no, Rosier doesn't have access to my body. I only trusted one person enough for that!"*

"I'm sorry, I'm sorry!" His demon, whom he persisted in thinking of as 'she', sounded nothing like her usual polished self.

"Then let me go!"

"I can't!" He closed his eyes to see her shaking her head violently, her long dark hair whipping about her panicked face. *"He'll kill you if he has to—he swore as much. But as long as you don't interfere—"*

"Then Mircea will kill me!"

"He can't blame you if you're not involved!"

"What the hell do you call this*?"*

"Is there something wrong?"

Casanova opened his eyes to find Marlowe regarding him from barely a foot away. The chief spy was inside his comfort zone, sharp brown eyes steady on his, but at the moment it hardly registered. "Wrong?" he heard himself say. "What could be wrong?"

Marlowe's lips twisted. "Around here? Virtually anything."

Casanova usually found Marlowe's suspicious nature a trial, particularly when his people were poking around the casino, looking for God-knew-what. But today he could have really used some of that perpetual paranoia. So, of course, Marlowe gave him one last considering look and turned to go.

"Rian!" Casanova thought urgently.

"Mircea won't kill you. He . . . he's not that vindictive." She sounded as if she was trying to convince herself, and doing a poor job of it.

"And you're willing to bet my life on that?" Casanova hissed.

"I don't have a choice!"

"Not a chance," he thought fiercely. *"He doesn't control you. He can give you commands, but you decide whether to follow them or not. And I want you to remember that, when this is over, when I'm paying the price. I want you to remember that you* chose*."*

Marlowe reached the door and "Pritkin" moved to Cassie's side.

"Could I have a word?" the fake mage asked pleasantly.

Cassie looked up, obviously still preoccupied by her little ethics problem. "What? Oh, sure."

"In private? It won't take a moment."

Cassie nodded and got up, starting for the bedroom. She didn't notice, Casanova realized, his stomach sinking. She might have, under other circumstances, but she was preoccupied and her guard was down because she was in a place that she believed to be safe. And that damn demon would have her dead before she ever knew otherwise.

Rian must have thought so, too, because he could feel her panic, like a tremor down his spine. *"I don't know what to do!"* she said desperately.

"I said the same to you once, do you remember?"

"Yes." Her voice shook slightly.

"And do you remember what you told me?"

She was silent for a long moment, while Cassie reached the door to the bedroom and a vampire opened the one to the hallway for Marlowe. *"That you would never regret it,"* she whispered.

"Well? Will I?"

"I hope not," she said fervently.

And then she let him go.

What followed couldn't have taken more than a few seconds, but it was blazoned on Casanova's memory nonetheless. He sprang for the girl, screaming his head off. "Not Pritkin, *not Pritkin!*"

Marlowe spun before he'd even gotten all of the words out and was across the room, leaping for the demon while the guards were still trying to figure out what was going on. He almost made it. Rosier flicked out an arm and Marlowe went flying backwards, barely missing Casanova as he hurtled across the room in his own leap.

But Casanova wasn't going for Rosier, because he'd last even less time than Marlowe had, and because he didn't matter, anyway. His job wasn't to kill the demon but to rescue the girl. So that was what he did, using the split second it took Rosier to deal with the chief spy to snatch Cassie and—

The room shimmered around him as they tumbled forward, bursting through the bedroom door and hitting the floor—and then kept on going into the middle of a very hard, very cold street. For a moment, there was nothing but confusion—Cassie struggling and Rian screaming and a horrible stench flooding Casanova's senses, making him want to gag. And then he looked up to see a huge, gelatinous blob of a creature bearing down on him.

Despite vampire vision, he couldn't see it very well, the edges going all fuzzy and vague as his eyes tried to focus. But that wasn't such a bad thing, considering that what he could see was making his flesh want to crawl off his bones and go whimper in a corner. It looked like a man, if men were six hundred pounds of pale, jelly-like flesh that was transparent enough to show another creature crouched inside, surrounded by its host's ropy intestines.

Casanova stared at it in disbelief, caught between paralyzing terror and an absurd urge to laugh. It was ghastly and yet unreal, like something out of a bad fifties' horror flick, its translucent skin gleaming in the dim light of a nearby streetlamp. But then the hunched passenger's dark red eyes swiveled in his direction, and he suddenly found that he could move, after all.

"Where the hell are we?" Cassie demanded, pushing tumbled curls out of her eyes.

"Yes," Casanova breathed. Then he snatched her up, threw her over his shoulder and ran like all the demons of hell were after him.

Or one of them, anyway.

Chapter Five

The shop looked a little different from the back, with the shades drawn and the lights extinguished. But Sid's shiny bald head was the same as it poked out a crack in the door and stared around nervously. "Hurry up!" he hissed, catching sight of John. "Before anyone sees you!"

John felt like pointing out that he'd just cut through a maze of side streets and across two marketplaces before doubling back, just to ensure that no one *would* see him. But he didn't. Because Sid could have left him to find Ealdris on his own, instead of scribbling 'meet me out back in half an hour' on the edge of the map.

He stepped through the door to find that the lights were off inside, too. But the softly glowing contents of the rows of apothecary jars provided just enough illumination to see by, throwing a watery rainbow over the walls, the floor, and Sid's anxious face. "I couldn't talk before," he said, wiping his hands down his apron front. "If Ealdris heard I helped you—"

"Tell me where to find her and you won't have to worry about it for long."

Sid snorted. "Typical human arrogance!"

"No. Knowledge she doesn't have."

The little demon didn't look convinced. "Such as?"

John spread the map on the counter again. "If she was hiding in the city, the Alû would have found her by now," he said, referring to the High Council's feared enforcement squad. "But they haven't, and none of the tracking spells they sent into the hinterlands returned anything. So, I know where she is."

"You think she's camping in the middle of the desert?" Sid asked archly.

"I think she's camping under it." John's finger traced an arc across a mountain range to the north of the city. "Long before there was a settlement here, there was some kind of mining concern in the hills. I don't know what they were taking out of there, but it was extensive. I came across a few of the tunnels as a boy—"

"That's what you were doing when no one could find you? Exploring the desert? You might have been killed!"

"But I wasn't. And that gives me an advantage she doesn't know I have. As do these."

Sid looked dubiously at the yellowish blocks of explosives John was pulling out of a backpack and piling on his nice clean counter. "And you think this lot will let you take her on?"

"If she's like most of the older demons, yes."

That won him a narrow-eyed look. "And how is that?"

"Powerful but not resourceful."

Sid huffed out a laugh. "I've never known your father to have a problem in that area. And he's nearly as old as our missing queen."

"The incubi are different," John admitted. "They have to build relationships with their prey unless they want to spend all their time hunting. And humans are nothing if not unpredictable. Interacting with them requires the incubi to be flexible, inventive, even somewhat open-minded."

"Unlike Ealdris. You think she won't expect an assault with human weapons."

John nodded, not wanting to elaborate and insult the creature. After all, Sid was fairly ancient, too. But as a shopkeeper, he also had to be flexible, at least to a point, to deal with so many different species. That wasn't true of most of the older demons, who tended to turn more and more inward as the centuries passed. By the time they reached Ealdris' age, they were virtually unable to comprehend any ways other than their own.

It was what had John worried, because she should have done exactly as she had last time and headed for Earth as soon as she broke free. Demons gained strength through one thing and one thing only—feeding. She needed food, and quickly, if she was to maintain her independence. And Earth was by far the richest source available.

But instead, she'd come here. It was like a starving man passing up a banquet hall to search for scraps in the Dumpster outside. It didn't make sense, and every time an ancient demon surprised him, John got edgy. And when he got edgy, he tended to hedge his bets, which was why he'd packed enough C-4 to bring down a mountain.

"Preferably right over her," Sid said, when he'd finished explaining.

"That's the plan."

"It's a good one," Sid admitted, frowning. "The wards she's familiar with guard against magic. Like as not, this. . . stuff . . . won't even register."

"But?" John asked, because there clearly had been one in the little demon's tone.

Sid sighed and started returning a few scattered jars to their appropriate shelves. "Nothing. I'm just a foolish old man who remembers another time."

"Meaning?"

"That in my day we did things differently. We faced our enemies."

John stared at him incredulously. "You think I'm being dishonorable? Knowing what she's done? What she'll do again given the slightest—"

"No, no." Sid shook his head. "I didn't mean anything. You're only half-demon and incubus at that. I don't expect you to understand." He caught John's expression. "No offense."

"None taken," John said curtly. Not being mistaken for a demon was hardly an insult. And standing and dueling a being as powerful as Ealdris wasn't honorable, it was stupid.

"And you're little more than a child," Sid said, looking down at the jar he held. A hazy smear of deep magenta curled and twisted inside, painting his skin a livid hue. "You don't know what it was like, in our day. And how could you? Seeing what we've become."

"You mean it was worse?" John asked cynically.

Sid glanced up at him, and smiled slightly. "You'd probably think so. It was certainly more savage, more raw. But infinitely more glorious, too. You should have seen it, John," he said, his voice going dreamy. "There weren't as many of us then, so you might think we were weaker, but it wasn't so. Huge armies we had, glittering in the night, under commanders worthy of the name, marching off to victory or death—"

"Mostly death," John interjected, because there had been nothing glorious about the ancient wars. Just century after century of bloody chaos, as each race struggled for existence in a never-ending competition for food and resources. Ending them had been one of the few things the High Council had ever gotten right.

"Yes, yes, but you miss the point," Sid said irritably. "The chaff was winnowed out, but the best survived, thrived, grew stronger by their ordeals. Instead of the weakest being rewarded for how well they can toady, like today."

"I never took you for a Social Darwinist."

"I'm not anything human," Sid told him, with a bite to his tone. "We were stronger without them, back when every resource was scarcer, every meal more hard won. Then we found their weak, soft, rule-bound race, and everything changed."

"I'm sure they felt the same," John said curtly, not interested in a debate. "I'm also fairly certain that Ealdris is where I say she is. But there could be miles of tunnels through these hills and I don't have time to search them all. I need you to narrow it down."

Sid stared at the map, but didn't say anything.

"Before the rest of your clientele goes missing," John added.

The little demon sighed fretfully and flapped a hand at the windows. "Check the shades, would you?"

"I promise you, I *will* find her," John said, turning to look for gaps in the dark green cloth.

And then dropping to his knees when something slammed into him with the force of a dozen sledgehammers. It knocked him to the floor, his head reeling, pain shooting from temple to temple in a mind-numbing haze.

But not so numb that he couldn't make out the ancient being bending over him—who was suddenly glowing with a power he shouldn't have had.

"I believe I can guarantee it," Sid said, as the room exploded around him.

* * *

"I think I wet myself," Casanova said faintly, hugging a wall.

It was soot-stained brick, crumbling and moldy and cold against his shoulder blades. Or at least it was for the moment. Part of the illusion they used to keep people from running and screaming at the sight of this place didn't fool his vampire senses. But part of it did. The result was a mishmash of images that would have made his head ache if it wasn't already threatening to take off the top of his skull.

"We have to get out of here," Rian told him. "We've lost them for the moment, but I can't shield us for—"

"Then why did you bring us here?" he asked savagely.

"I didn't know what else to do! The girl didn't know she needed to shift and there was no time to explain and Rosier—"

"So, you brought us to his doorstep?" The wall was stucco now, he couldn't help but notice. Bright, buttery stucco, like on his home in beautiful Cordoba. Where he would really like to be right now instead of shivering in Hell.

It's freezing over, he thought suddenly, and had to bite his lip on a hysterical giggle.

"I don't have her power," Rian said, looking at him strangely. "I can shift between worlds, but not between places in a world. And she couldn't survive in most of our realms in any—"

"Survive? You mean I'm not dead?" Cassie suddenly piped up.

Casanova turned to stare at her, but there was no doubt about it, she was looking straight at Rian's hazy outline.

"Well? Are we in Hell or not?" she demanded.

Rian looked at him, apparently nonplussed herself, and then back at Cassie. "You can see me?" she asked hesitantly.

"Clairvoyant," Cassie snapped.

"But I've known clairvoyants before, and they couldn't—"

"I'm Pythia. It comes with more power."

"We know," Casanova said, scowling. "That's what's drawing them. Demons feed off human energy and you're lit up like a Vegas buffet."

"I can't help it!"

"You never saw me before," Rian accused. "Did you?"

"You were in a body before. I see spirits. And will somebody please answer the damn ques—"

"Yes, you're in hell," Rian told her. "*A* hell, in any case, there are a number of them."

"Hundreds," Casanova interjected absently. He was watching the wall out of the corner of his eye, and he was pretty sure it was playing with him. Because now it was covered in the hideous wallpaper one of his mistresses had had in her bedroom in Seville. The one in which she'd entertained three other men, occasionally at the same time, whenever he chanced to be out of town . . .

"More than that," Rian said. "But it doesn't matter now. What matters is—"

"Then I *am* dead," Cassie said hollowly.

Casanova reached over and pinched her, hard. "Do you feel dead?"

She jumped. "Cut it out!"

"Yes," Rian agreed, shooting him a look. "We have to decide what to do."

"Yes, I'm *dead*?" Cassie said sharply.

"I was talking to him," Rian told her, starting to look confused.

"What to do is obvious," Casanova said impatiently. "We need to find somewhere to hide. As soon as the mage kills Ealdris—"

"And if he doesn't?"

"He will. He's good at killing things."

"Most things. But you know as well as I do that Ealdris isn't just any—"

"*Will somebody please tell me if I'm dead or not?*" Cassie yelled, before Casanova clapped a hand over her mouth.

"Do you *want* to be something's dinner?" he hissed.

Rian shut her eyes for a moment, and then spoke very slowly and distinctly. "You are not dead. Humans come here from time to time. Powerful mages can transition to the upper hells and back—the ones which can support human life, at least—and occasionally someone is brought here—"

"As a snack," Casanova finished for her, "which is what we are going to be if we don't get out!"

"That's what I've been saying!" Rian tossed her hair agitatedly. "But we can't go back to the casino. If Rosier isn't still there himself, he'll have people—"

"Then take us somewhere else!"

"I just told you, if I transition back to your world, it will be where I left it. I would need a portal to go somewhere else, and the master knows that. He'll have someone—"

"Another hell, then. Somewhere safer."

Rian looked at him like he might have lost his mind. "A safer *hell*?"

"We won't be there long! We only need to hide until Pritkin deals with this."

"Deals with what?" Cassie asked.

"He's supposed to kill Ealdris," Casanova informed her shortly. "As soon as he does, Rosier can't hurt you. He swore a binding—"

"Who's Ealdris?"

"What difference does it make? All you need to understand is that Rosier blackmailed him into going after her, thinking that he'd kill you while Pritkin was on his little errand. But the mage anticipated that and sent me to watch you. And now all we have to do is stay out of the way until—"

"Who. Is. Ealdris?" Cassie was looking strangely red in the face.

"An ancient demon battle queen," Casanova said, right before he was slammed against a wall for the second time that day.

"*And you let him go?*"

"*¿Cómo?*"

"You let Pritkin go after this thing, knowing the risk—"

"He's doing it to protect you—"

"How many times do I have to say this?" Little fingers dug into his flesh, surprisingly hard. "I don't want to be protected! Not if it costs someone else's life! *Don't you get it?*"

"Of course."

"Of course? Then why—"

"I 'get it'," Casanova told her nastily. "I just don't care. I don't work for you, *chica*, and for that matter, neither does the mage. It's his life. If he wants to risk it, I don't see where that's any concern of—"

"It's my concern because I'm the *cause*!" Cassie whispered furiously, her hands letting go of his arms only to bunch in the expensive fabric of his lapels. "And you do work for Mircea. And by vampire law, I'm his wife, so you work for me. And if you'd like to continue to work for me, you had damn well better learn to care!"

Casanova glared at her. "Why, you vicious, ungrateful little—"

"Will you two stop it?"

Casanova ceased prying Cassie's hands off his jacket and looked at Rian. Because she never used that tone, much less with him. But then, she never glared at him like that, either.

"We have to decide what we're going to *do*," she said severely. "The master will be here at any moment, and I cannot hide us from him!"

"How could he possibly know where you took us?" Cassie demanded.

"Because there aren't that many options. Most of the hells require permission to enter—"

"And this one doesn't?"

"It's neutral ground, a meeting place, a market—" she waved a restless hand. "Anyone can come here. And as soon as he does, he'll follow my trail right to you. All incubi can sense another's presence. But if I leave, I can't shield you from—"

"Can you do it?"

Rian looked confused again. "Can I do what?"

"Find another incubus."

"Yes, but what does that—"

"Then I know what we're going to do," Cassie said, jerking Casanova's face down to hers. "And I know who's going to help me."

Chapter Six

Bump, bump, bump.

It sounded like someone was hammering on a door, John thought vaguely. He wished they'd stop. Or that someone would answer the damn thing. He couldn't sleep with all this pounding going on.

Bump, bump, bump.

Or with all this pain. Every thud made agonized lightning zigzag behind his eyeballs, to the point that he was getting nauseous with it. It reminded him of a few of the hangovers he'd had in the bad old days, when he'd found solace, or what passed for it, in the bottom of a bottle.

Bump.

Except this hurt more.

Bump, bump, b—

Bugger it! If someone didn't get that damn thing—

John opened his eyes, just in time to close them again in a tortured wince as—*ump*—the back of his cranium came down, connecting with what felt like solid rock. A disoriented moment later, he realized that it was rock, specifically an uneven floor that he was being dragged across by the legs, his head allowed to bounce along behind the rest of him as best it could.

Which probably explained why it felt like a particularly ill-used football.

He tried to take stock, but it was a little difficult. He couldn't see bugger all, being in almost complete darkness; his arms were bound to his sides and his coat was gone, which explained the raw meat texture of his back. But his weapons . . . one of them was somewhere nearby.

He could feel it, the enchantment it carried chiming along his nerves like a glissando of bells. Cool and sweet, it was soothingly familiar. And loud, so loud that he had to be almost—

It was the small knife next to his right calf. John blinked, taking a moment to absorb the fact that some idiot had actually left his boots on. And had compounded the folly by not even checking them for weapons first. He didn't know whether to be pleased or insulted, but on the whole he thought he'd go with—

BUMP.

—seriously fucking up whoever was responsible.

He dragged the tattered threads of his concentration together, focusing them on that tiny chime. He could usually do this without thinking, an almost automated response after so long, like breathing. It was more difficult now, but he finally felt the connection snap into place and all that dormant magic spring to life, eager to leap to his defense at a whispered—

"No!" someone yelled, slinging him against a wall. Which hurt like the devil, since he had no way to avoid hitting face first. But on the whole that bothered him less than the supernova that suddenly erupted all around him.

John instinctively turned his head further into the wall, but that only seemed to make things worse. Light seared his eyeballs even through the lids, spearing straight through to his brain. For a brief instant he could see every blood vessel on the inside of his head, feel every scraped-raw nerve lit up in excruciating clarity.

And then something hot and intense shot though his body like a bolt of lightning before grounding itself in his spine.

Someone let out a not-so-manly mewl of pain and he hoped it wasn't him. He didn't think so, actually. Because he was fairly certain that his tongue had just fused to the roof of his mouth.

Someone else didn't have that problem. He recognized Sid's voice, cursing up a storm in some long-dead language, but he couldn't see him. Not even when the light finally dimmed, the wildly jumping aftereffects ensuring that John remained blind as a bat. Hoping that that was true for his attacker as well, John pried his tongue loose and started an incantation, only to stop when a knife was pressed hard against his jugular.

"Not if you want to live," Sid rasped, and the words died in his throat.

But not because of the threat. The blade currently denting his skin was well-oiled and razor sharp—and bleating at him alarmingly because it was his weapon. Sid must have caught it mid-flight, which would have been impressive except that a syllable from John would send it plunging into the demon's gut before he knew what had hit him. But John didn't utter that syllable. Because he didn't think the stark panic in Sid's voice was fake.

And a moment later he knew it wasn't when his eyes finally adjusted.

"Do you *see*?" Sid demanded.

John saw. It was rather hard to miss, since every surface of the low-ceilinged tunnel they were in had turned as translucent as alabaster, lit from within by hundreds of glowing red lines. They spidered through the rock like veins in marble—or under skin, because these pulsed with some strange, unearthly fire that brightened and dimmed, brightened and dimmed, as if driven by the beating of a distant heart.

It was like being in the belly of a huge, still-breathing animal, John's brain helpfully supplied, until he snarled at it to shut up. But the impression was damn apt, heightened by the unhappy rumbling in the stones around him and the heat generated by all that trapped energy. At least that explained why the shreds of his T-shirt were plastered to his body, he thought blankly.

Or maybe that was terror.

"To answer that question you asked earlier," Sid said, his voice dripping sarcasm, "they mined brimstone here. It's why I could magic you up here, but not in here." The little demon pulled the knife away from John's throat and shook it at him, before tucking it away in his waistband.

John's eyes followed it, but he made no effort to call it to him. Because the substance known on earth as 'brimstone' resembled the demon variety only in the overwhelming smell of rotten eggs. It didn't rain fire from the heavens, as some human legends insisted, or destroy entire cities. He'd always suspected that those accounts were ancient memories of the last of the demon wars, a few battles of which had been fought on Earth. Then the sky *had* burned, along with huge swathes of land, obliterated by single blasts.

Of the stuff glowing a few inches away from his face.

"It's laced all though these rocks," Sid informed him, slapping the side of the corridor hard enough to make John wince, even though he knew that wouldn't set it off. Sid could stick a pick axe through the wall and it would make no difference. Brimstone responded to only one thing.

Unfortunately, it happened to be the thing that John needed rather badly right now.

* * *

Casanova had spent years perfecting the alluring quality of his voice, imbuing it with the charm, the grace, the honeyed tones that often did much of his seduction for him. Rian had taught him some of that, but he was proud to say that much more came from his own Castilian roots, from a people who understood the lyrical potential of the spoken word in a way that few of the braying descendants of the British Isles ever would. He was an artist with his voice. He could make women, and the occasional man, weep with his voice.

And then there were times like these.

"Fuck it," he rasped, which would have made his point quite clearly had anyone been listening to him.

"I think I found something," Cassie's excited shriek drifted out of one of the rocks on this godforsaken hill.

Literally God forsaken, Casanova thought grimly, and he didn't blame Him one iota. Ugly, barren, and creepy as, well, hell—and he'd thought that the city was bad. Out here, nobody bothered with a spell to disguise anything, because there was nothing worth the effort. Just rocks, a little on-the-brink scrub, and a lot of dark, the latter broken only by the faint urban sprawl in the murky valley below them.

Why did anyone live here? Surely even demons could do better than this? And more importantly, what in the name of sanity was *he* doing here?

"Did you hear me?" Cassie demanded, and Casanova's hand clenched.

He knew what he was doing here. She was like a disease, a human virus that infected everyone around her, turning off their good sense and making them do things completely against their own best interests. Someone should lock her up, study her, figure out a vaccine before the whole damn world caught the madness—

A curly blond head poked out of a crack in the rock so that its owner could glare at him. "I'm not going in there," he said curtly.

Blue eyes narrowed. "Why not?"

"Why not? *Why not?* Because *this*—" his savage gesture took in the entire train of events that had led him from a warm, soft bed in Vegas to a frigid, rocky mountainside *in Hell*— "is insane. The only thing that could possibly make it more insane would be to crawl inside an unexplored hole in the ground after a mage who, on a good day, is suicidally reckless and who on this day is chasing a *demon battle queen*."

Cassie looked at someone over her shoulder. Rian, he assumed, since his traitor of a demon had floated in after her a few minutes ago. "I thought you said he'd calm down once we got out of the city."

Rian murmured something reassuring.

"Well, I don't know," Cassie told her. "He's getting pretty shrill."

"I am not shrill!" Casanova said, and all right, perhaps that had been a little shrill, but if so, he thought he'd earned it. "I am the voice of reason—"

"Well the voice of reason needs to get his butt in here."

Casanova didn't even bother to respond to that. Instead, he pulled the little silk pocket square out of his coat and made a point of placing it exactly in the center of the nearest sort-of-flat rock he could find. He smoothed it out, sat his Gucci-covered ass on it, and looked at her. Calmly, considering that he really didn't see how this could get any worse.

"Okay, fine," Cassie said. "I just thought you'd prefer it to the alternative."

"What alternative?"

"I think she means me," Rosier said gently, from behind him.

Casanova spun, but even vampire reflexes weren't fast enough this time. A blast of power picked him up and sent his body hurtling backwards through the air, right at the wretched little cave. And for a moment, things became a bit blurred.

That was possibly because his head hit the overhang hard enough to send his brain cavorting around inside his skull. Or because the impact half collapsed the structure on top of him. Or because he was grabbed by the shirt and jerked *into* the falling mass of debris, half of which put dents in his already abused body, while the rest rapidly blocked the way behind him.

Which bought him perhaps seconds with the power Rosier had at his disposal.

That thought had Casanova staggering off the remaining wall, which for some ungodly reason appeared to be glowing, with his brain still sloshing about between his ears. But despite that, and the mountain of dirt he'd just swallowed, and the fact that he appeared to be missing maybe half a pound of flesh, he somehow got fumbling hands on a certain blond-haired menace. And shook her like a maraca.

"Shift us out of here!"

Burning blue eyes glared at him through the dust. "I can't!"

"You shifted us in!" Her power wasn't supposed to work outside earth, but that hadn't stopped her from hopping them in stages across the damn desert, following the sight trail Rian had laid out.

"I shifted us *outside*."

"Then shift us outside again—far outside!"

"Are you listening? I *can't*," she repeated, jerking away from him.

"It's a form of magic," Rian told him agitatedly, "when she shifts, I mean, and right now—"

"What difference does that make?"

"A great deal," she said, her dark eyes on the cave-in behind him, as if she could see right through it. And maybe she could, because he'd never seen her that upset. "You need to listen, Carlos—"

His real first name usually got his attention, but not this time. "What I need," he said, his voice trembling only slightly, "what we all need, is to get out of here, now, before—"

"I'm not going anywhere without Pritkin," Cassie informed him, making Casanova want to scream. So he did.

"He's a war mage! He can take care of himself!"

"Not if he can't use magic!" she said heatedly, while scrabbling for something in the debris on the floor. "If he doesn't know the risk, he could blow himself up. And even if not, he's stuck down there facing that . . . that thing . . . with nothing more than a gun that probably won't even dent it. And I won't—"

He didn't hear what the wretched woman wouldn't do this time, because the rock fall took that moment to implode, sending a dozen shards of whatever made up this blasted hill into Casanova's backside. But he'd grabbed the girl, covering her body with his as he tumbled to the floor. Which promptly cracked and dropped, and then gave way entirely.

Of course, it did, Casanova thought, as they plunged into darkness.

Chapter Seven

"No magic," Sid said, spelling it out. "No type, no amount. Not unless you want to get yourself killed!"

"I thought that was the idea," John slurred, causing the demon to shoot him a look, as if suspicious that he was pretending to worse injuries than he had.

If only.

"No, wouldn't be much use then, would you?" he finally said.

"Use?"

"It was supposed to be your father," Sid complained, bending over to tug at John's boots. "We specifically waited until it was his turn. But I should have known that Rosier would find someone else to do his dirty work. He was always like that, even as a child."

"Why doesn't that surprise me?" John muttered, trying to work the ropes over his chest loose while Sid was busy examining his footwear.

But while Sid obviously didn't know much about tying someone up—he'd left John's wrists free—he'd made up for it in sheer enthusiasm. John was cocooned in rope from nipples to ribs, and it wasn't the kind with much in the way of give. Every movement just made the damn cords eat deeper into his flesh, threatening to cut off what little air supply he had. Without some way to cut the bonds, his arms weren't going anywhere.

Which left his legs.

Despite common perceptions to the contrary, it was perfectly possible to be deadly without using the upper body at all. John could almost see the maneuver he needed—a sweep outward to dump Sid on his ass, then a quick scissoring movement to trap his neck between John's feet and ankles. And then it was merely a matter of an abrupt twist and listening to the bones crunch. It wasn't the easiest of maneuvers, but it was doable, and it would also be pretty damn satisfying right about now.

Unfortunately, it would also be pretty damned useless.

Killing a demon as old as Sid was never as simple as snapping a neck. But that was especially true when they happened to be one of the two-natured—demons who could take both spectral or physical form. In Sid's case, he was an Uttuku, a type the Sumerians had once mistaken for ghosts due to their ability to leave their bodies behind. So even if John managed to kill Sid's body, he'd be left tied up and weaponless, facing a very unhappy ancient spirit with who knew what kind of abilities.

Frankly, he'd had better odds.

Of course, he'd had worse ones, too, but he shoved those thoughts away. Things weren't that bad. Yet.

"And you needed Rosier for what?" he asked, while trying to come up with another option. He didn't really expect an answer, since Sid had no reason to tell him anything.

Except for what John belatedly recognized as the intensity of a zealot.

The little demon looked up from ripping apart John's boots, and his whole face lit up with it. "It's what we were talking about before. You saw the potential—you even had the right idea. Merely the wrong *target*."

"The wrong target?"

"It's not Ealdris and the ancients who are the problem. It's the bloody council."

John felt his blood pressure increase a little more, if that was possible. Because as corrupt, self-seeking and generally appalling as the Demon High Council often was, it did serve one vital purpose—it was the one thing keeping the species from running amuck. And it was based here, in the Shadowland.

He thought he might finally understand what Ealdris wanted with the place.

"Even Ealdris can't take on the council," he said, fear making his voice harsh. "They're too powerful—"

"We'll see."

"They're the ones who imprisoned her in the first place!"

"Through trickery!"

"It was that or a blood bath in which thousands would have died! What would you have had—"

"I would have had them face her!" Sid screamed, suddenly in John's face. And while the small man's features hadn't changed, it was amazing how much he currently looked like a demon. "Properly, honorably—on the field of battle! There would have been no tricks then, no deception. If there is such now, they have only themselves to blame!" He hurled John's boots at the still-glowing wall.

John met his glare squarely, not flinching. Of course, the ropes helped with that. But it seemed to be the right move. Because after a moment, Sid calmed slightly.

"No honorable death this time, then?" John asked.

"She's learned," Sid said shortly. "I told her, times have changed. To survive, we have to change with them."

"I didn't think the old ones were good at that."

Sid sat back on his heels, the genial mask slipping perfectly back into place even though he didn't need it anymore. John supposed it got to be habit when you wore it for something like six thousand years. "She always did adapt well. You have to in battle, you know. But she still didn't believe me, when I told her that an incubus could be our salvation. In our day, your lot were considered rather . . . hopeless."

"And we're not now?"

"Oh, no," Sid said, an edge creeping into his tone. "Rosier has a finger in every pie these days, an ear in every court. Your kind have made a profession out of weakness, gaining power through soft words and pretty speeches, lies and deception, while being too innocuous for anyone to worry about. Ironic that it's your only strength that will bring you down!"

John didn't have to think it over, as there weren't a lot of options. Unlike most families, the incubi hadn't been blessed with an arsenal of weapons. "We can feed from anyone?" he guessed.

"It makes you unique among the races."

John licked his lips, wishing his head didn't hurt quite so much. Because he was fairly certain that he was missing something important. "And how does that help you?"

"Me?" Sid shrugged. "Not at all. There's only so much energy I can absorb at one time. Any surplus is wasted, I'm afraid. But Ealdris now . . ." He suddenly scowled. "They sent her to an awful place, John; you should have seen it. There was almost nothing to eat. It was supposed to keep her too weak to find a way back, but she almost went mad with hunger—"

"She didn't stay that way for long. She killed dozens before I trapped her!"

"Dozens, yes," Sid nodded. "But what she needed was thousands. Tens of thousands. There's no limit on her ability to absorb power. That's what made her so formidable once—and will again."

"Unless history repeats itself."

Sid suddenly laughed. "I don't think so."

"And what's to stop it?"

His head tilted, as if surprised that John didn't understand. "You are, of course. We tried it with a few other incubi, but they weren't strong enough. The effect lasted seconds only, and we're going to want more than that. That's when I realized, we needed someone of the royal line."

He waited, but John still didn't get it. Until suddenly he did. Sid saw when his eyes widened, when the beauty and horror of it hit him, all at once.

"Perfect symmetry, isn't it?" Sid asked. "She can absorb an unlimited amount of power, but only of certain types. You can absorb any type, but only in limited amounts. But put the two of you together . . ."

"You're mad!" John said, struggling uselessly against the damned ropes.

"And you are what you eat—isn't that what the humans say?" Sid asked mildly. "In the past, we hunted only the strong, we hunted each other, and so we were strong, too. But then we find a perfect feeding ground, with plentiful, prolific, stupid prey, and what happens? The feeble are elevated beyond their station; the greatest among us are hounded almost to extinction. The easy hunting has ruined us, made us soft, made us weak!"

"You're going to blow it up," John rasped. "You're going to use the brimstone to destroy the city."

"And the council along with it. And thanks to that royal blood of yours, when all those souls are released, Ealdris will have the ability to absorb every single one. It will wipe out her enemies and return her to her former glory, all at the same time."

"But the council is the only thing keeping the races in line! Without it—"

"Everyone will be free—free to feed, free to gorge. And once the humans are gone, we will go back to preying on each other." Sid grinned, baring a lot of teeth, none of which looked like they belonged in the mouth of a shopkeeper. "Until only the strong survive."

And all right, John decided. Maybe things were that bad.

And then he dumped the demon on his ass.

* * *

Rian screamed, Cassie cursed, and someone kicked Casanova in the head. That last was Rosier, who had leapt into the hole after them, even as Casanova hauled the damned girl against his side, preparing to jump back up. But they were falling too fast, the rock rushing by in a blur, the square of slightly less dark above their heads rapidly diminishing as his feet struggled for purchase on nothing more than—

Than a solid piece of perforated metal.

He stared at it for a split second, uncomprehending. It was dull gray, except for splotches of rust and bits of red soil that were flying up to hit him in the face. It suddenly dawned on him that they were on some type of platform—it was too kind to call it an elevator—that was plunging with wild but possibly not life-threatening speed into the heart of the mountain.

Which would have been quite a relief if their passenger wasn't about to murder them all.

"Why are you just standing there?" Cassie yelled, as Rosier got unsteadily back to his feet.

This is it, Casanova thought blankly. He was going to die. He was going to die hearing that voice bellowing at him, and the knowledge that she would probably swiftly follow him into the hereafter was exactly no consolation at all.

"Where do you go if you die in Hell?" he wondered aloud, only to have her sink those tacky pink nails into him.

"Do something!"

"What would you suggest?" Casanova demanded.

"Beat him up!"

"Demon lord," he pointed out, and Rosier grinned.

"Not now! He can't use magic!"

"Like hell he can't!" Casanova had bruises that said otherwise.

"Not in here!" she said furiously. "Rian said—"

Casanova didn't get to hear what wisdom his demon might have imparted, because Rosier took that moment to spring across the platform and take a swing at his head. Which, for a being as powerful as he was supposed to be, seemed a little clumsy. Casanova ducked with vampire speed and glanced at the girl.

"Can't use magic?" he asked. She shook her head frantically, as the demon snarled and spun on a dime, coming back at Casanova.

Who calmly punched a hole through his face.

Or, at least, he would have, had the creature been human. The blow didn't appear to have had the same effect in this instance, although it did send him flying back against a rusted support beam. Casanova couldn't be sure, because they were moving too swiftly, but he rather thought that particular beam might have a Rosier-shaped dent from now on.

But the demon shook it off and staggered back into the middle of the platform, glaring and holding his jaw. "Bastard," he snarled.

"Vampire," Casanova smiled and spread his hands.

So Rosier kicked him in the kidney.

Casanova gasped and thought about throwing up, while the girl grabbed a lever on the floor of the contraption and gave it a jerk. The platform shuddered, jolting them all and throwing the demon off his pale gray Prada loafers. *Nice*, Casanova thought, before picking him up by the lapels and shoving him into the side of the now even more briskly streaming rock face.

And holding him there.

The demon spat something Casanova decided to ignore because he was enjoying the sound of jagged rock grating his victim's backside. It made up for some of the pain in his own. At least it did until the vile, unprincipled son of a bitch kneed him in the nuts.

Casanova stared at him out of watering eyes. "Who *does* that?" he screeched, in disbelief.

"Demon," Rosier said pleasantly. Then he did it again.

Casanova staggered back, trying to tell if he was still intact, only to have his arms grabbed by the girl. "You can take him!" she said, turning him back around.

"You take him!" he told her shrilly, as Rosier sprang off the wall.

He landed on his feet, like the cat he had always vaguely resembled, and he was in a cat-like crouch, too. Making it impossible for Casanova to return the favor. So he kicked him in the side of his perfectly coifed blond head instead, sending him sprawling. And then the girl surprised him by copying his action, only aiming for the villain's side, obviously trying to shove him through the narrow gap between the platform and the wall.

And all right, she occasionally did have a good idea, Casanova thought, moving to help. Only to have Rian grab him in a metaphysical clinch, freezing his legs halfway through a step. *We're going to have to talk*, he thought grimly, as he toppled to the floor right by her master.

Who promptly poked him in the eye.

The demon cackled, Casanova cursed, and Cassie grabbed him by the arm, trying to haul him back up. But only succeeded in ripping the sleeve off a very expensive shirt. "She's the gift that keeps on giving, isn't she?" Rosier asked, and punched him in the throat.

"What is your problem?" Cassie demanded, glaring at him.

Casanova glared back out of his one good eye, tempted to tell her exactly what his problem was, assuming he could still talk. But then the infernal device they were on came to a very abrupt halt. The three of them with bodies went tumbling off the platform and into the middle of a rough stone floor.

It was warm for some reason, and was giving off a strange sort of ghost light that sent grotesque shadows jumping along the walls. But Casanova barely noticed. He also wasn't paying any attention to the girl's shrieks or the demon's curses. He was too busy staring at the half-eaten face that was all of an inch from the end of his nose.

It didn't move, which was the only thing that kept him from gibbering. But he was close, thanks to the greenish color of the rotting flesh. Not to mention the missing eye, the caved in nose and the cracked skull that had oozed something he deliberately didn't look at all down the still mostly intact side of the face . . .

"What is that smell?" Cassie asked, grabbing him. She sounded a little freaked.

Join the club he thought, noting that the corpse hadn't died alone. Half rotten bodies littered the floor of the not-insubstantially-sized room. More lay slumped against the walls or piled in heaps, like so many empty bottles, tossed aside after the yummy contents were consumed . . .

"*Casanova*," she said urgently. She apparently couldn't see too well, even with the faint light. And didn't he just envy her that right now?

That was especially true after he caught sight of a couple of bodies sitting against the nearest wall. Some of the corpses were old enough to be truly putrescent, but these were newly dead, their blank, staring eyes shining in the dim light, the shadows painting little half smiles on their faces. Like they were welcoming him to the party—

"Did you hear me?" Cassie demanded, shaking him. And something in Casanova finally snapped.

"Shut up!" he screamed, rounding on her. "Shut up, shut up, shut up! Or I swear I'll save Rosier the trouble and kill you my—"

"Be silent!" someone hissed, and a hand clasped over his mouth, causing his eyes to bulge in sheer unadulterated fury. Until he realized that it was far too large to be Cassie's. But before he could throw it, and the demon it was attached to, against the nearest wall, he heard something that would have stopped his heart in his chest had it been beating.

"What was that?" Rian whispered, sounding a lot more nervous than a demon had any right to.

Casanova didn't answer. His vocal cords didn't seem to work all of a sudden, but it didn't matter. He doubted that she wanted to know that the faint shushing sound was the drag of scales over an uneven floor. A lot of scales.

Dinner is served, he thought blankly, as something huge blocked out the faint light from the corridor.

"Well, fuck," Rosier said.

Chapter Eight

John smacked the floor like a sack of sand. *That went well*, he thought, as a pair of dusty boots stopped by his head.

"You're braver than your father," Sid said, kicking him over. "I'll give you that."

How kind, John didn't say, not being quite up to sarcasm at the moment. He settled for palming his knife out of Sid's waistband when the demon bent over to pick him up.

"But not as bright." Sid looked at him in amazement as John went scuttling backwards, all feet and elbows, like a particularly inept crab. "What do you think you're going to do with that little thing?" he demanded. "You can't kill me with it, and even if you manage to get your arms free, what then? Do you really think that will improve your odds?"

Can't hurt, John thought hysterically, and rolled to his feet, which is harder than it sounds when you're basically a sausage with legs.

"What's the plan, John?" Sid demanded. "You're underground, lost in a maze, which—believe me—you are not going to find your way through. You can't use magic, your human weapons are gone, and in the last two minutes, I've had no fewer than four opportunities to kill you."

Five, John thought irrelevantly, but he guessed Sid had missed one. It was the only thing he'd missed. For someone who swore he wasn't a warrior, Sid was doing okay.

"Why make this harder than it has to be?" Sid asked. "I'll knock you out; you won't feel a thing—"

"But you will," John snarled. "After I bring this place down on your head!"

It was pretty much the only card he had to play. Thanks to the no-magic clause, his options had been narrowed to two: get out—which meant getting past the brimstone so he could transition back to earth—or make sure that neither of them did. The former was looking less and less likely all the time, and the latter . . .

A lot of people believed that John had a death wish. Even some of those closest to him acted like they suspected it, despite denying it when anyone else brought it up. But it wasn't true. There had been times when he could honestly say that he hadn't cared much, either way, but it wasn't in him not to go down fighting, not to struggle for every last breath, not to take as many of his enemies as he could along for the ride.

But suicidal or not, his line of work ensured that he'd faced death any number of times. And he thought he'd at least come to terms with it. Damn it, he *had* come to terms with it. He knew the feeling like an old friend—the hard ache of despair, the iron strength of resolution, the cold calm of acceptance.

Only he wasn't feeling so much that way right now. Which was a problem, since the acceptance of death was one of the few things that had so far helped him to avoid it. *Get a grip*, he told himself savagely, as Sid slowed to a halt.

But despite his lack of forward momentum, the little demon didn't look impressed. "And then what?" he asked. "If you collapse the corridor with some spell, what happens?"

"We die!" John spat, sawing frantically at the acre of rope the bastard had cocooned him in.

"No, you die," Sid said blandly. "I am . . . inconvenienced . . . for a time, while forming another body. Which I have more than enough power to do. You'll delay this, nothing more."

"But I don't get another body," John reminded him sweetly. "This is it. And without me—"

"What?" Sid looked at him impatiently. "John, I didn't even know you were coming until you walked into my shop! We were planning this for

Rosier, all along. You were a happy coincidence, yes, but if you die, we'll merely go back to the original plan."

"Assuming the council doesn't find out about it in the meantime—"

"They haven't so far, and we've been planning this for months."

"—and assuming your partner survives the explosion. If brimstone really is laced throughout these rocks, setting it off here might bring down the whole mountain!"

He'd expected that to hit home, since Sid's plan pretty much required keeping his battle queen alive until she returned to her former strength. But ether the little demon had a damn good poker face, or John had missed something. Because there was no flutter of those short eyelashes, no slight flush to those plump cheeks. Just a slight moue of irritation.

"She's two-natured," Sid reminded him, "or have you forgotten?"

"No. I also haven't forgotten that she's weak. She was almost starved, you said so yourself. And I doubt the council was kind enough to feed her before they threw her back in prison!"

"She doesn't need her full strength to best you," Sid said dryly.

"But I'm not the scariest thing out there, am I?"

It was what John had been betting on when he'd formulated his plan, in case she got past him. Of course, in that happy scenario, he'd also had a cadre of the council's elite guards to back him up. But even without them, the Shadowland wasn't the place to be an unhoused spirit—not unless you were a great deal more formidable than Ealdris was at present.

But Sid brushed that argument away like the others. "You aren't scary at all," he said frankly. "And this has gone on long enough."

John backed up again as the demon resumed advancing, wondering if he could risk a glance behind him. All he needed was a distraction and an open corridor. He might not be able to outfight Sid under the circumstances, but bare feet or no, he was willing to bet that he could still outrun him. And he didn't need to make it all the way back to the surface; he just needed—

To not fall on his ass. A piece of the damn uneven floor tripped him up, sending him staggering backwards—into a solid wall of rock. He felt around frantically with his foot, but there was no opening.

Dead end, his oh-so-helpful brain quipped.

He was going to have the damn thing examined if he ever got out of this.

"There's nowhere to go, John," Sid said, echoing his own thoughts. "Now, why don't you give me the knife—"

"My pleasure," he hissed, and threw it with the arm he'd finally worked free of the damn rope.

He saw it connect with the flabby fold of Sid's neck, saw blood spew in a pinkish mist—and then nothing. The knife had barely left his hand when something that looked like black smoke boiled out of Sid's pores, his eyes, even his mouth, as if he'd caught fire on the inside. In an eye blink, it had enveloped the two of them in a color so thick, so dense, it almost had substance.

Almost nothing, John thought, as something latched onto him, like a thousand tiny barbs sinking into his skin. His shields should have stopped it, but he hadn't been able to use them here. And without them, there was nothing to prevent the horrible sensation of something other slithering in through his skin, sinking inside him through a million tiny invasions, draining him dry. He sank to his knees, a scream unable to get out past the suffocating mist pouring down his throat.

And he finally realized why Sid hadn't seemed too concerned about his partner.

* * *

Casanova had never been much for sports. It had mostly been viewed as training for war when he was young, and even before he met up with the incubus who had once possessed his namesake, he'd always thought of himself as more of a lover than a fighter. But he would have been willing to bet that he broke Olympic speed records getting back to the elevator.

Which meant that he hit it about the same time as the cowardly bastard of a demon lord.

Rosier slammed the heel of his shoe back into Casanova's face while simultaneously leaning on the lever to raise the elevator. Which went up all of two inches, because Casanova was holding it down with the hand that wasn't cradling his broken nose. "Going thomewhere?" he asked viciously.

"Bite me!"

"My pleathure!" Casanova snarled, and jerked him off the platform.

Unfortunately, he didn't also remember to hold down the elevator, which shot up like a rocket, leaving the two of them looking at it in horror. And then at the wall, for a recall lever that wasn't there. And then simultaneously diving for the only exit that wasn't currently being blocked by a monster.

Rosier reached it first, only to slam into the floor when Casanova tackled him. "Let me go, you fool!" he grunted. "You can't outrun her!"

"And you can?"

"I don't have to outrun her," Rosier hissed. "I only have to outrun you!" Which was when he flipped over, got a foot in Casanova's stomach and used it as a lever to throw him over his head.

Straight at the monster.

"*Bastardo!*" Casanova breathed, even as he grabbed onto Rosier's leg halfway through the arc, skewing it and sending them rolling and sliding and kicking and biting almost back where they'd started.

And where the blonde whose existence he'd briefly forgotten was still standing, staring death in the face.

Shit. She couldn't see worth a damn down here, Casanova reminded himself. He was trying to work out how to grab her, lose the villain currently trying to eviscerate him, and make It back to the damn door, all in the second or so he probably had left, when the daft girl suddenly reached out a hand.

And gave death a little push.

Which surprised Casanova almost as much as when death quivered and wobbled and toppled over onto its side.

He froze in shock, allowing Rosier the chance to take a vicious shot to his ribs. Casanova didn't retaliate, being too busy watching Cassie squat beside an acre or so of gleaming lavender scales. And do it again.

"Thop poking that thing!" he told her wildly.

She looked up, and apparently her eyes had adjusted somewhat, after all, because she found his easily. "Why?"

"Why?"

"I think it's dead." She stood up and nudged the horror on the floor with one small shoe.

"What are you—oh," Rosier said, his head poking out from underneath Casanova's arm. "Well, look at that."

Casanova slammed his face into the ground, just because.

Rosier looked up, nose bloodied and teeth bared in a rictus, but his eyes were fixed on the thing on the floor. And Casanova had to admit, it was rather hard to look anywhere else. It had a Medusa-like head, human and reptilian all mixed up in an extremely unfortunate way, only the things poking out of it weren't snakes. Not that tentacles were a great improvement, particularly not when the body ended not in legs, but in a long spiny tail.

And there's another fetish ruined, he thought wildly. He'd always found mermaids faintly erotic, or at least the idea of them, since they didn't actually exist. At least not as far as he knew, and if they did, he wasn't keen to meet any after today. Because it turned out that a scale-covered tail actually looked pretty damn obscene sprouting out of a naked human torso.

"What did it die of?" he asked hoarsely, before he managed to finish horrifying himself.

"Nothing," Rosier, said. "And get off me. Unless you're planning to make me an offer."

Casanova practically wrenched something getting back to his feet.

"What do you mean, nothing?" Cassie asked, before he could find something vile enough to say to the creature. "She isn't dead?"

"See for yourself."

And to Casanova's utter disbelief, she did, squatting beside the body to feel for a pulse at the pale gray skin of the neck. The scaly, scaly neck, right next to where some of those tentacles were slightly moving, like seaweed in a current. Or unnaturally long fingers reaching out to—

"There's a pulse," Cassie said, frowning. "But it's faint. And she's cold. And barely breathing. Of course, I don't know if that's normal or—"

"It is," Rosier had gotten to his feet and moved over to the thing's other side, where he crouched opposite the girl. "For stasis."

"Stasis?"

He looked heavenward, why Casanova didn't know. It wasn't like he was on speaking terms with anyone up there. "Demon bodies aren't like human ones," he told her. "Ours don't require a soul *in situ* to continue functioning, albeit on a low level. Some of us can shrug off our bodies like a set of clothes, and return to pure spirit form for a time."

Cassie blinked. "That's . . . really weird."

"Unlike being trapped in one body, one world, one plane of existence, unable to see or experience anything except the trickle of information supplied to you by your so-called senses?" He barked out a laugh. "'Weird.' As with most words you humans use, you don't know the meaning of the term."

Casanova didn't comment, but he swallowed thickly. He had absolutely no problem believing that, after today.

Rosier glanced at him, amused, and then back at Cassie. "You know, if you're going to hunt demons, girl, you should perhaps take a moment to find out something about us."

"I wasn't hunting her!" Cassie said, scowling. "I wasn't even hunting you. I wasn't doing anything—"

"Except risking my son's life—again. I don't know why you don't simply put a knife in his ribs and be done with it." The last was said with a tone that had the girl practically apoplectic.

"Like you care! Like you've ever cared! You sent him here to die!"

"I sent him here to get him out of the way. He wasn't supposed to find anything this quickly—"

"But he has! And if her body's here, her spirit probably is, too. And if she's like most demons, that's just as—"

"She isn't," he said grimly. "She's worse."

Cassie sneered at him, and it was a pretty good effort, Casanova thought. She clearly didn't lack courage. Intelligence, prudence and a healthy sense of self-preservation, yes; courage no.

"What's the matter?" she demanded. "Afraid somebody else will kill him before you get the chance?"

Rosier's eyes narrowed. "Coming from the person who has done more to put him in an early grave than anyone in centuries—"

"I've been trying to save him!"

Rosier glanced around, his expression eloquent. "And this is what you call a rescue, is it?"

Casanova didn't get a chance to hear what from Cassie's expression would have been an interesting comment, because the next moment Rian was back. Which was a bit of a shock since he hadn't noticed her leaving. "There's no way through," she said, and for some reason, she was looking at Cassie.

Who transferred her scowl from one incubus to the other. "There has to be!"

Rian shook her head agitatedly. "I checked in every direction. The demons she didn't consume she put to work. There has to be two, perhaps three dozen, just in the corridors near here, and who knows how many between us and—"

"Put to work on what?"

"Brimstone. They're mining it. I don't know why, but—"

"Brimstone?" Casanova asked, confused, only to have everyone turn to look at him with varying expressions of incredulity. "What?"

"Do try to keep up, old boy," Rosier said, with a sigh.

"It's an explosive," Rian said, getting between Casanova, who had about had enough, and her boss. "Like TNT—"

"I know what it is!" Casanova snapped, glancing around. The glowing striations in the stone suddenly made a horrible kind of sense. "That's why we can't use magic?"

"Yes!" Cassie hissed. "And without it we have no way to get through the tunnels and find—" she stopped abruptly. And looked at the crumpled body on the floor. And then she slowly raised her head and looked at Rosier, her eyes narrowing.

And for some reason, his widened. "No."

"You said it was like a suit of clothes."

"It isn't my suit!"

Cassie smiled, and it was vicious. "It is now."

Chapter Nine

"**N**o, no, no!" Sid yelled. "The charges aren't set yet! Consume him now and we'll have to start all over!"

The pressure abruptly released and John hit the ground, hard enough to rip the air from his lungs and to stab him in the side with his own broken rib. But the outward pain was nothing next to the emptiness inside. Dark and cold and echoing, it made him want to curl into a protective ball around his terrified, savaged soul.

But he couldn't. He couldn't even manage to lift his head when someone grabbed him, jerking him off the floor. "I wanted you fresh," Sid hissed. "You're more powerful that way. But I'm not going to lose you after this much trouble!"

John found himself slung over a shoulder and carted back down the hall, then dropped in a heap on the floor. It hurt, but not nearly as much as it should have. Which was a bad sign for some reason he couldn't seem to concentrate on at the moment.

His head lolled to one side, seemingly of its own accord, but he couldn't see anything. Until he switched to demon sight, but that was little better because the glare of Sid's power practically blinded him to everything else. It glowed through the demon's skin like a searchlight through cheesecloth, turning the veins of ore in the walls into a web of silver fire, revealing their true color instead of the tint they borrowed from the stone.

And yet, there was a gleam of red, a faint flicker against all that light.

John transitioned back to human sight to find that the darkness had retreated into its host, leaving the corridor dim and prosaic-looking except for that coil of angry red. It was coming from the small jar Sid had just pulled out of a backpack. John watched, mesmerized, as the contents gleamed and twisted, sending hellish flames dancing across the stones.

Sid sat it down on a flat piece of floor and pulled out another one, this one empty. John didn't ask what it was for. He didn't have the strength, and in any case, he had a pretty good idea.

He forced himself to look away, to search for some avenue of escape. But and all his peripheral vision showed him was more of the same: a small, rock-cut tunnel, a few distant shadows that might have been exits he couldn't possibly reach, and Sid, muttering to himself. If there was anything helpful in that, John didn't see it.

Except, of course, for the obvious.

"Experience is the best teacher," Rosier had said, leaning back in his chair. "Why read about something when you can live it?"

"Because it kills them!" John held out the jar that had contained his latest acquisition.

It had been a special order, one he'd been so eager to get his hands on that he'd paid a premium for a rush job. Perhaps that was why the hunters had been a little careless, why they'd left some of the final memories intact. Or perhaps their usual clients wouldn't have cared.

But whatever the cause, John had experienced everything, just as if it had been happening to him: the desperate flight, the heart pounding terror, the cold wash of disbelief when they cornered him. The hopeless cry—what had he done? And finally, the veil of pain that fogged his senses, as he clung to consciousness, to life, with a frightening effort of will, even as his soul was ripped from his body—

John had come out of it in a cold sweat, hands shaking, stomach churning, unsure for a moment who he was, where he was. He'd run into the next room in a blind panic, trying to hide from soul hunters who weren't there, before reality finally caught up with him. He hadn't found it a great improvement. In the end, he'd lain on the floor in his bedroom, sick and shaken, and stared at the ceiling for a long time.

Then he'd gone to see his father.

"So does butchering a cow," Rosier had said, impatiently. "And I haven't noticed you becoming vegetarian."

"A cow is an animal—"

"As are some of these."

"But not all! Not most! Many of them are sentient beings—"

"Who have the most to teach us."

John had looked at the creature he'd once so admired, and for the first time, seen him for what he was. "Even if doing so destroys them?"

Rosier saw his expression, and his face closed down. "What did you expect?" he demanded. "A library full of books? We're demons."

"You are," John had breathed. And walked out.

It had taken him years, and a wealth of pain, to understand that he'd been right that day, in what he'd told his father. But he'd been wrong, too. Because part of him was demon, with the same unending hunger as all the rest.

He could feel it now, not taste or scent or any other sense a human would have understood. Just desperate, all-consuming need. It was mewling in his gut right now, begging piteously for just one taste of all that exotic power, that deadly strength, that . . .

Irin.

He didn't know how he knew. But the part of him that was incubus identified it unerringly. He even knew which one, the memory of its power still fresh from their brief meeting in the shop.

John supposed he knew what Sid had done with those thirty minutes.

He didn't know why, because Irin were not easy prey. They had abilities that might have turned the tables on Sid very handily. But then, that was true of John, too, before he lost his magic, and it hadn't helped him. He could see Sid, the trusted shopkeeper, running after one of his best customers, having forgotten to tell him . . . something. It didn't matter; it had obviously worked. And now they had the perfect test subject.

And that's what he was, John realized, watching the color thrash uselessly against the glass. They couldn't risk implementing their plan without being sure that John's watered-down blood would do the trick, so they needed a test. He assumed that, after Ealdris got done with him, she would try to absorb the contents of the jar. Which had to be something unusual. Something exotic. Something most demons couldn't possibly ingest.

But John wouldn't have that problem.

John never had that problem.

He stared at the jar.

He didn't often get this close to temptation anymore. Incubi needed their victim's lust, like vampires needed blood; without it, they had no conduit into a person's power, no way to feed. But there was no body here anymore, no barrier, and thus no need for a conduit. All he had to do was reach out. All he had to do . . .

John closed his eyes, but the color swirled through his lids nonetheless, sharper, richer, clearer in his demon senses than it ever could be in human sight. It was breathtakingly beautiful, as they all were. And sweet, so sweet, every single one.

Even the last.

You are what you are. Someday, you're going to have to come to terms with that. His father's voice echoed in his head, but it lacked any weight. Because Rosier had never understood: John *had* come to terms with it. He knew what he was, what he would always be, no matter how far he managed to run. He'd had that demonstrated one horrible night in the most vivid way possible. And for years, he'd believed that it was all he ever could be.

Until he'd met someone who refused to see him that way. Who argued and fussed and tried her best to boss him around, but who never shrank away. Who relied on him and needed him and called him friend. Who touched the scars on his body, and other places, as if they were just another part of him, not evidence of where he'd been, what he was.

And lately he'd begun to hope that perhaps, just perhaps, there was something even a monster could contribute.

He stared at the jar.

And then slowly, shakily, he held out his hand.

Chapter Ten

*T*his is never going to work, Casanova thought, panicking, as several nearby demons turned their way. They were short and squat and had too many limbs, and he had no idea what either of them were. But they looked suspicious.

Or maybe that was him. He couldn't tell anymore. He was pretty sure he was having a nervous breakdown, but since that wouldn't help he concentrated on ignoring them. And on personifying his role as a recruit being escorted to the job by the big boss herself.

Which would have been vastly easier had said boss not hit the damn wall every five seconds.

"Stop it!" Casanova hissed.

"I don't know how to drive this thing," Rosier complained, his tail making little furrows in the dust as it swished back and forth, propelling him into a corner.

"Then figure it out!"

"There's a bit of a learning curve," he muttered, slithering back a few steps. And then smacking straight into the wall again.

Casanova leaned over and grabbed a scaly arm, jerking him back into the corridor. It was a broad one, which would have done positive things for his claustrophobia if it hadn't been full of demons. And the hellish equivalent of TNT. And a ten-foot-tall half-snake that was weaving drunkenly along, as if coming back from a night on the town.

God. That's where he should be, right now, on the town. Any town. Or better yet, enjoying the nightlife in his beautiful casino. Pressing the flesh with high rollers, schmoozing with starlets, making sure it all ran smoothly, effortlessly. He was good at that—no, he was *great* at it, maybe better than anything he'd ever done in his life. He wasn't so good at this, particularly not when it involved touching that hideous thing in order to keep up some semblance of—

"What are you doing?" he demanded shrilly, catching sight of Rosier's current activity.

"Nothing."

Casanova was momentarily speechless, disbelief and revulsion warring for dominance on his tongue. Revulsion won. "You were *feeling it up?*"

"She."

"What?"

"Well, she's obviously female," one hand glided over evidence of that fact with every appearance of appreciation. "And I was merely trying—"

"It's a *snake*," Casanova said, horror making his voice quake.

"It's a lamia, which makes it—her—a sentient being."

"It has *scales.*"

The disgusting creature licked his lips. "Quite."

"And it's *dead!*" *Dios*, how many perversions was that in a single—

"It's in stasis," Rosier said calmly, "it isn't dead. Although we're likely to be if I don't figure out how this body works."

Casanova was beginning to think that was inevitable anyway. He'd been envisioning a quick trip through a few short tunnels, grabbing the damn mage and heading straight out the nearest exit. That rosy little vision had lasted all of five minutes, until the small side tunnels let out into increasingly larger ones, populated by pick-wielding demons who couldn't all be mind-controlled. There was just too many of them; at least some had to be in on this, whatever this was.

He still hadn't figured it out and he really didn't care. Right now, he cared about exactly one thing. "Where is that blasted mage?" he said savagely, as he turned a corner.

And had the damn man slam into him, hard enough to knock him off his feet.

Casanova hit the ground, Cassie yelled "Pritkin!" and Rosier cursed. And then the crazy bastard was gone again, as if jerked back by some unseen wire. Leaving Casanova sprawled in the dirt with his ass in the air.

Which was not such a bad thing considering what was spread out all of a foot in front of his nose.

"Dios," he breathed, his fingers digging into the rock as he stared at the lip of a very narrow ledge, over what appeared to be nothing at all.

Casanova peered cautiously over the rim to see a cavern the size of an airline hangar, if they were also a mile deep and carved out of glittering rock. Demons lined the deeply grooved sides, where jagged streaks of pure ore glistened silver-bright against the stone, like captured lightning. It looked like half the damn mountain was hollow, he thought, awed.

Right before he was hit by the rest of it.

He heard Cassie scream as their ledge was engulfed by an avalanche of debris, including dirt, rock and several sharp little pick axes, one of which bounced off his already abused ass. It took him a moment to dig himself out, only to find that everyone else had been smart enough to hug the wall. And were now staring with varying expressions of horror at something behind him.

He whipped his neck around in time to see that, for once, the danger wasn't to him. The mage had just hit the wall in a billowing explosion of dust—on the other side of the cavern. How he'd gotten all the way over there, Casanova didn't know, since he didn't see a bridge. But that was less of a concern than the fact that they'd come all this way to rescue someone who had just gotten himself killed.

Only he hadn't.

He *should* have been dead; hell, he should have been a greasy streak on the rock face. But instead, Casanova watched him spin, snarling, and launch himself off the side of the cave—straight into thin air. But instead of instead of plummeting who knew how far to his death, he soared up, which was clearly impossible unless the Shadowland had some crazy rule on gravity he'd yet to—

"Wait. Are those . . . *wings*?" Casanova asked stupidly, as Pritkin hit a fat little demon who had also been hovering with gravity-defying ease in the middle of a lot of nothing. And sent him smashing into the wall above them.

Most of which came down on Casanova's head.

"Carlos! Get off the floor!" Rian told him, as he struggled to fight himself free a second time.

He pulled his face out of the dust to glare up at her, grateful that he didn't actually need to breathe. "You know," he said sarcastically. "That never would have—" he cut off as Cassie stepped on his head, scrambling over the mountain of debris towards Rosier.

She'd survived the double avalanche, but she looked a little worse for the wear, with a bloody streak glistening on one cheek and red dust coating her like a film. But that was nothing compared to her just-shy-of-crazed expression. Which might explain why she grabbed a fistful of those horrible tentacles, jerked Rosier down to her and screamed in his face.

"Do something!"

"What would you suggest?"

"Anything! Everything! He's going to get himself killed!"

"He looks like he's doing all right to me," Casanova said sourly, dragging his filthy, torn and bloody ass over to the minutely safer area by the wall.

"He isn't," Rosier said shortly.

"How can you tell?"

"Watch."

Casanova was, but it looked to him like the mage was winning. The fat demon dove for Pritkin, the air boiling around him like an angry black cloud, only to be sent flying into the midst of a half dozen miners. They'd been hugging a ledge, watching the show, but should have picked a better vantage point. Because they toppled like bowling pins, the pudgy demon sprawled in the middle of them, bloody and obviously hurting.

But Pritkin was, too, either that or he needed a breather. At least Casanova assumed that was why he didn't immediately follow up his advantage. He hovered in the middle of the cave, the great white wings that he'd somehow acquired beating the air, while his opponent writhed in pain and black smoke boiled around him.

Only it didn't look so much like smoke anymore. More like a swarm of angry insects, which were pursuing the miners the demon had toppled. And while Casanova couldn't tell what it was doing, every time it caught one, the miner screamed and dropped—and didn't get back up.

"What's happening?" Cassie demanded.

"Ealdris," Rosier said grimly. "She's feeding."

"Now? But why—"

Rosier glanced at her impatiently. "Every time her associate is injured, she pulls energy from the surrounding life forms and feeds it to him. He can keep going indefinitely—or as long as the food holds out, at least. Emrys can't."

"Emrys?"

"John then," Rosier said, gesturing violently. "Call him what you will, he is going to die if we don't find a way to separate those two. Soon."

"And how do we do that?"

"I'm thinking," Rosier snapped.

"I can try," Rian volunteered. "If I could drain her—"

"You're not powerful enough," Rosier said curtly. "I might be, but not through a body. That's Ealdris's talent, not mine."

"But she doesn't have a body right—"

"As soon as either of us attacks, she'll simply draw back into Sid." He made a disgusted noise. "Sid. You can't trust anybody anymore."

Casanova stared at him, a little awed at the arrogant irony in that statement. But he didn't think this was the moment to point it out. Not when the fat demon—Sid, he assumed—suddenly jumped up and threw himself back into the fight, slamming into Pritkin and sending the two of them swerving and looping and diving around the space. And everywhere they went, the black cloud followed, buzzing around the war mage just as it had the demons who were now bleeding out on the ledge.

"He doesn't have much time," Rosier said harshly. "If we don't do something soon, he won't—"

He stopped on a gasp, a look of surprise coming over his features. Casanova didn't know why until he looked down. And saw the gore-coated end of one of the picks sticking a good two inches out of Rosier's middle.

It was a shock, but not as much as who was holding it. "What are you doing?" he asked Cassie blankly.

"Getting its attention," she said savagely, and ripped the pick back out.

Rosier made a choked sound, everyone in the vicinity got sprayed with hot green blood, and an ear-splitting shriek echoed around the cavern. Right before the cloud whipped about in a swirling mass of vengeful fury. And dove straight for them.

"Thanks," Rosier told Cassie, staring at it.

"Any time."

He turned around and fled, and he must have figured out something about how his new body worked, because he wasn't hitting any walls this time. Casanova felt a chill, deathly wind ruffle his hair as the cloud streamed past, ignoring the girl holding the gory pick in favor of the demon making off with its body.

And then, for a split second, there was nothing. At least, not in the threat category. Casanova stared around, first at Pritkin, who was currently making mincemeat of the small demon, then at the three of them, all of whom were still more or less intact, and finally at the distinct lack of any enemies that weren't running for their lives.

And all right, he thought, straightening his tattered jacket. This was more like it.

And then the cave blew up.

Chapter Eleven

Everything happened between one heartbeat and another. Sid's body falling, broken and bloody and beaten, to spin away into darkness. His spirit rising out of it and moving, but not up, as Pritkin had half expected, in order to attack him. Not even out, toward one of the tunnels and freedom. But down.

To where the biggest vein of brimstone ran in a glittering ring around the cave.

Pritkin had no time to stop him, no time even to brace himself, before he was hit by a vast wash of air from the explosion. It sent him tumbling helplessly backwards, head over heels, with no way to right himself or even tell where he was going. Until he crashed into a wall like a bird hitting a window.

He slid down to a ledge, body bruised and wings askew, in time to glimpse Sid streaming past, a faint outline against a curtain of silver fire. But he didn't pursue. Not because he couldn't have caught him, but because whatever spell Sid had used to ignite the brimstone had caused a chain reaction, exploding vein after vein, one right after the other like a massive firework pinwheel, all the way back to—

"Cassie!" He hadn't seen her before, hadn't had time to see anything in the life or death struggle with not one but two ancient horrors. He would have thought he was hallucinating, but Casanova was there, too, screaming his fool head off as the ledge they were on cracked and splintered and—

"No!"

Pritkin saw them fall, saw Rian grab Casanova, saw her reach for Cassie—who was too far away. Rian stared up at him for a split second, horrified and apologetic, and then she and Casanova winked out. While Cassie fell into a pit straight out of a medieval vision.

John dove, not knowing if she had enough strength left to shift, not betting on it because the damnable, damnable woman never held anything back, never once put her own safety ahead of anyone else's, a fact that was going to get her killed one day, but please God, not this day. But he couldn't see anything through billowing clouds of red dust, could barely breathe through the waves of fiery heat, and there was no hope of hearing her cry out, not with the roar of all that raw power being released, the crack of huge swaths of stone as they calved off the sides of the cave and fell, many exploding from the inside as they did so.

"Cassie!" It was a desperate, stupid, useless. Because he hadn't caught her, and if she hadn't shifted, somehow holding concentration in the midst of an inferno, there was no chance left—

"Over here!" He heard it, faint, so faint, that it might have been a figment of his imagination. But he turned anyway, banking left, barely missing a mass of burning stone with a few screaming miners still clinging to it as it fell, and then he saw her.

She was half on, half off a ledge, one leg dangling over nothing, rivers of molten brimstone cascading on either side, the whole shelf ready to blow at any moment. But she was alive. Somehow, despite all possible odds—and then he had her.

"I . . . tried to shift to you, but I landed . . . here—" she broke off, choking, as a stinging cloud of gas and debris showered them, seemingly from all directions.

The whole place was imploding, with huge gouts of fire belching out of tunnels, molten brimstone dropping like silver rain, and falling boulders shattering off pieces of the overhang above them. Shifting back to Dante's while surrounded by this much explosive was impossible; they'd be dead before he could finish the spell. But staying put was equally out of the question.

A great wash of air boiling up from the inferno below buffeted them as he took off once more, launching them toward the only halfway clear air he could see. And then there it was: a piece of sky, blessedly dark against the searing light, just a crack far, far above his head. But a second later there were two, and then a dozen, and then the whole top of the mountain was cracking and fissuring and falling in.

He pulled Cassie's T-shirt over her nose and mouth, raised one forearm over his eyes to shield them, and strained upward. Sparks showered down everywhere; smoke masked the only way out after barely an instant; and the heat was unbelievable. He couldn't reassure Cassie, even if he'd had the breath, because close as she was, she wouldn't have heard him. He had never before been inside an explosion as it was happening, but it was deafening. It cracked and rumbled, whistled and roared, thundered and boomed, on all sides, as it consumed the mountain from the inside out.

Even the knowledge he'd gained from the Irin was insufficient to chart a course through something like this. The demon had never done it, so there were no memories to plunder, no visuals to guide him, no anything but desperate clawing against air so dry, it had hardly any lift. John had the impression that the only thing he was doing was managing not to fall, while the headway they gained was mostly from the huge surges of air rushing up from below.

He had been riding the edges of most of them, but one finally caught him full on, picking him up as if he was no heavier than the burning bits of ash glittering through the air, and then throwing him up, up, up— and out.

They burst out through the remains of the mountaintop, just as what looked like a volcano erupted below them. The whole mountain breathed in for one last great gasp before bursting outward, the colossal explosion throwing huge burning pieces of rock high into the sky. But not as high as John flew, his borrowed wings beating the air in time to the rapid pace of his heart.

He didn't stop, didn't even slow down, until they had put whole mountains between them and the smoking hulk behind. He finally set them down on a blessedly cold, dark hillside, far enough away that he couldn't even feel the heat anymore. Only then did he sink to his knees, gasping for breath, the great singed wings falling around him and still smoking slightly.

But he didn't let his passenger go.

For a long time, they just stayed like that, John eventually moving into a sitting position, pulling Cassie's body back against him as they watched the awesome power erupting on the horizon. She kept swallowing, tiny little gulps that John could barely hear, which could have been from a parched throat or too much smoke or a thousand other things. But he didn't think so. Because she was also trembling.

"Close your eyes," he told her softly, and she did, tilting her head back against his chest, her breath hitching again. But she didn't cry, didn't go into hysterics, didn't do anything. Except stay there, her hand tight on his thigh, her breath hot against his chest, until her own slowly evened out again.

After a long time, one small hand moved, slowly, tentatively, tracing the feathers falling around her, stroking the black slashes along one huge wing. She didn't ask where he'd gotten them, didn't ask why they mimicked the marks on his shoulder, didn't ask anything. Just kept running those soft fingers through the down, along the spines . . .

"How long will they last?"

"A few hours," he said hoarsely. He should tell her, he thought, that the feathers weren't just a projection. That for the moment, for however long the Irin's essence held out, they were an innate, physical part of him. And that her fingers stroking along the marks felt just like they once had, moving over his scars.

He ought to tell her, ought to ask her to stop. It's what a gentleman would do, he knew that. But then, he was half demon.

And tonight, he thought maybe he'd just go with that.

"They're nice," she murmured, pulling one around her.

"Yes." One hand tightened in her thick, soft hair. "Yes."

* * *

"It was epic," Rosier said, as they watched Cassie sitting in her living room, opening more gifts. John scowled. His father was incorporeal today, not having had time to replace the body he'd lost in the explosion. John could barely see him, just a smudged outline against the gaudy wallpaper the casino deemed elegant. But he was looking smug.

"You mean you got lucky."

Rosier looked offended. "Luck had nothing to do with it. I drained her during the whole chase back to the elevator, until her body bled out, and by then I was close enough to pop back into mine. And even Ealdris has trouble leeching a soul through the protection of a body. It gave me the few seconds I needed to finish the job." The smug look spread. "I was awesome."

"You were lucky," Pritkin repeated, not that it was likely to do any good. Nothing, to his knowledge, had ever dented his father's overweening arrogance, and he doubted anything he could say was likely to do so now. And in any case, that wasn't why he had asked to see him. "Are you going to tell me why you came after Cassie?"

"Oh, yes, that." Rosier shrugged, as if it was a minor detail. "The high council had a meeting a few days ago. After some deliberations to which they did not bother to invite me, I was summoned. They informed me that we were in mortal peril, and that your precious Pythia was the cause."

"There have been Pythias for thousands of years," John said, his eyes narrowing.

"Not one allied with a homicidal half-demon best known for killing one of the High Council," Rosier said dryly. "They were convinced that you had seduced her with the intent to use her power against them."

"That's ridiculous!"

"Not at all. Your well-known hatred for our kind coupled with her ability to time shift—the one power we do not possess—makes the two of you a formidable threat. You possess enough information about our history to know exactly where and when to strike. With her power at your disposal—"

"It isn't at my disposal, and it wouldn't work in the demon realms if it were!"

Rosier shrugged. "Perhaps, perhaps not, but it is immaterial. It works perfectly well here on Earth. If she wanted to attack us at a previous point in our history, all she would have to do is to shift backwards in her own time stream, and then enter our realms from there. That would effectively put her back in our time, too, would it not?"

John didn't answer. His mind felt strangely numb. Like he'd been hit by a blow so hard, he had yet to feel it.

"I can't say I was surprised," Rosier continued, sounding aggrieved. "I saw this coming some time ago. If you'd stayed out of the way I could have dealt with it before it became an issue—"

"By killing her, you mean," John grated.

"I will never understand the attraction you have for those things," Rosier hissed, leaning forward. "Time after time, you choose their side over ours, when you know perfectly well they. Die. Anyway. A year from now, a hundred—what difference does it make?"

"A great deal to them, I should imagine."

"And none at all to us! We will be here when they are dust, when their civilization—or what passes for it—is dust. Do you have any idea how many of their petty little kingdoms I've seen rise and fall?"

John couldn't have cared less. "And how does the council feel now that this great threat saved their asses?"

Rosier scowled. "You mean, after I saved—"

"You wouldn't have been on hand to do anything if Cassie hadn't led you there!"

"She's human. We do not consider their actions worth—"

"But I am not, as you so frequently point out. And she wouldn't have led you there if she hadn't been looking for me. So in a way, you could say that *I* saved their asses."

Rosier's eyes narrowed. "Do I need to ask what your price is?"

"I think you know."

"It appears you did get something from me, after all," he said bitingly. "Fine time to recall it."

John smiled as his father abruptly winked out, and dropped the silence shield he'd had up. For the first time since this whole mess started, he allowed himself to unwind, relaxing back in his chair as Cassie finished opening her latest gift. And then sitting up abruptly again when he saw what it was.

"What is this?" she asked, pulling out a length of gleaming lavender scales, fine as silk and far more precious.

Marlowe, who had shown up a few minutes before searching for answers he wasn't going to get, raised an eyebrow. "Lamia scales," he breathed. "Now that's a bribe worth having."

"Lamia?" Cassie said blankly, and then flinched back when it hit her, dropping the shimmering length in a puddle on the floor.

"There's no card," Marlowe said, frowning, as he searched through the box. His dark eyes met hers. "Who would send you a priceless gift and not claim credit?"

"It isn't priceless," Cassie said, in disgust. "It's horrible."

The chief spy's eyebrow climbed a bit higher. "Most people wouldn't think so. You might not either, one of these days."

"I doubt that," Cassie said, staring at it in revulsion. John was having much the same reaction, unsure whether this was his father's idea of a gruesome joke or a peace offering. Knowing him, it was a bit of both.

"Lamia scales are supposed to be good for—how should I put it? Aging skin," Marlowe told her.

"Aging?"

"Not that you have anything to worry about for many years to come," he added reassuringly, because her eyes had narrowed.

But not at him. Pritkin didn't understand the odd look she was suddenly giving the softly gleaming pile. Until a few days later, when he happened to be in the suite when Mircea burst in the front door.

The vampire was looking less than pleased, and he had the glimmering lavender length with him. He held it out, his hand shaking slightly. "Cassandra! What on earth did you send to Ming-de?"

Wide blue eyes met his, guileless and sweet. "Why, just a thank you gift, Mircea."

John turned away, hiding a smile. She was learning.

Author's Note: "Shadowland" is the sequel to "A Family Affair".

SHADOWLAND

Chapter One

John turned off a side street onto Las Vegas Boulevard, the early morning sun already hot enough to soak his singlet in a dark line down the front. He dragged the arm of his hoody over his face, ignoring glances from the few tourists sober enough to be up at this hour. Most of whom were doubtless wondering why he hadn't driven two miles to run the treadmill in an air-conditioned gym.

He dropped his speed to a more pedestrian-friendly four miles per hour, and lifted a hand at a street vendor who had waved at him. He didn't know the man, but he'd learned that it was expected. Like people asked him how he was as a casual greeting, despite not knowing him or giving a fig how he was. John felt it was too personal of a question to ask a stranger and didn't like the insincerity of it.

There were plenty of other things he didn't like about Las Vegas: the otherworldly heat and arctic air conditioning, which seemed designed to give everyone pneumonia. The paucity of sidewalks and, especially, of crosswalks, which explained why his coworkers regularly took a car to go two blocks. The fact that everything seemed new. He'd never experienced a physical craving for old buildings before living here.

Some old buildings, he amended, as his run brought him back to a new structure that had deliberately been designed to look old.

Dante's casino, hotel and generalized debauchery den loomed large at the end of the Strip, like a bad dream. Even in Vegas, a town not known for the subtlety, or indeed the sanity, of its architecture, the place stood out: a faux stone monstrosity with fake mold, fake turrets, fake everything except for the monsters. They were real enough.

He should know.

He was one of them.

But right now, he was a hot and sweaty monster badly in need of a drink. And not of water. The hotel doors showed him back a flushed face, sweaty blond hair and somewhat evil green eyes, because he hadn't had his morning fix yet.

He jogged in between the writhing eight-foot statues that guarded the entrance and through an eye-wincing lobby intended to resemble someone's idea of Hell. Which one? he'd almost asked on first arrival, before stopping himself. But at least it was mercifully clear of damned souls at the moment, being barely seven a.m.

Getting up early in Vegas meant you practically had the place to yourself. But newly arrived sheeple off the latest red-eye and hardened gamblers weaving their way back to bed at dawn had prompted the casino to keep a few breakfast options open. One of them had turned into John's favorite way to reward himself for a good, long workout. He could smell it from here, the siren call of his drug of choice, suffusing the air all the way out into—

He stopped in his tracks, just inside the main drag. It was always a bit of a shock, designed to look like an Old West ghost town with the ghosts still in residence. But for once it wasn't the fake wood buildings or the fiberglass tumbleweeds or the dancing neon skeletons over the casino coffee kiosk that had him stopping abruptly. And doing a double take.

The front counter of the little booth was lined with cobweb doilies on which sat the usual diabetic-coma-inducing pyramids of doughnuts and pastries. And something new. Something awful.

"What is *that*?" he demanded, transferring his glare from the case to the Goth girl standing behind it.

She looked like an extra from Beetlejuice, all wild black hair and dead white makeup except for raccoon-dark circles around her eyes. But her expression indicated that he was the one being scary. Her gaze dropped to the item in question, which was wedged between a tower of zombie cake pops and a bunch of "fruit cups" laced with custard and cream.

"M-muffin?" she asked, as if she wasn't sure.

He couldn't blame her. The monstrosity spilling over the edge of a shiny gold baking cup was big as a couple of clenched fists, a bloated alien of a sweet menacing the other nearby treats. And then he noticed the little heart-shaped sticker that someone—some *fiend*—had attached to the front of the foil.

"*Heart healthy?*" he asked, outraged.

"It—it has fiber," the girl insisted weakly.

"Where?" All John saw was candied fruit, crystallized sugar and what looked to be toasted almond slices sticking out of the dessert for a family of four disguised as breakfast.

And then he bent closer.

"Is it leaking something?" he inquired pleasantly, meeting the girl's eyes through the curved glass of the bakery case.

She swallowed nervously. "R-raspberry jam?"

"Good God."

"Watch your language," someone said from behind him.

John glanced over his shoulder to see the casino's dandified manager standing there, in a summer-weight off-white suit and dark tie. It made him look like a young Mr. Roarke, an image helped by his Spanish coloring. And hurt by his dyspeptic expression.

The expression was not unusual when its owner was looking at John. But it was odd that a four-hundred-year-old vampire had yet to learn to control his face better than that. Especially when said vampire was possessed by a demon who had once shared body space with the illustrious Casanova.

John glanced down at his sweaty khakis and oversized hoody. The latter was hot and was usually stuck to him by the time he'd gone half a mile in the desert heat, but it was necessary to conceal accoutrements of which the local police might not approve. The butt of one of them was peeking out from under his left arm.

He pushed it back into place. "Better?"

"No!"

Casanova had adopted the name of his demon's old host, but had clearly failed to master the man's charm. Or perhaps he had, and John simply didn't rate the gold star treatment. Which was actually somewhat refreshing after all the faux American niceness he encountered. Some days, John became quite tired of being smiled at.

And Casanova's mood meant that he didn't have to bother with the social niceties, either. They loathed each other. It would only make the creature nervous.

"You look like a refugee from *Platoon*," Casanova snapped.

An evil thought occurred.

John activated the appropriate facial muscles, as wide and as charmingly as he could manage with a distinct lack of practice. The creature paled. His work done, John returned his attention to the girl hovering behind the case.

"Two coffees," he told her. "A sixteen-ounce espresso and—" he broke off at her look. "What?"

"I . . ." she spread hands covered in black, fingerless gloves. "We don't have . . . I mean, an extra-large espresso is four ounces . . ."

She must be new. "Yes, I know," John said impatiently. "Give me four of them in a cup."

"*Four* of them?"

"In a cup. And one medium coffee with cream and sugar. A *small* amount of sugar," he added.

"Four double shots and he's worried about sugar," she muttered, wandering off in the direction of a silver machine in the corner.

"All right, what is it?" Casanova demanded.

John ignored him in favor of deciding on breakfast. Not his own; he didn't eat this much sugar in a year. But for a certain blonde-haired menace with a sweet tooth, who was perfectly capable of popping down here and ordering the raspberry monstrosity if he didn't come up with a suitable substitute.

"Well?" The shrill demand came almost immediately. Patience wasn't one of the creature's virtues.

Of course, John had yet to discover anything that was.

"Well what?"

"Well, what are you up to now?" A slim hand descended on John's shoulder with the crippling grip of a veteran rugby player.

And was abruptly removed, smoking slightly, when John sent a pulse of energy through it. The creature cursed.

"Nothing," John said mildly. "You're paranoid."

"*I'm* paranoid?" Casanova hissed. "You're the one jogging with no fewer than five weapons—"

"Six."

"—and then coming in here to terrorize my staff!"

"I'm here to buy breakfast," John pointed out, as the girl came back with a drink holder that smelled like heaven.

Not that he would know.

He took the coffee with a junkies' thoughtless smile. It caused her to blink again, but for a different reason this time. Damn it.

"Or seducing them," Casanova muttered.

"I'll leave that to you," John said dryly, transferring his attention back to the case.

"There's a coupon special on today," the girl offered, suddenly friendlier. "Four mini blueberry for two dollars."

"I don't have a coupon."

She smiled. "I might could find one for you."

"No, you can't," Casanova said, shooting her a glare. Which she didn't see because her eyes had never left John.

"That won't be necessary," he replied, as repressively as possible.

Which obviously wasn't repressive enough.

"Hey, where are you from?" she asked brightly.

Britain by way of Hell. "Ohio."

"Really? Cause you sound English or something."

"I sound Welsh."

She looked confused. "Isn't that the same thing?"

"No!"

"Are you going up there?" Casanova demanded, before John could elaborate. Just as well.

He wanted to discourage the girl, not traumatize her.

"What about that one?" he asked, pointing at the least unhealthy-looking item he could find.

"That one?" She looked doubtful.

"Yes, what is it?"

"Applesauce donut," she said disapprovingly, as if wondering how something without icing, coconut or any type of sprinkles had gotten in there.

"I'll take it. The one in front," he added, since it looked to be the smallest.

The girl might have rolled her eyes, although it was hard to tell through that much makeup. But she found the tongs and fished it out. The casino manager's grip, meanwhile, returned to John's arm.

And sent up sparks this time because John hadn't bothered to lower his shield.

The creature cursed some more and snatched it back. "Answer the question!"

"What question?"

"Are you going up there?"

No, I thought I'd drink both coffees myself, John didn't say, since the vampire had no sense of humor. And since it wasn't entirely unknown. "If you mean to Lady Cassandra's rooms, yes."

"Lady Cassandra."

There was no doubt about the eye roll this time. But Casanova knew better than to elaborate. "Then take her a message."

"Take it yourself."

"I have! And been ignored. In my own hotel!"

John scribbled his name and room number on the pay slip and handed it back, in exchange for a small white bag. The girl glanced a little too long at the number, and then smiled at him again, this time long and slow and deliberate. And *bugger*.

The familiar yearning pain slammed into John, hard enough to make his breath catch. He *wanted*, just that fast, just that stupidly. And he saw that want reach out and touch her, staining her cheeks, quickening her breath, causing a small pink tongue to flicker out to moisten ridiculous black-dyed lips—

He closed his eyes. He didn't know her; wasn't interested in her. But the starving thing that lived at his core didn't care. And he couldn't even blame his reaction on a parasitic infection like Casanova. The vampire could banish his other half, should he ever tire of it, but John didn't have that option. An incubus didn't possess him. It *was* him. And one of these days, it would destroy him.

But not today.

He slipped an arm around Casanova's waist, and leered into the surprised demon's face. "All right then, why don't we go up together?"

"What the—"

He leaned in. "You can carry the coffee, darling."

"Go to hell!"

John watched the girl turn away, frowning, and shove the pay slip into the cash register. "Not for her."

Chapter Two

didn't think you had a problem with men," John said, amused, as Casanova pushed past him into an elevator. And shoved the coffee carrier into John's chest as he went.

"I don't have a problem with men! I have a problem with you! And with *her*." The vampire glared skyward and punched the button for one of the upper suites. "Why is she still here?"

John didn't bother pretending not to know what he meant. Lady Cassandra, AKA the Pythia, AKA Cassie, was the newly appointed chief seer of the supernatural world and Casanova's reluctant guest. But she wasn't half so reluctant as her host, who had been hinting broadly about a move for the last two weeks.

It seemed he had decided on a more direct approach.

"You know why," John told him shortly. "The casino has the best wards available."

The vampire said a word that didn't go with the soigné façade he cultivated in public. "She's a witch. She belongs with the Circle," he snapped, talking about the Silver Circle, the magical authority who usually guarded the Pythia. "And who was it who did the wards around here? Oh, that's right—the Circle's mages! They must be able to protect her!"

"Don't pretend you're concerned about her safety," John said dryly. The creature made sociopaths look altruistic.

"Of course, I'm not concerned about her," Casanova said, looking incredulous. "She has a brigade of senior masters watching her every breath. She sneezes and ten people offer a hanky. She stubs a toe and they order an evac team! She's perfectly fine!"

"Do you have a point?"

"Yes! That my hotel isn't!"

"It isn't your hotel."

"And it never will be if I don't manage to turn a profit—and keep it from burning to the ground," Casanova said passionately. "And your precious Pythia is doing nothing to help with that. Half the people on the planet want her dead—"

"Hardly."

"—and a fair number from other worlds—"

"Not anymore."

"—and every damned one of them tromps through here—"

"Is that a word?"

"—and trashes this place in the process. I want her *gone*!"

"Is that what you want me to tell her?" John asked archly. "To get out?"

Casanova fidgeted, brushing down a wrinkle in the otherwise perfect drape of his coat. And noticing a singe mark the sparks had left. He frowned at it.

But he didn't answer, too busy recalling, no doubt, that his master was also Cassie's current protector. Mircea Basarab owned the hotel, a senior spot on the powerful vampire senate, and—if John understood the hierarchy properly—Casanova's Armani-covered arse. And Basarab wanted Cassie right where she was.

It was one of the few things they agreed on.

John normally trusted vampires about as much as the demons he'd grown up with, which was to say not at all. And that went double for the oily Mircea. But at least he seemed sincere about protecting her, which was more than could be said for the Circle, which was preoccupied fighting a war and dealing with a recent coup among its leadership.

The coup had been fortunate for Cassie, since the old guard had not been fond of their new Pythia's raised-by-vampire-mobsters credentials. Or the fact that she couldn't be relied on to turn a blind eye to some of their illegal activities. Not only would they have failed to weep had an accident befallen her, they hadn't been above trying to arrange something of the sort themselves.

The new government had a different view, and had purged many of the old regime's supporters. But no one believed that they had found them all. And until they did, Cassie was better off where she was.

Only it seemed that Casanova didn't agree.

"Do you know what a third of my guards—guards that I am paying for, mind you—are doing?" he asked severely. And then didn't give John a chance to reply. "Because it isn't watching the dealers, who are likely robbing me blind. Or attending to intoxicated patrons or breaking up fights or escorting my money. Or even dancing attendance on their lordships up there—"

John assumed he meant the Vampire Senate, which had taken over a large part of the hotel's nicer suites when their previous base became an early casualty in the war. Since the hotel was owned by one of their own, they did not see any reason to pay for the rooms, or for the food consumed by their human entourages, or for much of anything else. John suspected that the dent they had made in Casanova's income was primarily responsible for his current mood, but he couldn't very well yell at them.

"—oh, no. They're too busy running errands for Her Highness!"

"They're assisting the guards," John pointed out, "not running errands. And that isn't her title."

"I don't care about her title!" Casanova slammed his hand down on the STOP button, why John didn't know. That only worked in the cinema.

Unless, of course, you didn't mind setting off an alarm.

"Bugger it!" Casanova snarled, looking around as a klaxon blared like a ship about to go down.

"I thought that was my line," John said, leaning back against the wall as Casanova pressed buttons and snatched the phone out of its box and yelled at it, and then at the ceiling when that didn't work. Finally, one of the overworked security guards called in to ask if there was a problem.

"Whatever gave you that idea?" his boss snarled. "Yes! Yes, there's a problem! Turn off the damned alarm!"

Which the man did.

And which resulted in the elevator proceeding on its previous course.

Casanova cursed some more until John leaned over and pressed the Door Closed button as they glided to a halt. It wouldn't avoid eavesdropping from Cassie's vampire bodyguards, but Casanova looked to be beyond caring. And John didn't want him ranting in front of her.

"What?" he asked flatly.

Casanova regarded him for a second, lips pursed, as if actually wondering if charm might work. He wisely decided against it. "She's a sitting duck here," he said finally. "You know that."

"You just pointed out that she's surrounded by guards."

"Yes, but why are they necessary? Because every damn body knows where she is. Smart money is to get her somewhere they don't know, at least until the war is over. A safe house—"

"There are no houses safe enough for Cassie."

"Well, neither is this. Everyone knows she's here, and despite everything, more than a few have managed to get at her. And your . . . and certain people . . . can be persistent."

"Yes, they can," John said, letting his voice go clipped. "Dangerously so."

It was Casanova's turn to just look at him.

He didn't say anything else.

He didn't have to.

If there was one thing he and the vampire shared, it was antipathy for the head of their dysfunctional clan. John wasn't completely clear what Rosier, Lord of the Incubi, had done to offend Casanova, but it was probably a long list. For a creature whose stock in trade was charm and seduction, Rosier managed to make a lot of enemies.

Including his own son.

John had a list of grievances against his father longer than his arm, and at one time had actually believed that he couldn't hate him any more. Until a little over a month ago. Until Rosier joined the queue of people trying to kill Cassie.

It hadn't helped that it had been partly John's fault.

The demon council, of which Rosier was a member, was afraid of the influence Rosier's disaffected son might wield over an impressionable young woman—one who possessed a power they lacked. Cassie didn't just see the past, she was able to visit it as well, and to take a person or two along for the ride. The council was afraid that John would be that person, and that the knowledge he had of their activities would allow him to destroy them before they even knew he existed.

It was absurd. Not his antipathy for the council, which was well-known and well-founded. But the idea that he would move against the only power keeping the other demons in line—demons who would like nothing better than to descend on Earth en masse. Or that he would risk involving Cassie if he did. But convincing his father of that might have been difficult.

For all his centuries, there were certain concepts that Rosier would never understand.

Fortunately, Cassie did. And when, in the process of trying to kill her, Rosier almost managed to let Sid, another disgruntled family member, destroy the entire demon council, Cassie had intervened. And John had made damned sure that his father returned the favor. Namely, he'd forced the slimy son of a bitch to take a vow to never again lift a hand against her. And knowing Rosier, he had made it as air-tight as possible.

If he broke it, he died.

John was sure of it.

Well, as sure as he could be when dealing with someone who'd had had thousands of years to create a new definition for deviousness . . .

"We both need her out of here," Casanova said softly, watching him. "For different reasons, perhaps, but does that matter? You could talk to the Circle. They can protect her against almost anyone . . ."

Yes, except themselves.

What was the world coming to, John wondered, when Cassie was safer with a bunch of blood sucking fiends than her own kind?

Speaking of which . . .

A huge hand inserted itself between the crack in the silver doors. The thick black hair dusting the knuckles told John who he would see before a single black eye peered through at him. "You guys making out in here, or what?" a deep voice asked.

"He would be so lucky," Casanova sneered, and pushed his way into the small, marble-tiled entry leading to one of the Casino's nicer suites.

John was glad to see two guards, upper-level vampires judging by the fact that they were active in broad daylight, lounging by the door to the suite, having a smoke. Not that they were needed with the huge bear of a creature facing him. Six-foot-five and not slightly built with it, Marco liked to think of himself as Cassie's senior bodyguard. John let him since it was easier, and since he rather liked having something the size of a Mac truck guarding Cassie when he wasn't around.

Marco might be one of Basarab's creatures, but he was competent. He also wasn't stupid, which was probably why John was getting the hairy eyeball as he stepped out in Casanova's wake. "Something got you spooked?"

"No." No more than usual.

Marco looked like he was going to say something, but stopped when another vampire poked a head into the hall. "She's up."

They all went inside, except for the two smokers, who would remain in place until they were relieved by the next crew. And if someone managed to get past them, they would be met by the most formidable wards the Circle could devise, which John had augmented by a few tricks of his own. Not to mention a dozen more master vampires in a very bad mood.

And a half-demon war mage in an even worse one.

Cassie was as safe as he could make her, which was pretty damned safe, he told himself, trying to stop the frisson crawling up his spine as she came out of the hall leading to the bedrooms. She was yawning and still pink-cheeked with sleep, all tumbled blond curls and drowsy blue eyes, and dressed in a rumpled, oversized tee that declared: 'Stressed spelled backwards is desserts'. She looked about twelve, not like someone who should have the weight of the world on her shoulders.

The impression heightened when she noticed the white bag perched between the coffee cups. "Whaddjabringme?" she demanded.

"Some stress."

He didn't know if she got the reference, or just didn't care. She grabbed the bag and poked her nose in. And came out with a little powdered sugar clinging to the end, and a disappointed expression. "Pritkin?"

"Yes?"

"You brought me one doughnut?"

"Yes."

"One?"

He crossed his arms.

"I didn't think they even came like that," she muttered.

"I can take it back—"

Cassie snatched the bag and took it off to the bedroom, along with her coffee. She often did that, despite having both a dining room and a breakfast bar in the suite. He had the impression she didn't like to eat in front of the vampires, or perhaps she just tired of all the eyes on her all the time. But it had become a habit for him to drop by with something appropriately caloric every morning, and for her to eat it while they discussed the day's schedule.

He followed her down the hall and into the large bedroom, where she began pushing some gaily wrapped packages off a small table by the window.

"More bribes," she said, plopping the bag down in the cleared spot.

John settled into his usual chair. "It's traditional for the leaders of the magical community to give the Pythia gifts on her accession," he reminded her, not for the first time. "They're not all bribes."

"Oh, of course they are," she said, wolfing down the pastry in a couple of bites. She had to take big ones, but she was trying to make a point about the paucity of his offering, and by God she managed it. "They figure they have to play nice until somebody kills me."

John had just taken his first caffeine-laced sip of the day, which was usually something approaching nirvana. But that one didn't go down well. Damn it, he hated when she did that. They were busting their arses to keep her safe, and she talked like it was only a matter of time.

"Now you're mad again, aren't you?" she asked, reading him easier than he'd prefer.

"No. I simply wish you wouldn't plan your funeral quite so soon."

"Well, somebody has to," she joked, and then caught his expression. And stopped.

"Nobody is going to kill you," he said shortly. "They've tried and they've failed—"

"There's always the next time," she said, in a smaller voice. The kind that was worse than the bluster and bravado. The kind that let him know she meant it.

"There's not going to be a next time," he said harshly. The brief euphoria from his run had just taken a nose-dive.

"Okay," Cassie said softly, because she'd just gotten up and she didn't want to argue, either. She drank coffee and pulled over the nearest gift. "Hey, maybe it's something fun this time. They keep sending me god-awful jewelry and I already have more of that than I—"

"*No!*"

Chapter Three

John had perhaps two seconds notice before Cassie died. It was enough to allow him to jerk up his head, to let the coffee cup fall from his fingers, to start up from his chair. It wasn't enough to save her.

"No!" he shouted, diving for the chair where she sat. She looked up, blue eyes wide and startled, and the pretty package she'd been unwrapping fell from her fingers. *"Don't touch—"*

A tremendous blast interrupted him, tearing through the suite. His shields slammed into place automatically, but not before he was sent hurtling backwards through the bedroom wall. He hit something on the other side, hard enough to shatter his protection and to push all the air out of his lungs. Then everything went black.

A stabbing pain in his right leg dragged him back to consciousness. Acrid black smoke boiled through the air, threatening to choke him, and when he tried to move, he discovered that he was half buried in debris. He groped about for a hand-hold only to have his fingers slip on what he vaguely identified as piano keys. It took him a second to realize that he'd been blown almost to the foyer, landing near the baby grand.

"Cassie!" He struggled to his feet, listening for a response, any response, but heard nothing. The loud ringing in his ears left him all but deaf, like the smoke deprived him of sight, but there was a slightly lighter patch of air ahead. He started that way only to have his leg spasm and collapse beneath him.

His groping hands discovered a piece of rebar making a bloody mess out of his upper calf. He couldn't walk on it, and with the rod in place, he couldn't heal. His hand twitched, clenching on the rough surface for a moment as he took a steadying breath. And then he jerked it out.

The spike of pure agony that followed made the room swim sickeningly around him. He dropped forward onto his hands, panting harshly and fighting a strong urge to vomit. But the panic twisting in his gut was worse than the pain. As soon as his head cleared enough, he slapped a shield patch over the wound and staggered back to his feet.

Casanova pushed past as he neared the bedroom, disappearing into the smoke. A moment later, it cleared enough for John to see him, clutching what remained of the bedroom doorframe with both arms and a leg. His mouth was moving in creative curses and it wasn't hard to see why.

His other leg dangled over nothing but air.

The master suite wasn't destroyed; it was gone. Only a few smoking shards of once expensive flooring remained, clinging to the space in front of the miraculously still-standing door. Below, it looked like a large bite had been taken out of the building, with nothing for several floors besides tumbled concrete, twisted rebar and expensive rubble.

"What happened?" Casanova mouthed, but John didn't answer. He also didn't try to stop. His shields clamped back into place and changed shape as he slid across the floor and off the side of the building.

Eighteen floors was a difficult height—too long to fall without a shield chute and too short to give it time to deploy properly. He landed on top of a Mercedes hard enough to cave in the hood and to send a lance of agony from his leg up into his chest. But he'd missed the majority of the wreckage, landing beyond the smoking pile below the casino's jagged wound.

He strongly suspected that he'd just cracked a rib, but at least his hearing was improving. It still sounded like he'd stuffed cotton wool in his ears, but the dozen or more car alarms screaming on every side were audible. But they receded into the distance for him, like cries on a battlefield, as he rolled off the car and scanned the parking area.

It was hard to know where to even start looking. The debris was scattered widely, all the way to the fence at the far end of the lot. And thanks to the nature of the bomb, every bit of it was potentially deadly.

He saw several pieces of glowing balcony railing eat through the roof of a Lexus and drop onto the seat below, immediately starting a conflagration within the car. He saw one of the ornamental topiaries that ringed the casino, this one shaped like a satyr, writhing in almost human-like agony as it was turned into ash by strange silver flames. He saw a couple of vampire security members hacking at the limb of one of their own, whose hand had come into contact with the wrong bit of rubble.

He saw no sign of Cassie.

Panic, horror, pain—his body was screaming with all of them but he forced himself to focus on the search. Wrapping an extra layer of his shields around his hands, he started throwing aside piles of blackened furniture, ruined clothes and the remains of once-expensive drapes, some of which were still burning. But there was no spill of blond curls anywhere, no stupid pink tee, no—

No thrumming feel of feedback from the trace charm he had on her.

The thought slid sickly across the panic, stopping him in his tracks. She could have shifted, he told himself, as ice settled into the pit of his belly. She could have used the ability she possessed for traveling through time to go almost anywhere. To outrun the blast.

A blast she hadn't known was coming?

He shoved the small voice away and shouted her name, trying to listen over the sound of blood rushing in his ears. There was no answer. But a faint trace of familiar magic tugged at his senses, leading him like a rope to the far end of the lot.

Blown up against the chain link fence, like flotsam after a storm, was a twisted snarl of blackened metal. It was only just recognizable as mangled box springs, warped into modern art by the force of the blast. And underneath, barely visible through a layer of grime, was a dull glint of red. It was just one shard among many, but this one wasn't glass.

The chill settled into his bones, threatening to paralyze him, as he picked up the charred remains of a once-potent talisman. The chain was missing, the gold filigree of the setting half melted and the stone cracked and dark. Useless.

He stared at it blindly, outwardly calm. But inside his head every curse and prayer he'd ever heard roared like a gale force wind. It scoured him out, swept through all the corners of his mind and threw open the doors, leaving nothing but the bitter truth behind.

She hadn't shifted. There hadn't been time. Even more telling, she wouldn't have done it, wouldn't have left all of them to die in her place. She was far too stubborn for that. If she'd shifted, she would have taken the bomb with her.

And she hadn't.

Everything went a little vague after that. There were flashes of people shouting, of the parking lot filling up with useless emergency personnel, of the hard asphalt giving way to the sponginess of earth beneath his boots. He slowly sank to his knees in the dirt of the empty lot behind the parking area, his right leg throbbing with every heartbeat.

Shields were not meant to be used as field dressings, and his was leaking badly. His rib was also stabbing him in the side, making each breath painful. But he couldn't seem to care very much. It was like being high, or really, really drunk.

He sat there, scraping flakes of dried blood off his hands, while sweat rolled down his neck and adrenaline went stale in his veins. Nearby, part of a corpse sizzled in the sunlight, the smell both nauseating and strangely familiar. The smell of home, he supposed, and felt a hysterical laugh building somewhere in his chest.

Until the corpse grabbed his pant leg.

He lashed out automatically, before belatedly recognizing one of Cassie's vampire bodyguards. Or part of one, as everything below the waist appeared to be missing. A single column of naked spine twisted in the dirt, glistening wetly in the sunlight, like a pale snake.

"Where?" Marco asked, blood spilling down his chin. "Where is she?"

John tried to answer, but the words wouldn't come. He silently held out the remains of the talisman she never took off, the one who linked her to her ghost servant. And saw when it registered.

"What was it?" Marco asked harshly.

"Brimstone." John left it stark, as there was no point in softening it. Humans used the name as an alternative to sulfur, probably because the pungent smell was similar. But this wasn't nearly so benign. Found solely in an obscure demon realm, real brimstone burned with an unquenchable fire. It wouldn't extinguish until it had finished consuming whatever living flesh it encountered. There was no antidote.

Marco closed his eyes.

"How did it get in?" he demanded, after a moment. "We checked everything. Every single goddamned—" he broke off, choking.

John stared at the anthill of activity the parking lot had become and didn't answer. He didn't have one to give. They opened each and every gift before Cassie ever saw it, looking for booby traps, for poison, for malignant spells. And that was after the boxes had been gone over with a fine-toothed comb by Casanova's people in the lobby. Yet somehow, he'd still managed to miss it, until the unmistakable smell of brimstone hit the air.

Somehow, he'd still managed to get her killed.

"Pritkin—"

He glanced down to see that Marco's eyes had gone wide and glazed with shock. John stared at the creature, feeling a surge of unaccustomed pity. The vampire's body was trying to repair the massive damage, but the brimstone was eating his flesh faster than his system could knit it back together. He would lose, but it would be a long, agonizing battle.

"What do you want?" he asked quietly.

"Not to lie here for hours like a stuck pig!"

John nodded and pulled a knife from under his coat, before kneeling beside the dying vampire. He didn't usually carry a stake, since vampires were allies these days, and they'd never been his usual prey, in any case. But there was no need to worry. Half the yard was covered with slivers of once-costly flooring and John snapped off a jagged piece.

Marco grasped his arm. "Who did this? You know, don't you?"

John didn't answer.

Brimstone was an ancient weapon, almost obsolete these days. Like a modern human using Greek fire. There were few even among the demons who would have thought of it.

But one would. One who had been reminded of its existence forcefully just a few weeks ago. One who had seen it in action the last time he tried to kill Cassie.

John felt the bottom finish falling out of his world. How could he have been so sure that an oath would stop an ancient demon? One who had survived on dirty tricks and vile cunning for so long? It seemed absurd now. Laughable. Naïve. And of course, Rosier hadn't had to violate his oath at all, had he? All he had to do was post the gift prior to taking it, and it would count him blameless.

Ancient magic was helpful like that.

But that didn't explain how he got it past security, John thought, his head spinning. It didn't explain--

"John!"

"Rosier," he rasped, his voice sounding like rust on old hinges. "Lord of the Incubi."

"A demon?"

"A demon prince. Cassie made a fool of him recently, and he doesn't forget a slight."

Marco's hold tightened. His hand was cold and trembling, but his grip was still surprisingly strong. "You're going to find him. You're going to get him."

"Yes."

In an eye blink, Marco sprang, sending the stake flying with one hand, while the other clasped like a vise around John's throat. The creature was inches from his face, his eyes staring directly into John's own. And for an instant, a crimson flash outlined the pupils, like the corona about an eclipse.

"I wouldn't be too sure of that, Emrys," the vampire said, his voice suddenly deeper, more resonant, totally inhuman. "But do feel free to try."

John's lips formed the most hated name he knew, but he didn't have the breath to utter it. The vampire stretched his lips in a parody of a smile, a slash of bloody teeth against swarthy skin. And then the world around him shattered like a bullet through glass, the shards of it falling away into darkness.

Chapter Four

"That was less than wise," Rian sighed, as Casanova gave another twist to the shard of wood sticking out of Marco's back.

"I wasn't taking any chances," he replied impatiently. "We don't use that sawdust crap in the nicer suites. This is hard wood." He threw aside what had been part of a very nice mahogany armoire. Goddamnit.

"I was referring to your attack on the master," the mellifluous voice said, taking on the patient tone he particularly hated.

"Screw your master," he hissed, struggling to heave aside what remained of Marco's smoking corpse.

"I have. I do not think it will help us in this instance, however."

Casanova narrowed his eyes. Sometimes, even after this long, he couldn't tell when she was joking. And then he noticed that his coat was on fire.

"We need to discuss this," his demon continued calmly, as Casanova danced around, trying to get the coat off without letting any stray sparks touch his body.

He finally fought his way free and threw the jacket onto the ground, resisting the urge to scream. He stripped off his fine cotton shirt and wrapped it around his hand, running it nervously over his pale slacks. If one little ember touched his flesh, it would be enough to start a conflagration that would consume him. Mercifully, he didn't find one.

It was the only mercy he was likely to receive today.

He stood there, feeling the sun bake his brain and grimly watching $2,000 worth of couture go up in flames. Brimstone. Typical. They'd layered enough spells over that room to make the air thick from all the magic floating around. An alarm went off every time that damn girl got a hangnail, yet not one of them had managed to detect the real threat.

"The master never ceases to surprise," Rian murmured. "I would not have expected this of him."

Casanova scowled. "Don't talk to me about your master. I have one, too, remember?"

"But hardly on the same level of menace."

"Oh, no?" He kicked what was left of Marco's body aside. Then, just for the hell of it, he kicked Pritkin, too. "Tell that to my staked corpse!"

"I do not think our body is in any immediate danger. At least, not from Lord Mircea."

"It's not 'our' body," he reminded her. "It's mine. You can go get another, but I'm stuck with this one. And I prefer it in one piece!" He kicked Pritkin's limp form again.

"Did you save him merely to kill him yourself?" his demon inquired mildly.

"No. Although the idea does have a certain charm."

"Why did you do it? You obviously have no love for him."

"Exactly." Casanova started waving an arm, trying to flag down one of his employees to help drag the man inside. Of course, it didn't work. Damn useless things. "Mircea is going to want blood for this. Better the mage's than mine."

"You plan to blame this on him, then?"

"It's his fault!" Casanova snarled. "Everything has gone to shit since he arrived."

"He always was a great deal of trouble," Rian agreed. "And is about to be more so, if you persist in helping him. The master clearly wants him dead along with the girl."

"He can have whatever Mircea leaves." Casanova threw the body over his shoulder in a fireman's carry and headed for the back door. One of his security members finally saw him when he was two-thirds of the way across the trash heap of a parking lot. The man held up a cell phone, but Casanova ignored it. For right now, if it wasn't Mircea—and it wasn't—he didn't care.

"How do you know it isn't?" Rian asked curiously.

"You know, sometimes I wonder what you do all day," he snapped. "How long have we been together now?"

"Over two hundred years."

"Yet you still don't understand how this whole thing works."

"How what works?"

"Masters. Their reputations. Revenge," Casanova waved a hand, but had to stop or risk dumping Pritkin's heavy ass in the dirt. "For this, Mircea won't use the phone. I'll either get a searing mental message soon, or—worse—I won't hear anything at all. I'll just disappear one night."

"Are you certain you are not being slightly paranoid?" Rian's voice was soothing. "I've always been under the impression that Lord Mircea is quite lenient."

Casanova closed his eyes and there she was, sitting on her favorite rock by the sea, combing out her long, dark hair. Normally, the sight of that tall, slender body, clad only in moonlight, was enough to calm him. It wasn't working so well today.

"Yes, because that's how you get a senate seat. By being a nice guy."

"There's no need for sarcasm," she chided. "And I have always found him charming."

Yes, particularly when he was about to go for the jugular, Casanova thought, right before something slammed him in the face. He shrieked and dropped Pritkin, preparing to flee. Then his eyes popped open, bringing him face to face with—his own face. It took him a few heart-clenching seconds to realize that he'd run into the mirror on the side of a truck.

"You need to calm down," Rian said mildly as he leaned against the vehicle, trying to swallow his heart back down where it belonged.

"You calm down! Your neck isn't on the line!"

"Neither is yours unless you persist in involving yourself in this," she said, more sharply. "Emrys and his father have been feuding for centuries. No one who gets between them ever prospers."

"At the moment, I'd settle for survival."

"That is why you need to listen to—"

"No, you listen," he hissed, crouching behind the truck. "The master and the girl had a bond. At the very least, he knows that something has gone terribly wrong. At worst, he already knows she's dead. If he's decided I'm at fault, there could be assassins on their way here even now."

Or perhaps there was no need to send any, he thought, spying a few of his men loitering suspiciously nearby. Maybe some of his own people had taken the job, the ungrateful bastards. He wouldn't put it past them.

"They're your vampires," Rian admonished.

"That's the point! As my master, Mircea can control them. Any minute, one of them might sneak up on us and—augghh!"

He broke off as he was slammed into the side of the truck, hard enough to rattle his teeth. He shrieked again and tried to crawl over the hood, but was jerked back down. And found himself staring into a pair of furious green eyes.

His spine sagged with relief as he recognized the mage. Which only made it hurt more when the slamming motion was repeated. "You knew what he planned," Pritkin snarled. "You knew he was coming! That's why you wanted her gone—to save your precious hotel!"

Casanova would have answered, but at the feel of a sliver of wood denting the skin right over his heart, all his saliva dried up. It didn't help that the mage was looking fairly crazed. His face was red, his short blond hair was standing up in tufts and his eyes . . . his eyes did not look entirely sane.

What else is new, he thought hysterically.

"He knew nothing," Rian said, answering for him. "For that matter, neither did I."

She had used Casanova's vocal cords, but Pritkin seemed to know who was speaking, because his scowl deepened. His hand came up, threatening to crush Casanova's throat. "You're one of his creatures. You do as he commands!"

"But he didn't command."

"Why should I believe you?"

"You know our Lord better than anyone. Would he trust me with a mission likely to put me at odds with my host?"

"You are far more ancient than your host," Pritkin spat. "In a battle of wills, you might well prevail."

"I might," she agreed. "And I might not. Age is not the only factor. This body belongs to another, and ownership grants certain privileges. Now release him, unless you wish to have the blood of an innocent on your hands."

"I already have that." The mage's voice went suddenly cold, but Casanova found himself abruptly let go. He stayed sprawled against the truck anyway. His knees felt a little weak for some reason.

"It was not your fault, Emrys," Rian said, sounding sad.

"Do not call me that!"

"As you wish. What will you do?"

"What do you think?" He used a knife to slice away his right trouser leg, revealing bloody, mangled flesh beneath.

"You're injured," she pointed out, kneeling to examine the wound.

"And he's drained." Pritkin tossed his coat on the truck's hood and stripped off his shirt.

"You can't be sure of that."

"If he wasn't, he would have jumped to another body and continued the fight. In spirit form, he can possess anyone he chooses."

"Anyone except vampires," Rian said thoughtfully. "Yet he controlled Marco, a powerful master. I did not think even Lord Rosier so strong as that."

"He isn't." Pritkin pulled out a knife and began to savage his shirt. "That is one reason we had only masters guarding her. But Marco insisted on coming back to work early, despite being almost killed recently. Now we know why. His injuries made him vulnerable and that thing took full advantage."

"You still cannot kill him, Em—John. He'll be at court, and you are barred from that place."

"Save your breath, Rian," the mage said coldly. "You know as well as I do, he isn't going there."

"And of course, you're going to follow him," Rian said, sounding resigned.

She stood up as the crazy bastard began binding his wound with the remains of his shirt. Like there weren't perfectly good, sterile bandages available at first aid, Casanova thought resentfully. Probably thought it made him look macho, all hairy-chested and sweaty, his torso crisscrossed by scuffed leather holsters and old bandoliers.

Muscle bound Neanderthal.

"I'm not afraid of death," Pritkin said curtly, and Casanova rolled his eyes.

"That's not courage, John; it's suicidal ideation."

"Spare me the pseudo-science."

"Death wish, then. Do you like that better?" Rian challenged, grasping the mage's wrist.

Uncharacteristically, Pritkin didn't bother to shake off the hold. "Say what you will," he told her coldly. "But you will not save him. Not this time."

"Even should you manage it, killing him will not change what has happened. You know this!"

He raised his head, the impromptu patch up job complete, and the eyes had gone olive and frighteningly blank. "I also know that if I had ended his existence centuries ago, as I should have done, this never would have happened."

"You can't be certain of that," Rian said softly. "None of us can know the future."

"One could," the mage said, a strange, savage smile twisting his lips. "But she is dead. As her murderer will soon be."

"John—" Rian cried, but it was too late. The mage didn't move, but Casanova felt the wrist he held disintegrate under his fingers. A moment later, he closed his hand on nothing but air.

"All right," Casanova said in disgust. "At least there's no way today could possibly get any—"

A wave of disorientation interrupted him, and when it cleared, he found himself back in the casino, in one of the back stairwells. Before he could even frame a question, the door to the flight below opened. He caught a glimpse of bronze faceplates and huge curved swords, and then his head was bouncing down the stairs like a gory soccer ball.

"I think I know a way," Rian said.

Chapter Five

In an instant, John was swept from a blindingly hot morning into a dark, cold night. His breath frosted the air in front of him, half obscuring what looked like a composite of every city he'd been in during the last fifty years. It had the same grimy buildings, the same smog-filled air, the same dark streets filled with dangers. Only the creatures who prowled these alleyways wouldn't just pick your pocket and shiv you in the side for good measure.

They'd stay to dine on the corpse.

Of course, hell didn't really decorate with Dumpsters and graffiti. But the city, or rather, the ancient ruins on which it was built, had been created by beings who didn't rely on boring old three dimensions. Viewed without a filter, it made his head feel like it was about to explode.

Fortunately, the current inhabitants felt the same way, and had laid a spell that supplied a generic environment to keep everyone from going mad. It pulled images from the viewer's memory, meaning that everyone saw it slightly differently.

The last time he'd visited, it had looked like Victorian London. The time before that, it had been Revolutionary France. Still earlier it had been an Iron Age village on the edge of a forest, where the trees looked back at you if you stared at them for too long. And while the basic layout never changed, the human mind relied on visual cues that shifted greatly in between incarnations.

He therefore needed a moment to get his bearings, but found that he didn't have one.

The runes he'd used to transition were still glowing faintly in the air when he heard it—a sound like leather sheets flapping in the wind, followed by a screech that rent the night. Something huge sailed by overhead as John sprinted for the cover of a nearby alley. He moved as quickly as his leg would allow, even knowing that it wouldn't be fast enough.

It wasn't.

A tattered shadow rippled grotesquely over the surrounding buildings as the creature banked and turned. This time it was a hunting scream that echoed off the buildings on either side—it had spotted him. John cursed himself for a fool and felt around under his coat, finally locating the right vial about the time the creature landed a few doors down.

Vetalas had notoriously bad eyesight, relying mostly on an acute sense of smell for hunting. That could be an advantage—unless you happened to be covered in sweat and gore. John dashed the neutralizer potion all over himself, then held his breath, not knowing if it would be enough.

He didn't normally come here drenched in blood. Of course, he didn't normally come here at all anymore. A death order signed by the demon high council was something of a deterrent.

Not that there weren't plenty of others.

For a long moment, there was nothing but the sound of slow, heavy pants and the incongruous tap, tap, tap of claws on cement as the creature prowled up and down the sidewalk, looking for the tasty tidbit it had glimpsed from above. John stayed utterly still, not even breathing. It wasn't likely to help.

Vetalas were rare in the city, preferring the wild hinterlands beyond. But when they did come in, no one challenged them. They were frighteningly fast, immensely strong, and cunningly smart. And they could hone in on human magic as easily as scent. Throwing a silence shield or a cloaking spell over himself would only help it to find him faster.

But not being able to move was driving him crazy. His hand itched to tense, to grab a weapon, to *fight*. But vetalas hunted in packs, and the others wouldn't be far away. And meeting a group of flesh-eating predators in his current condition would make this a very short trip.

Finally, through the cobweb strewn packing crates at the entrance to the alley, he glimpsed it—a fantastic beast, sleek as a viper and built for raw power. Like a nightmarish cross of hyena and bat, it was a mass of contradictions—silky russet fur that melted into leathery black wings, a delicate, fine-boned head that ended in a razored snarl. Grace seamlessly combined with terror, it was the perfect instrument of death.

And it was wagging its tail.

John slumped against the cold bricks behind him, faintly dizzy from relief and lack of oxygen. He decided that perhaps God didn't hate him as much as he'd always believed. Because of the thousands of the creatures who ravaged this strange world, he'd stumbled across the only one he knew.

Or perhaps it had stumbled over him, because before he could emerge from the alley, it bounded over the crates, knocked him to the ground and deposited a ton of enthusiastic slobber onto his face.

"Beren—Beren get *off*," he growled, which did no more good than it ever had.

Glossy fur gleamed over hard muscle as a monster the size of a large car slumped in a playful crouch. It thought he wanted to wrestle, which was more than a little dangerous in the confined space. The vetala's heavily barbed tail had gotten caught in one of the packing crates, a problem Beren solved by thrashing it back and forth against the two sides of the alley. Nails and shards of wood went flying everywhere—including into John's flesh.

It occurred to him that it would be exactly like him to get killed in a city full of enemies by a friend.

In desperation, he made one of the sounds he'd perfected as a young man, a pretty good approximation of the cry young vetalas used to let their nest mates know when they'd bitten too hard. He'd hardly begun the haunting mewl of distress before Beren was pulling back in an undignified waddle, until only its head was in the alley. It snuffled around his hurt leg, its muzzle careful not to nudge the wound, its body language apologetic.

"It's all right," John said, sitting up. "I'm glad to see you, too."

The great head pushed its way under his arm, pretty much forcing him to scratch it behind the ears. He obliged, and found the rumble of its breath and the impression of barely contained violence familiar and soothing. He'd never been able to own a dog. After Beren, they seemed so cringing, so subservient. They were carrion eaters and beggars of scraps; Beren was a proud member of an ancient race of hunters, and he preferred his food alive.

Fortunately, he'd never viewed John as food. Why was still open to question. Beren hadn't been an abandoned waif John had rescued or a starving outcast. He'd been pretty much as he was now when they'd met, after Rosier had moved his son to his secondary court in the demon realm humans called the Shadowland.

It had been the second upheaval for John, who had been snatched from life on Earth to Rosier's main court only a few years before. That had proved to be a hot, brightly lit desert world, full of spice and color and debauchery—and intrigue and danger and hatred for the half-human child who was suddenly the focus of his father's interest. After the fifth failed assassination attempt, Rosier had moved him here.

John hadn't found it much of an improvement, other than for the fact that he saw his father considerably less. He'd taken to exploring the outer city, mainly to avoid the court. It was no less deadly, but at least out here, he'd known who his enemies were. Until he'd met Beren, and unexpectedly found a friend.

"What have you been doing?" he asked, and received in return a joyful tumble of images, straight into his brain: of hunting little scurrying things, of russet-coated babies all in a knot, of soaring high above the claustrophobic lid of clouds, into the star strewn sky.

Beren's head tilted to the side, obviously returning the question, and John felt a gentle probe against his mind. He rejected it fiercely, feeling suddenly, strangely vulnerable in a way that made him want to lash out at the world, to rip something apart with his bare hands, to do anything to stop the images that iced his veins. Beren gave a bleat of distress and John abruptly shut down his thoughts.

"I'm not good company today," he said briefly, and pulled a few shards out of his skin so that he could examine his leg.

It hurt like a bitch after his mad scramble for cover, but there didn't seem to be any additional damage. Unfortunately, there also wasn't any noticeable improvement. Pretty much the only good thing about his heritage was an ability to close most wounds within moments. But that wasn't happening here.

He tried a healing spell, but other than for a faint lessening of heat radiating from the wound, nothing happened. He swore. He must have had an ember of brimstone caught in it during the blast. His body would compensate—probably—but it meant that he would be stuck limping about on the thing until he could visit a healer and get it dug out.

He looked up at Beren. "My luck isn't improving."

Beren didn't say anything. It was one of the things John liked best about him.

John got to his feet, testing his leg for strength. It held, but ached every time he put any weight on it. Just standing was painful; walking any distance was likely to be excruciating, and he had a long walk ahead.

For security reasons, transitioning into the heart of the city was forbidden. Of course, considering that John was already under a death threat, that wouldn't have worried him overmuch—if the caretakers hadn't backed the law up with a very nasty spell. As a result, he'd had to enter the Shadowland on the very outskirts of the city, nowhere near the areas his prey was likely to be.

John glanced at Beren, who was watching him expectantly, the great tail whisking slowly back and forth on the street. Its head tilted, as if wondering what he was waiting for. John decided it had a point.

"Feel like giving me a lift?"

The joyful cry of assent shook nearby buildings and echoed for blocks.

John gingerly climbed onto the broad back, his feet automatically hooking under the huge wings, his hands finding purchase in that luxurious fur. He was barely in place when Beren was off, bounding in quicksilver leaps down the street, before surging with terrible grace into an arcing spring. And then, with an enormous whoosh, they were airborne, fast enough to have John's eyes watering from the speed.

In minutes, the glittering city center spread out below him, an irregular, starfish-shaped sprawl of light in the gloom. It was bigger than he recalled. Either his memory was faulty, or the Market had engulfed even more blocks since he'd been here. That wasn't surprising, as it was the main reason the Shadowland existed.

A minor demon realm with no riches, no natural resources, and a damn depressing atmosphere, it had never been deemed worth anyone's time to conquer. For millennia it had remained a stretch of twilit, rocky nothingness, populated only by the vetalas and the small mammals that were their natural prey. Until someone, ages past, had seen opportunity in its poverty.

Suspicion and distrust had long stymied trade among the demon worlds, with most demons barred from each other's realms except for the occasional heavily guarded ambassadorial delegation. Those traders who did attempt to move about were often regarded as spies and treated accordingly. From a merchant's perspective, the whole situation was, well, hellish.

Then somebody stumbled across the Shadowland. No one recalled who the commercial genius was anymore, although almost every major court claimed to have produced him. John doubted that, as none of them would have let a gold mine like this slip through their greedy hands, and they didn't control it. More likely, it was one of the guild of traders who still ran the place who had had the epiphany: an area not worth attacking might be perfect as a much needed meeting place.

It was an immediate hit, not least because of the way it had been set up. Unique amongst a species known for bureaucratizing everything, the Shadowland had few rules and restrictions. As long as everyone paid the guild's taxes and didn't cheat their customers badly enough to prompt retaliation, they were free to barter, gamble and whore together to their heart's content.

That last was the reason John was here.

Rian had been trying to spare her master, but she'd known as well as he did—Rosier wouldn't go near either of his courts so dangerously drained. Too many of his higher ranked creatures were just waiting for an opportunity to dispose of him, and to elevate themselves in the process. No, he'd replace the strength he'd lost first. And for an incubus, that only meant one thing.

John patted Beren's gleaming left flank and it banked and turned toward the Market's most notorious district.

Chapter Six

Cassie woke up screaming bloody murder. It felt pretty good, so she did it some more. She'd had nightmares before, but God *damn*—

Somebody grabbed her and she looked up into Marco's concerned eyes. "What is it?" He gave her a little shake. "What's wrong?"

She blinked and looked around, breathing hard, but saw only a ring of tense vampires.

A couple had dropped hands onto their weapons, and were darting glances around the room. Others had their eyes fixed on her, as if waiting for something to sprout out of her chest like in *Alien*.

She wasn't sure that would be any weirder than waking up in a body already in progress.

Instead of finding herself lying in a dark room, enjoying a lazy Sunday morning—the only day of the week Pritkin didn't roust her out of bed to go jogging in a heat wave—she was sitting up in bed. Early sunshine was leaking around the blackout curtains the vampires insisted on. A bunch of gifts were piled on the table by the window and more were on a cart near the bed. One of which had fallen off the tottering pile and landed near her feet.

She gave a little shriek and reflexively kicked it at the wall, then screamed again and ducked under the covers as everything came pouring back.

"If you don't tell me what's wrong right now, I'm calling a healer," Marco told her, lifting up the edge of the sheet.

Cassie just stared at him, wishing she knew. She'd had visions, plenty of them, and okay, that had been one hell of a lot worse than most, but she could deal. *If* it had been a vision. Only it hadn't felt like one. It had felt like her flesh was being stripped from her bones, which were being blown apart and simultaneously seared into charcoal, before everything went very, very dark. Not dark as in night but dark as in dead, and no one knew dead like she knew dead and that, friends and neighbors, had very definitely been—

"Are. You. All. Right?" Marco demanded, enunciating like he thought her problem might have to do with her hearing.

"Do I look all right?" she snarled, as Casanova ran into the room.

One look at his expression was enough to convince her, if she'd needed any help, that a vision was not what had just happened here. "Alû!" he yelled, sounding winded, which was ridiculous since he didn't breathe. But Casanova wasn't looking his usual suave self at the moment.

"Hello," one of the other vamps said, causing Casanova to turn on the unfortunate man with a screech.

"*Alû!* Not *hello*, you incompetent—"

The sound of gunshots from outside drowned out whatever else he might have said, and caused several of the vampires to draw their weapons and run out the door. Only to get blown back into the room in pieces as several large somethings rushed inside too fast for the eyes to track.

Oh, shit, Cassie thought blankly. "Not ag—

*   *   *

Cassie woke up with a scream lodged in her throat that she mostly swallowed back down. Her eyes were closed and she didn't really want to open them, because if she did, there might be a ring of vampires staring at her like she was crazy. But it got a little tiresome, sitting there looking at her inner eyelids, so eventually she did crack one lid halfway.

There was a ring of vampires staring at her like she was crazy.

"Is there a problem?" Marco asked, after a minute.

Well, clearly.

Cassie swallowed and opened both eyes, because she probably looked a little strange peering around with only one. And no one appeared to be trying to kill her just at the moment. She licked her lips. "What's an Alû?" she asked. "Just for information."

"Alû?" Marco asked, giving it a slightly different pronunciation.

"Close enough."

He tensed. "I think they're a type of demon, why?"

"Because there may be a slight chance that—"

Casanova ran into the room, looking freaked. "Alû!" he shrieked.

That time, five guards made it out the door, not that it made any noticeable difference. Cassie tried to shift, but absolutely nothing happened. Of course, she thought, as a dark wind blew inside. That would be far too—

* * *

Cassie woke up fairly calmly. She opened her eyes to see Marco standing by the door, talking to one of the other vamps, and the rest lounging around in deceptively casual stances. That could change in an instant into high alert status, but that didn't seem to be helping much lately. "I have to go to the bathroom," she said to no one in particular, threw back the covers and ran like all hell was after her—which apparently, it was.

Marco grabbed her before she made it out the front door. "The bathroom is back that way, princess."

"I don't like that one."

"You have three."

"I don't like any of them."

Marco sighed. "You want to tell me what's going on?" he asked calmly.

"Sure thing. As soon as I figure it out."

"Don't take this the wrong way, but you get weirder every day."

"It's the days that are getting weirder," she snapped, as Casanova came bolting in the door. "Alû?" she asked.

"Alû."

"Fuck."

Cassie tore away from Marco and sprinted across the entry to the fire stairs. "That won't work," Casanova breathed, right at her back. "They're coming up that way."

"Then where?"

"Would somebody tell me what the hell is going on?" Marco asked, as she and Casanova came running past him, back toward the suite.

"I can't get killed again," she told Casanova confidentially. "It's starting to give me a complex."

"Tell me about it," he snarled, pulling her into the elevator and then out the floor below and shoving his pass key into a random room. Marco had gone down the stairs, and was waiting on them, but Casanova slammed the door in his face.

Normally, that wouldn't have worked for longer than it took Marco to put his number thirteen boot through the foam core. But Casanova had barely had time to clap a hand over her mouth when the sounds of running feet were heard outside. They were followed by a shout and a squelching grunt and a body falling heavily against the floor.

Cassie swallowed hard, but didn't scream. She was all screamed out. What she wanted was some answers.

She indicated this by pushing an elbow into Casanova's ribs until he let go. "What is your problem?" he hissed.

Cassie stared. "What is my problem?" she whispered savagely. "Really, Casanova? *Really?*"

"All right," he straightened his tie, and brushed down a few wrinkles that had dared to show up in his nice off-white suit. "All right," he said again, which Cassie didn't find all that helpful.

"What is going on?" she demanded.

Casanova licked his lips. "I was actually hoping you'd know."

"Well, I don't! I just keep waking up and somebody kills me, over and over. Who the hell are these Alû?"

"Demons." Casanova swallowed. "They're the elite guard of the Demon High Council, to be precise. Faceless and merciless, in case you didn't notice."

"I didn't notice the faceless part. I never got a chance."

"Obviously, the council has decided it wants you dead."

"You *think*?"

"There's no need for sarcasm."

"No? People always say that, but you know what? If ever there was a need, I think this qualifies. I think this qualifies like gang busters." Cassie sat down on the sofa in their borrowed suite and hugged herself. "How long until they find us?"

"Not long, if their reputation is anything to go on. The council only sends them out on important missions."

"I feel so special."

"What I want to know is what you did," he said accusingly. He must be recovering, Cassie decided. That sounded more like the guy she knew.

She was feeling slightly better herself. A little shaky from the adrenaline but, overall, not too bad for someone who'd been a corpse three times today. She decided it was Casanova. He wasn't that great of a fighter, but then, she hadn't noticed anybody else doing any better. And at least he didn't act like she'd lost her mind along with her head.

"The only demon I've pissed off is Rosier," she told him. "At least that I know of. But Pritkin said he wasn't going to be a problem anymore, and I haven't so much as heard a peep from him since—"

"No!" Casanova slashed a hand through the air. "What you did. Why aren't we dead?"

Cassie started to point out that one of them was, but saw his expression and decided against it. "I didn't do anything," she told him honestly. "I didn't have time. I saw Pritkin jumping at me with that look on his face and screaming and I knew something was about to hit the fan, but—"

"You must have done something," Casanova said nastily. "Unless you have a fairy godmother hiding in the wings."

"No, the fey pretty much want me dead, too. At least some of them."

Casanova put a hand to his forehead and left it there for a long moment. "Any second now," he finally said, his voice very calm, "a group of Alû is going to come through that door and kill us. Again. Before that happens, I would like very much to know that I will continue to come back until we figure this out. I need you to concentrate and tell me what you did."

Cassie looked at him soberly and spoke in the same measured tone he had used. "I didn't do any—"

"I want to know!" Casanova screamed.

"So do I! Only I don't have anyone to ask," Cassie snapped, before remembering that she did. A heavy fist landed on the door. "If we come back again," she told him as it blew open. "I need to make a phone call."

Chapter Seven

An open door flooded the street with orange light, turning the shadows shades of umber and gray. One of the lampades, a type of minor demon the Greeks had called the nymphs of the Underworld, lounged in the doorway. The light added an incongruous halo to her long dark hair and shone through the diaphanous slip she was wearing, highlighting the curves beneath.

She looked bored until her sloe-eyed gaze fell on him, and then she smiled beguilingly. It might have made more of an impression if her eyes hadn't stayed dead. John went over anyway.

"I'm looking for someone," he told the girl, without preamble.

The ruby lips curved a bit more. "Of course, you are. Everyone who comes here is."

"Someone in particular."

"Naturally. Or why not slake your lust with a human?"

"You don't understand—"

"But I do." Soft little hands slipped under his coat, smoothing over bare skin. The edge of a nail scraped over a nipple, sending a frisson hurtling down his spine. He started to push her away, but she held on, her hands curving around his biceps. "I felt it from across the street. The hunger, the anger, the *pain*. But I can help with that."

"Save the speeches," he said harshly. "I want—"

"I know what you want." And in an instant, the dark hair faded, shortened, curled. The figure altered as well, becoming suddenly more voluptuous, more fragile, more recognizable under his hands. "I know what you need," she murmured, her lips pressing where her hands could no longer go.

And when she looked up, her eyes had gone a perfect, cloudless blue, with that guileless expression that said she'd been up to something. John went stock still; even the voice had changed. From the scent of the citrus bath wash she used to the feel of her body under his hands, it was all familiar, all known, all *Cassie*.

One glimpse of her and everything came rushing back, hitting with a rawness that made it all new again. He'd worked so hard to protect her, to teach her how to protect herself. Yet all the while, an icy knot of fear had clenched in his gut, because he knew it might not be enough. He knew the kind of things that stalked her.

And it had played out exactly as he feared, almost as if pulled from one of his own nightmares. All his training, all the meticulous plans and preparations, had been useless when it counted. The knowledge of his failure writhed through him, the pain more shocking, more intimate, than the deepest wound carved into his flesh.

"Shhh," she murmured, and he must have released her, because those small hands suddenly closed around his face. "It's all right. I'm here now. I'm fine."

With her words, something cold in his chest uncurled at last, bright relief slumping his shoulders. He felt a moment of calm, of peace, cocooned in drifting warmth. "You came back." His thoughts were slow, sluggish, but that one came through with crystal clarity.

"I always do."

His forehead wrinkled. That wasn't what he wanted to hear. He wanted "I always will," he wanted promises she couldn't make, he wanted certainty. What he received were lips against his throat, feathery-soft, a tongue that licked the salt of his sweat away, and hands that branded their touch into his flesh.

His arms clenched fiercely around her, reassuring himself that she was solid, real. Their lips met in a kiss that melted down his spine and coiled in his gut, but it wasn't the passion that undid him. It was the breath in his mouth, the feel of that small heartbeat against his, the knowledge that she was alive and that it had all been just another nightmare . . .

And then the warm lips suddenly fastened onto his with the hunger of a leech, the wet tongue probing further than it should have been able to reach, further than a human organ could go. And suddenly it didn't feel like it was probing into his flesh, but into his soul. He could feel each heart-deep tug as she ripped part of him away, and he was gasping on a voiceless scream in seconds. It felt like being flayed alive, like his soul was being skinned away in flinching strips.

Which is exactly what was happening, he vaguely realized. She was peeling his spirit out of his body in great bloody rents, and yet he couldn't reach his weapons, couldn't fight, couldn't move. Until his bad leg suddenly gave out.

His knee hit the sidewalk, hard enough to shoot a spike of agony through his body—and to shatter the spell. When he looked up, there was no Cassie, no lampade. Instead, a creature with a snarled mass of magenta-red hair stood over him, watching him hungrily. He'd seen wolves with that very expression, godless and cold, completely devoid of even the concept of mercy.

Just a narrow-eyed watchfulness as they sized him up for the kill.

"Well, shit," she said, as he scrambled away, getting the brick wall of the building at his back. Not that he trusted it; not that he trusted a god damned thing here.

The creature facing him pulled a pack of cigarettes out of her rat's nest hair. She lit up, leaning against the wall before taking her first drag. "So, you want to do business, or what?"

"Rakshasa," he spat, as he held himself upright with an effort of will.

She looked down at her blood-streaked form, naked except for the usual necklace and a belt. In the habit of her kind, the necklace was strung with trophies she'd taken from her victims—tufts of hair, small finger bones, and what looked like a withered tongue. The belt was worse.

Rakshasas were soul hunters, living off the life essence of others. This one had three tattered remnants hanging from a worn leather strap, the ghostly forms writhing gently as if in an unseen wind. They were so decayed that it was impossible to tell what kind of bodies they had once inhabited before she ripped them free. One still moaned softly, hopelessly.

She looked back up at him. "What gave it away?"

A killing fury leapt up white-hot inside him. He didn't go for a gun; they were useless against such creatures. But there were things on his potions belt that were far more effective. His fingers closed over one, itching to use it, even knowing that it would open him up to a retaliation he might not survive.

She noticed the movement and sneered. "You can't hurt me."

"We're not in the human world now. I assure you, I can."

"Yes, but then the pack will be on to you, and we wouldn't want that." Her free hand spread the gore over her body in what he assumed was supposed to be a sensual slide. It made his gorge rise. She sighed and dropped the act. "Look, you can't have the one you want, but you can have me. It's not a bad deal. I won't take that much—"

"You've taken enough!" He could feel the rents she had made in him, the coldness where there should have been warmth, the void where something he would never get back was missing.

She looked at him cynically, through a veil of smoke. "Will you miss it?"

"Will you miss yours?" he snarled.

"Never had one to worry about." She crushed the cigarette under her bare heel. "If you didn't come for the usual, why are you here?"

He dragged the back of his hand across his face, smearing the spattered blood that stained his skin. It was always the same, every time he came here, the taste of blood in his mouth, the scent of death in the air. He hated this place and everything in it.

But he hated his bastard of a father a little bit more.

Normally, it would not have been difficult to trace him. Incubi could feed from virtually anything that could feel human-like lust, but his father had high standards. There were only a few establishments he was likely to view as fit for his personal patronage.

KAREN CHANCE

But the higher-end houses were also frequented by the types Rosier would prefer to avoid just now, including some of his own nobles. And he was desperate enough not to be picky. That left John with block after block of low-rent brothels to check.

He had to narrow it down or he'd never find him in time.

"If you can read minds, you already know," he said harshly.

She lit another cigarette with nicotine-yellow fingers. "That's the problem with minds. They don't hold thoughts all nice and indexed. I just get flashes," she waved a hand tipped with long black nails. "Here and there."

He carefully did not think his father's name. Some bands of Rakshasas had entered into an alliance with him recently, and with John's luck, this would be one of them. "I need to find an incubus," he said instead. "He was badly drained in an accident and needs help."

He thought he'd phrased it in such a way that it might sound as if he wanted to assist him, but she wasn't fooled. "Plan to finish him off, huh?" She didn't look concerned.

"Where would he go?"

"I might have an idea, for a price." She bared her teeth at him.

"You've had your price—without permission. If you do not wish me to lodge a complaint with the guild . . ."

Of course, he couldn't go to the guild, not with a price on his head. But apparently, that was one thought she didn't pick up. "He won't be in one of the regular places," she said sourly, crushing out her second cigarette.

"How do you know?"

"Because they won't let him in. In that state, he's likely to drain somebody. If he's one of the higher ranked of his kind, maybe the whole damn house. They won't want him near the merchandise."

"Then where would he go?"

She smiled, her eyes flicking over him contemptuously. Then she decided it deserved better than that, and she laughed. And then she told him.

Chapter Eight

"So that's it," Cassie said, squatting in the darkness and clutching Casanova's cell phone. "I don't know what I did, but I must have done something because we've looped like six times now and nothing seems to help. Every hour and fourteen minutes—"

"—and twenty-nine seconds," Casanova added, poking her with his bony finger. As if a few seconds more or less mattered. But nitpicking the details seemed to be some kind of crutch for him.

Sad, Cassie thought, and ate more chocolate.

"Anyway, we loop. And my power doesn't work and Pritkin's run off somewhere and nobody but me and Casanova seem to remember what's happened! And before I can get Marco or anyone to *listen* those things show up and *kill* us all again and—"

"Cassie, calm down." The warm, composed tones on the other end of the phone were a balm to her frazzled nerves. "We'll sort this out. Give me a moment."

She waited, heart pounding, as the magical community's version of a president thought things over. Jonas Marsden was the second smartest man she knew when it came to magic—and her best hope considering that the absolute smartest had gone AWOL. If Jonas didn't know how to fix this—

Cassie shut down that line of thought fast. No, Jonas would know. Jonas knew everything. Of course, it would be exactly her luck if the first problem to stump him was the last one she ever had.

"What's he doing?" Casanova demanded.

"He's thinking."

"Well, tell him to think faster! If we run out of time we'll have to explain all this to him again and we'll never get anywhere."

"I'll get right on that," Cassie snapped, and pushed his elbow out of her ribs. They were in a janitorial closet on the sixteenth floor. It wasn't roomy or comfortable, but it had the huge advantage of being the one place they'd found so far that the Alû hadn't.

And a cleaning cart stocked with Godiva's didn't hurt.

"We've been working on freezing time," Jonas said thoughtfully. "It's arguably a Pythia's greatest weapon, and I wanted you to concentrate on it until you're comfortable."

"Which I'm not."

"Yes, but you've practiced that spell more than anything else you've done with your power, other than shifting. And in a time of crisis, we gravitate toward what is familiar."

"But I didn't freeze time, Jonas. I . . . looped it. And I didn't even know that was possible."

"It isn't. That is to say, there isn't a spell for it that I'm aware of. And I think it unlikely that you perfected an entirely new one on the spur of the moment."

"Then how do you explain this?" she asked, trying to sound calm and in control. In reality, she thought she might be going back into the screaming phase again, because she really wanted to yell the place down, or punch something, or—

She ate more chocolate.

"Do you recall what I told you about that particular spell?" Jonas asked. "About what it actually does?"

"You said it temporarily removes me and whoever I cast it on from the timeline."

"Yes. Everyone isn't really frozen around you; you simply aren't immersed in the time stream anymore, therefore it appears so. You are the one who is stationary, not them."

"Like an island in the middle of a creek."

"Yes, only now I fear you are in a whirlpool, endlessly circulating a single point in time, that of your death."

"Yes, but *why?*"

"You knew something was wrong, knew from John's expression that it was potentially catastrophic, but you didn't know what it was."

"Yes." Casanova was poking her again and tapping his watch. She was going to rip that finger off his body later, but for the moment, she refrained. It sounded like Jonas might be onto something.

"I believe you wanted to give yourself a chance to figure it out," he continued. "Consciously or unconsciously, you knew you needed more time."

"But time. Isn't. Frozen."

"Because you did not complete the spell. You began it, but you died before you finished."

Cassie frowned. "That can't be right. When a Pythia dies, her power goes to her successor. But mine is still here. I can't shift or do anything else with it, but it keeps on pulling us back."

"Exactly. You died, but your power did not go to another, because it was busy."

"Busy?"

"Trying to complete your last spell. That is why Pythias traditionally pass their power to a successor *before* they die, to prevent that sort of thing."

"I think I have a headache."

"Think about it like this," Jonas said, with that infinite patience she'd come to rely on. "You were dead. Taking your body back in time would have been useless—"

"Assuming it could have found anything to take," Casanova muttered.

"Your power therefore took *itself* back, to a time when you were alive and could complete your command. And when it reintegrated with you, you received the memories of what had happened."

"But I can't complete it!" Cassie said, feeling herself start to panic. "I told you, I can't do anything. The power just ignores me. I can feel it, but it won't—"

"If that were true, why do I also remember everything?" Casanova interrupted. "The power didn't "reintegrate" with me."

"In a way it did," Jonas argued. "You were pulled onto that island with her. And as to that, where were you when the bomb went off?"

"Coming down the hall towards the bedroom. I'd had to get permission from Marco to ask her High—to ask Cassie something. And it had held me up."

"And where was he?"

"Right behind me. Why?"

Jonas didn't answer. "Cassie, you said John is missing?"

She nodded, even though he couldn't hear it. "Casanova thinks he's in the demon realms, chasing Rosier."

"I beg your pardon?"

Casanova made an impatient sound and plucked the phone from her fingers. "Lord Rosier possessed the leader of Cassie's bodyguards," he said rapidly. "I would guess that was how he smuggled in the bomb, since it should have been caught long before it made it to her. And he must have also turned off the wards, because they haven't so much as hiccoughed all through this. In any case, Pritkin jumped what was left of Marco after the explosion and figured it out. Then he pursued Rosier to the demon realms when the bastard decamped."

Jonas was silent for a moment, absorbing this. "I didn't think it possible to possess a vampire," he finally said.

"Normally no, not without permission. But Rosier is a demon lord—considerably more powerful than most. And Marco nearly died in the last debacle around here. He was ordered to take a month off but instead of staying in bed, swilling vodka and smoking those horrid cigars of his, he insisted on coming back to work."

"His illness made him vulnerable, and Rosier took advantage," Jonas summarized.

"Essentially. But Rosier isn't here now; my incubus can detect him and she swears Marco is clean. And even weirder, the Alû weren't here before. The bomb caused the problem the first time, not those head-lopping maniacs! They didn't show up until Cassie dragged us back in time on the first loop."

"You're sure? Perhaps you merely did not notice them before then."

"I tend to pay attention when someone is trying to cut my head off!" Casanova said, a little shrilly.

"Yes," Jonas said. "Quite." And then, "I think I may have it."

"Have what?" Casanova asked, before Cassie snatched the phone back.

"You know what happened?" she asked. They were almost out of time, and there was no way of knowing if Jonas' epiphany would strike him again next go around.

"I know you said you cannot remember, Cassie," he said gently, "but it would be very helpful to know if you focused the spell on yourself . . . or if you perhaps left it open."

Cassie gripped the phone tighter. It was slick with sweat and kept threatening to shoot out of her palm like a bullet. "And if I did leave it open?"

"Your power might have thought you meant to include everyone in your vicinity."

"Meaning?"

"Everyone near you at the time." Casanova looked confused, but Cassie felt her stomach drop. This was starting to sound terribly familiar.

"When a spell doesn't conclude, there are usually only three possible causes," Jonas continued. "It was cast improperly, someone is blocking it, or an element is missing. We know the spell was cast properly, because it is working—repeatedly, in fact. And I do not see how anyone can be blocking you when no one else realizes you are looping. We are therefore left with the third option: something, or in this case, someone, is missing."

"Wait. Wait, wait, wait," Casanova said, catching up and stealing back the phone. "Are you telling me that the spell can't complete itself until that little prick gets back?"

"If you mean John, yes," Jonas said, sounding disapproving. "And Rosier, too. They were both in the vicinity when the spell was laid and are likely vital parts of it."

Casanova broke into a string of Spanish curses and Cassie grabbed the phone again. "But . . . if we keep going back in time, why isn't Pritkin here? He should be downstairs, buying me a donut, but he isn't. We've looked!"

"You aren't going back in time, Cassie," Jonas explained patiently. "Your power removed you from the regular time stream. You're on that island we discussed earlier. And without John's presence, you have no way off it."

"But *he* got off it!"

"Yes, by transitioning to the demon realms. And time doesn't function there the same way as here. They are like Faerie, with their own, separate time line. Therefore, when John entered the Shadowland, he left the island, removing him from the spell temporarily and causing the problem we have now."

"Great," Cassie grumbled, and felt around for another chocolate. Only to find out that she'd eaten them all. No wonder she felt queasy.

Well, that and the whole death thing.

"What about Marco?" Casanova demanded, wrestling back the phone. "If your theory is right, he should be looping along with the rest of us."

"It is an interesting question," Jonas agreed. "If a spell is cast on a possessed person, whom does it affect: the person or the spirit possessing him?"

"Both, obviously!"

"Ah, but magic is rarely obvious. It has its own rules; even when a spell is carefully thought out and rigorously tested, unexpected events can arise. And Cassie's spell was neither carefully planned nor perfectly executed. It wasn't even completed. Under the circumstances, it is possible that the spirit possessing Marco, in this case Lord Rosier, was caught in the spell instead of the body he was using. But, like John, he left for the demon realms shortly thereafter, and is thus unaffected—for now."

"For now?" Cassie asked.

"All right, all right, but what about the Alû?" Casanova persisted. "None of this explains why they're here."

"They are under the council's control, are they not?" Jonas asked. "And Rosier is a member of council. Perhaps he had them along as backup, as it were, in case something went wrong."

"Then why aren't they waiting for the big explosion? Instead of making mincemeat out of us?"

"Because something did go wrong," Jonas pointed out. "From their perspective, Rosier disappeared without warning, and John along with him. Perhaps they think John detected the demon's presence and attacked him. Perhaps they think that their master is dead, or that he fled to the demon realms with John in pursuit—which is, in fact, what happened. Either way, it would be enough to engage Plan B—"

"—with Plan B involving our heads on a platter!"

"Cassie is the target," Jonas demurred. "You're merely in the way. But otherwise, yes."

"In the way?" Casanova blinked. "You mean . . . if I get away from her, I'm not going *to die every five minutes*?"

"Every one hour and fourteen minutes."

"And twenty-nine seconds," Casanova added automatically. And then he grinned, huge and euphoric. "Who cares? It doesn't matter anymore!"

"I am afraid it does, old boy," Jonas said grimly, as Cassie wrenched back the phone.

"So you're saying what? We just have to wait for Pritkin to get back?" she asked hopefully.

"No, that is what we cannot do. At the moment, John is outside the spell. But once he returns to this time stream, he will be caught in the same loop as everyone else who was in that room—unless he returns with Lord Rosier. Only once all components are back in place will you be able to access your power and end the spell."

"Then we have to go get him," Cassie said. The Shadowland wasn't her favorite place, but right now, it was looking pretty damned good.

"There is no 'we'," Jonas said, his voice sharpening. "Once you leave the loop, the protection it offers is left behind as well. If you die outside this time stream, you will stay dead. As bad as it may seem, you are better off where you are. Casanova can go."

The vampire in question was halfway to the door at this point, but supernatural hearing had him whirling in outrage, nonetheless. "Casanova can do no such thing! I had nothing to do with any of this!"

"Perhaps not," Jonas agreed. "But you are involved now, trapped on that island along with Cassie, in a hotel filled with homicidal demons. And you will remain there until you retrieve your missing pieces, and their corpses will not do. You need them in the same shape they were in when the spell was cast. If either succeeds in killing the other before you reach them, the spell will never complete itself."

"And we'll be stuck," Cassie said numbly. "We'll be stuck here forever."

Chapter Nine

Well. It looked like he'd finally found the right place, John thought, as a familiar blond came crashing through the door in front of him, staggered out into the street, and hit a wall on the other side. Hard.

John smiled.

He'd already been in ten of these dumps tonight, looking for Rosier in the last places anyone would expect to find him. He'd begun to think the Rakshasa had been playing him, as he checked off possibly venues, one after the other. He'd left this street for last, since it was considered beyond the pale even by the kind of places that knifed you in the side for a hello. He'd assumed his father had better taste.

He should have known better.

He started forward, but before he'd taken two steps, something else came out of the door. It was huge, yet moved in a blur of speed that left it little more than a pale smudge against the night. Until it grabbed their mutual prey by the throat.

"Unhand me this instant, you cretin," Rosier spat, a lock of the pale hair he wore longer than John's falling into enraged green eyes. "How dare you put a hand on a member of council!"

The creature—a ten-foot-tall demon of a type John didn't recognize, but which looked alarmingly like a huge, yellowish snake—did not seem impressed. "You pay," it rumbled, twining the end of a tale as thick as a wrestler's torso around Rosier's legs.

"I've already told you. I didn't remember to bring my purse. I was in a bit of a hurry!" Rosier said scathingly. "Now release me, and I'll send someone back with—"

That was as far as he got, before the creature flicked the tale, throwing Rosier off his feet, and then slamming him face-first into the wall again. It looked like the bouncer didn't believe him, John thought idly. Or maybe it just didn't understand the language.

Not too surprising around here, where half the denizens probably weren't even literate in whatever tongue they called their own. The brothel seemed to bear this out, lacking even a name over the door. Of course, that would have been hard, since it didn't have a door anymore, either. What it did have was a hole in an old brick wall, a straw-strewn, dirt-floored room on the other side, a rickety-looking set of stairs, and a pungent mix of grime, sweat and sex.

Charming, John thought. Right before he was grabbed from behind.

"Hello, handsssome." The sibilant voice went with the off-white, scaly flesh on the hand that slipped onto his shoulder. And then splayed on his chest. "Niccce," was hissed—literally—in his ear.

John turned his head to see a body that matched the hand—vaguely humanoid, with an impressive set of curves, most of which were currently on display. But they weren't compensating for the slit of a nose, the hairless, reptilian head or the black, forked tongue that slithered out to graze his cheek. He managed not to shudder—just.

"Looking for something in particular?" The madam asked.

"Found it," John said, watching Rosier peel himself off the grimy wall.

The madam looked back and forth between John and his doppelgänger, and then she smiled. "We could possibly make that happen," she offered.

"Oh, yes?"

"He owes a debt," she confirmed. "Came in here not two hours ago and drained half my girls. And then demanded the other half!"

"And, of course, you demanded payment first."

A scaly shoulder raised in a shrug. "Naturally. The girls he finished with won't be any use for days. I couldn't have the rest in the same condition, not without more than a councilor's promise." She hissed the last contemptuously; apparently, people around here had about the same respect for the council that John did.

"And now you want him to wash dishes to pay for his supper," he guessed.

The madam didn't look like she understood that, but she didn't get a chance to answer anyway. Because Rosier had spotted him. "Emrys," he gasped, hitting the ground again.

He was dressed in a suit that a self-respecting bum wouldn't have worn, with frayed lapels, a dirty shirt and holes over the knees. Like the rest of the city, it was an approximation, designed to go with the mental image his brain had settled on for the evening's activities. But the fact remained: he was looking rough. Yet his usual air of faint disgruntlement, caused by a world that inexplicably failed to acknowledge his greatness, remained.

The madam said something to the bouncer, who had started toward the deadbeat again. Didn't want to damage the merchandise if there was a potential buyer on hand, John assumed, as his father started crawling over the stones toward him. "Emrys! What are you doing here?"

"Accepting your invitation."

"What? What invitation? Have you gone mad?"

"Possibly," John growled, wondering if he should just let the snake finish him.

It was alarmingly tempting.

"Oh, never mind that now," Rosier said peevishly, flailing about in a puddle. "Help me up! We have to—"

"How much?" John asked, glancing at the madam. Because if he looked at his father for another second, he was going to simply walk away. And that wouldn't do.

That would be too easy.

She named a figure and John snorted. "He's not worth that."

"Stop messing about!" Rosier demanded, tugging his now quite filthy trouser leg off of whatever it had snagged on. "Pay the creature what she wants and let's get out of here! You have no idea what I've been through!"

John felt his fists clench involuntarily, and closed his eyes. He needed to remain in control, or this would be over far too soon, and he couldn't afford that. He wanted some answers first. He wanted—

"How much to finish him for you?" he rasped.

"What? What are you talking about?" Rosier squawked.

"You think I'm a fool?" John opened his eyes to find the madam looking at him contemptuously. "You're an incubus, too. Think I can't feel it? You pay me a fraction of what he owes and then drag him off, saying you'll finish him, only to set him free! Then where will I be?"

"Good point," John said, turning to look at Rosier. Who had opened his mouth, to make another demand no doubt. Until something in his son's face caused him to shut it abruptly.

"Emyrs?" he asked, unsteadily this time.

"What about if I do it here?" John asked softly.

*   *   *

"Augghhh!" Casanova breathed, trying to push his body into the scant cover afforded by a crack in a wall.

That didn't work very well, even though the "wall" gave slightly in a way that real brick never did, hugging his back like warm pizza dough. He tried to not think about it, which turned out to be astonishingly simple. Maybe because what mind he had left was focused on the writhing mass of huge warriors just down the street.

They were standing at a junction where five roads met, where he'd desperately tried to lose them a few moments before. He didn't know what they used for senses, but sight didn't seem to be foremost. They reminded him more of bloodhounds on the scent—or at least he hoped so.

On Rian's advice, he'd run up and down every street before choosing this one, leaving multiple, overlapping scent trails. Of course, the idea had been to be gone before they came across his sensory snarl, but he'd been too thorough or they'd been too fast and now he was caught.

Like a rat in a trap, he thought, too panicked to be original while watching them poke into every nook and cranny.

It's all right, he told himself. He had super senses, too, but they didn't work so well in the Shadowland, where smells seemed as malleable as everything else in this not-quite-real landscape. Maybe the trails he'd laid would be enough to—

His brain froze as they suddenly stopped, all at the same time, some halfway through a step. And slowly turned as one being. And looked right at him.

His eyes closed and his chest seized up, trying to hold a breath he hadn't taken. He was in a shadow, but he never for a moment thought it would be good enough. He braced for the worst, since it wasn't like he didn't know what was coming.

Only this time, there was no reset button.

This time, he wouldn't be coming back.

He thought about running, but he couldn't seem to move and anyway, he'd already tried that. Though a maze of narrow, dirty streets with high walls, shuttered shops, and swinging oil lamps shedding puddles of light Casanova didn't need across the gloom. It only added to the insanity since, for some reason, his brain had settled on medieval Rome for this trip, despite the fact that he'd obviously never been there.

"My bad," Rian admitted, her voice a whisper through his mind. "It's the Great Market. It always reminds me . . ."

"Shut up!" he hissed, and then they were on him.

He might have whimpered slightly as the mob surged into the confines of the alley, so closely packed that their scabbards scraped along the narrow walls. But his spine stiffened as he felt their approach, and his chin came up. He was the scion of an ancient house; he would die as one. Alright, not like that bastard of a father of his, God rot his soul, but he'd been a terrible drunk so Casanova didn't know what anyone had expected. But he'd be goddamned if he went cowering like a little—

Oh. Oh, God, he thought, as he felt them surround him on all sides.

There was a wash of heat from the torches they carried in the hands that weren't busy with those scimitar-like swords. One of which was placed under his chin a moment later, forcing his head up even more. His eyes flew open involuntarily, and he found himself face-to-face with one of the warriors. Or rather, face-to-polished-bronze-faceplate, because he could finally see that there was nothing behind it.

Nothing at all.

What was it Nietzsche had said? he thought dizzily. Some warning about looking into the abyss and having the abyss look back, although why he cared he didn't know. Who took life advice from a man who died penniless in an insane asylum? That had never made sense to Casanova, who'd always had far loftier goals.

Although he didn't suppose it mattered now.

Now, all his hopes, wishes and dreams had coalesced down to just one thing: managing not to soil himself before he died again. Although they really needed to hurry up with it or he was going to be denied even that small—

He blinked, because suddenly the sword was withdrawn. And the Alû were on the move again, the wind of their passing ruffling his hair, the light from their torches splashing his face, the rough wool of their tunics brushing the fine linen of his jacket. As they just kept going.

It took him a second to realize that they weren't attacking, weren't breaking stride, weren't so much as looking his way again, if 'look' was the appropriate word with nothing in the place of eyes. Just more of those creepy face plates, leaping with flames from the torch light, heartstoppingly dreadful if he'd still had a heartbeat.

And it felt like he did. It felt like it was in his throat as they pounded past, iron tipped boots ringing off of stones half buried in the muck. Until they were gone, as suddenly as they'd come, the sound of their feet almost immediately muffled by the height and thickness of the surrounding walls.

Abruptly, the alley returned to darkness, to silence, to calm. And Casanova sank down onto all fours on the cold stones, hands shaking, chest hurting. And wondering if he needed new trousers.

"I think they're all right," Rian said quietly, appearing like a lovely vision in front of him. She was suspiciously blank-faced, which could mean a lot of things, but which usually meant—

"If you laugh," he told her shakily. "So help me . . ."

"I assure you, I don't find this to be funny." A frown appeared on the lovely forehead as she stared after the Alû. "Something is wrong."

"Wrong?" Casanova quavered, trying for heat but mostly managing a breathless sort of wonder. "We're alive! I'd say something is very right!"

"We're alive because they weren't after us," Rian countered. "If you had not run, they might not have chased you at all."

"Well, forgive me for panicking a little," Casanova said, regaining some of his indignation. "When suddenly confronted by a group of the things that just killed me half a dozen times!"

"I was not assigning blame, simply offering an explanation," she said mildly. "But they are looking for someone. I've never seen so many of the council's guards deployed at one time before."

"One guess as to who the target is," Casanova muttered, struggling to get back to his feet. Trust the damned mage to already have the whole guard after him. Like his father, he seemed to attract trouble.

Rian didn't comment, but her lips tightened. And her eyes got that faraway look that meant she was communicating with one of her own kind. "It's worse than that," she told him, after a moment.

"How does that work?" Casanova asked, honestly bewildered.

"He's found Rosier."

Chapter Ten

"You raving lunatic!" Rosier said, diving for cover behind a stack of trash cans.

They smelled foul, but not as much as when John sent a fireball into them, causing a burning wash of overripe fruit, spoiled meat and who knew what else to cascade across the already filthy alley. It also tipped a crate of empty bottles over onto its side. Mostly empty, John amended, as the superheated remains of whatever poison the locals imbibed blew out the sides of their receptacles like a line of firecrackers going off. And imbedded most of their remains into Rosier's shins.

"Son of a bitch!" he snarled, glaring from his bloody calves to John. "What the hell is the matter with you? I took an oath, remember?"

"After you posted the bomb that killed her," John snarled back.

"Don't be ridiculous!" his father told him, right before throwing a spell so bright, it looked like a flare had gone off in the alley.

John managed to get a shield up in time, but was nonetheless blown off his feet by the impact and back several yards. He flipped and jumped back up—and then had to throw himself down again as the deflected spell hit the side of the brothel. A blast of old bricks and mortar shrapnelled the alley, and the madam cursed.

"Hey! Hey, you gonna pay for that!"

But John wasn't listening. He was too busy hugging the ground to avoid the trash can lids, which had flown up in defiance of gravity and sailed at his head. They came out of the dust cloud like so many burning UFOs, but mostly missed him, skimming by overhead. And his shields deflected the ones that didn't.

Right into the group of bouncers, who had just muscled their way out of the brothel.

"Well, shit," Rosier said, staring at them. And then at John. "Look what you did!" he said accusingly.

John didn't answer, being occupied evading the huge tail that had just lashed out at him, lightening quick, and threatened decapitation with a single stroke. And then the odd shaped spear that came crashing down onto the stones, striking sparks off where his body had just been. And then the screaming mass of girls and their clients who started pouring through the now defunct wall, desperate to get away.

"No, no, no!" the madam yelled, wading into the fray and trying to direct her people. "They pay first. They pay first!"

John saw an opening and jumped onto the back of the nearest spear carrier, who was bent over trying to pull his weapon out of the pavement, and from there to the top of the Dumpster. His knee almost gave way again, but he managed a flying leap off the other side, tackling the slimy bastard who was trying to use the confusion as a cover for a quick retreat. And who didn't make it.

"Get off me!" Rosier snarled, rolling over and trying to smash him the face with a boot.

John returned the favor by throwing him into the wall, which turned out to be lucky for more than one reason. It shut his father up momentarily, and allowed them both to roll behind the Dumpster and avoid the fight that had erupted between the bouncers and some of the patrons. The bouncers were bigger and better armed, but the patrons were more numerous and determined not to pay for a truncated good time. The alley was fast turning into a war zone.

And that included his makeshift bolt-hole, where John found himself hit with a paralysis spell.

It didn't take completely, his shields still being up. But it left him sluggish and caused the knife he'd been planning to put through his father's eye to hit the wall instead. It stuck in some of the old mortar, and his wrist was captured in an iron grip before he could yank it back out.

"Listen to me!" Rosier hissed. "I haven't harmed that annoying child. I don't know what's going on, but you have to believe—"

John stopped his lying mouth with a fist.

He would have followed up the advantage, but a man with trousers around his ankles kicked him in the head on his way past, and then tripped and staggered into the nearest bouncer. Who sent him flying into the Dumpster with one arm, and in the process spied the two people hiding behind it. Bugger!

John threw a spell that stopped the creature's spear all of a foot from his face, and then reversed it, sending it back into the huge, thrashing tail. It pinned its owner to the ground momentarily, and before he could wrench free, he was jumped by a bunch of disgruntled patrons. John didn't wait around to see who won, but dragged his bastard of a father inside the brothel and slammed him against the wall.

"Are you a fool?" Rosier demanded wildly. "Why would I go after her again? What could it possibly gain me?"

That made John pause for an instant, since Rosier was entirely self-serving. It was his most defining characteristic. "She almost killed you once."

"You've almost killed me half a dozen times," was the angry response. "And yet you're still alive. And she also saved my life, if you'll recall. I believe that makes us even."

"The council hates her. You said so yourself!"

"Yes, and they'd love a replacement. Someone more . . . sane. But they recognize that she did them a favor, and they're willing to wait and see."

"You lie!"

"Why? In the name of whatever you hold holy, why would I want to have anything to do with that walking time bomb? Every time I get near her, this," he waved an arm wildly. "This is how I end up."

"If you didn't try to kill her, why are you injured?"

"Because you just slung me around an alley for five minutes?"

"Don't give me that! You were hurt before! Why else would you be here?" John gestured around at the bare, unpainted walls, the chandelier composed of a dozen strings of bare bulbs knotted together, and the graffiti-covered bar. Even for hell, the place was a pit.

"You'd know why," Rosier said heatedly. "If you'd bothered to go by my court before trying to kill me!"

"And what would I know?"

"That it isn't there anymore! It was firebombed a few hours ago by the damned Alû. And no, I don't know why. I was rather more concerned with getting out alive, and then eluding a few of my loyal servants, who decided to see the disaster as an opportunity for promotion! I barely managed to make it here alive."

John stared at him, his head reeling, and not just because of the kick. Rosier sounded sincere, but of course that meant sod all. Like most of his kind, he had elevated lying to an art form. One he had long ago perfected.

John wanted to end him. He'd rarely wanted anything more. His head hurt; his leg throbbed with every heartbeat; but neither was anything close to the pain of knowing how badly he'd failed. Cassie's death was his fault as much as his father's, and it burned like brimstone in his gut.

"Emrys, listen—"

But John wasn't. The image of another young woman he'd cared about, and also utterly failed, rose up in front of his eyes. And it was suddenly all he could see, her screams all he could hear.

"You expect me to believe that someone attacked you," he rasped. "At the exact moment that Dante's was also being hit? You actually expect me to *believe that*?"

"I expect you to use your head," Rosier said, eyes flickering oddly. "Cassie has enemies; I have enemies. But we only have one enemy. Damn it, boy! I taught you better than this! Stop wallowing in sentiment and *think*."

But John couldn't. He heard the creature's words, but the meaning hit the old well of anguish and self-hate and seething, simmering resentment he carried around like a weight. One that, right now, was threatening to crush him. He needed to throw it off, but the rage that had been building since he found that cracked and ruined necklace rose up with irresistible force.

And swamped him.

"You lie!" he breathed, and readied the spell that would end this. Finally, utterly—

And had a blinding pain shoot through his head, hard enough to drop him to his knees.

"Cut it a little closer next time, why don't you?" he heard his father snarl at someone behind him.

And then nothing.

Chapter Eleven

"He's coming around," a woman said.

"Where is it?" a man's voice demanded sharply.

"I don't . . . give me a second," another man said, sounding distracted.

"Damn it! Why don't you have it ready?"

"Well, don't blame me! He has the hardest head in existence. He should have been out longer than this."

"You're lucky he had the shield up, or he would be out permanently. And then I would be forced to gut you. Now give it to me!"

John opened his eyes to see something dangling in front of his face. It was gold and red, and glinting in the low light of a bare bulb overhead. And cold like everything in the Shadowland when it grazed his cheek. It was also hauntingly familiar. He tried to raise a hand to grasp it, but nothing seemed to happen.

"Give it a moment. The vampire almost took your head off," someone told him.

John didn't think he had much choice. The combination of two head knocks in a row on top of blood loss, a soul hit, and a stun spell had him swimming around in the realm of the barely conscious. But after a few seconds, his flailing hand managed to bump into the prize, and it swung closer to his face. Just about the time his eyes uncrossed.

And saw the impossible.

"It's a trick," he rasped, after a stunned second, and someone sighed.

John focused on Rian, in the form of a hazy outline of a beautiful woman. She was standing to the left of the bed he appeared to be lying on. It was Spartan and roughly twin-sized, and barely fit a tiny closet of a bedroom. One of the brothel's, he assumed, judging by the smell. And if Rian was here—

"I told you so." Casanova's scowling form came into focus on the other side of the bed, standing in front of a small window. He wasn't dangling anything, though, and neither was Rian. Which meant—

"Hold him!" Rosier's voice said sharply, as John tried surging up. But Casanova had his arms, holding him down as Rosier shoved what John now identified as a gaudy necklace with a dull red center stone at him. "It's real," he said urgently. "Test it for yourself. The vampire brought it."

"It's true, John," Rian chimed in, loyal as ever to the creature who'd spawned her.

"You lie!" John said, struggling against the vampire's strength. "I saw the real one. It was broken, cracked, ruined—"

"That was only the first time," Casanova said, and then glared as John got in a good shot to the jaw.

Some of the fog in John's head seemed to clear, as the vampire's words penetrated. "What first time?" he panted. "What are you talking about?"

"If you'll cease trying to murder everyone, we'll explain," his father said dryly, coming into view on Rian's side of the bed.

He looked slightly more beaten up than before, with a dirty face, a puffy jaw and two black eyes that ran together, like a superhero mask. But otherwise, he was right as rain. John growled.

"Oh, come off it," Rosier said, sitting on the bed, and tossing the necklace onto John's chest. "What? Did I pull that out of my ass?"

"Bet it wouldn't be the first time," Casanova muttered, as John closed his hand on it.

There was no way to tell if it was real. It looked the same, but of course it would. Rosier had seen Cassie's talisman more than once. Despite what he claimed, for someone of his skill, reproducing it would be easy.

"We don't have time for this," Rian warned, glancing out the window.

"Do you have an alternative?" Rosier asked. "We can't drag him through the streets unwilling, and we can't transition in the heart of the city."

"It wouldn't do us any good if we could," Casanova muttered. "The damned casino is full of Alû, too."

Rian looked at John, her pretty face worried. "Your father is telling the truth; we brought the stone, Carlos and I. Your Pythia put it in his hands herself. She said it would convince you. Was she wrong?"

"You do yourself no credit, Rian," John sneered. "I know what I saw!"

"And you saw truly. But you did not see all."

"Oh for—just tell him already!" Casanova said, breaking in. And then he did it for her. "Cassie did something at the last second, some kind of spell. It stuck us in a time loop with everything repeating every hour and fourteen minutes and twenty-nine seconds, including the bunch of maniac Alû going around collecting heads! We finally found a hiding spot they mostly overlooked and Marsden said—"

"Jonas?" John frowned. He wouldn't have expected them to bring him into their lie. "What does he have to do with this? And why would the Alû—"

"I'll tell you if you shut up!" Casanova said, a little wildly. John belatedly noticed that the vampire was looking almost worse than Rosier. His jacket was missing, his hair was covered in dust, and his face and shirt were filthy. And there was an odd odor clinging to—

Rian cleared the throat she didn't have.

"It comes down to this," she told him quickly. "Lady Cassandra is trapped in a time loop made of her own power. The only way for her to be free is to complete the spell. But she can only do that if all the people on whom it was inadvertently cast are once more assembled."

"What people?" John asked.

"The ones in the damned room with her at the time," Casanova said. "That's why her Loftiness dispatched me to hell, in order to find you and whoever was possessing Marco—"

"That's easily done," John said, grabbing his father by the shirt front.

"It is no such thing," Rosier said testily. "Let us try this again, and do see if that vaunted intelligence of yours can grasp this one simple concept, would you? *I. Was. Not. There.*"

"Then who was?"

"Sid, presumably."

"Sid?" John stared at him in disgust.

"Think about it. Who thwarted his well-laid plans to destroy the council, and half the city along with it? I did, with some help from you and the girl. And, of course, he wants revenge."

John didn't bother commenting that, as usual, his father had managed to make himself the hero of the piece when he'd actually been a villain. Instead, he concentrated on the more relevant point. "If he so much as shows his nose here, he's dead. How—"

"But he didn't show it, did he?" Rosier asked. "He's likely been on Earth, feeding up and plotting revenge. And somewhere along the line, he realized that he couldn't pick us off one by one without the others getting suspicious. If he killed me, you'd know something was up, and vice versa. Therefore, he decided to take us all at once."

"But he didn't take us," John gritted out. "The bomb was meant for Cassie—"

"And in the process, Sid no doubt hoped that you would die as well. But he couldn't be sure that she would open the bomb in your presence, therefore he took back up."

"In the form of the council's own guards?" John looked at him incredulously. "Where did he get them?"

"From the council. He was pretending to be me, after all."

"How could he possibly—"

"He's an old adherent of our house," Rosier reminded him. "It wouldn't be difficult for someone who has known me for a few thousand years to impersonate me convincingly."

"Except that no one goes around impersonating council members!"

"Which is likely how he got away with it. It would be a death sentence if caught, so as you say, nobody does it. But what if someone doesn't care if he's caught? What if all he really cares about anymore is revenge?"

Casanova shook his head. "If the Alû believed Sid to be you, then they're your allies. Why turn on you?"

"Turn on you?" John demanded. "What—"

"They're asking the locals about both of you," Rian confirmed. "Searching the streets around us right now."

"What? Why? They just went with him," John hiked a thumb at his father, "to help kill Cassie!"

"We've discussed this before," Rosier said, slipping back into the lecture mode that John especially hated. "Not all creatures think like you do. Your viewpoint isn't the only viewpoint; your logic isn't the only logic."

"Then what is Alû logic?"

"To do the will of the council. And a council member had told them to come along on the assassination of a known threat." He shrugged. "They went."

"But you had taken an oath—*on* the council itself—not to hurt Cassie!"

"Yes, but that was my look to, wasn't it?" Rosier asked, as if that were obvious. "It wasn't up to them to keep my oath for me. If I broke it, they would kill me, certainly, as the vow demanded. But until then, I was perfectly within my rights to require their assistance."

"But they didn't kill you—or Sid or whomever—"

"Because he disappeared. Which is when they communicated with their counterparts here, instructing them to attack my court."

John blinked, because that made an insane sort of sense. "Because you were then viewed as a traitor for breaking your oath."

"It has a certain beauty to it," Rosier said admiringly. "Sid assumed the bomb would take out the girl, but if not, the Alû would. He probably hoped the explosion would also kill you, and that the forces he'd prepped in the Shadowland would kill me, making for a nice, tidy operation. But he had an alternative plan, in case that didn't happen."

"To make me believe that it was all your doing." John was beginning to see where his father was going with this.

Rosier nodded. "At which point, you could be relied on to do exactly what you did, and come after me in a murderous rage. Thereby ensuring that you broke *your* oath not to enter the demon realms without the council's express permission, and forfeited your life in the process."

"He thought that I would kill you if the Alû failed, and that they would then end me," John said, fist clenching around Cassie's talisman.

Rosier nodded. "He planned this perfectly, with layer upon layer of assurance that, no matter what we did, we ended up dead."

"But we didn't. Cassie lives, and so do we! He failed."

"Yes, well. That remains to be seen," Rosier said dryly. "The problem is to get him to show himself. We need him, and not only to break the spell. We have to—"

Casanova cut him off with a curse. "Details can wait! Rian already told you—we don't have time for this. The Alû are everywhere in the streets below—to the point that we barely made it through. And there's more of them now than before!"

"They're searching every house," Rian acknowledged. "They aren't familiar with this area—no one who lives here is usually important enough to come to the council's notice—but they learn quickly."

"And too many people saw that display you two put on," Casanova added. "Someone's bound to turn us in. I'm surprised they haven't done it already."

"The Alû aren't popular," Rosier said grimly. "But it doesn't matter; they'll find us soon enough, and I can't hold them off in the shape I'm in. I expended what little energy I had left in the fight—"

"You're an incubus," Casanova said impatiently. "In a *brothel*! Feed, for the love of—"

"Now, why didn't I think of what?" Rosier asked sweetly.

"It wouldn't be sufficient, Carlos," Rian told him. "The Master was almost drained by the wounds he sustained at court. He needs a proper feeding, more than any of the workers here could provide, even if we could find them again . . ."

"Then what about you?" Casanova asked. "Can't you loan him enough—"

She shook her head sadly. "I do not have a body on which to draw. And a spirit feeding will not be enough."

"No," Rosier mused. "I need to feed from a body, but a normal one won't do. This calls for someone old, rich, powerful. Someone who has been storing up energy for centuries. Someone like . . ."

He suddenly looked up, and met John and Rian's eyes. And then they all turned to look at the vampire. Who was still staring worriedly out the window.

"And how are we supposed to find someone like that around here?" Casanova demanded.

Rosier smiled gently. "I may have an idea."

Chapter Twelve

"I hate you," Casanova said weakly, grasping hold of a roof tile.

"Which one?" Pritkin asked, grabbing his forearms. And hauling him roughly onto the roof.

"All of you," Casanova gasped. "Every single . . . damned one . . . of your hateful, misbegotten clan!"

"You're part of that clan," a loathed voice reminded him. He turned his head to see Rosier—God damn him—vault up from the room below like an Olympic gymnast.

And why not? That was his power the bastard was using. Almost all of his power, judging by the way he felt. Casanova groaned and rolled over, wishing he still ate so that he could throw up.

"Don't be such a drama queen," Rosier said, clapping him on the shoulder.

"Pudrete en el infierno!"

"Too late."

Rian came up and slipped a cool hand onto his shoulder, but wisely didn't attempt anything else. He'd had about enough of incubi for the moment. He'd had more than enough.

"Well, that's less than encouraging," Rosier said, after a moment, and his tone caused Casanova's head to come up.

"What is?" he demanded.

But nobody was paying him any attention. They were all staring over the edge of the roof, including Rian. She'd moved from his side to peer between Rosier and his spawn's shoulders. "Oh, dear."

"What?" he asked again.

And was again ignored.

"Hijueputa," he muttered, dragging his exhausted body up and over to the edge, which was crumbling like the rest of the building, and didn't sport anything like a proper guardrail. Casanova scowled. He hated heights.

Especially ones looking out over torch-wielding mobs.

"What the—what is that?" he demanded, grabbing Rosier's shoulder so the bastard couldn't avoid answering him this time.

"What does it look like?" Rosier turned to Pritkin. "Any ideas?"

"Yes," Pritkin said shortly, and wandered off somewhere, making some weird kind of trill.

They were all mad, Casanova decided. Every damned one of them. "If someone doesn't tell me what the hell—" he began dangerously.

"It's the locals," Rian said. "It seems the madam has convinced them that the disturbances in the area are all to be laid at our door."

"Which in fairness—" Rosier began.

"Shut up!" Casanova snarled. He turned back to Rian. "We have to get rid of them. They'll lead the damned Alû right to us!"

"I think it's a little late for that," she said softly, staring down at the street.

It was a long one, running the length of this sordid little part of hell, but something seemed to be going on near the end of it. Something that resolved into a bronze-colored wedge driving through the crowd like a bulldozer, or like the cow catchers on the front of old trains. A hateful, murderous train that was going to kill them all, Casanova thought blankly. There had to be a hundred of the council's damned guards down there.

"One hundred thirteen," Rian supplied unhelpfully.

"Do something!" he told Rosier.

But the demon—damn his hide—was just standing there, lighting a cigarette. "And what would you have me do?"

"You're a council member!"

"Yes, and I would normally call on that body's guards to protect me." His lips twisted. "Unfortunately, they're already here."

"Then . . . then use magic! Do some sort of a curse. You're a demon!"

"I'm one demon. They are many demons. See how that works?"

"Then why the—what was all—why did we—" Casanova spluttered.

Rosier let out a smoky breath. "At the time, I assumed I'd only have to deal with small groups dispersed throughout the area. That seems to have changed."

"Then . . . then all that was for *nothing*?"

"Don't be like that," Rosier reproved. "I'll always cherish our time together."

Casanova let out a little screech and went for the creature's throat, intending to throw him off the roof. At least he'd have the satisfaction of watching him die first. But then a horrible shriek rent the air, right behind him, like a thousand nails on a hundred chalkboards.

He spun and saw something out of a nightmare, which completely matched the sound. It was huge and deadly and spreading massive, leathery wings against the night. And Pritkin . . . was on its back?

"Get on," Pritkin told him shortly.

"Die in pain!"

"The idea is to avoid that," Rosier commented, climbing up behind his bastard of a son.

"Carlos, please," Rian tugged on his hand.

"You're planning to fly that thing out of here?" Casanova asked, horrified. Torchlight glistened off a maw of eight-inch fangs. It could devour them all, any second.

"Unless you have a better idea?" Pritkin asked.

"Give me a minute," Casanova said desperately.

But they didn't have a minute. One glance over the roof was enough to show a mass of homicidal demons flowing through what would have been the front door, if the place still had one. And he didn't need vampire senses to hear them tearing through the house below. Or to feel them shaking the very walls by the number of their boots on the stairs.

"Get on, or we're leaving you," the infernal mage said.

Like it was just that easy.

"Get on Carlos," Rian begged. "Please!"

Casanova glanced over the roof again, only to meet the faceless mask of one of the Alû, looking up from the window below.

"Oh, just leave him," Rosier said carelessly. "Once we're gone, I'm sure he'll be fine."

"They've already seen me!" Casanova said shrilly.

"Oh, well. Probably not then." Rosier shrugged.

Casanova screamed and went for the demon, and Rosier grabbed his arm as soon as he was close enough. And then—

"Mierda," Casanova gasped, feeling his feet leave the roof, just as three Alû crawled up on top of it. And lunged for them, almost too fast to see. But a beat from the great wings knocked one of them down, and the wind of it tumbled a second off the roof, and a third had to whip up his shield to defect a fireball somebody threw.

For a moment, it looked like they might make it. But then a fourth Alû Casanova hadn't seen snuck up from the other side, and threw what looked like a fiery lasso around the great beast's back paw. It roared in pain, getting the attention of the Alû still in the street, who raised their heads in one, bronze ripple.

And then a barrage of thrown swords came flashing at them through the air. Casanova screamed, the damned beast flapped harder, almost bucking him off, and they jerked slightly higher in the sky. Making them an even better target for the swords that were about to—

Disintegrate a few yards out?

"Pretty, isn't it?" Rosier yelled, as the weapons hit a barely perceptible bubble in front of them.

"Pritkin—" Casanova gasped, ready to forgive the man for everything he'd ever—

"Nope," Rosier yelled cheerfully, to be heard over the beat of massive wings shredding the air. The beast they were riding gave a tremendous heave and surged upward, taking the Alû trying to restrain him right along for the ride. "That's your power! Feel better about our time together now?"

"Get your hand off my butt," Casanova snarled, and kicked the Alû back into the crowd below. And then the great wings caught an updraft, and they were spiraling hundreds of feet skyward, at an angle that left them almost perpendicular to the rapidly receding ground. Casanova screamed.

"If you don't start holding on, my arm may get tired," Rosier warned him.

"Hijo de mil putas!" Casanova gasped, but somehow, he dragged his tired, bruised body further up the beast's huge back, clinging there like a limpet.

"No, just one," Rosier laughed.

And then they were gone.

Epilogue

"You had better be right about this," John said, as they rematerialized in the middle of the main drag at Dante's. He glanced about, but the only one in sight was the girl at the coffee kiosk. And she just looked bored.

"Sid's a vindictive little shit," Rosier said confidently. "He'll want to watch us die. My bet is that he rejoined the hunt for Cassie, after ensuring that you were on your way to finish me off. Speaking of which—" he glanced at Rian, who nodded and disappeared.

John clutched Cassie's talisman inside his pocket, hard enough to leave an impression on his palm. But he didn't move. As a spirit, Rian could check all the little spaces where Cassie might be hiding in a matter of seconds, far faster than he could hope to do.

She would find her; of that he had no doubt.

The question was—in what condition?

Yes, the spell might have kept her alive, but at what cost? How long had they been gone? With time looping here, there was no way to tell, and the demon world worked so differently as to give no point of reference. It could have been hours, as it felt to John, but it could also have been days. Or weeks. Or . . . or it could have been years.

What must it have been like, he wondered, being all alone, battling for her life, hiding or running or dying, over and over again, for what must have seemed like infinity? With no way out and with no one to even share the burden? He couldn't imagine.

He wasn't sure he wanted to imagine.

What would he find, back in that damned hotel room, or in that dark little closet Casanova had described? She might be alive, but would she be alright? Would she be sane?

Would she still be *Cassie*?

"We need to find Sid first," John heard himself say. "If he never left, then I was the only missing piece of the puzzle, and my return just broke the spell. If he kills her again . . ."

"Yes, but where to start looking?" Rosier asked. "He could be in spirit form still, or have possessed someone, anyone. I say we find the girl, and then let him find us, assuming the Alû don't do it first—"

"Like that?" Casanova croaked, from the floor. Which he appeared to be clutching.

John followed the vampire's gaze to see one of the Alû coming at them at a run. He grabbed one of his potion vials and prepared to throw, only to have a hand descend onto his shoulder. "Wait," Rosier said softly.

It was then that John noticed something odd about this particular Alû. Its once bright armor was battered and dented, one side was singed almost black, as if an explosion had hit it, and it was limping badly, essentially just dragging its left leg behind it. But it was limping fast.

"Please . . ." The creature called out, its voice as scratchy as its armor, cracked and helpless. And the hand it lifted out to them, as if in supplication, was shaking.

"Cassie?" John asked carefully, wondering if she'd somehow managed to disguise herself as one of the enemy. But no. Because a moment later, he saw her flying across the lobby, blond curls bouncing, pink t-shirt crisscrossed with weapons, and half a dozen Alû right on her tail.

"Cassie!" he yelled, but she didn't hear.

"Now!" she screamed, running onto the drag. And the words had no sooner left her mouth than the windows on the upper floor of the Old West buildings slammed open, almost in unison, and she hit the deck. A second later, a massive barrage of gunfire erupted in the space in between, catching the Alû completely off guard.

"No," Casanova said pitifully, crawling past John. "No. No, stop it!"

But nobody heard. And then Cassie flipped back to her feet, right on the edge of the gunfire, and tossed something into the hellscape that the center of the drag had become. "Yippie Ki Yay, Motherfuckers!" John thought he heard her say, although clearly, he'd been mistaken. And then she turned and ran behind an overturned wagon at the edge of the street.

Rosier looked at John, and then they both grabbed Casanova and dove in behind her. Just as the street erupted in a massive explosion. The ground trembled, the shop windows blew out, and something caught the hay spilling out of the front of the wagon on fire.

The automated sprinklers started up, making it look like it was raining indoors, as Cassie bounded back to her feet. And lunged at the battered single Alû, which had followed them over, and which John had managed to totally forget. "Get away from me!" the creature screamed. "Get away!"

It ducked behind Rosier, pawing at him pathetically, while dozens of vampires poured out of the ruined storefronts on either side, weapons and fangs out.

"Cassie?" John asked again, confused.

She jerked her head around, teeth still bared from glaring at the Alû, and for half a second, she looked alarmingly like one of her vampires. And then she recognized him. "You're back!" And suddenly he found himself with an armful of Pythia, warm and breathless and alive. And almost immediately squirming away.

"Sorry, but I don't want to miss this," she told him. "It's my favorite part."

"What is?" John asked wonderingly, as Rosier pushed the Alû off him with a look of refined disgust. The movement snapped the already battered face plate in two, and beyond it—

A terrified elder demon stared out at them.

It looked like Sid had been right, John thought, when he once said that he could make a body for himself at will.

"John?" he wavered, looking at him pleadingly. But, apparently, he didn't see anything helpful. Because he let out a wail and started limping down the drag again, toward the back stairs.

"Wait," John said, catching Cassie's arm as she started after him. "Where's Jonas?"

She looked confused. "No idea."

"He isn't . . . coordinating this?"

She shook her head. "I tried calling him a few dozen times. But it always takes too long to get him to believe me. And when he does, he just wants me to hide away somewhere."

"That sounds like a good—"

"I tried that. But it's unbelievably boring. I don't need to sleep—time isn't passing for my body, so I don't get tired. I don't get hungry—well anymore hungry," she said, shooting him a look. The sad excuse for a donut had apparently not been forgotten. "I don't even need to pee. And there's never anything new on T.V."

"You've been doing what, then?" he asked, in disbelief. "Killing demons?"

"Well, it occurred to me sometime back in the sixties—"

"The sixties?"

"The sixtieth go 'round," she said, matter-of-factly. "Anyway, I knew that when you got back, the spell would break. But then we'd be right back where we started. We might dodge the bomb this time, but we'd still have a casino full of demons."

"You therefore decided to take care of that," John said, his head spinning. "How many times?"

"I don't know. I lost count a while ago. Duck."

"What?"

Cassie shoved his head down and let off a barrage from an M-16 that strafed a new group of Alû that had been trying to sneak up on them. She grinned at him, a little manically. "They hate it when I do that."

Her vampires let out what sounded like battle cries, and jumped the disoriented demons. That included Marco, John was relieved to see, back hale and hearty enough to rip one's head right off its body. But unlike with Sid, there was nothing underneath.

John looked back at Cassie. "Where—" he cleared his throat. "Where did you get the weapons?"

"Downstairs," she told him happily. "The senate's using this as a base now, remember? It's like Guns R Us down there."

"But they must have guards—"

"Of course."

"—and you're without your powers. How did you get in?"

She looked at him like he might be slow. "I'm Pythia. I told them to unlock the goddamned door."

And then she was off, leaving John staring after her, his stomach falling, but a strange sort of smile twitching at the corner of his mouth.

"I suppose I shall have to go rescue Sid," Rosier sighed. "We need him to tell the council that neither of us was really at fault here."

"Uh huh." But John made no move to help. Instead, he turned and started toward the coffee shop, where a dazed-looking Goth girl was pouring something into an overflowing cup.

"Where do you think you're going?" his father demanded.

"To buy someone the biggest damned pastry in the world."

Author's Note: This is the Pritkin POV requested by the winner of the Pritkin swag bag that I put together for the Read for Pixels charity event in March, 2017. It contains Pritkin's take on a couple of scenes from *Tempt the Stars*, and will make very little sense unless you've read that book. It also contains spoilers for that novel, so it should be read afterwards, not before.

PRITKIN POV

The first was pathetic. So much so that it took John a moment to realize what he was seeing. But his body seemed to be ahead of his mind, because he felt his face flush and his hand clench on the door to his suite, while a blonde in a slinky satin gown simpered at him. She had red-gold curls done in an artfully mussed style, bright blue eyes gunked up with mascara, and a feather boa, of all things, sliding alluringly off one shoulder. The absurdity of it was the only thing that saved her.

"John—"

He slammed the door in her face.

The second was better. The second was much better. He was fairly sure the first was just his father being a cunt. John wouldn't sleep with the bevy of beauties he kept sending? Wouldn't help the family business? Wouldn't, as his father had memorably remarked, get his head out of his ass and grow *up* already?

Fine. Then send him a reminder of what he'd lost. Of what he would never see in the flesh again.

But, in that split second of confusion, John must have given some sign of exactly how deep that particular knife had dug. Or perhaps the night of drunken despair that followed and the trashing of his well-ordered suite had given Rosier a clue. Because, when everything else proved fruitless, his father tried again.

And, this time, it almost worked.

Even the scent was perfect, John thought, as she grabbed his biceps. Not the perfumed musk of the first Cassie-clone, but a lingering freshness from purloined Dante's toiletries, panicked girl-sweat, and an underlying sweetness that was all her own. Addictive, Pritkin thought, breathing it in.

Until she shook him, and even that was familiar.

"We need to get out of here!"

"There's no way out," he heard himself rasp. "Not for me."

"Don't say that." She looked up at him, tears shimmering in her beautiful blue eyes. "I can help. I have transport, and supplies. We can make it—"

"Back into the desert."

"Yes!"

"And to the portal."

"Yes!"

"And back to Earth."

A couple of tiny teeth bit her bottom lip appealingly. "Not yet. The demon council still has a price on your head, if you leave this place. But we could hide, discuss what to do. I have supplies for weeks—"

"Weeks."

And, for a moment, he actually let himself think about it. Weeks in the desert under star-strewn skies. Weeks of nothing except the two of them, away from any possibility of interruption. Weeks with a few guards showing up to lackadaisically search the area, giving them some pulse pounding excitement for a moment or two.

Before they went back to their tent and found another way to raise their blood pressure.

His eyes closed, but he felt his hands clench on her arms. And if he'd needed confirmation that she was not who she appeared to be, that would have done it. That grip would have bruised a bodybuilder, yet she never so much as flinched. But when he opened his eyes, hers were even bluer: suddenly, impossibly, inhumanly blue.

Yes, he knew what she was.

Yet still he just stood there.

She nodded, missing the undercurrent in her eagerness. "Yes! I've thought of everything." She took his hand. "But we have to go now or your father will find me—"

"He already found you." John knew his voice was harsh, even cruel. He didn't care. "Tell me, was it a street corner or a bordello?"

The blue eyes flashed dangerously for a second, before the deceptive sweetness flooded back. Along with enough power to make him blink. No wonder that barb had hit home.

"What are you?" he demanded, pulling away. "Not Rakshasa. They're not this strong."

"I'm Cassie, *your* Cassie—"

But this time, the illusion didn't work. A sudden flood of rage swamped it. "Not on your best day," he snarled, and slammed the door before he did something stupid.

And then he did it anyway, taking a bottle of whiskey out to the balcony.

It was almost nightfall. Dark ribbons of orange and pink and red played around the horizon, and back lit the desert-colored buildings and craggy mountains beyond. He fell into a chaise and plunked his bottle onto a handy table, without even checking to see that it was there. He just knew it would be, just as everything else a man could want or need, every physical thing at least, had been thoughtfully provided.

Even company.

Especially company, John thought, with a twist to his lips. But the spell that had dragged him back here, to the world the incubi called their own, couldn't force compliance, could it? It could deprive him of the life he'd chosen, could force him away from everyone who mattered, could destroy any chance he'd ever had at happiness. But that wasn't enough for the old man. He hadn't waited hundreds of years and coaxed his son back from the Demon High Council for the pleasure of his company.

He wanted a return on his investment, and there was only one way to get it.

But the parade of lovelies his father had sent to tempt him hadn't worked, so Rosier had decided to get tricky. It didn't matter who John coupled with, after all. Not now. The big clients would come later, after he'd remembered his place in the natural order of things, and sloughed off the myriad rough edges that made him who he was.

After he'd become the clone of himself that Rosier had always wanted.

For now, it was enough to get him feeding again, as his father's people did, to remind him of the added power it gave, to make him crave it . . .

And anyone would do for that.

Anyone at all.

Well, anyone who could break his resolve, that is. Anyone whose face he saw in dreams every night, and missed every morning when she wasn't there. Whose absence had made him feel loneliness, true, aching loneliness, for the first time since . . . well, possibly ever. He had felt many things for his dead wife: anger, regret, guilt. And they had lasted, for there was no getting closure from a dead woman, was there? But loneliness?

No, he'd never felt that. Because how did you miss someone who'd never existed, except in your imagination? The real woman he'd known remained a mystery, one skilled at eliciting the desired reactions from men and bending them to her will. But Cassie . . .

Yes, Cassie he missed. More even than he'd thought possible, and he had expected it to hurt. But not like this, not like a part of him had been carved out by an exceptionally dull blade. Leaving an ache that went on and on, unlike anything he'd ever known, save for that horrible time all those years ago after his father first pulled him from Earth, and introduced him to his personal little corner of hell.

John poured himself another drink.

So, yes, this imposter had had a real chance of success. Because his biggest fear was that the real madcap blonde he knew wouldn't leave well enough alone, but would try some damned fool rescue that would only put her back into danger—serious danger—yet again. Despite the fact that he'd just sacrificed his life to get her out!

It battled with his other fear, one that grew bigger as day slid into long, interminable day: the idea that maybe she wouldn't. Because why the hell should she? The real Cassie Palmer was Pythia now, chief seer of the supernatural world, with responsibilities and petitioners and factions clawing at her every day, not to mention a war against gods to fight. She had plenty to do and plenty of people to make sure she did it, and that she forgot all about him—

A sudden image of shrewd brown eyes rose up in front of his vision, ones in a darkly attractive face. Her vampire mentor, as smooth and suave as any incubus and twice as deadly. John's hand clenched on the bottle. He wanted to hurl it over the balcony, wanted to scream, wanted to fight—for her. More than he'd ever wanted anything in his whole, misbegotten life. Wanted to get her away from all of them, Circle and Senate alike, before they succeeded in tearing her apart like dogs fighting over a particularly meaty bone. Wanted—

He poured himself another drink.

So yes, it might have worked. Because this imposter had been smarter than the other, arriving not in silk clad finery but in denim shorts and a simple tee, a smear of something dark on one slightly pinker than normal cheek, and her breath coming fast and panicked. "I found you," she'd said, throwing herself into his arms. "Oh, God, Pritkin! I've missed you so much!"

And, for a moment, it *had* worked. For a moment, he'd felt his arms tighten around her, felt the soft, warm body mold itself against his, felt a wave of emotion start to swamp him. And then she'd pulled his head down into a kiss, one full of passion and fire, igniting almost as hot as his own.

But it had none of the hesitancy, none of the internal conflicts writ large in clear blue eyes, none of the bundle of contradictory emotions that Cassie, the real Cassie, somehow managed to hold all at the same time. Ones that mirrored his own snarl of jumbled feelings that, until he came here, he'd never had a chance to sort out. But he'd had nothing else to do for six months, and there was no more confusion now, but it didn't matter because it wasn't *her*.

It would never be her.

He tried to pour another drink, but he was drunk and his hand slid on the wet glass, leaving him fumbling for it awkwardly. He gave up and set the bottle down on the tiles between his feet, and put his head in his hands. And wondered, briefly, why he hadn't run off with her as she'd asked.

How long would it be before he took someone else up on the offer? Until he believed because he wanted to believe? Because if he didn't there was nothing else but this, long nights and regrets and endless what-ifs, and alcohol that wasn't nearly strong enough to blot out the memories that amounted to torture now.

I should have told her, he thought for the hundredth time, watching the whiskey throw strange shadows over the tiles.

He was still in the same place an hour later, the glass held slack in a trailing hand, the stars well up and the night air growing cold, when he heard it. Bells, a few at first, then more and more, loud, insistent, and then almost frantic, pealing from every corner of the city. He looked up, bleary eyes blankly registering the fires spotting formerly quiet streets, and people screaming and something exploding—

He shot out of his chair, his heart hammering as it hadn't since he came to this infernal city. And then he all but ran back into his room, in time to see the door slam open and a wild-eyed vampire spill in, with that half-crazed look that only one person in the universe could inspire. And lurch in his direction, babbling something John couldn't hear over the damned bells and didn't care about anyway.

"Is she here?" he demanded, snatching the creature down to him. And despite the fact that Casanova had at least three inches on him, the man looked terrified.

"This isn't my fault!" he kept babbling over and over. "They kidnapped me! They made me march through the scorching desert until my feet bled, they—"

"More than that will bleed if you don't answer me!"

"Yes, all right? But you don't under—"

"Where?"

"I don't know where she is!" the vampire shrilled. "Rian took off and left me once I started fighting her, but by then we were halfway across—"

"You brought her here and left her *alone*?" Pritkin heard himself roar, before shoving Casanova back through the still open door. And smashing a fist into the creature's face as he bounced off a wall, only to hear—

"Pritkin!"

He looked up, his vision tunneling and his ears ringing. Because it was her, standing at the end of the hall in a ridiculous outfit like the ones the dancers wore in the souk, with no makeup and dirty feet and her hair everywhere and slightly smoking. And her expression—

He'd never seen her look that furious.

A moment later, they were back in his room, and she was glaring at him for no reason he could see. He was the one who had the right to be angry; angry that his sacrifice had meant nothing, angry that she'd come here. Angry now that doubts were creeping in.

"I knew it was you," he told her, even as he wondered if it was. His old friend Caleb was with her, or someone who looked just like him. And that ridiculous Casanova. And Cassie, barefoot with terribly chipped toenail polish that looked like it had been through a war or two. It was all completely believable . . .

But maybe that was the point. To send an obvious fake, and then almost immediately follow it up with an illusion so good, he couldn't find a crack or a flaw. Maybe this was how his father finally won, when she threw herself into his arms, proclaimed her undying love, said all the things he wanted to hear, but never had and never would because she was fake, fake like the others, and he had been a fool to hope, even for a moment—

She slapped him.

"You son of a *bitch*!"

And then her face wrinkled up and he was holding her, unsure whether to laugh or scream, fear clutching his heart like a vise, but a strange, ebullient joy flooding his veins.

Everything since had been a blur. The escape from the city, the battle with his father, the demon council imprisoning him again as he'd known they would. They'd wanted him dead for centuries, deploring the potential power of the hybrid creature his father's ambition had created. And now they had the perfect excuse.

What chance was there that they wouldn't take it?

Yet Cassie couldn't see that. And, frankly, John was having a hard time concentrating on it himself. They were in a bar somewhere in the Shadowland, the demon world where the council met, waiting to be summoned. At which point he would come face-to-face with the fate he'd avoided all these years, and with the terrifying creatures chomping at the bit to dole it out to him. Yet, none of it seemed to matter next to the thought that kept ringing in his head.

I should have told her.

And now he could. She was right there, glaring at him again, and fighting with his father, because the fact that Rosier was a member of the Demon High Council seemed to matter exactly fuck all to her, and it was glorious. But not as much as the look in her eyes, the expression John could swear he saw now and again, slipping past her formidable defenses. Only he couldn't trust himself. He couldn't trust himself about anything anymore, much less to parse reality from his desperate desires, desires she might share.

Only she didn't.

She couldn't.

Could she?

John stared up at her in a mixture of bewilderment and resentment and anger and terrible affection, and, yes, that was it, the snarl of emotion he remembered so well. The snarl that wanted him to jump up and shake her and slam her against the nearest wall and kiss her quiet. Because she didn't get this, didn't understand that, no matter what she or some dead goddess said to the council, it wasn't going to work.

Only maybe she did understand, because she was suddenly looking miserable, too. Like some of the hard truths he'd been telling her were finally getting through. As if perhaps she was finally realizing just how bad the odds were.

He already had, but he still didn't care. Wouldn't have even if they'd been worse, even if they'd been certain, because death might be preferable to the alternative he faced at his father's court. He found he only cared about one thing, *that* thing, and suddenly, she was looking unsure for the first time since she broke into hell to free him, with only a terrified vampire and a crusty war mage at her side.

Suddenly, she was looking very worried indeed as he started backing her around the table. And, for some reason, that had John's heart feeling lighter than it had in months. Maybe because it was accompanied by more of that odd expression again, the one that had his pulse pounding and that odd rushing sound flooding his ears, which was inconvenient because he wanted to hear her *say it.*

"Then give me a reason," he said, watching her face. She'd just claimed that he couldn't leave with his father because she needed him. What *he* needed was for to realize *why.*

"I . . . there's so many." She almost tripped over a chair.

John took no mercy. "Name one."

"I can name a hundred—"

"I didn't ask for a hundred; I asked for one. And you can't give it to me."

"Yes, I can!" She was looking angry again.

"Then do it!"

He heard the anger in his own voice, and the almost pleading, and the edge that dared her, for once, to face her emotions head on, and put a name to what they had between them, and *say it.*

But she couldn't. Because she hadn't had those months, all the interminable days and endless nights, all the silence and loneliness, all the *time*, an endless ocean of it, stretching out as far as the eye could see in all directions, none of which contained her. He'd broken before the first month was out, in realization of what he'd lost, and despair at what he'd never have again.

But now he did, and he could push it, could make her see . . .

But she wasn't there yet, if she'd ever be, and all he was doing in his desperation and hopelessness was making her miserable. Was making her cry, and he'd never wanted—God!

"I don't know how to say it right," she sobbed. "I don't know what you want. I just know I need you. I need *you*; I can't do this without you—

"Oh, spare us," Rosier said, sounding disgusted. For an incubus, he had always had a serious lack of sentiment.

But his attempt to pull John away had an effect, just not the one he'd intended.

Because Cassie suddenly went from misery to something that looked like panicked terror. "No! You can't go! You can't!"

John gripped her hands harder, because she looked like she was about to pass out. "Cassie—"

"Just try. You just have to *try*."

"It isn't that simple. Even if—" He stopped, trying to come up with something, anything, to wipe that look off her face. But, like his father, emotions weren't his strong suit. He didn't know what to tell her, how to make this easier, just as he'd never managed to make anything easier for her. He'd told himself it was for her own good, everything he'd put her through, that she had to toughen up in order to survive. But, looking back, all he could remember was how cruel he'd been, the things he'd said, the way he'd pushed her—

God. Maybe this was for the best, after all. Maybe his father was right, and she'd be better off without him.

But how to make her see that?

"Even if *what*?" she demanded, staring up into his face.

"Cassie," he forced himself to focus. He'd been thinking about himself long enough; it was time to think about her. To make her understand that she had to leave. "The council . . . it isn't like a human court, with rules and procedures and some semblance of justice. They are arbitrary and capricious at best, and at worst . . . they're the definition of chaos."

She blinked up at him, and the panic abruptly cleared. Her pleading, tear-streaked face became calm, and quietly brave. Just as she'd always been the bravest damned soul he'd ever known.

"Mother said chaos is like jumping off a cliff," she told him softly. "Not knowing what's at the bottom. But she didn't seem to think that was so bad. I didn't understand what she meant then, but I think . . . maybe I do now. Sometimes there are no guarantees. Sometimes, if you want something badly enough, you just have to *jump*."

He stared at her for a moment. And, suddenly, it really was just that easy. Suddenly, it didn't matter if she felt the same, didn't matter if he was going to survive this, didn't matter at all. Because he simply couldn't leave. Not and wipe that look of hope off her face, or go back to that sterile room, to a life that had never been his and was almost obscene now.

Suddenly, he couldn't do anything but jump, right along with her.

And, for the first time in months, John Pritkin smiled.

Author's Note: This was the first Cassie Palmer short I ever did, about Tomas, a central character is the first two Cassie novels, *Touch the Dark* and *Claimed by Shadow*. It should be read after those two books or, alternatively, after *Shatter the Earth*, the tenth Cassie novel, with which it coincides.

THE DAY OF THE DEAD

"I'm looking for my brother," the girl repeated, for the third time. Her accent was terrible, New Jersey meets Mexico City, making her difficult to understand, but Tomas doubted that that was the problem. The largely male crowd in the small cantina weren't interested in a *gaba* with a sob story, even one who was tall and slim, with slanting hazel eyes and long black hair.

Japanese ancestry, Tomas decided, or maybe Korean. There might be some Italian, too, based on the slight wave in her hair and the Roman nose, which was a bit too prominent for her slender face. She was arresting, rather than pretty, the kind of woman you'd remember, although her outfit would probably have ensured that anyway. He approved of the tight cargo pants and the short leather jacket. But the shotgun she wore on a strap slung over her shoulder and the handgun at her waist took away from the effect.

"He's nineteen," she continued stubbornly. "Black hair, brown eyes, 6 foot 2—"

The bartender suddenly snapped to attention, but he wasn't looking at her. His hand slid under the counter to rest on the shotgun he kept there. Tomas hadn't seen it, but he'd smelled the gun oil and faint powder traces as soon as he walked in. But the man who slammed in through the door was nothing to worry about, being merely human.

"*Hijole*, Alcazar!" the bartender shouted, as the room exploded in yells of abuse. "What do you mean, bursting in here like that? Do you want to get shot?"

The man shook his head, looking vaguely green under the cantina's bare bulbs. "I thought I heard something behind me," he said shakily, joining a few friends at an already overcrowded table. "On the way back from the cemetery."

"You shouldn't have been there so late," one of his friends reproached, sliding him a drink. "Not tonight."

"I lost track of time. I was visiting Elia's grave and—"

"*¡Aguas!* You will do your daughter no good by joining her!"

There was frightened muttering for a moment, and several patrons stopped fingering their weapons to actually draw them. Tomas had the distinct impression that the next time the door opened, whoever stood there was likely to get shot. Tension was running far too high for good sense.

Then the bartender suddenly let out a laugh, and slid another round onto the men's table. "I wouldn't worry," he said heartily. "From what I hear, even your Consuela doesn't want you. Why would the monsters?"

The room erupted into relieved laughter as the man, his fright forgotten, stood up to angrily defend his manhood. "She ran off with some wealthy bastard," he said, shooting Tomas an evil look.

Tomas calmly sipped mescal and didn't respond. But he wished for about the hundredth time that he'd given a little more thought to blending in. His reflection in the chipped mirror behind the bar, while not Anglo, stood out almost as much as the girl's.

The high cheekbones and straight black hair of his Incan mother had mixed with the golden skin and European features of his Spanish father, resulting in a combination that many people seemed to find attractive. He'd always found it an inconvenient reminder of the domination of one half of his ancestry by the other. The conquest of a continent written on his face.

He couldn't honestly blame the locals for mistaking him for a wealthy city dweller, despite the fact that he'd been born into a village even poorer than this one and was currently completely broke. He'd picked up his outfit, a dark blue suit and pale grey tie, at an airport shop at JFK. He'd needed a disguise, and the suit, along with a leather briefcase and a quick session with a pocket knife in front of a men's room mirror, had changed him from a laid-back college student with a ponytail to a thirty-something businessman in a hurry.

He'd eluded his pursuers, but with no money he'd been forced to use a highly illegal suggestion on the clerk. Since then, he'd lost track of how many times he'd done something similar, using his abilities to fog the minds of airline employees, customs agents, and the taxi driver who had conveyed him a hundred miles to this tiny village clinging to the side of a mountain.

Every incident had been a serious infraction of the law, but what did that matter? If any of his kind caught up with him, he was dead anyway. He just wished he'd thought to find something else to wear after landing in Guadalajara. There weren't a lot of locals in $1200 suits.

Tomas couldn't see the outfit that helped him stand out like a sore thumb, because an altar to the souls of the dead had been placed in front of the mirror. Hand carved wooden skeletons in a variety of poses sat haphazardly on the multi-tiered edifice, each representing one of the bartender's family members who was gone but not forgotten. One hairless skull seemed to grin at him, its tiny hand wrapped around an even tinier bottle of Dos Equis – presumably the man's favorite drink. A regular-sized bottle stood nearby, a special treat for the spirit that would come to visit this night, for it was *El Dia de la Muertos*, the Day of the Dead.

A particularly fitting time, Tomas thought, for a vampire to return home.

At least resentment of the city slicker gave the men something to talk about other than their fear. They didn't relax, being too busy shooting suspicious glances his way, but most of them let go of their weapons.

Which is why everyone jumped when a shot exploded against the cracked plaster ceiling.

It was the girl, standing in the middle of the cantina, gun in hand, ignoring the dozen barrels suddenly focused on her head. "My. Brother," she repeated, pointing the gun at the bartender, who had lost his forced joviality. "Where is he?"

"Put your weapon down, *senorita*. You have no enemies here," he said, eyeing her with understandable concern. "And I told you already. No one has seen him."

"His car is parked by the cemetery. The rental papers have his name on them. And the front seat has his handprint – in blood."

She threw the papers on the bar, but neither they nor her speech seemed to impress the bartender. "Perhaps, but as I told you, this is a small town. If he had been here, someone would know."

The glasses on the shelf behind him suddenly exploded, one by one, like a line of firecrackers. The gun remained in the girl's hand, but she hadn't used it. Tomas slowly set his drink back down.

"Someone here does know. And that someone had better tell me. Now." Her eyes took in the bar, where most of the men's weapons were still pointed at her. That fact didn't seem to worry her nearly as much as it should have.

"I saw a stranger." The voice piped up from a table near the door, and a short, stocky man, dressed in the local farmer's uniform of faded jeans, cotton work shirt and straw hat, stood up. "He was taking photographs of the ceremony, out by the graves."

"He's a reporter," the girl agreed. "He was doing a story on . . . something . . . but said he'd meet me here."

"I told him to go away," the man said. "This is a day for the dead and their families. We didn't want him there."

"But he didn't leave. His car is still there!"

The man shrugged and sat back down. "He said he was going to photograph the church, and I saw him walking towards town. That's all I know."

"The church is the white building I saw driving in?"

"Yes." The bartender spoke before the man could. "I can show you, if you like." He motioned for the boy who'd been running in and out all night from the back, clearing off tables and wiping down the bar. "Paolo can take over for me here."

"You're going out?"

"But it's almost dark!"

"Are you mad?"

The voices spoke up from all directions, but the bartender shrugged them off. He brought out the shotgun and patted it fondly. "*Ocho ochenta.* It's only a short way. And no one should go anywhere alone tonight."

The murmuring didn't die down, but no one attempted to stop him. Tomas watched them leave, the bartender solicitously opening the door for the girl. His broad smile never wavered, and something about it made Tomas's instincts itch. He gave them a couple of minutes, then slid off his stool and followed.

There was little light, with the sky already dark overhead, the last orange-red rays of the sun boiling away to the west. But his eyes worked better in the dark. And in any case, he could have found his way blindfolded.

The village looked much the same as it had for the last three millennia. Many of its people could trace their ancestry back to the days when the Mayan Empire sent tax collectors here, to reap the benefits of the same plots these farmers still worked. The 500-year-old village where he'd grown up in what was now Peru seemed a young upstart by comparison. It was gone now, bulldozed to make way for a housing development on the rapidly expanding outskirts of Cuzco. But although he hadn't been back here in almost a century, this place hadn't changed.

A trail of bright yellow petals led the way to a small church with crumbling stone steps overlooking the jungle that floated like green clouds against the mountains. The church was still draped with the *flor de muertos*, garlands of marigolds, from the morning service. He went in to find the same old wooden crucifix on the altar, surrounded by flickering votive candles and facing rows of empty pews. He edged around it and paused by the back door, where the sweet, pungent smell of incense mingled with the damp, musty odor of the jungle. Somewhere, out in the twilight, he caught a whiff of the girl's perfume.

The church faced the red earth of town's only street. Behind it, the jungle washed up almost to the steps, except for the area where a small cemetery spilled down the hillside. It had never been moved despite each summer storm threatening to wash the bodies out of their shallow graves and into the valley below.

Tomas picked his way down a marigold-strewn path to the cemetery gate, pausing beside a statue of *La Calaca*. The skeleton lady was holding a placard with her usual warning: 'Today me, tomorrow you.' In many such villages, families stayed all night at the graves of their dead, waiting to welcome the spirits that returned to partake of their offerings. But not in this one. Only four people stood among the flower decked crosses and scattered graves, and only two of them were alive.

There was little light left, other than a few burning votives here and there, shining among the graves. But Tomas didn't need it to recognize the new additions. The wind was blowing towards him and it carried their scents clearly: Rico and Miguel, two thugs in the employ of the monster he'd traveled a thousand miles to kill.

"I saw her. She shattered them with some kind of spell." The bartender was talking, while Rico held onto the girl.

"Why carry all this?" Miguel held one of the girl's guns negligently in one hand, with the rest tucked into his belt. "If she's so powerful?"

"I'm telling you, she's some kind of witch," the bartender said stubbornly. "That mage I sent you this morning was her brother. She came looking for him."

"Where did you take him?" The girl demanded, her voice full of cold, brittle anger.

Everyone ignored her. "Her aura feels strange," Miguel said, running a hand an inch or so above her body. "Not human, but not exactly mage, either."

"What are you girl?" Rico demanded, his breath in her face. She didn't flinch, despite the fact that she had to be able to see his fangs at that range. If she hadn't known what the villagers feared before, she certainly did now.

"Tell me what you've done with my brother or I'll show you." She sounded no more concerned about her predicament than she had at the bar. Tomas couldn't tell if that was bravado or stupidity, but he was leaning toward the latter. Her heart rate had barely sped up, despite the obvious danger.

"What about me?" the bartender demanded. "You said if I brought you the mage, I was safe. I want my nephew's safety in exchange for this one."

"That will depend," Rico said, jerking her close, "on what she can do. You had better hope one of them is what the master wants, or we'll be taking out the price for our inconvenience in your blood."

Tomas didn't move, didn't breathe, a lifetime's habit keeping him so still that a small bird lit on a tree branch right in front of his face. But inside, he was reeling. It wasn't the cavalier kidnapping that surprised him. The men's master, a vampire named Alejandro, had been organizing hunts on the Day of the Dead for as long as Tomas had known him.

While families across Mexico were busily collecting delicacies for the dead—chocolate for *mole*, fresh eggs for the *pan de muerto*, cigarettes and mescal for the long-departed—Alejandro was collecting treats of his own. Strong, smart, cunning—they'd all had some advantage that made them attractive prey. Assembled together, they were always told the same thing: last until morning, or escape beyond the borders of Alejandro's lands, and win your freedom. They were given flashlights, weapons and maps showing the extent of the ten-mile square area he claimed. Then, at midnight, they were released.

No one had ever lived to see dawn.

The participants had changed over the years, from Aztecs to conquistadors to local farmers sprinkled with the occasional American tourist. But one group Alejandro had always left strictly alone were magic users. He liked a challenge, but not prey capable of bringing down the wrath of the Silver Circle, the guardian body of the magical community, on his head. He was twisted, cruel and sadistic, but he wasn't crazy. At least, he hadn't been before. It seemed that some things had changed around here, after all.

"I told you to let go of me."

The girl's heart rate had finally sped up, but Tomas didn't think it was from fear. Her complexion was flushed and her eyes were bright, but she wasn't trembling, wasn't panicking. And there was something wrong about that. Because even if she was a witch, at three to one odds, with two of the three being master vampires, most magic users would be more than a little intimidated. His estimate of her intelligence took another dive, just as what felt like a silent thunderclap exploded in the air all around him.

A shockwave ran across the ground and shivered through his body like a jolt to his funny bone. It shook the surrounding trees and caused the dusty soil to rise up like steam. The little bird took off in a startled flutter of wings and Tomas made a grab for the limb it had been sitting on, catching hold just as the ground beneath his feet began to buck and slide. Within seconds the slide became a torrent of red earth heading for the side of the mountain—and a drop of more than a mile.

The bartender lost his footing and went down, hitting his head against the side of a massive oak. It must have knocked him out, because the last Tomas saw of him was his body tumbling over the cliff, still limp as a ragdoll. The two vampires jumped for the trees on the opposite side of the path, out of the main rush of earth. They made it, but the girl wasn't so lucky. She fell into the crashing stream of rocks, foliage and dirt, her scream lost in the roar of half a mountainside sluicing away.

Tomas hadn't wanted to get close enough for the vampires to scent him, but it meant that she was too far away for him to grab. She managed to catch hold of a tree stump in the middle of the sliding mass, but she was getting pounded by a hail of debris. Tomas tried to tell himself that she could hold on, that he didn't have to risk being seen by Alejandro's men on a dangerous rescue attempt. He didn't mind the thought of dying so much—considering what he was about to face, that was pretty much inevitable anyway—but he was damned if he wasn't going to take Alejandro with him.

Then the church bell began to chime, its plaintive call cutting through the sound of the earthquake, reverberating across the valley only to be thrown back by the nearby hills. Tomas glanced behind him to see the back end of the old building hanging precariously over nothing at all, its foundation half gone in the landslide. With a shudder and a crack, the church broke in half, the heavy stones of its colonial-era construction beginning to crumble. Some of them were ancient, having been looted by the builders from nearby Mayan ruins, and weighed hundreds of pounds apiece. Even if the girl managed to hold on to her precarious perch, they would sweep her over the mountainside or break her into pieces where she lay.

Bile rolled up thick in his throat. Alejandro had wanted to make a monster of him, a carbon copy of himself. But he'd probably be pleased enough at the thought that he'd turned Tomas into someone who would stand by and watch an innocent die because saving her might cost him something. He might never live to kill that creature, but he wouldn't give him that satisfaction.

Tomas let go of the limb and leapt for the one spot of color in the darkness, the girl's pale face, using her as a beacon to guide him through the hail of falling debris. He reached her just before the first of the ancient stones did, grabbed her around the waist and leapt for the side of the path that remained half stable. It was the one where his old associates were trying to scramble to steadier ground, but at the moment, that seemed a minor issue.

Despite senses that made the falling hillside look as if it was doing so in slow motion, he couldn't dodge everything. He twisted to avoid a stone taller than him, and slammed into a smaller one he hadn't even seen. He heard his left knee break, but all he felt was a curious popping sensation, no real pain—not yet—and then they were landing on a surface that wasn't falling but was far from steady.

Tomas rolled and got up on his good knee in time to block a savage kick from Miguel. He'd hoped that, in the confusion and danger, his old comrades might not have recognized him, but no such luck. Miguel hit a nearby tree hard, but flipped back onto his feet almost immediately and was back before Tomas could regain his stance.

Powerful hands choked him, setting spots dancing in front of his eyes as he grabbed his assailant's arms, trying to keep his throat uncrushed. He pushed Miguel's arm the wrong way back until he heard the elbow crack. The vamp didn't let go, but his hold weakened enough for Tomas to twist and get an arm into his stomach, using all his strength to send him staggering into the path of the falling church. One of the tumbling pews caught Miguel on the side of his head, knocking him back against the newly created embankment, where the heavy wooden cross from the altar pinned him with the force of a sledgehammer.

It wasn't quite a stake, but it seemed to do the trick, Tomas thought dazedly, right before something long and sharp slammed into his side. "So the traitor has come back at last," Rico hissed in his ear, twisting a shard of wood so that it scraped along his ribs, sending stabs of hot pain all up and down his midsection. "Allow me to be the first to welcome you home."

Tomas jerked away before the sliver could reach his heart, but his knee wouldn't support him and he stumbled. He felt the hillside disintegrate under his foot, then he was falling, tumbling halfway down the side of the embankment. He grasped the top of a coffin, one of many now sticking out of the newly churned earth, and the lid popped open just in time to intercept another slice from Rico's stake. A pale, silverfish-grey arm flopped out of the tilted casket, and Tomas sent its owner a silent apology before breaking off the limb to use as a makeshift weapon.

He spun to see Rico a few feet away, his hand raised as if to strike. Only the blow never fell. Rico jerked once, twice, then he dropped, falling along with the last of the debris into the valley below. For a moment, Tomas didn't understand what had happened. Then a cascade of spent shotgun shells tumbled down the embankment, rattling against the coffin lid like bones, and he looked up to see a pair of slanting hazel eyes staring down at him.

"Are you all right?" The girl's blood was dripping onto his face, a soft wet plucking like a light rain.

"I should be asking you that," he said, struggling to get back over the edge with only one good leg.

He felt it when his skin absorbed her blood, soaking it up like water on parched earth, using it to begin repairs on the damage he'd suffered. But it wasn't enough to do much good. What he needed was a true feeding, something he hadn't taken time for recently. It had cost him in the fight; he couldn't afford to let it lessen his already slim chances against Alejandro.

He paused by Miguel's impaled body, still full of the blood he'd recently stolen, some of it already pooling in his eye sockets. The sight worked on Tomas the way the smell of a feast would on a starving human. His mouth began to water and his fangs to lengthen without any conscious command from him. He would have delayed it, would have gotten rid of the girl first, but he couldn't risk having the blood coagulate and lose the energy it contained.

"I have to feed," he said simply.

Instead of recoiling as he'd expected, she merely took in his injuries with an experienced eye. "Yeah. Heroics have a way of coming back and biting you in the ass. But when you're done, we need to talk."

He nodded and hunched over Miguel so at least she wouldn't have to watch. Tomas couldn't remember the last time he'd fed from another vampire, but he quickly recalled why it wasn't a common practice. The reused blood nourished him, the lightheaded rush of feeding giving the same almost narcotic high as always, but the taste was like metal in his mouth.

He forced himself to finish, trying to concentrate on the feel of his cracked ribs re-knitting, on the tear in his side mending and on the grating sensation in his knee slowly fading. The healing of wounds, especially if done so quickly, was excruciating and this was no exception. Tears had leaked out of the corners of his eyes by the time he was finished, forced out by the pain, but Tomas didn't mind. Pain was good. Pain meant he was still alive.

"I hate it when that happens."

Tomas looked up to find the girl scowling around at the cemetery. Or what was left of it. A huge swath had been carved out of the middle, where nothing but slick red earth remained. On either side, coffins stuck out of the ground like bony fingers, with a few marigold crosses scattered here and there haphazardly.

Up above, on the crest of the hill, the remaining half of the church swayed dangerously on its ancient foundations. One last pew teetered precariously on the edge of the abyss, half in and half out of the structure. Inside the church, a single candle still burned.

"You handle yourself pretty well in a fight," she continued, as Tomas rose from Miguel's exsanguinated corpse.

"I've had some practice."

She gave a sputtering laugh, short and mocking. "Yeah. I bet."

Tomas pulled himself over the edge and examined her. Amazingly, she seemed to be all right. There was a shallow cut on her forehead and few scrapes and scratches here and there, but nothing serious. It was little short of miraculous.

"We need to talk, but we ought to get out of here," she said, slinging her shotgun over her back again. He'd heard her reloading while he fed. "Half the village is likely to be here any minute."

Tomas sat down on the edge of a stone bearing weathered Mayan hieroglyphs. "I doubt it," he said wryly.

She studied him silently for a moment, then plopped down alongside. "Want to fill me in?"

"This is the Day of the Dead. And in this area, that term has always had more than one meaning." He spent a few minutes sketching out for her Alejandro's idea of a good time, making it as clinical and unemotional as he could. It didn't seem to help.

"Let me get this straight. That son of a bitch has taken my brother to use in his stupid games?"

"Possibly," Tomas agreed. "Although I can't understand it. He never took magic users before."

"Maybe he got bored. Wanted more of a challenge."

"Does a cat get tired of playing with lizards or mice, and attack the neighborhood dog instead? Preying on weaker creatures is Alejandro's nature. But if your brother is a mage, he wouldn't fall into that category."

"His type of magic isn't likely to help him much," she said curtly.

"I don't understand."

"You don't need to." She stood up. "Just tell me where I can find this guy."

Tomas shook his head. "I can't do that."

"Why not? Based on how his vamps treated you, I got the impression you weren't all that close."

He smiled at the understatement. "We aren't. But helping you commit suicide won't aid your brother."

"Tell me where to find this Alejandro, and the only one dying will be him."

Tomas got slowly to his feet, gingerly putting his weight on the injured knee. It held. "For what it's worth, I've come to kill him. If I succeed, it may cause enough chaos to allow your brother to escape. Wish me luck."

He started to go, but a hand on his arm stopped him. "I'll do better than that. I'll go with you."

"I told you—that would not be wise."

"Really? And you think you'd have survived just now without me? It sounds like you going alone isn't so wise, either."

Tomas turned to face her, already exasperated. He had enough on his plate tonight. He didn't need this. "You may be good with a gun, but that won't keep you alive. Alejandro was once my master. I know what he's capable of."

"Uh huh. And can he break off half a mountain because he loses his temper?"

Tomas regarded her narrowly. "You're saying that was you?"

"That's what I'm saying. I'm a jinx."

"I beg your pardon?"

"Jinx. J.I.N.X. A walking disaster area. Fault lines love me. Of course, so does just about anything else that can go wrong."

"An inconvenient talent."

"And an illegal one. If the magical community ever finds out a jinx as powerful as me is walking around, they'll kill me. Which is why I got really good at protecting myself—and other people—a long time ago. This vampire has bought himself more trouble than he knows."

"Bringing down a mountainside won't help your brother. If he's where I think he is, it would only bury him as well."

"I can control it. And this isn't exactly my first time at the rodeo. I can take care of myself."

Tomas hesitated, instinct warring with dawning hope. "I tried to draw someone else into this recently, and almost got her killed," he finally admitted. "I swore that I'd never do that again. This is my fight—"

"It *was* your fight. Once that bastard took Jason, he made it mine." When Tomas just stared at her, trying to think of some way to get rid of her that did not involve actual violence, the ground grumbled beneath him. The precariously perched pew gave up the struggle and slid down the hillside, only to go sailing off into the void like a huge wooden bird. "Look, I'm not asking you, I'm telling you. You think you've got troubles now? Try leaving me behind. My brother is all I've got, and he is *not* dying tonight."

"It will not be easy," he said, wondering how to even begin to explain what they were up against.

The girl snorted. "Yeah. I kind of got that." She held out her hand. "Sarah Lee. And no, I don't cook."

"Tomas."

"Well Tomas. We gonna stand here exchanging pleasantries all night, or go kill a vampire?" Tomas didn't say anything, but he slowly took her hand. She grinned. "Well, all right then."

* * *

"Jason is a reporter for the *Oracle*," Sarah said, as Tomas hotwired her brother's rental car. Hers had been parked in the part of the cemetery that hadn't survived and was currently exploring the bottom of the valley. "We were supposed to meet up in Puerto Vallarta for a vacation, but when I got to the hotel, he'd already left. All I found was a note telling me he'd got a lead on a story and asking me to meet him here."

"If Alejandro has started kidnapping magic users, it would be front-page news," Tomas agreed, as the engine on the old subcompact finally turned over. "Or your brother could have found out about one of his other businesses. He controls everything from magical narcotics to weapon sales in much of Central and South America."

"I know. I've dealt with his people before." At Tomas's sideways look, she shrugged. "I can't buy weapons from legitimate sources, not in the quantities I need. The authorities monitor that kind of stuff."

"Why would you need huge quantities of magical weaponry?"

"Why do you want to kill your old master?" she countered. "I didn't even think that was possible."

They bounced out onto the main road through the village, with only the weak light of a quarter moon to see by. "It wouldn't be, if he were still my master," Tomas said. "I challenged him to combat, but he wouldn't face me. He brought in a champion, a French dueling master, instead. But rather than kill me as Alejandro had wanted, after Louis-Cesare defeated me, he claimed me as his slave. I only recently escaped."

"And came straight back here."

"Yes."

"That's very . . . heroic."

Tomas didn't think it qualified as heroism if he had nothing left to lose. But he didn't say so. Her tone made it clear that the word she'd really been searching for was 'stupid'.

"Alejandro killed the entire population of my village. There isn't anyone else." If the dead were ever to be avenged, it was up to him to do it. And after four hundred years, they'd waited long enough.

"So you came back alone." She shook her head. "People like you are bad for business."

"You're a mercenary." Tomas supposed he should have figured it out before.

"We prefer the term 'outside contractor'."

"I couldn't afford to hire a team," Tomas said, turning onto the pitted road leading into the mountains. "And you also came here alone."

A dark shape suddenly loomed in front of them, forcing Tomas to squeal tires and practically stand the car on end to avoid hitting it. The shape resolved itself into a tall, gaunt man with the brilliant eyes of a fanatic set deep in the hollows of his craggy face. "Not so much," Sarah said, climbing out of the car. "Boys, glad you could make it."

"Looks like we already missed some of the fun," another man commented, stepping out of the jungle that hedged the road on each side.

Tomas stared hard at the new arrival. He hadn't heard him approach, and that was unacceptable. Unless he was a mage using magic to mask his breath, the sound of his heart beating, his footfalls—all would have alerted Tomas to his presence.

But he didn't look like a mage. He had a jagged, ugly scar on his right cheek, as if someone had dragged a fork with sharpened tines over his skin. It was the sort of thing that could be fixed by magical healers or covered by a glamourie. Unless, of course, its owner preferred to look like an extra from a horror flick.

"Meet my knife and gun club," Sarah said, slapping the man on the back. "At least the ones close enough to get here in time for the festivities."

The men didn't greet him, and nobody offered any names, but they also didn't demand to know what Sarah was doing with some strange vampire. Of course, she didn't give them much of a chance, launching directly into an explanation of the problem. If Tomas had had a doubt about their profession, it would have been quieted by their reaction to the news that they were about to raid a vampire stronghold.

"Can I keep the bones?" the fanatic hissed, speaking for the first time. "They're useful in some spells."

"Knock yourself out," Sarah said, shrugging. "But no collecting until we have Jason, understood?"

The man gave a quick nod that reminded Tomas of a lizard or some other kind of reptile. It wasn't a human movement. The other man didn't say anything at all, just switched out a couple of the weapons in the collection draped over his body for several others he drew from a pack on his back. Then everybody got in the car.

Tomas pulled off the road a few miles to the north, where a burbling stream snaked its way through the dense jungle. "We walk from here," he said, pushing the car off the road in case any of Alejandro's men were out a little early.

"I don't see a house," Sarah had pulled night- vision goggles out of her associate's pack, and was staring around.

"There isn't one. Alejandro lives underground."

"Come again?"

"There are some Mayan ruins near here, with a maze of underground passages beneath them. He's lived there for centuries."

"Great." She sounded less than enthused.

"What is it?"

"Nothing. What about guards?"

"Normally, the entrances are all watched. That's why I picked tonight to return. They will be open for the hunt, as the prisoners' first challenge is to find their way out of the maze. Many never do."

"We need to reach them before they're released, then. Otherwise, they'll be scattered in the tunnels, in the jungle—we'll never find them all."

"I thought the plan was to rescue your brother."

"Yeah. Like I'm going to leave you and the rest to be prey to that thing."

Tomas glanced at her, but it was difficult to see much of an expression behind the absurd goggles. She'd sounded sincere enough, though. And he couldn't let her go in thinking that way.

"I know where they used to keep the prisoners. We'll go there first. And if we're lucky enough to locate your brother alive, you need to take him and go."

"I don't abandon a colleague in the middle of a mission. We go in together, we leave together. That's how it works."

"Not if you want to stay alive!" Tomas grasped her arm. "I have the best chance of reaching Alejandro alone. If you stay to help me, both you and your brother will die. Not to mention that you will almost certainly cause me to fail at my task."

She stopped, looking from the hand on her arm to his face. He released her, but the steady stare didn't change. "If you don't want my help, why are you taking me along?" she demanded.

"You wouldn't find your brother alone. Not in time."

"And why would you care about that? You don't even know him."

"I might not know your brother, but I've known plenty of others." A thousand faces, ten thousand, he'd lost count over the years. All of those eyes begging him to help them, to save them. They'd seen his face, the one that had prompted Alejandro to nickname him 'my angel,' and assumed he was their savior. Only to realize with horror that he was one of those hunting them.

"What?"

"Alejandro forced me to help with the hunts," Tomas said bluntly, "because he knew how much I hated it." Telling her was unnecessary, but it was probably his last chance for confession. He didn't remember the last time he'd talked with a priest, not even the last time he'd wanted to, and she couldn't absolve him anyway. But then, considering some of the things he'd done, he doubted that anyone could. "I've killed hundreds just like Jason," he added, trying to keep his voice neutral. "And the only mercy I could show them was to make it quick. For once, I'd like to help someone survive. And to have Alejandro be the one wallowing in his own blood."

"That's a plan I can get behind," she said, fingering her automatic.

Tomas shook his head and didn't comment. Once she saw what was waiting for them, her bravado would fade. Just like everyone else's always did. The two men didn't say anything. But when he and Sara stepped into the undergrowth, they followed.

The next hour was taken up with slipping through a jungle through which no paths had ever been carved, followed closely by a damp cloud of mosquitoes. Sara managed it better than Tomas had expected; it wasn't easy going even for him. Alejandro had left the jungle intact for exactly that reason: it formed an added layer of protection. It also added to the fun of his hunts, watching mere mortals flounder around in the endless green sea until he chose to put them out of their misery.

They finally reached an old temple on the edge of Alejandro's lands. The place was beautiful, silvered with moonbeams, the stones seeming to glow with a delicate light just bright enough to pick out shapes. Weeds and vines had half obscured the entrance and small trees were growing out of the tumbled stones over the lintel.

A crop of wild orchids had moved in, settling among the ruins like nesting birds, their white and orange petals spotted with brown like freckles. Tomas reached out to touch one and found it softly furred beneath the pad of his finger—like skin. A sudden shiver flashed up and down his spine, before twisting like a snake in his gut. For a moment, it felt like the last century had never happened, like he was returning from a mission for his master with blood on his hands, and all the rest was merely a dream.

"This it?" Sarah asked briskly, breaking the mood.

"Yes," he said, and for some reason it hurt to talk, like he was scraping the words out of his throat.

They ducked under deeply sculpted reliefs and entered the main hallway, leading to a chamber with a stone altar. Like his own ancestors, and unlike the Aztec, the Maya had rarely practiced human sacrifice. It was far more common for their priests and kings to use their own blood as the sacrifices their gods required, letting it flow when crises occurred or when the auguries deemed it necessary. Tomas had always been proud that he came from a people who understood the real nature of sacrifice—and it wasn't having someone else bleed for you.

The altar sat in front of a raised dais, behind which was a small room where he supposed the priests might have once readied themselves for ceremonies. It was empty now, except for a set of rock-cut stairs leading down into darkness. Below were a series of *chultuns*, old underground storage chambers for water and food, and beneath them the reason Alejandro had chosen this site in the first place: naturally occurring limestone caverns that even Tomas had never explored in full. It was like an underground city, part of which the Mayans had used as a refuse dump, part of which had held some type of mystical significance, with carvings on the walls showing ancient ceremonies and still partially covered in molding paint.

"This is one of the lesser used entrances," he told them, as Sarah drew out a flashlight. "But we shouldn't risk the light. Alejandro's men don't need it, and if they see it, it will only draw them to us that much faster."

She nodded, but she didn't look happy. Tomas wasn't surprised. Descending into an unknown labyrinth that probably looked pitch dark even with her goggles would have upset most people. But there wasn't much to see, unless she liked the look of striated stone and deep, dark holes branching off here and there. That was all until they reached the populated areas. And then, she was probably better off if she couldn't make out what lay ahead.

The four of them entered the tunnels, and almost immediately Tomas found himself struggling to breathe against a thick, smothering pressure, voices rising like a tide in his head. He'd killed before he came to Alejandro, fighting against the men who had come across the sea to steal his homeland. But those deaths had never bothered him, he'd never lost one night of sleep over them, because those men had deserved everything he did to them. The ones he'd taken in these halls were different.

Taken. It was a good word, he thought bleakly, seeing with perfect clarity the bodies, pale and brown, young and old, faces spattered with blood, bodies cracked and split open. They had bled out onto the thirsty earth because the ones who hunted them had been so sated that they could afford to spill blood like water. And none of it had been due to the hand of God, through some natural, comprehensible tragedy. No, they had died because someone with god-like conceit had stretched out his hand and said, *I will have these*, and by that act ended lives full of hope and promise.

More often than not, Tomas had been that hand, the instrument through which his master's gory commands were carried out. He hadn't had a choice, bound by the blood bond they shared to do as he was bid, but that had somehow never done much to soothe his conscience. He had known it would be hard to return, but he hadn't expected it to be quite this overpowering. Four hundred years of memory seemed to permeate the very air, the taste of it thick and heavy, like ashes in his mouth.

He glanced at his companions. Forkface had an utterly blank stare, cold as ice, while the fanatic kept muttering silently to himself and fingering a necklace of what looked like withered fingers around his neck. Sarah was looking a little green, as if something about the atmosphere was getting to her, too. He swallowed, throat working, and said roughly, "Are you all right?"

She nodded, but didn't try to reply. He decided not to press it, struggling too much with the weight of his own memory. They silently moved forwards.

It was deeply strange to walk through the familiar halls, the bumps and jagged edges of the lintels stretching out claws of shadow that even his eyes couldn't penetrate. He'd done so much to try to forget this place, but he'd been branded by Alejandro's mark too long for that. The feeling of familiarity grew with every step, like each one took him further into the past. He kept expecting to meet himself coming around a corner, as if part of him had never left at all.

Tomas wondered what he might have been like, if he'd never been taken. Or if his first master hadn't decided to show off his new acquisition at court, where Alejandro had chosen to claim him. Once, he'd yearned for freedom with everything in him, hungered for it as he never had food, lusted for it as he never had any woman. But it didn't seem to matter how long he waited or how much power he gained, the story was always the same.

He'd had three masters in his life, but had never been master himself. The idea of being free was like an old photograph now, faded and dog-eared, and Tomas didn't think he could even see his face in it anymore. All he wanted now was to end this.

Sarah stopped suddenly, breathing heavy, her hand gripping the wall hard enough to cause bits of limestone to imbed themselves under her nails. She saw him notice and tried to smile. It wasn't a great attempt. "God, it's hot." She ripped off her jacket, tying it in a knot around her waist, and gathered her hair into a ponytail to get it off her neck.

Tomas hadn't noticed much of a fluctuation in temperature. Usually, the caves were cooler than aboveground, not the reverse, although this time of year the transition was less noticeable. But patches of sweat had already soaked through her shirt and glistened on her skin, and her hand left a wet print on the wall where it had rested.

"This way," he said, leading them into one of the outermost rooms branching off the main hallway before stopping dead.

"What is it?" Sarah had noticed him tense, instantly aware of a change in the atmosphere.

"Something's wrong," he said softly.

"Like what?" The three mercenaries had drawn up in a defensive wedge and were scanning the room, their weapons in hand. The two mages seemed to see fine in the dark, courtesy of a spell, Tomas assumed. But there was nothing *to* see except a few rat bones and a scrap of ancient material.

"There are supposed to be mummified bodies here."

"Great," Sarah muttered. "For the extra creepy this place was missing."

"This was where Alejandro kept the remains of ancient Incan kings," he explained. Alejandro had acquired them as trophies shortly after following Pizarro to the New World, and had brought them along when he finally decided on a permanent residence. Once they were settled in, however, they'd largely been forgotten, left to mildew in dank, underground cells.

Tomas had been one of the few to ever visit them. They had been venerated by his people even after death, remaining in their palaces, supported by their lands, just as they had when alive. Each new Incan monarch had to wage his own wars of conquest to fund his rule, because what had been his ancestors' remained theirs and beyond his control. Legions of servants had daily draped their withered corpses in the finest of garments and prepared lavish meals for them. On important occasions, they had been brought out to sit again in court, giving council to the living and presiding over the festivities.

There had always been something uncanny about them—brown, almost translucent skin stretched over old bones, empty eyes and hollow mouths, with shadows inside like parodies of human organs. Tomas had come this way knowing it was usually avoided by the court. That still seemed to be the case, but for some reason it worried him that the kings weren't there. It made something cold go running along his spine.

"I'm more concerned about the living," Sarah said, eyes on his face. "Are we close?"

Tomas swallowed. He was imagining things. The kings had just been moved, that was all; or perhaps Alejandro had finally decided to rid himself of his macabre trophies.

"Yes. The holding cells are down there." He pointed out a small hole in the wall, about two feet square.

"Down there?" Sarah peered into the darkness, her hand tightening convulsively on her gun. "You're kidding, right?" she sounded hopeful.

"No. There is another way in, but it involves going through much more populated areas. This is safer."

"Safer." She didn't look convinced. She peered inside the small, dank, black hole for another moment, then muttered something that sounded fairly obscene. "Stay here—keep watch," she ordered her men. Then she stowed her gun in its holster and went in head first, on hands and knees. Tomas followed close behind.

The tunnel slanted sharply downwards, leaving behind the mildewed plaster of the *chultuns* for true caverns. Tomas could sense the room's emptiness almost as soon as they entered the small tunnel—there were no whimpers, no cries for help, no rapidly racing heartbeats. But before he could tell Sarah, she was already out the other side.

He emerged in a dark cave half-filled with ancient garbage, with deer bones and pottery shards crunching under his weight. His foot slipped on an old turtle shell, causing him to almost lose his balance, and then there was a rumbling that set half the room's contents jittering.

"There's no one here!" Sarah whirled on him, her face livid.

"They must have moved them."

"A convenient excuse! I swear, vampire, if you've lied to me—"

"To what end?"

"To get me down here alone—"

"I had you alone in the cemetery," Tomas pointed out, with barely concealed impatience. The rumbling just got louder, with rocks and small pieces of pottery stirring uneasily. "If I meant you harm, I would have acted then."

"You said they would be here! That you knew where they were!"

"If Alejandro had followed the usual practice, the prisoners would be here," he replied, trying for calm. "But the contents of the room above were moved, and if they changed one long-standing practice, they may have changed another. I haven't been back in a century—"

"Something you might have mentioned before now!" she was sweating harder, with a few drops glistening along her hairline before falling to stain her shirt.

"We will find your brother," he told her. "I swear it."

"Why should I believe you?" she sounded frantic.

"Why shouldn't you?" Tomas asked, bewildered. "What reason do I have to lie?" A crack formed in the ceiling overhead, raining dirt and gravel down on them. "I thought you said you could control this!" The caverns weren't entirely stable, as multiple cave-ins had demonstrated through the years. If she didn't cut it out, she was going to bury them both.

Sarah looked around, as if she honestly hadn't noticed that the entire room was now shaking. "I can! Usually."

"Usually?"

"I'm a jinx. My magic isn't always . . . predictable. I've learned some control through the years, but it's harder when I'm angry." She paused, her breath coming hard. "And I really don't like being underground."

"You're claustrophobic?"

"I have a small problem with enclosed spaces." There was a badly-concealed edge of panic in her voice.

"But you're a mercenary! Surely—"

"I'm a mercenary who prefers to fight in the open!" she snapped, her face scrunching up with effort. The shaking didn't noticeably diminish.

"Something you might have mentioned before now!"

"Very funny."

The crack widened, dirt and rock exploding inwards, peppering them with pieces of rock as sharp as knives. "Do something!"

"I'm trying!"

She was almost doubled over in effort, pain written on her face, but whatever she was doing wasn't working. A huge crack reverberated around the small space, knocking them both to the ground, hands pressed against their temples. A moment later, a chunk of the ceiling the size of a sofa broke away and came crashing down, missing them by inches.

Tomas stared at it for a split second through a haze of dust before grabbing her around the waist and dragging her back to the entrance. "Hurry! Back up the tunnel!"

"It won't help." She'd braced herself against the wall. Her face was pinched and white and her eyes wide and panicky as they met his. "Hit me."

"What?"

"I need a distraction! Something else to think about. Pain sometimes works."

Tomas could feel the pressure building in the room, like a storm in the distance, about to break. "Sometimes isn't good enough! I can put you under a suggestion—"

"No, you can't."

"I assure you—"

"I'm a jinx!" she repeated furiously. "My magic doesn't work like most people's! I'm not susceptible to suggestions, vampiric or otherwise. Now hit me, goddammit!"

"No," he said, and kissed her. It was an instinctive reaction, something unexpected that might shock her enough to stop this without actually hurting her. But then she shuddered slightly and her mouth opened under his and her hands clenched on his shoulders and somehow he was kissing her savagely, this woman he barely knew who might be the last person he ever touched, the last warmth he ever felt.

Sarah's heartbeat was hard against his hand, the urgent thump resonating through his body. They stumbled back into the cavern wall, Tomas cradling the back of her head to save her from a concussion, trying to remember to be careful when his hands were so hungry that he couldn't hold them still. Sarah was shaking almost as hard as the room. And, for a moment, it was the most natural thing in the world to be kissing her desperately, both hands locked around her head, the long hair coming loose under his fingers, while the mountain threatened to fall in around them and death lay waiting, sure and inevitable, only moments away.

Tomas hadn't realized fully until that moment how certain he'd become that he wouldn't survive the night. He felt the knowledge settle into him now along with her breath, and instead of sadness or regret, he found himself just overwhelmingly grateful that, if this was the end, at least he wasn't facing it alone. It was, all things considered, more than he deserved.

And then Sarah pulled away, her eyes wide open, shocked and angry, and struck him hard across the mouth. It was enough to rock his head back, to make him taste the rich, metallic tang of his own blood. He wiped a smear off his lip with a thumb as she pushed at him, hard.

"I said *hit* me! Are you deaf?" She didn't wait for an answer, but launched herself towards him, fist clenching.

Tomas caught her hands, effortlessly holding her away from him. "Vampires don't get in fights with humans unless we intend to kill. You're too vulnerable, too easily broken."

Another rock hit the floor, hard enough to send bones and debris flying. Sara looked around wildly. "If you don't, we'll both be broken! Nothing else works!"

He grabbed her by the hips, swinging her against the wall, slamming her backwards into it. Startled out of fighting for a moment, she just stood there, panting and staring up at him as he pressed against her. "If I misjudge, there will be no one to stop this hillside from erupting just as the cemetery did. You'll be unconscious or worse, and we'll both die—as will your brother."

His hands were busy as he spoke, and with a sharp tug on the hem of her blouse, he sent the buttons flying. By the time he'd pushed the cloth out of the way, getting his fingers on the living warmth beneath, her nipples had gone tight and pebbly and she was gasping, her hands fisting in his shirt. But she wasn't pushing him off. She was kissing him brutally, lips and teeth savage, pressing hard against his body while her hands clawed at his back.

"Are you distracted yet?" he breathed, as she ripped open his shirt, pushing his undershirt up to his neck and biting at a nipple.

"I'll let you know," she said roughly, dragging their lips together again.

Her mouth tasted of the sharp, sweet tang of mescal, or maybe that was him. Her lips were sweet, but her body was shaking and her eyes were darting everywhere as if certain this wasn't going to work. And it wasn't, if he couldn't get her mind off the room and onto him—and keep it there. The room was coming down in chunks around them and the only thing that kept running through his mind was that it would be truly typical to come a thousand miles to die in some deserted anteroom.

He was breathing hard, adrenaline pumping through him, as he managed to get a hand between them. He dipped his head for another kiss, hands slipping away from hot, damp skin to tug impatiently at the button on her jeans, to work at the zipper. He pushed the maddeningly tight material down her thighs, his hand clenching on the soft flesh of her hip, rounded and warm for his palm. He pulled her closer, fixed the angle between them, and pushed into her.

Her legs wrapped around his thighs, clenching, as he began moving. He'd been careful because he hadn't prepared her, but she gasped out, "I won't break," her voice low and rough, and he began thrusting hard and fast, the way his body craved. His only concession to her comfort were his fingers working between her thighs roughly.

Within moments she was shuddering, her breath fracturing into harsh, quick gasps, panting, "*Harder*, damn you!"

"Make me," he growled, and in one quick movement she shoved him back, her foot behind his, tripping him, sending them both falling to the floor and driving herself onto him. Tomas barely noticed the hard floor or the pottery shard that was gouging him in the back or the unstable ceiling hanging above him. He was too busy watching her face. He kept his hands on her hips, guiding her, but not giving in to her gasped commands. Instead, he deliberately slowed down, then abruptly stopped, waiting.

"Tomas!" He ignored her, even though she wouldn't stop squirming, pushing the jagged pot shard further between his shoulder blades. She shifted, pulling back enough to rip open his shirt, to rain biting kisses all along his neck, to lick the hollow of his collarbone and mouth, his shoulders. Tomas's hands scrabbled desperately at the rubble beneath him, but he didn't move. He just lay there and took it, amazed at how much he needed this, until she let out a frustrated scream and raked her nails down his chest. "Move, damn it!"

He just stared up at her, at her glittering eyes and sweat drenched, dusty hair, her blouse open and her jeans around her knees, giving him a view of the dark stain of his hands against the pale skin of her hips. He wondered how he'd ever thought her less than stunning. She glared at him and then pulled farther back, letting him almost slide out of her, then suddenly forced herself back onto him. She did it again and Tomas bit back a groan, but he held himself completely still.

"Some help here!" she demanded, and did something with her hips that made his eyes roll into the back of his head.

He slid his hands down the curve of her back and tightened them on her slim waist. He could feel the tremors in his frame the longer he held on and knew he'd soon have no choice but to move. And she knew it, too–she was laughing when he finally gave in, an exultant sound that ran like fire through his veins.

He let her have her moment of triumph, before suddenly stopping once more. It took her a second to notice, then she stared down at him, momentarily speechless.

"That's inhuman!" she finally hissed.

He grinned. "So am I."

She wrapped her hand around his tie and jerked him upwards, the new angle forcing a moan out of them both. "Finish this or I swear—"

Tomas was moving before she completed the sentence, ignoring caution this time, fast and furious, glad that he didn't actually need to breathe because she hadn't let go of the tie. And then her hips were jerking in a way that was making it hard for him to focus, her gasps loud in his ears, her body's pleasure doubling his own. He felt her shudder her release and the clenching of her body triggered his, making them both groan deep in the back of their throats—and a great mess of pebbles and dust poured out of the ceiling.

It took Tomas a few seconds to realize that he wasn't trapped beneath a ton of dirt and rubble, that this wasn't a cave in, just the result of one final tremor. He dug himself out to find Sarah staring about room, which was, surprisingly, mostly still intact. It was also blessedly quiet.

Those hazel eyes came back to rest on him and she smiled a little crookedly, teeth a shock of white in her dirty face. "Okay. I guess that method works, too."

* * *

Instead of having to fight their way to the center of the complex as Tomas had expected, their path was unobstructed, the halls echoing, silent and empty except for the carved faces of long forgotten gods staring down from the walls and lintels. That was more than strange—it was unprecedented. And very bad.

Tomas had always known that his only real chance was that he knew this place, and its master, better than anyone. But nothing had gone as planned all night. He honestly didn't know what to expect when they finally made it to the huge natural cave that Alejandro used as an audience hall.

He brought them in through a little-known side tunnel that let out onto a set of steps about a story above the cave floor. There were guards at the entrance, finally, who Tomas dealt with by simply ordering them to sleep. He was a first-level master; he hadn't been worried about them. But the creature sprawled on the throne-like chair at the head of the room was first-level also, and far older than he.

As usual, Alejandro was dressed like a Spanish nobleman of the conquest period, which he'd once been. He didn't look like a monster, with an attractive if florid face and bright, intelligent black eyes. But then, the worst ones never did. Seeing that face again brought a sudden, miserable lurch, a shuddering memory of centuries of heartbreak and horror and nauseating fear. Tomas had to clutch at the door jamb, feeling the rock crumbling beneath his fingers, to keep silent.

Nobody else said anything, either. Tomas had warned them that even a whispered word was likely to be overheard, as beyond the excellent acoustics of the room itself was the small factor of vampire hearing. So Sarah was quiet as they surveyed the scene spread out below, although her face was eloquent.

Tomas now knew why they hadn't met anyone on the way. The prisoners should have been downstairs, while the vampires were disbursed throughout the property for the hunt. Instead, the entire cavernous space was crammed with people, mostly human, but with a ring of vampires circling them. It took Tomas a moment to understand what was happening, because none of this was normal.

A young Mexican man stumbled forward, pushed by one of the guards. He landed near a group of five bodies. There were lined up in a row at the front of the hall, their throats slashed down to the bone, white gleaming through red flesh in wide, jagged lines.

The floor beneath them was not the chipped, angular surface of the outer halls, but worn to a smooth, concave trough by generations of feet. A small stone altar had been found when Alejandro moved in, leading to speculation that this had once been the site of sacred rights. Blood from the latest corpses had run down the central depression, looking like a long finger pointing the way to the altar and to his throne above it.

Standing to the side of the carnage were two men and a woman, all human, with expressions ranging from dazed to disbelieving to horror struck. Tomas felt a hand grip his arm, and looked down to see Sarah clutching it hard enough to bruise had he been human. "To the right," she mouthed, and nodded to indicate the tall, lanky young man at the end of the lineup, his face dead white and smeared with blood.

He looked like he'd put up a struggle, but there was nothing of that spirit visible now. He was swaying slightly on his feet, mouth slack, and blinking slowly behind his glasses like a sleepy owl. Shock, or close to it, Tomas thought; so much for hoping he could run on cue.

"You want to save the life of this man?" Alejandro asked, addressing the young brunette on the other end of the line. "If so, you know what I want."

Instead of answering, the young woman giggled, a nervous, high-pitched sound that warned of incipient hysteria. It reverberated oddly in the high vault of the room; laughter wasn't a sound that lived here, and the echoes came back with sharp, mocking edges. She stopped, cutting it off abruptly.

"We told you already," the older man next to her said, his salt and pepper beard quivering more than his voice. "What you ask is impossible. Even if we could create that many—which we can't—keeping them under control would be—"

"They're zombies!" Alejandro screamed, cutting him off. He gestured savagely to a row of odd-looking spectators assembled behind his throne. The missing kings looked out with dead, empty eyes onto the crowd, assembled once more in an audience chamber, as if to give their advice. "They'll have no more mind than these! A child could control them!"

"If the child had multiple souls," the older man snapped. "We're necromancers, not puppeteers! To raise a zombie, we must lend it part of our soul—that is the only way to direct it. I can create one or two zombies at a time—no more. An especially-gifted bokor might be able to manage as many as five, but a whole army?" he gestured to the mass of waiting humans. They were there, Tomas realized with a sickening lurch, to be turned into more troops for Alejandro's growing megalomania. Troops who wouldn't question his orders, wouldn't challenge him as Tomas and a few others, had dared. "You ask the impossible!"

Alejandro didn't move, didn't blink, but Tomas knew what was coming. A flick of a guard's wrist broke the man's neck, his body tumbling to the floor to join the others. The young man who had been intended as the next victim fainted and was dragged back into the waiting throng.

"Do it," Alejandro told the girl, who was staring at the body of her fallen colleague as it was arranged in line with the others. "Now."

She transferred her stare to the creature on the throne, and Tomas knew she couldn't do as he asked. It was written on her face, along with horror and revulsion and abject terror. She was shaking just standing there, and he doubted she could concentrate enough to remember her name at this point. Much less how to manage a complex spell.

"She'll fail," Sarah said suddenly, "and my brother will be next."

Tomas looked around frantically for any sign that she had been overheard, but there was nothing. The closest vamps, two guards a few yards away at the bottom of the stairs, never even flinched. They were watching one of the captives, who was busy vomiting up his dinner, the gasping, wet sounds followed by painful dry gasps.

Tomas glanced at Sarah, who nodded at the fanatic. He was clutching his bones and murmuring something with a distracted air, as if everything below wasn't enough to hold his attention. "Silence shield," she explained. "Have any suggestions, or do you just want to wing it?"

Forkface had taken off his bulging pack and was systematically tucking stoppered vials into his already weapons-filled belt. It was pretty obvious how he was voting. Too bad they'd all be dead within half a minute of an attack.

"This is Alejandro's power base," Tomas said, struggling to explain in terms a human could understand. "In addition to his own, he can draw power from every vampire in the room. A frontal assault will not be successful."

"Any idea what will?"

Tomas's eyes were on the woman necromancer, who was crying and chanting at the same time, with theatrically raised arms but no discernable effect on any of the bodies. "Can he do a spell to allow you to move through the crowd unseen?" Tomas nodded at the fanatic.

"The best he can do in full light is a shadow spell to make us less obvious. It works on humans by redirecting attention away from us. But I don't know what effect it will have on vamps."

She glanced at her colleague, who was still muttering to himself but was now staring at an old inscription in the rock. She kicked him. "Yes, yes. Will not work on master-level, but all else, yes."

Tomas nodded. "I will distract Alejandro. While he is occupied with me, slip through the crowd and get your brother."

"That won't help everyone else."

"If I can defeat him, his position will devolve onto me and they'll be safe." But the odds were a lot less in his favor than he'd hoped. Catching Alejandro somewhere in the tunnels or the jungle, alone except for a few of his closest attendants, he might have stood a chance. But nowhere in his plans had he figured on anything like this.

His voice must have reflected some of his doubt, because Sarah narrowed her eyes. "And if you can't?"

"Once they see me, the court will likely have eyes for nothing else. Get as many people out as you can while they are distracted."

"Distracted killing you, you mean. Bullshit."

"I came here knowing this was the likely outcome."

"Another little thing you forgot to mention. We're gonna have to work on our communication."

Tomas decided he couldn't waste more time arguing. The woman necromancer had failed and Alejandro's power was boiling through the room, hot on his neck. He was furious. And when he lost his temper, people died—a lot of them. It would be perfectly within character for him to simply order every human in the room put to death.

As if in response to Tomas's thoughts, the guard behind the woman started forward, hand raised.

Tomas was grateful for vampiric speed, which allowed him to reach her before the guard could snap her neck. He caught the vamp's arm, but he needn't have bothered. The room had frozen.

"Tomas." The voice was the one he remembered, echoing inside his head like cool silver, but crawling under his skin like something alive. But the power behind it, the force compelling him to do Alejandro's will, was gone. For the first time, Tomas had reason to be grateful for his current master. As much as he hated the man, Louis-Cesar's ownership ensured that Alejandro's unspoken command exerted no more pull than that of any other first-level master. A rank he currently shared.

Tomas opened his hand and the guard retreated in an undignified scramble. The rest of the court was moving closer, not attacking, not yet, but on high alert. No one had any doubts about why he was here.

Apparently, neither did Alejandro. The moment Tomas made a move in his direction, a strong force pushed against him, like a hundred invisible hands holding him back. Make that two hundred, he thought, glancing about at the family he'd once called his own.

The fifteen feet to the bottom of the stairs felt like miles; he had to fight for every inch with eyes burning into his spine like acid and a thick, roiling nausea in his gut. He had a moment of vertigo, swaying on his feet like a drunk trying to dance, and someone laughed, high and cold and mocking. It wasn't Alejandro. His eyes were glittering dangerously and he'd lost the faintly amused smile that was his usual armor.

The stairwell leading up to his throne had twenty steps. By the time Tomas reached them, he was panting like he'd run a mile. "I challenged you once before," he said, around the mass that had risen in his throat, huge and cold and sickening. "But you were too cowardly to face me. I have come—"

It was a good thing he hadn't worked too hard on his speech, because he never got to give it. The vampires had closed in on every side, jostling each other, trying to get up the courage to attack him. Tomas had hoped that Alejandro's pride would force him to fight his old servant himself, especially with the odds so heavily in his favor. But Alejandro remained seated, letting his men get more and more worked up until, finally, two broke away from the crowd and dashed in, snarling.

They came from opposite sides, and while Tomas was dealing with the one on the left, turning his own knife back against him, the one on the right smashed something heavy against his leg. It was the one he'd injured earlier, the one that had yet to completely heal. He fell to his hands and knees, the jar of landing on the shattered kneecap turning the whole room white hot with blinding pain.

He pulled the knife out of the first vamp, who retreated back into the crowd, howling and clawing at his wound, and rolled in time to slash at the second's throat. He missed because the man dodged, lightning fast, at the last minute. But Tomas didn't need weapons to crush his throat with an application of raw power.

The vamp was young and that effectively put him out of commission. But it also used up power Tomas couldn't afford to lose. And there were plenty more that the family would consider expendable if their deaths served to further weaken him.

Tomas dragged himself back onto one leg, momentarily crippled while his system fought to rebuild torn cartilage and shattered bone. Alejandro leaned forward, still not bothering to get to his feet. "Do you really believe you will make it all the way up here, Tomas? Because I believe I will sit here and watch them gut you as you try."

Four more vampires rushed him, all from the same side, and although he dealt with them and with the low-level master who had waited for them to distract him, he missed the ax that someone threw from the crowd. Alejandro made a small gesture and the assault halted, for the moment, while Tomas shuddered and leaned his forehead against the slick, cold surface of the third step, a buzzing uproar surging all around him. On the third or fourth or tenth try, Tomas managed to take a couple of shallow breaths. He brought up shaking hands and tore the weapon out of his belly.

"Really, Tomas. I'm disappointed. I remembered you as better than this." Alejandro had finally bothered to get out of his seat, but he didn't come any closer. "And to think, I was contemplating offering you a position at the head of my new army. I really will have to reconsider."

Hot tendrils of agony shot out from his stomach wound as he tried to stand. At least he couldn't feel the throbbing in his leg anymore, Tomas thought, and laughed to cover the scream that wanted to tear out of his chest. An all-out assault on Alejandro was the only chance he had. If he hurt him badly enough, the family might back off, waiting to see the outcome before they risked attacking the man who might be their new master. Slogging slowly up these steps, one by one, being battered from all sides and buffeted by Alejandro's power, was a sure recipe for disaster. But it was also the only hope the humans had.

He couldn't hear anything from the back of the cave, from the mass of four or five hundred people who had been corralled there. And there was no way so many could remain silent while witnessing something like this. Not unless they were being shielded and hopefully guided out.

But it was a long way through the maze of hallways, as countless mortals had learned to their terror, and even further to the town beyond. He had to give them time, if they were to have any chance at all. And in this slice of hell, time meant pain.

Pain wasn't a problem, Tomas decided, looking into Alejandro's amused black eyes. He'd brought it to enough people through the years. It was his turn.

"Still a coward posing as a gentleman," Tomas gasped, and threw the gory ax straight at Alejandro.

His old master turned it aside with an elegant wave of his hand, but anger and surprise caused his attention to waver slightly, allowing Tomas to make headway against the stream of power opposing him. He made it to the tenth stair before the world spun around and dropped out from under him, and he hit something hard and unyielding. Only when the pain receded a fraction did he realize he'd been dumped on the floor by another ax, this one to the spine.

And master or no, no one healed a wound like that instantaneously. Suddenly, his limbs didn't work, his arms and legs flopping uselessly around him, his head falling back into a puddle of his own blood. Alejandro waved off the guards who were rushing in to finish him, as he slowly descended the remaining stairs.

He stopped directly in Tomas's line of vision, his booted feet just touching the bloody pool. He unsheathed a rapier, good quality Cordoba steel instead of wood, making it obvious that this wasn't going to end quickly. "How the mighty have fallen. That is the phrase, isn't it? From my lieutenant to this, all because of ambition."

Tomas tried to tell him that ambition wasn't the point, that it never had been, but his throat didn't seem to work either. Although that might have been because of the sight that suddenly loomed up behind his former master. At first, Tomas was sure he was imagining things. But not even in a pain-induced near faint could his brain have come up with something like that.

Behind Alejandro, a withered arm encased in a few rotting rags appeared, a tracery of thin blue veins pulsing under the long dead skin. A head followed, cadaverous and brown, but with two enormous, glittering eyes rolling in the too large sockets. They stared at Tomas for an instant, full of terrible, ancient fury, before the arm caught Alejandro around the waist and a mouth full of cracked and yellowed teeth clamped onto his neck.

Alejandro gave one sharp gasp before the others were on him, a crowd of dry, old bones and tanned leather skins that glowed slightly from the inside, like someone shining a flashlight through parchment. And although Alejandro's power still surged around Tomas like a hurricane, his attackers didn't seem to feel it. There was a crack, a thick, watery sound, and then silence—except for the ripping, chewing noises coming from the middle of the once human mass.

The kings had returned.

Another pair of feet came to rest beside him, just brushing his hair. Tomas looked up to see Jason, slack-jawed no longer, but with a quiet intensity his eyes. It seemed Alejandro had kidnapped one necromancer worth his salt, after all.

"You brought them back," he managed to croak after a moment.

Jason didn't look away from the creatures and their meal. "They brought themselves."

Tomas didn't have a chance to ask him what he meant, because the earth began to move in a very familiar manner. Jason grabbed him under the arms and pulled him backwards down the stairs. No one tried to stop him. It was as if the court was frozen in place, staring in disbelieving horror at the sight of their master being attacked by supposedly harmless sacks of bones.

They made it to the edge of what had been the holding pen before Alejandro's power suddenly cut off, like someone throwing a switch. A ripple went through his vampires as they felt it too and realized what it meant. They came back to life with a vengeance, but too late; half the roof collapsed in a cascade of limestone.

Sarah and one of her men ran up, dirty-faced and panting. Forkface grabbed Tomas, yanked the ax out of his back and threw him over a shoulder. Then they ran.

The doorway collapsed behind them, dust billowing into the air while rocks and gravel nipped at their heels. The entire tunnel system was buckling, the floor heaving, the ceiling threatening to crush them at any moment. His helper lost his footing and they both went down, Tomas managing to catch himself on arms that, while unsteady, actually seemed to work again.

He grabbed Sarah, attempting to shield her, at the same time that she grabbed for him. And amid stones falling and dust clouds choking them, they braced together, Sara saying things that Tomas couldn't hear over the roaring in his ears. But their small patch of ceiling held, and after they limped across the boundary from the caves to the old temple, the rumbling gradually petered off.

They emerged at last into the jungle, where a mass of dazed people huddled together in small groups under the dark, star-dusted sky. Forkface dumped Tomas unceremoniously beside a small pool just inside the temple, where people were scooping up water in hats, hands or flasks. It was a green and it stunk, with slimy ropes of algae clinging to sides, and nobody seemed to mind. Some were hugging, more were crying and one, amazingly, was laughing. Tomas blinked at them, disbelieving, seeing for the first time in four hundred years the Day of the Dead celebrated in this place by the living.

Jason brought him some water in an old canteen, and while Tomas didn't particularly need it, he drank it anyway. The fanatic came over to join them after a moment. It seemed he'd been delegated to lead the way out while Sarah and her remaining associate remained behind to rescue Tomas. He seemed perturbed that they hadn't brought him any bones, and eyed Tomas speculatively for a moment before moving off, muttering.

Tomas's whole body hurt and he was ravenously hungry, but he was alive. It didn't seem quite real. "How did you do it?" he finally asked Jason.

"I didn't. I only woke them up."

"I don't understand."

"The Incan kings were believed to watch over their people, even after death, and to demand good behavior of the living. Any who defied them soon learned that they also had within their power to reward or to punish."

"That's a myth."

Jason smiled, an odd, lopsided effort. "Really. It seems strange, not to mention expensive, to tie up most of the revenues of the state in the care of creatures who have no ability to hurt you." He shook his head. "The ancient priests prepared the royal dead well. I only had to give them a nudge."

"You mean—"

His eyes went soft and dreamy. "They said they had been watching Alejandro for a long time. And they were hungry."

"Well, they'll have the whole court to snack on now, once they finish with him," Sarah commented, stopping by after locating enough local people to serve as guides for everyone else. Tomas had a sudden image of vengeful Incan monarchs pursuing Alejandro's vampires through the halls where they had once done the same to humans. He smiled.

"Attacking that thing on your own was insane," Sarah said bluntly. "I like that in a person. Want a job?"

Tomas just looked at her for a moment. He was a first-level master, one of only a handful in the world. The rest at his rank were either sitting in governing positions over his kind, or were powerful masters with their own courts. They were emphatically not running around with a motley crew of mercenaries carrying out jobs so crazy that no one else would touch them.

He'd killed Alejandro, or close enough by vampire law. He could assume his position, round up whatever vampires had made it out before the cave-in, and claim to be the new head of the Latin American Senate. That would put him beyond the jurisdiction of the North American version—which wanted him dead—and his master—who wanted him back in slavery. He could rebuild Alejandro's empire and walk these halls once more, this time as their master. He would be rich, powerful and feared . . .

And, in time, just like Alejandro.

"Well?"

Sarah didn't seem to be the patient type. It was something else they were going to have to work on. They weren't touching, but she was standing so close that he could smell the vestiges of her perfume mingled with gunpowder and sweat. It was strangely comforting, like the lingering warmth of a touch even after it's gone. Tomas looked up at her face, surrounded by stars, and for the first time in longer than he could remember, he saw a future.

"Where do I sign?"

Author's Note: This is a Cassie Palmer holiday short. It is ahead of the current timeline for the series, which at publication had reached *Shatter the Earth*, so I put it here.

BLACK FRIDAY

"You don't see the irony, Cassie?"

I looked back at the walking bundle of presents that was following me. "What irony?"

"Shopping for Christmas gifts in hell."

I frowned. "Well, they have the best prices."

And I had a ton of people to buy for. Just so many. It almost made me wish for the days when—

I stopped myself. No, it didn't. Other people had happy memories of lying under the Christmas tree as a child, staring up at all the pretty lights, while the smell of peppermint eggnog floated through the house and a playful kitten batted at a low hanging decoration. Or so I assumed. I wouldn't know, since I'd been raised by a homicidal vampire who had been approximately the circumference of Santa, but resembled him in exactly no other way.

Fat Tony had not been a jolly old elf or any other kind of elf, unlike the guy in the next store.

Who was not on script, I noticed.

The Shadowland, the closest hell region to Earth, was basically a huge marketplace, with a vested interest in keeping its visitors happy. To help with that, it projected an image that fit the buyer's expectations, taking clues from their minds to form a version of itself that would make them comfortable no matter what world they came from. Or possibly to keep them from running down the street screaming at what it actually looked like. In any case, right now, to me, it looked like a Victorian Christmas, complete with snowy stoops, cobblestones, and old fashioned multi-paned shop windows through which bright yellow lamplight was streaming into the street.

I'd even changed myself, when I shifted in here a couple of hours ago, because they seemed to be doing a special, suped-up illusion for the holidays, maybe to encourage people to stay longer. Anyway, I'd found my t-shirt and jeans transformed into a bottle green Victorian skirted suit, complete with cute little jacket, frothy lace blouse, and a bustle. My companion, likewise, appeared to be wearing a suit coat with long tails, a pair of riding boots, and a ridiculously tall top hat which he'd repeatedly tried to take off, but which wasn't budging, probably because it wasn't actually there.

I'd stuck a sprig of holly in it anyway.

It looked quite festive.

Unlike the fey.

He should have matched the scene, with whatever he actually looked like overwritten by some version of a Victorian merchant, maybe with mutton chop whiskers and a snowy white apron, like the guy in the last place. Instead, long, pointy ears were sticking up around a bright red Santa hat, and his shining, silver hair was almost touching the old floorboards. He noticed my interest and smiled, showing off a mouthful of long, cracked and stained teeth.

Well, at least he got the Victorian mouth right, I thought, and went back to my list.

"What's a fey doing in hell?" the gift pile asked.

"No idea. Okay, the new nunchucks are for Pritkin—"

"You coulda bought those on Earth, and then I wouldn't have to lug them all over hell. My feet are killing me!"

"You're a vampire. Stop whinging." I'd brought Fred, my tiniest bodyguard, along as present-toter, because he was the least likely to freak out and start wailing on somebody. And while the Shadowland was generally friendly toward outsiders, at least until it relieved them of all their money, freaking out was not advised. Whinging, on the other hand—

"I'm not whinging—"

"You've been whinging for blocks."

"—and you're American. Stop using that weird British slang you picked up from lover boy."

I ignored the last comment, since it was none of Fred's business, and checked the list again. "The nunchunks are spelled. They'll fight with you or for you. Good for training as well as defense."

Pritkin would like them, I was pretty sure.

Anything lethal tended to go over well.

"And Jonas gets the doggy treats," I continued. He had a possessed bloodhound, so something from hell's bakery had seemed appropriate. "And Tami the new bakeware—"

"What does that do?" Fred asked suspiciously.

I looked up. "It's bakeware. It . . . bakes stuff."

"Hell pies?"

"Any kind of pies. The little cookie cutters take on any shape you want, and the Bundt pan—"

"Would madam like a free sample?" someone asked.

I glanced up. Oh, the fey. He had a glass of cider or mulled wine or something on his palm, which he was proffering to me with another hideous grin. Seriously, Faerie needed to invest in some dentists. Like now.

"Thanks."

I passed it over to Fred, who was a garbage disposal when it came to food. So far, our shopping trip had seen him consume five little peppermint sleighs, complete with Santa and reindeer, at the candy shop, despite the fact that they could fly and he'd had to chase one of them down the street. And a couple of hot dogs from a stand, loaded with sauerkraut and mustard and pickle relish and coleslaw and jalapenos and bacon, before he ran out of room—on the dogs; Fred didn't run out of room, or at least, I'd yet to see it. And an even dozen cookies which had been so freaking cute with their little animal faces that I hadn't been able to resist—until Fred snitched one and it started screaming.

Fred had ended up with the lot after that, because hell's return policy sucks.

"Bah!" he wiped his lips, and then beat the center of his chest with his one free fist. "That was spicy!"

"Well if you wouldn't chug it—"

"You keep saying you're in a hurry!"

"I'm not in a hurry; we just have a lot to—"

I cut off, because Fred had just belched—a plume of fire that set the fey's hair alight. I stared, Fred looked around in confusion, and the poor fey screamed and went running off to stick his head in a snowbank. I hesitated, but he looked like he had it handled, and the fey were pretty hardy, and we were starting to draw a crowd—

Screw it.

I grabbed Fred's hand and pulled him down the street. "Sorry!" I yelled behind us, before ducking into a cross road and whirling on him. "I told you—no assaulting people!"

"Well, it was his brew!" Fred looked indignant. "And it gave me heartburn!"

"Yeah, that couldn't possibly be the massive amount of crap you've eaten since we got here."

"Hey, I offered you a cookie!"

"A screaming Bambi pleading for his life!"

"It was a gingersnap." Fred grinned, showing a little fang. "Tasty."

"Oh, stop it!" I said, and pulled him into a toy shop.

I'd mainly been trying to get out of the street, before a seriously pissed off shopkeeper came after us. But then I looked up. And stopped, my mouth hanging open in wonder, because—

"Oh, hey," Fred said. "This is more like it!"

And it was, it really, really was. I caught sight of my own reflection in a bright silver Christmas ball, one of thousands festooned everywhere, and realized that I looked like that wide-eyed kid I'd never been: blue eyes bright, short blonde hair dusted with snow, cheeks pink from the cold, and face suffused with wonder. Because this shop was magical.

It was *magical*.

There were old wooden floors and flickering lantern light and berry covered garlands that smelled deliciously of pine. There were huge wreaths with big red Christmas bows, and a tree that stretched up to the exposed rafters, and a whole wall of exquisitely embroidered stockings that quickly rewrote themselves with my name. There were wooden bird ornaments on festoons of ribbon stretching from the tree to the shelves on either side that really sang, tiny drummers peeking out from the branches who really drummed, icicles that looked like the real thing and were cold when you touched them, and a miniature train, running on a track near the ceiling, complete with passengers drinking coffee, reading newspapers and walking clumsily along the jolting carriages.

And that was just the decor.

I moved on to the aisles of toys, passing down one entirely filled with marionettes in exquisitely made suits of armor, or military uniforms festooned with braid, or delicate ball gowns softly shimmering, or an amazing Balinese dancer's costume glittering with gold. There were snow globes showing all kinds of different scenes, including one as big as my head in which a perfect, miniature town was blanketed in white, complete with minute skaters on a frozen pond that actually skated—and leapt and twirled and danced—while the people in the stands above huddled together, drinking hot chocolate under snuggly blankets and watching their breath frost the air. I marveled at broomsticks that actually flew, at kites big enough and magical enough to carry you, at a costume box that could immediately put a child into any of a thousand different outfits, and on and on and on.

Here's the rest of my Christmas list sorted, I thought, thinking of how excited a bunch of little girls I knew were going to be on Christmas morning.

"You're gonna need to grow a couple extra arms," I told Fred, who laughed.

"Not in the skill set. I'll get a basket."

I nodded absently, already intrigued by a curious line of carved wooden boxes on a shelf, all beautifully decorated. Except that they didn't seem to do anything. Maybe they were just for looks?

"Can I be of service?"

I glanced up to see a roly-poly demon headed my way, with the cutest little baby horns sticking out of his head. He looked more the part, I thought approvingly, in Victorian appropriate gear over which a bright green apron had been stretched. It had "Merry, Merry!" written on it in flowing, cursive letters, and the expression matched the get-up.

Guy knew a sucker when he saw one, but right then, I didn't mind. "What are these?"

"Oh, good choice," he approved. "They're some of the finest memory spheres we've had in many a year."

He took a box down and opened it to reveal a softly glowing globe the size of a large Christmas ball. But inside was a scene more reminiscent of the snow globe, showing the interior of a cozy little house. A small family was gathered around a fireplace: mom, dad, a couple of kids and a pet dog, with the kids trying to open gifts while the dog wagged its tail and got in the way, and the parents laughed and sipped wine.

"It's nice," I said. And shook it. But nothing happened except that the mother spilled some wine and the dog stared around and started barking. I frowned. "Where's the snow?"

"There's no snow," the jolly little proprietor told me. "Haven't you ever used one of these before?"

I looked up. "One of what?"

"A memory ball. People come in and sell us their recollections of the most wonderful and enchanted times in their lives, when they were at their happiest. We preserve them so that others can experience them, too. Either to cheer up after a hardship, or," his head tilted, and he regarded me shrewdly. "To experience something they never had?"

I blinked. "You mean, it feels like . . . you're one of them?"

He nodded. "Say the password and you'll be transported into that exact scene—well, mentally, at any rate. Lasts for over an hour. And while you're there, you'll completely believe it. There will be no doubt in your mind whatsoever that it's all real."

"But it isn't," I said, looking back down at the happy family.

The little girl had left off opening her gifts to comfort the dog, who was now flopped over her lap, tongue out and tail wagging slowly in perfect contentment. The mother reached down and smoothed her hair lovingly, while the father batted the son's lightweight airplane away from the flames. After a moment, the two of them went outside to fly it, and the girl and dog climbed into the mother's squashy armchair, and promptly fell asleep.

"Well, it was for the seller," the shopkeeper said, looking confused, like he didn't see why that mattered. Or understand how terrible it would be to wake up from that cozy dream, and realize that it had all been a lie. "We have a two-for-one special going on right now, in honor of the holidays," he added.

"I'll think about it," I said roughly, and pulled out my list. "I need these things."

The shopkeeper and Fred, who had just returned with three massive baskets, moved off on a mission. I put the happy family back in their box, and back onto the shelf. Only to have my hand trapped by someone else's before I could finish the motion.

It was the fey, standing behind me with his hair all singed along one side, and his eyes more than a little wild.

Well, shit.

"Look," I told him, "I'm really sorry about—"

"Do you know," he panted, pulling the box back off the shelf. "These are really quite dangerous items."

"Are they?"

"Yes, yes. You can get trapped—trapped forever in memory— forgetting to eat or sleep or do anything at all, until you die with a smile on your face!"

"I . . . thought it only lasted an hour—"

"It all depends on how much magic is put into it," the creature told me, fishing out the globe once more. And holding it tightly between his hands, until spears of golden light began to sift through his fingers. "Yes, yes, quite dangerous!"

He was starting to look a little deranged.

"Yeah, well, maybe you should show the shopkeeper—"

He looked up, and the eyes were glowing, too. "I'll show you in a minute!"

"Hey, look what I found!" Fred said, from somewhere behind me.

And the next thing I knew, something terrible and fluffy was bounding down the aisle, barreling into me and sending me staggering into the fey.

Who dropped the little ball.

It shattered into a thousand pieces on the hardwood floor, and a brilliant flash of golden light surged around the room, gilding everything in the small shop for a moment before abruptly fading out. Only not entirely. Because, suddenly, all the toys were really, really . . . animated.

A bunch of tin soldiers jumped out of a box and scattered everywhere, one attacking Fred's shoe with a bayonet. "Hey!"

He stumbled back into a shelf full of a dolls, who a moment before had been sitting quietly, kicking their Mary Janes or occasionally brushing their hair. But I guess they didn't like being disturbed. Because they jumped onto Fred *en masse*, their faces suddenly a lot less angelic as they started to—

"Shit!" I yelled, when blood spirted.

But nobody heard me, because there was already a lot of yelling going on. The fluffy whatever had turned on the fey, and was currently trying to lick him to death on the floor. The tin soldiers were attacking everybody, except for me because I'd climbed onto a table like a sensible person. Although that didn't help with the toy birds that were currently zipping around, dive-bombing us.

And then the lights turned on in a nearby dollhouse, big as a dining room table stood on end, and painted to look like a perfect representation of a Victorian farmhouse. Complete with irate farmer, I realized a second later, when tiny bullets started spewing out of a miniature shotgun. Really painful bullets!

I grabbed a pretty tray to use as a shield, only to have it immediately indented with a bunch of little projectiles, because apparently this shotgun did not need to reload. But something stung my ankle anyway, and I looked down. To see the farmer's son, at a guess, who'd jumped to the table with a slingshot, and was targeting my big toe.

"Ouch!" I said, and kicked out reflexively, causing him to hit the floor and then just stay there, moaning softly. I immediately felt bad; he was so cute in his little torn jeans and straw hat, and looked to be seriously distressed. I was about to scoop him up when the farmer blew a whistle.

And a whole line of dollhouses lit up, everything from a brownstone to a castle to a Victorian fire station suddenly coming to life.

Uh oh, I thought, and started looking for an exit, only I didn't find one. Because while I'd been busy getting turned into Swiss cheese, things had deteriorated. Big time.

Fred was staggering around under the weight of what looked like every doll in the shop, with bloody bite and scratch marks everywhere that wasn't covered by frilly dresses and shiny shoes. The fey was still on the floor, and still being savaged by the fluffy thing—and beaten over the head by a clown with a club, and bayoneted by the soldiers, and nipped by a goose on wheels . . . thing . . . with a savage eye and a bloody beak. I opened my mouth to scream "run" at Fred, when I was almost washed off my perch by a blast from three fire hoses at once.

Then the shopkeeper barked a word I didn't know and everything paused—except for fluffykins, who didn't seem particularly well-trained. The shopkeeper pointed at the fey, who had his hands over his head and didn't see it. But I guess he heard when the demon yelled: "No! That one!"

The fey looked up wildly, just in time to see half the toys in the shop turn to look at him, including all the dolls on Fred's shrieking corpus.

Who promptly jumped onto his.

"Auggghhhh!" The fey scrambled up and ran screaming out the door, carrying a boatload of merchandise along with him. Including most of the dolls, who had latched on with their little baby teeth right before he fled. Except for one, who'd hit the ground but was nonetheless snarling and snapping and toddling for the door.

Until the shopkeeper scooped her up, and put her over his shoulder, patting her back comfortingly and glaring—

At me.

Well, crap.

Half an hour and some very poor bargaining later, Fred staggered out of the shop laden with three massive bags along with all our previous purchases. None of which I could help him with because I had doggo on a leash. A very flimsy-looking leash, considering the fact that doggo wasn't actually a doggo.

He was a hellhound.

A tiny, newborn hellhound, probably all of a few days old. Which is why he was only the size of a large Saint Bernard. Although he had the strength of a couple bull elephants as he went bounding down the street, towing me along behind him.

"Dig in your heels!" Fred said, puffing beside me.

"I am digging in my heels!"

"Well, it isn't working."

"I know it isn't working!"

"I'm just saying—"

"What?" I turned to glare at him, which I was able to do because doggo had just loop-de-looped around a streetlight, and been held up for five seconds.

Until he bit it in two and bounded off again, that is.

"Damn it!" Fred said, as the crashing light pole barely missed him. "We need to get outta here!"

"We can't get out of here! We have to take him back!"

"What?" Fred caught up with me. "To where? I got the impression demon dude was glad to get rid of him!"

"He shouldn't have had him in the first place!" I said, as we plowed through a couple more demons, who wisely jumped out of the way. "They're not pets!"

"I'll say. So what's the plan?"

"Find mama."

Fred's eyes got huge, but I barely noticed because I'd just seen—

Yes!

"Did you say 'find mama'?" Fred demanded, as I threw some gold at a guy renting scooters, to help people zip around the massive marketplace a little easier. This one had a sidecar, which Fred threw the packages in while I revved up the engine. Which is easier said than done with an overly enthusiastic hellhound threatening to rip your arm off!

But we got going, Fred jumping on behind me, still laden with what wouldn't fit in the sidecar, which was a lot. We'd had to buy out half the shop to keep the proprietor from reporting us, and we hadn't even done anything wrong! Crazy ass fey, I thought darkly, and hit the gas.

On the one hand, my shoulder thanked me, with the hound now loping just ahead of us, and more or less matching our speed; on the other—

He seemed kind of distractible.

"Auggghhh!" Fred said, when the hound saw something off to the left and went bounding after it, causing us to bound, too. And fly and jounce and floor it, because it was either that or get dragged through the handlebars.

As it was, we just got dragged through a fruit stand, sending oranges flying everywhere, and over a pile of rugs outside a carpet seller, who came out of his shop to screech at us and wave half a dozen fists, and down an alley where clothes were suspended on low hanging lines stretched between windows—

Or they had been.

"Damn it! I can't see!" Fred yelled, from underneath somebody's nightie as we trailed a couple of laundry lines behind us.

"Just as well," I said.

"What does that mean?"

"It means I think that fey might be trying to kill us," I said, staring at the crazy bastard just up ahead, who was blocking the alley and aiming what looked like a rocket launcher.

Straight at us.

Fred's head poked out the leg hole of somebody's panties.

"What? Why?"

"I don't know why!" I stomped on the brakes, which didn't help, and the hellhound took a swift turn into an alley, which did.

"Holy shit!" Fred screeched, as part of a building exploded behind us.

He tried to cover me from the flying bricks and dust and debris suddenly raining around everywhere, which would have worked better if additional shots weren't being fired at the same time. We zigzagged through a succession of interconnected alleyways, at a really ridiculous speed that was somehow still not enough to keep stoops from turning to rubble and the road from erupting in potholes the size of Pintos. A manhole cover went flipping through the air, barely missing our heads, and Fred cursed.

"Does the bastard have rockets on his feet?"

I slung around the latest hole on about a half inch of road, and stared up at a rectangle of stars—and a dark form leaping from one building to the next. "No. He's on the roofs."

I floored it, because outrunning him was about the only option here. And thanked god that I hadn't had money for a car when I was hiding from Fat Tony back in Atlanta. I'd had to make do with a used moped I picked up for sixty bucks off a crackhead, and which didn't have an actual second gear, so I'd learned to drive fast.

Real fast.

Super, duper fast.

"Ahhhh!" Fred said, as we took a corner on two wheels, slammed back down, lost the sidecar and shot ahead, juddering up an outdoor staircase beside a cafe, before crashing through a railing and flying off the side of the building—

To land clean in the street beyond.

"Yeah!" Fred screamed, as we bounced up and down. "Yeah! Did you see that? Did you fucking see that?"

"I saw it," I said, sounding a little wobbly, but I didn't care. That had been pretty damned sweet.

Or it would have been.

If the street hadn't been a dead end.

Fred was still yelling as I slung the scooter back around, but it was too late. The fey jumped down from a nearby three-story building like it was nothing, weapon in hand. And there were no convenient crossroads or alleys here, or rather, there were—behind him.

And I somehow didn't think we were going to make it that far.

"Oh, shit," Fred said, catching up.

The hellhound, which had been enthusiastically bounding along, easily matching our pace, had also turned around, and started whining.

Tell me about it, I thought, as the fey shouldered his weapon.

"A little holiday gift from my lord," he said, showing all those broken teeth.

"Aeslinn," I guessed. The head of one of the leading fey kingdoms wasn't a fan.

The fey inclined his head. "You've led him a merry chase, Pythia, but your power doesn't work here!"

That wasn't entirely true, but it was true that it came and went. The Pythian power that let me shift around space and time and go shopping in Hell was tied to Earth, and when I wasn't there, it was wonky. And, right now, I wasn't feeling it.

"But my money does! Whatever he's paying you, I can double it," I promised, while trying to pull my power up. It was sluggish, but something else wasn't. Something massive that suddenly blocked a whole street of starlight behind the fey.

"Don't bother trying to bribe me," he sneered. "I've worked for my master for more than a thousand years, and killed more of his enemies than I can count. But this—this will be my crowning achievement!"

"Okay," I held out my hands. "I get it. It would be a waste of time trying to bribe a loyal servant like you. And Fred and I knew the risks when we took this job. We're prepared to die—"

"Speak for yourself!" Fred said. He'd slipped an arm around my waist, obviously preparing to jump for the nearest roof.

He probably wouldn't make it, but damned if he wasn't going to try.

"—but, please. Let the puppy live."

The fey looked confused. "Puppy? What puppy?"

I gestured at the hellhound. "He hasn't done anything wrong—"

"He almost eviscerated me, the mangy cur!" The fey kicked a rock, and he had good aim. The jagged piece of stone whipped through the air and caught the hellhound in the thigh, causing him to jump and then yelp with pain.

"He was just confused! He's a baby—"

"He's an abomination that should never have existed, like everything here! Like you, and those vampires you lead! Like this whole misbegotten realm, filled with disgusting, filthy, vile, sinful—"

The cloud suddenly descended, swift as a lightning strike, and the fey's voice cut out.

Probably because he'd just been bitten off at the waist.

He collapsed to the ground, or what was left of him, while the massive hellhound behind him, big as a house and boiling with rancid black steam, swallowed. And then bent a huge head down to snuffle and lick her baby boy. Who was suddenly dancing around with joy, his little scrape forgotten.

Home for Christmas, I thought, and grinned.

* * *

"Are you all right?" I asked Fred, later that afternoon.

"No," he staggered against a wall. "How can you ask me that, oh my god."

"You're going to be fine," I told him, leading him to a café table, outside a tea shop.

The demon attendant bustled over with menus. "Just tea," I told him.

"Wait," Fred said weakly, and reached out a hand.

I slapped it. "No."

"I just wanna look—"

"No! He'll have tea," I said firmly. Fred groaned and stared at his stomach, which had pooched out over his sans-a-belt trousers so that the belly button could wink at me. "You'll make a good Santa soon," I told him, checking my list one last time.

"I don't know why I'm so sick," Fred complained.

"You ate the marketplace. Literally."

"I did no such thing!"

"I don't think we missed a stall."

"How often does a guy get to try so many new things?" he asked, eyeing a vendor across the street. Who was selling some kind of marshmallow concoction.

"You don't need it," I warned without looking up.

"The holidays aren't just about what you need. Every other time of the year it's the same thing: eat your vegetables, exercise, you don't need that entire package of double stuffed Oreos—"

"I hate double stuffed."

Fred looked at me like I'd blasphemed. "What?"

"They're too sweet. It throws the balance off."

"You know, some days I can't even talk to you." He peered at the list over my shoulder. "What did you get Mircea?"

"Demon ruby cufflinks. They light up whenever somebody lies."

Fred raised an eyebrow, but didn't say anything. And then our tea arrived, and damned if the waiter hadn't piled on a bunch of sandwiches and some Christmas cookies, too. I sighed. I wasn't gonna fit into any of my jeans after this, I just knew it.

We ate.

"Back there, did you really think you could make that jump?" I asked him, after a while.

"What jump?"

"When the fey had that gun on us. I was pretty sure you were about to try to jump us to the roof."

Fred looked up from picking the lettuce off a finger sandwich. "You really think I'd make a three-story jump while holding someone else?"

"Well, no. That's why I wondered . . ."

"I had my eye on his finger. Soon as it twitched, I was gonna throw you at the roof, and hope the explosion hid it. He'd think he killed you and head out, and you could go catch a portal or something."

I looked at him. "And what about you?"

"What about me?"

"Fred! You'd be dead!"

He shrugged. "Better than both of us."

He went back to eating sandwiches, now denuded of nasty green stuff. I finished my tea. And then snuck off when he went to the john and got him the biggest marshmallow thing they had, to surprise him with later when he'd actually enjoy it.

And just made it back to the table before he waddled back over.

"You know, this was weirdly fun," he announced.

"Was it?"

He slid into his chair, his top hat drooping down over one eye. "Yeah. I don't know what people are always going on about. Black Friday is the bomb."

"Maybe we'll do it again next year," I said, looking around at the glittery lights and the tacky decorations and the drunk group of demons lurching down the street and singing off key.

Maybe it was time I started making some holiday memories of my own. Not borrowed from somebody else's head, or with some stranger's family. But with my own, the one I'd somehow made without ever intending to.

The only one I'd ever been able to depend on.

"It's a date," he told me. And then looked alarmed when my hand covered his. "You know, the platonic kind. I don't need a pissed off war mage on my ass."

I rolled my eyes. "Fred?"

"Yeah?"

"Happy Holidays," I told him, and shifted.

The End

Made in the USA
Middletown, DE
14 January 2025

69397367R00222